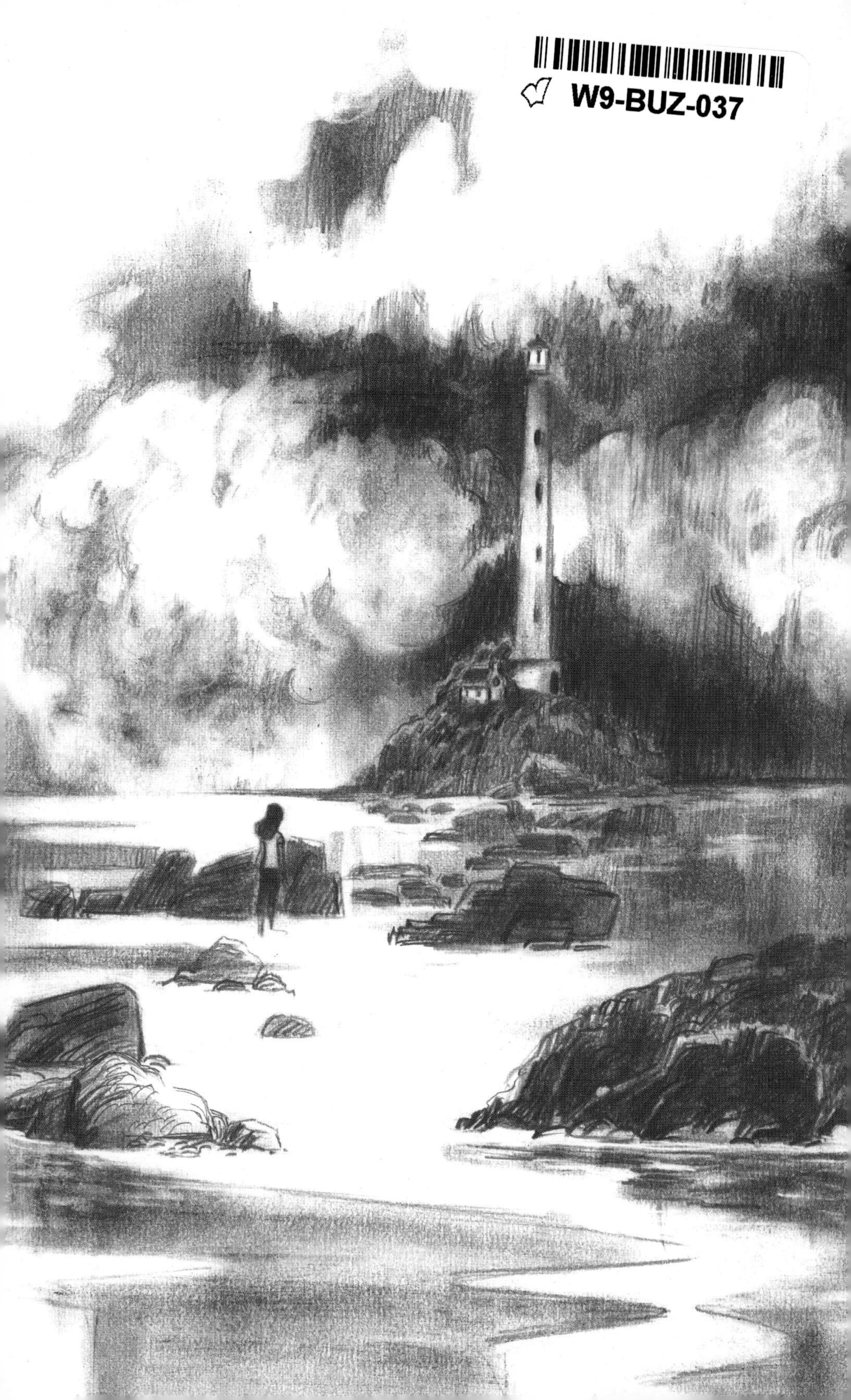

ROAR

Water Memory

Artist and colorist **Valérie Vernay**
Writer **Mathieu Reynès**

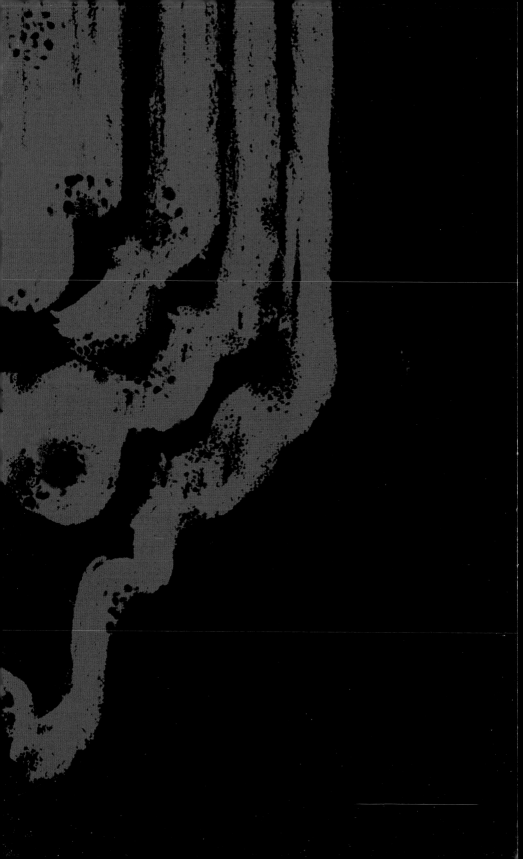

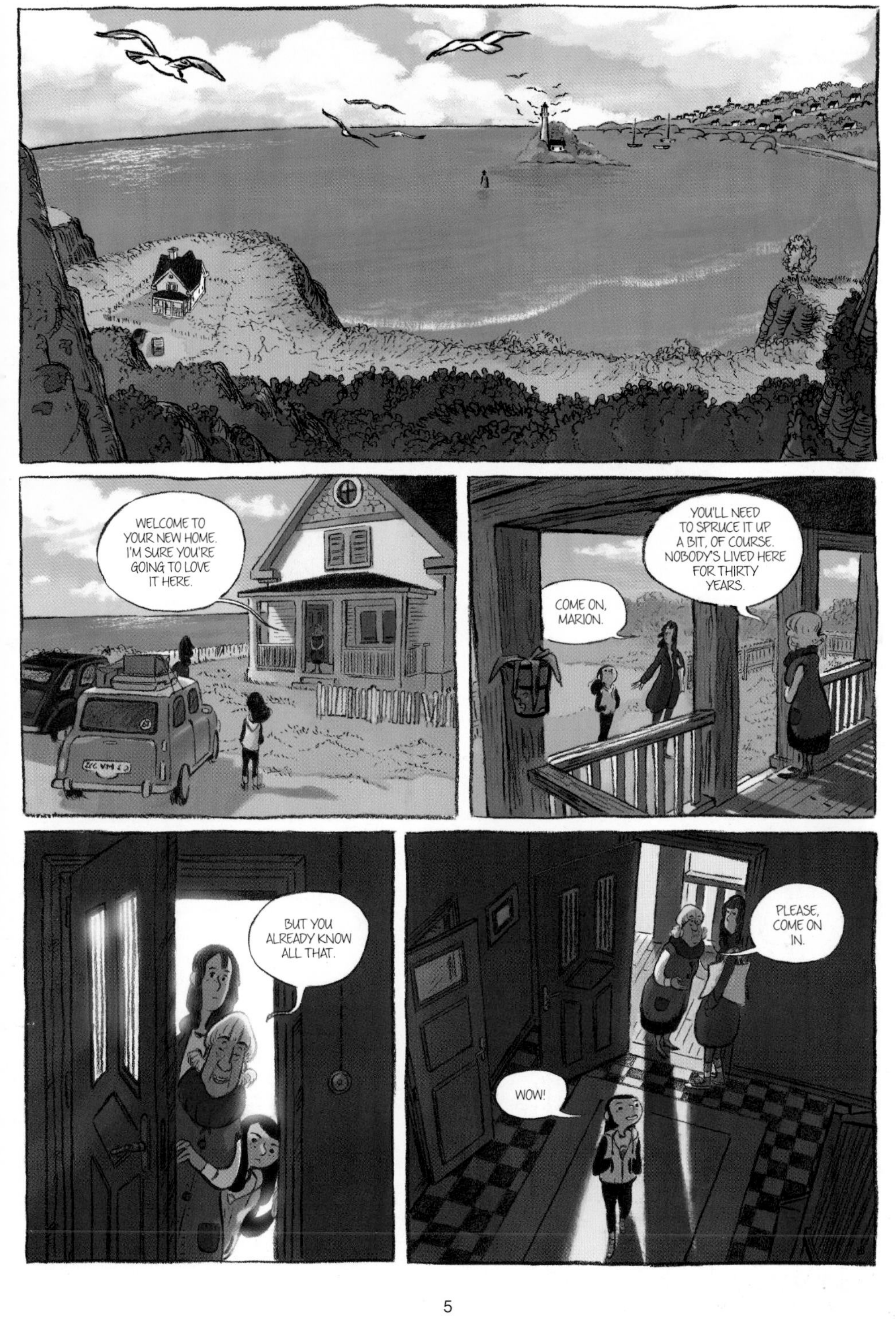
WELCOME TO YOUR NEW HOME. I'M SURE YOU'RE GOING TO LOVE IT HERE.
YOU'LL NEED TO SPRUCE IT UP A BIT, OF COURSE. NOBODY'S LIVED HERE FOR THIRTY YEARS.
COME ON, MARION.
BUT YOU ALREADY KNOW ALL THAT.
PLEASE, COME ON IN.
WOW!

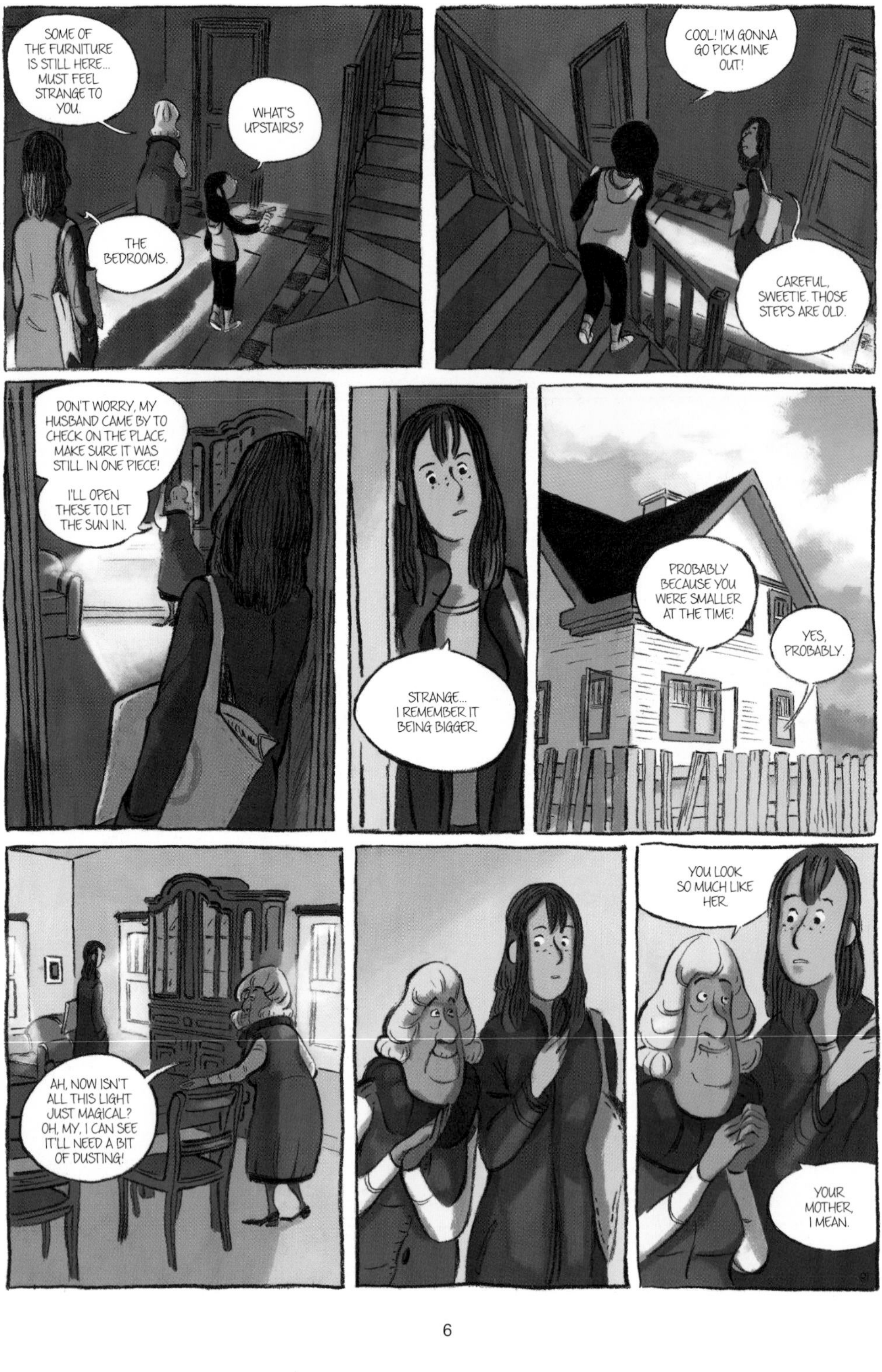
SOME OF THE FURNITURE IS STILL HERE... MUST FEEL STRANGE TO YOU.
WHAT'S UPSTAIRS?
THE BEDROOMS.
COOL! I'M GONNA GO PICK MINE OUT!
CAREFUL, SWEETIE. THOSE STEPS ARE OLD.
DON'T WORRY, MY HUSBAND CAME BY TO CHECK ON THE PLACE, MAKE SURE IT WAS STILL IN ONE PIECE!
I'LL OPEN THESE TO LET THE SUN IN.
STRANGE... I REMEMBER IT BEING BIGGER.
PROBABLY BECAUSE YOU WERE SMALLER AT THE TIME!
YES, PROBABLY.
AH, NOW ISN'T ALL THIS LIGHT JUST MAGICAL? OH, MY, I CAN SEE IT'LL NEED A BIT OF DUSTING!
YOU LOOK SO MUCH LIKE HER.
YOUR MOTHER, I MEAN.

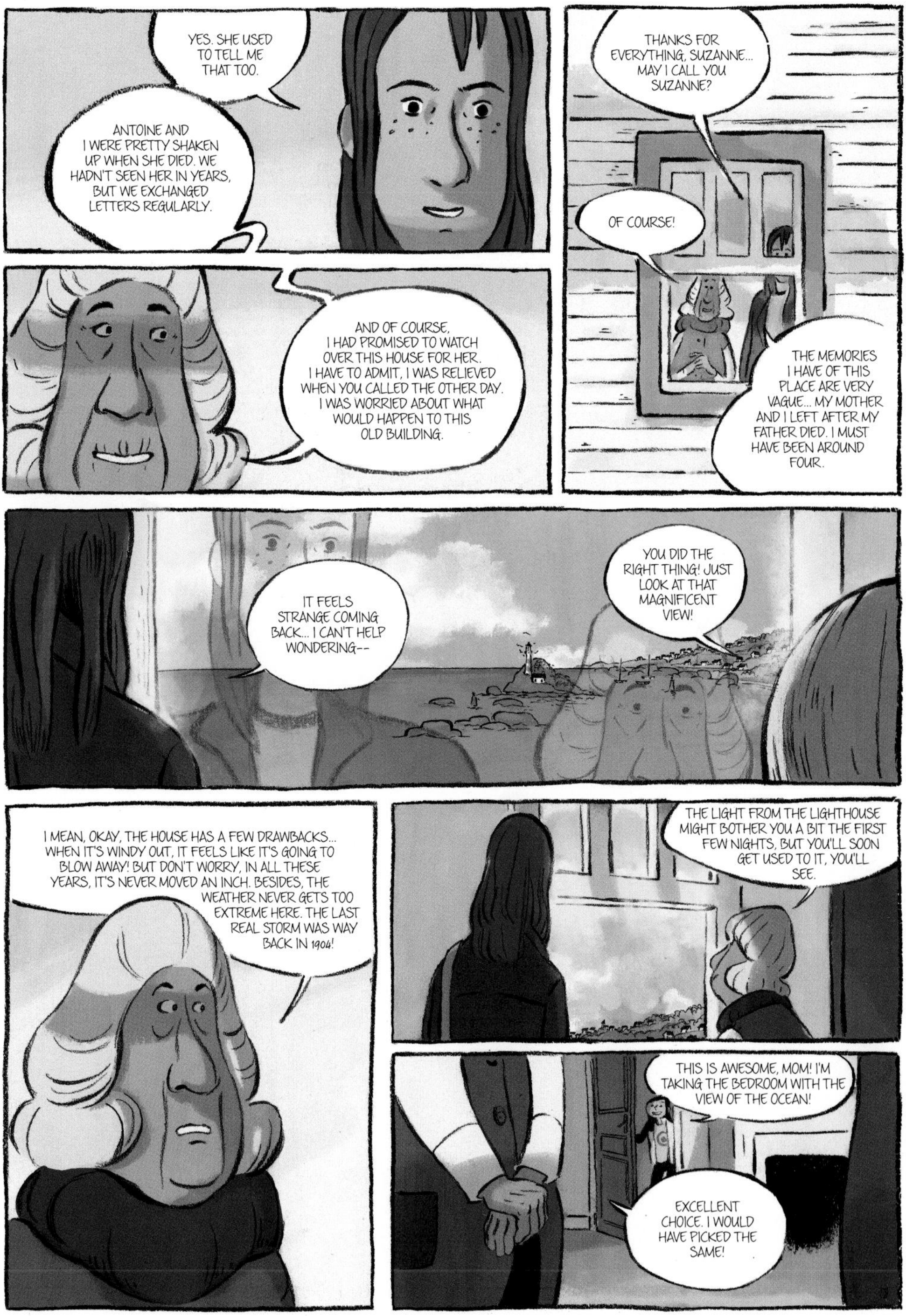
YES. SHE USED TO TELL ME THAT TOO.
ANTOINE AND I WERE PRETTY SHAKEN UP WHEN SHE DIED. WE HADN'T SEEN HER IN YEARS, BUT WE EXCHANGED LETTERS REGULARLY.
AND OF COURSE, I HAD PROMISED TO WATCH OVER THIS HOUSE FOR HER. I HAVE TO ADMIT, I WAS RELIEVED WHEN YOU CALLED THE OTHER DAY. I WAS WORRIED ABOUT WHAT WOULD HAPPEN TO THIS OLD BUILDING.
THANKS FOR EVERYTHING, SUZANNE... MAY I CALL YOU SUZANNE?
OF COURSE!
THE MEMORIES I HAVE OF THIS PLACE ARE VERY VAGUE... MY MOTHER AND I LEFT AFTER MY FATHER DIED. I MUST HAVE BEEN AROUND FOUR.
IT FEELS STRANGE COMING BACK... I CAN'T HELP WONDERING--
YOU DID THE RIGHT THING! JUST LOOK AT THAT MAGNIFICENT VIEW!
I MEAN, OKAY, THE HOUSE HAS A FEW DRAWBACKS... WHEN IT'S WINDY OUT, IT FEELS LIKE IT'S GOING TO BLOW AWAY! BUT DON'T WORRY, IN ALL THESE YEARS, IT'S NEVER MOVED AN INCH. BESIDES, THE WEATHER NEVER GETS TOO EXTREME HERE. THE LAST REAL STORM WAS WAY BACK IN 1904!
THE LIGHT FROM THE LIGHTHOUSE MIGHT BOTHER YOU A BIT THE FIRST FEW NIGHTS, BUT YOU'LL SOON GET USED TO IT, YOU'LL SEE.
THIS IS AWESOME, MOM! I'M TAKING THE BEDROOM WITH THE VIEW OF THE OCEAN!
EXCELLENT CHOICE. I WOULD HAVE PICKED THE SAME!

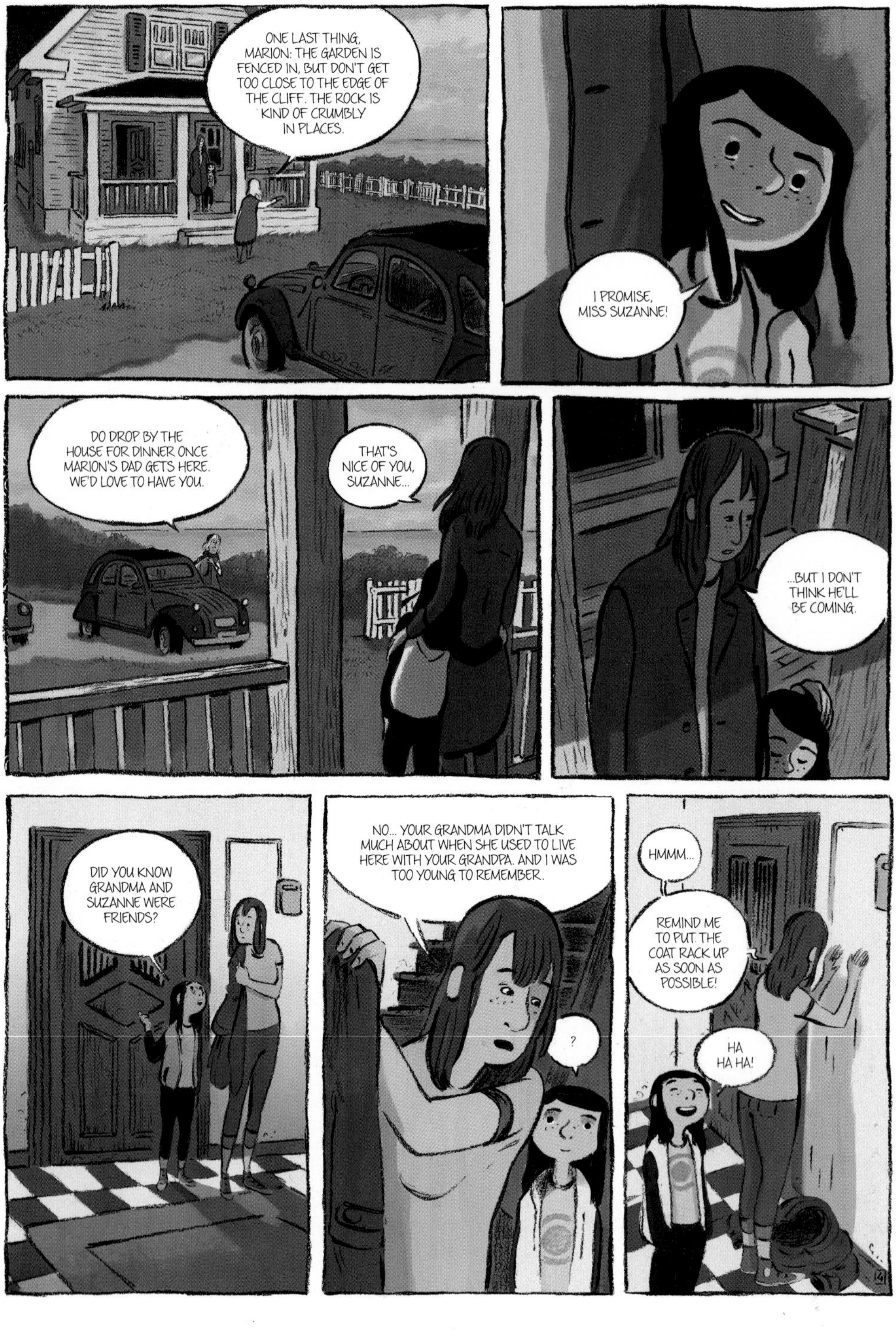
ONE LAST THING, MARION: THE GARDEN IS FENCED IN, BUT DON'T GET TOO CLOSE TO THE EDGE OF THE CLIFF. THE ROCK IS KIND OF CRUMBLY IN PLACES.
I PROMISE, MISS SUZANNE!
DO DROP BY THE HOUSE FOR DINNER ONCE MARION'S DAD GETS HERE. WE'D LOVE TO HAVE YOU.
THAT'S NICE OF YOU, SUZANNE...
...BUT I DON'T THINK HE'LL BE COMING.
DID YOU KNOW GRANDMA AND SUZANNE WERE FRIENDS?
NO... YOUR GRANDMA DIDN'T TALK MUCH ABOUT WHEN SHE USED TO LIVE HERE WITH YOUR GRANDPA. AND I WAS TOO YOUNG TO REMEMBER.
?
HMMM...
REMIND ME TO PUT THE COAT RACK UP AS SOON AS POSSIBLE!
HA HA HA!

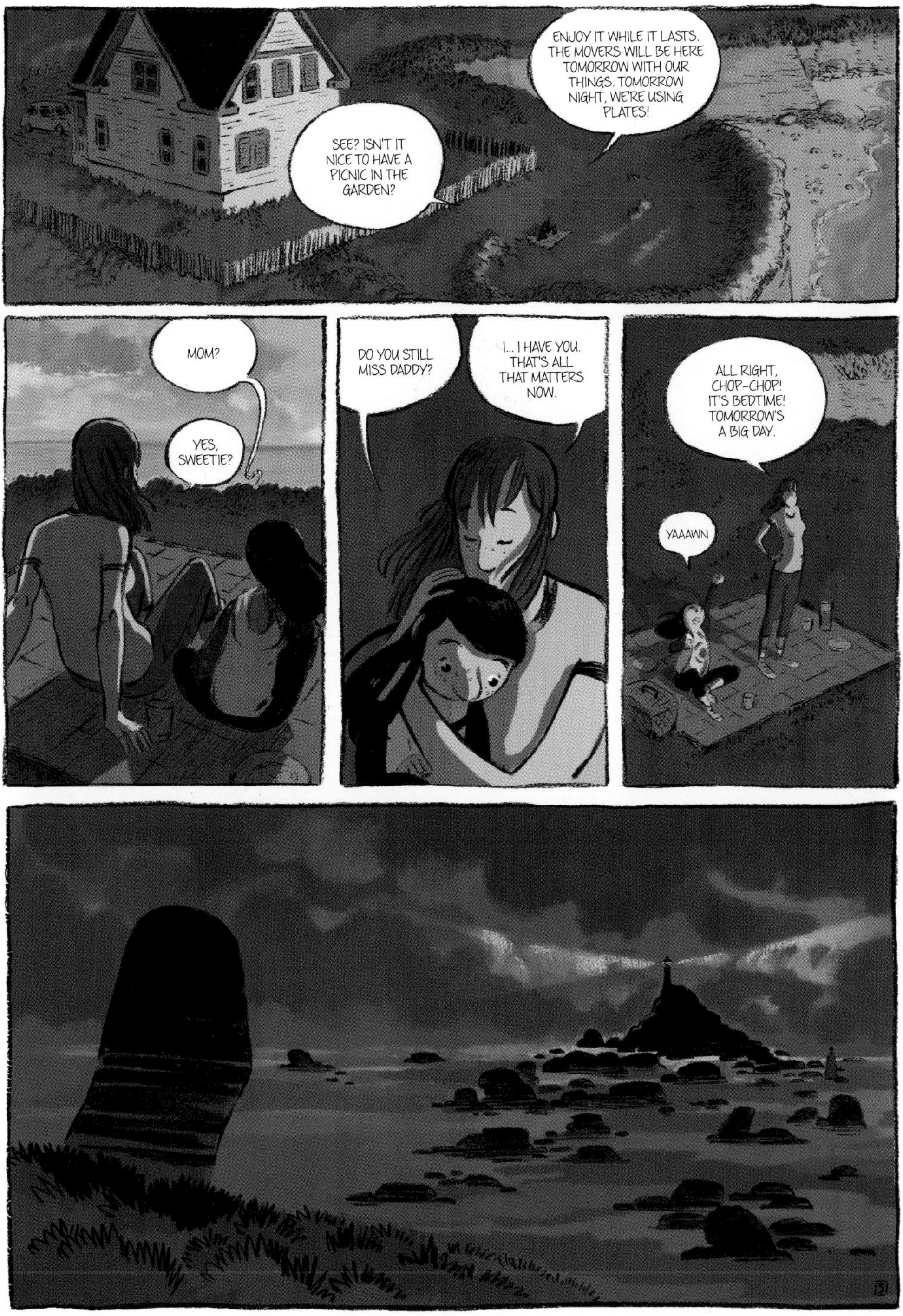
ENJOY IT WHILE IT LASTS. THE MOVERS WILL BE HERE TOMORROW WITH OUR THINGS. TOMORROW NIGHT, WE'RE USING PLATES!
SEE? ISN'T IT NICE TO HAVE A PICNIC IN THE GARDEN?
MOM?
YES, SWEETIE?
DO YOU STILL MISS DADDY?
I... I HAVE YOU. THAT'S ALL THAT MATTERS NOW.
ALL RIGHT, CHOP-CHOP! IT'S BEDTIME! TOMORROW'S A BIG DAY.
YAAAWN

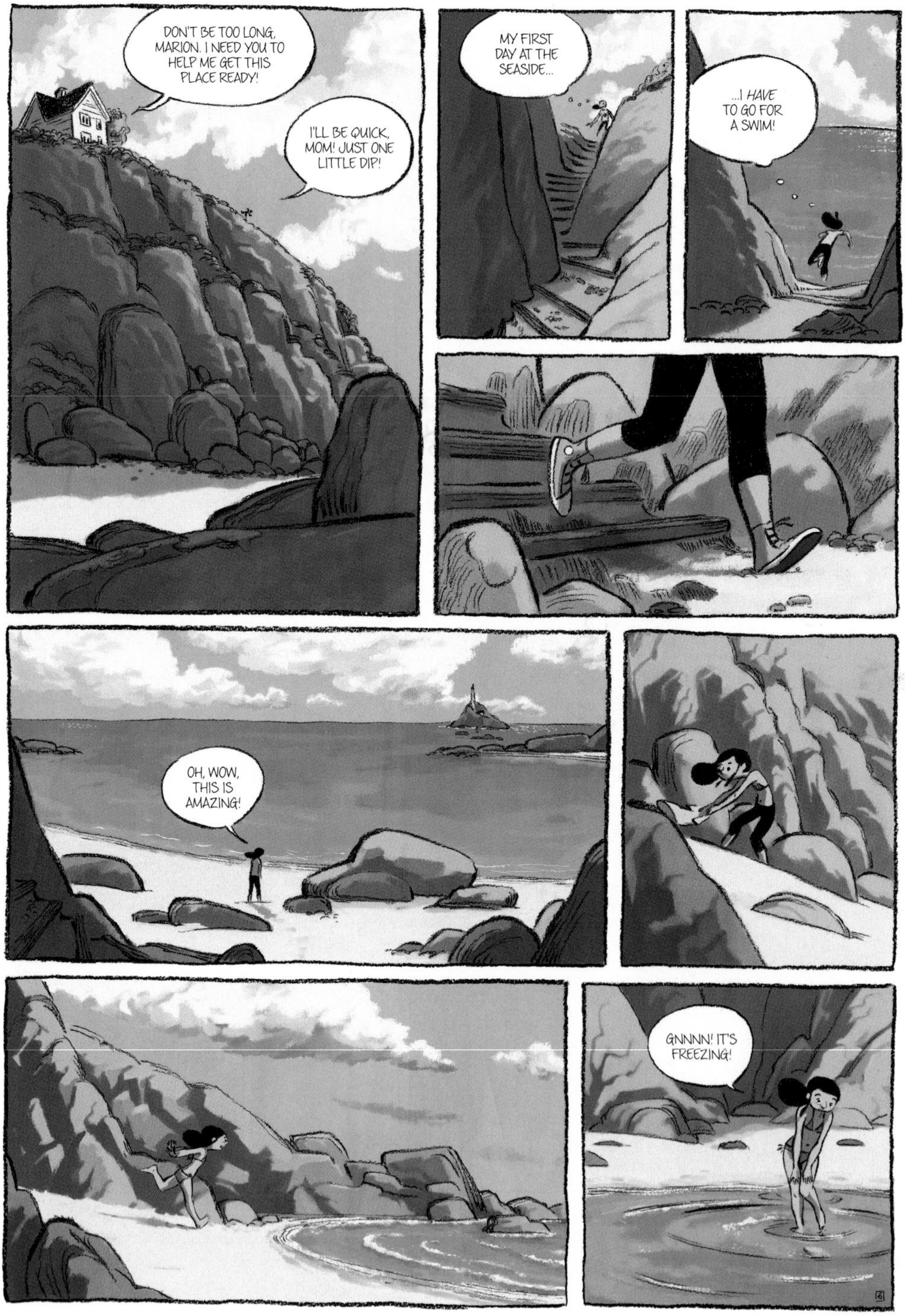
DON'T BE TOO LONG, MARION. I NEED YOU TO HELP ME GET THIS PLACE READY!
I'LL BE QUICK, MOM! JUST ONE LITTLE DIP!
MY FIRST DAY AT THE SEASIDE...
...I *HAVE* TO GO FOR A SWIM!
OH, WOW, THIS IS AMAZING!
GNNNN! IT'S FREEZING!

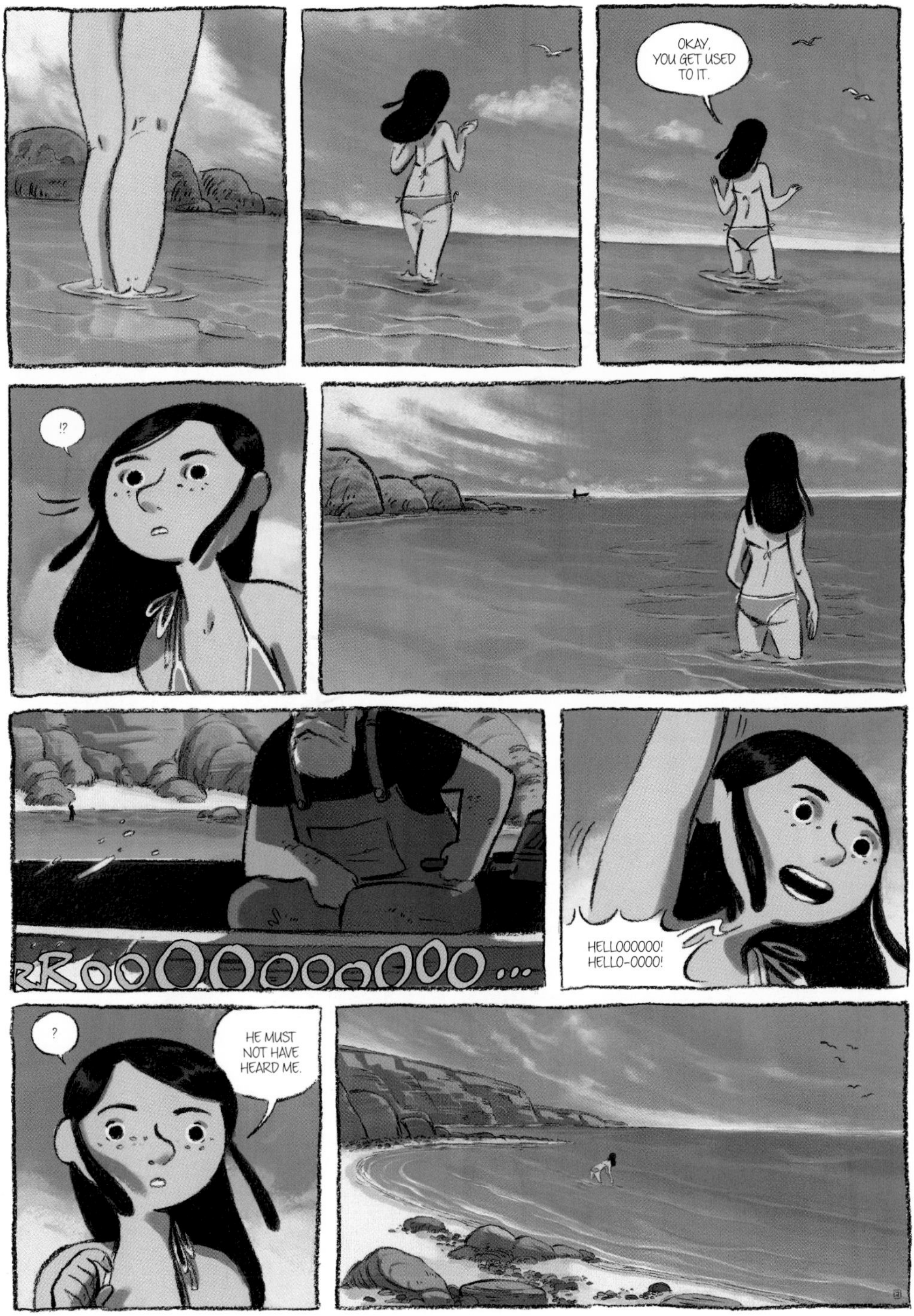
OKAY, YOU GET USED TO IT.
!?
RROOOOOOooOOOO...
HELLOOOOOO! HELLO-OOOO!
?
HE MUST NOT HAVE HEARD ME.

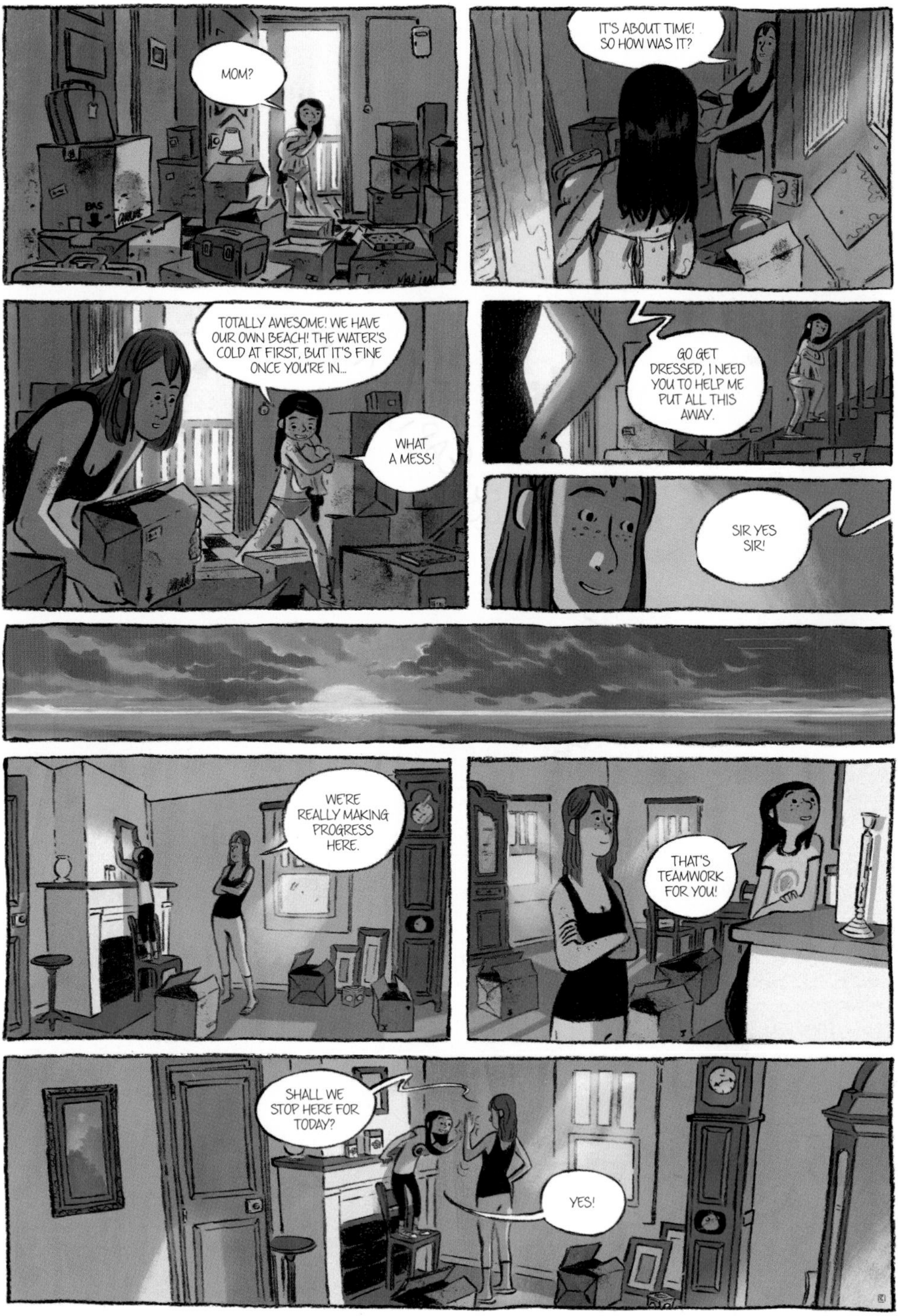
MOM?
IT'S ABOUT TIME! SO HOW WAS IT?
TOTALLY AWESOME! WE HAVE OUR OWN BEACH! THE WATER'S COLD AT FIRST, BUT IT'S FINE ONCE YOU'RE IN...
WHAT A MESS!
GO GET DRESSED, I NEED YOU TO HELP ME PUT ALL THIS AWAY.
SIR YES SIR!
WE'RE REALLY MAKING PROGRESS HERE.
THAT'S TEAMWORK FOR YOU!
SHALL WE STOP HERE FOR TODAY?
YES!

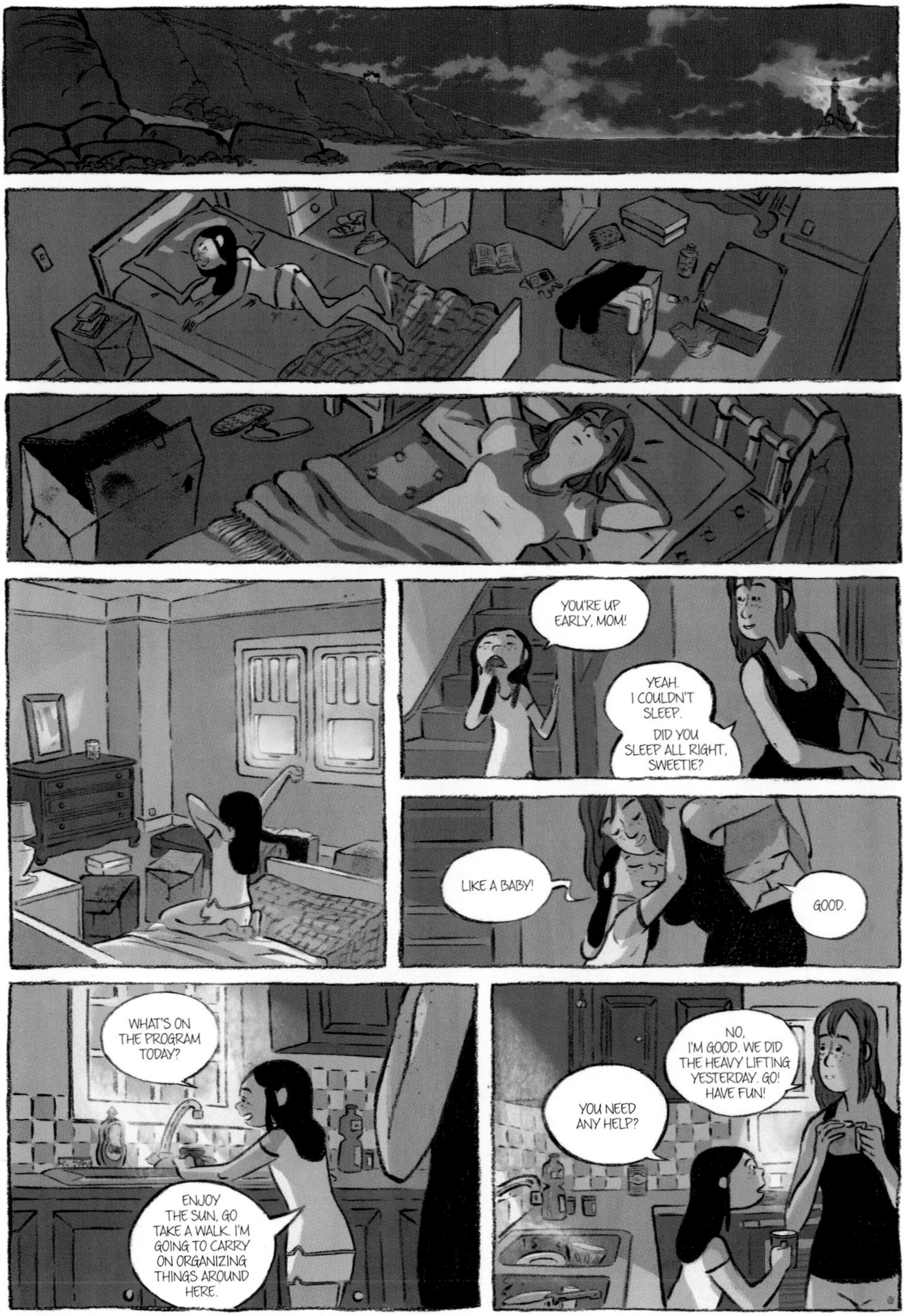
YOU'RE UP EARLY, MOM!
YEAH. I COULDN'T SLEEP.
DID YOU SLEEP ALL RIGHT, SWEETIE?
LIKE A BABY!
GOOD.
WHAT'S ON THE PROGRAM TODAY?
ENJOY THE SUN, GO TAKE A WALK. I'M GOING TO CARRY ON ORGANIZING THINGS AROUND HERE.
YOU NEED ANY HELP?
NO, I'M GOOD. WE DID THE HEAVY LIFTING YESTERDAY. GO! HAVE FUN!

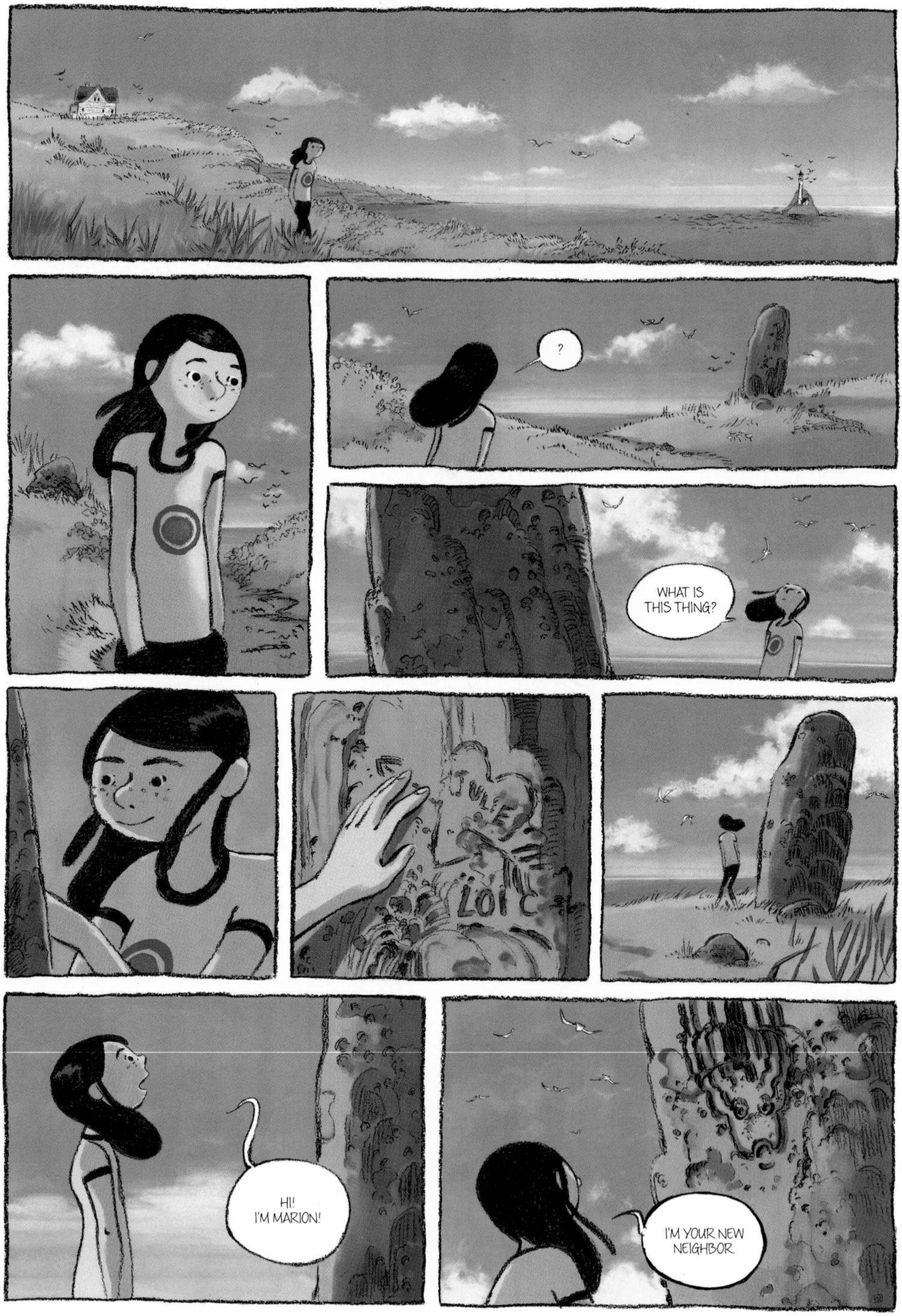
?
WHAT IS THIS THING?
JULIE
LOIC
HI! I'M MARION!
I'M YOUR NEW NEIGHBOR.

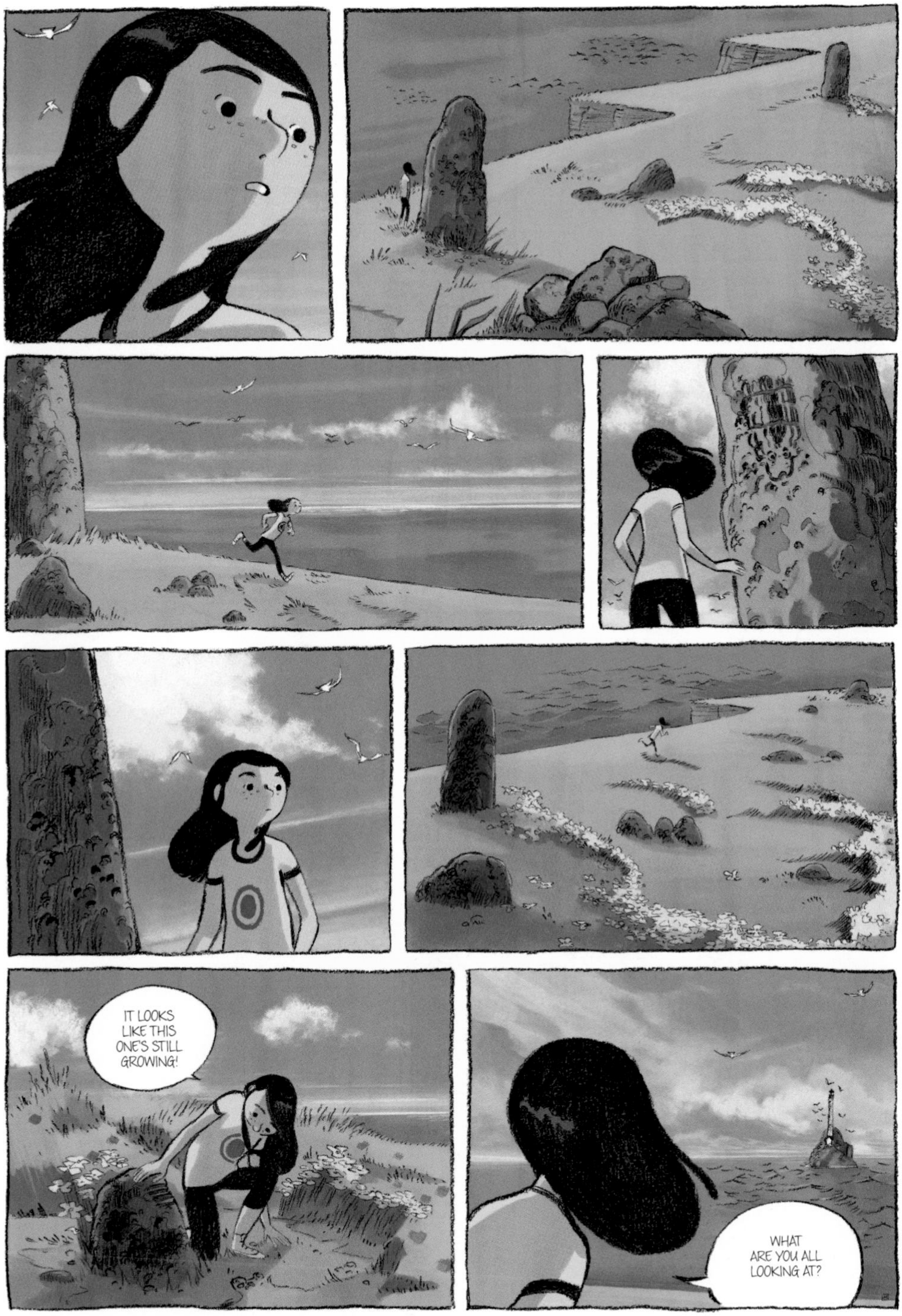
IT LOOKS LIKE THIS ONE'S STILL GROWING!
WHAT ARE YOU ALL LOOKING AT?

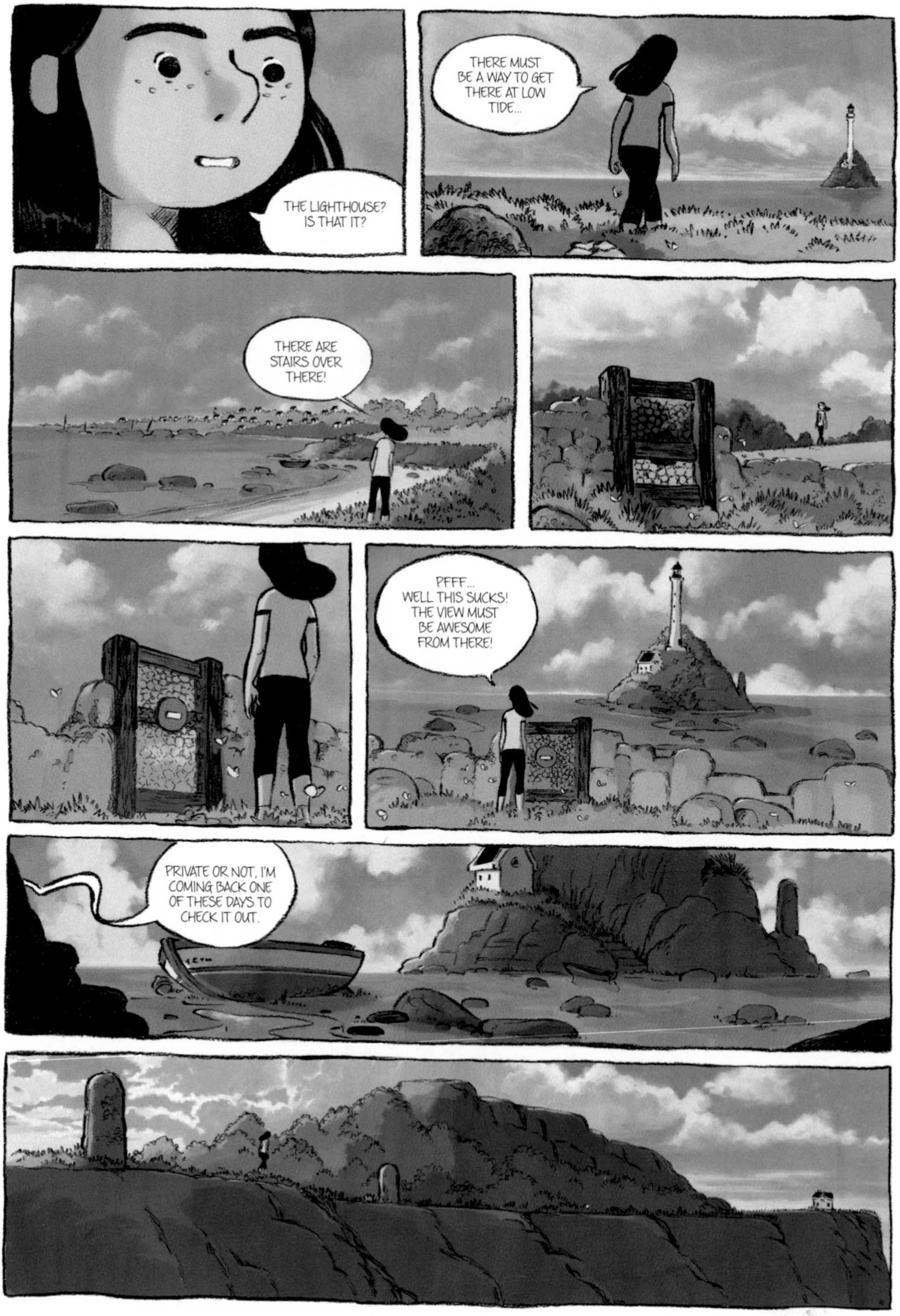
THE LIGHTHOUSE? IS THAT IT?
THERE MUST BE A WAY TO GET THERE AT LOW TIDE...
THERE ARE STAIRS OVER THERE!
PFFF... WELL THIS SUCKS! THE VIEW MUST BE AWESOME FROM THERE!
PRIVATE OR NOT, I'M COMING BACK ONE OF THESE DAYS TO CHECK IT OUT.

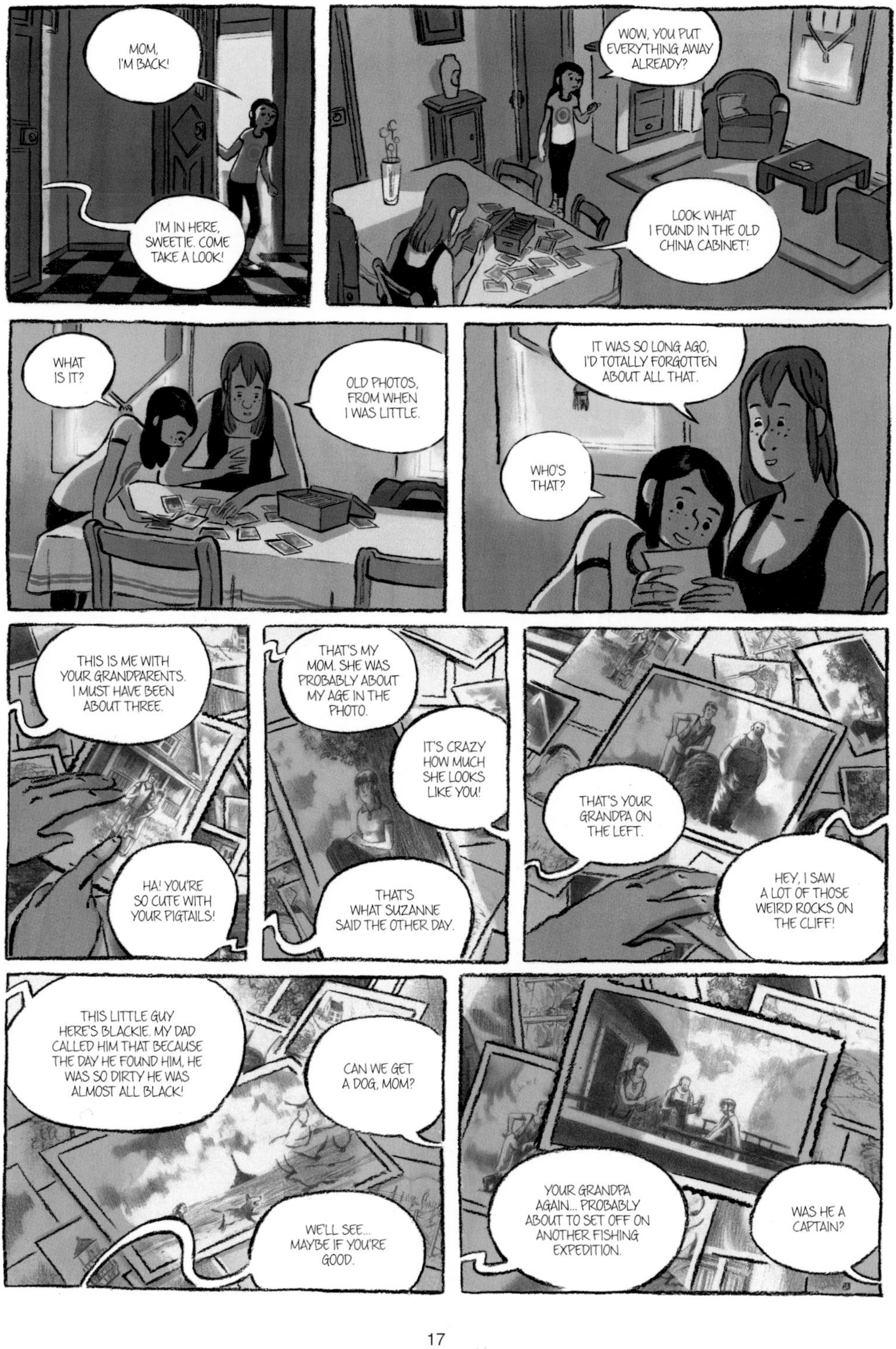
MOM, I'M BACK!
I'M IN HERE, SWEETIE. COME TAKE A LOOK!
WOW, YOU PUT EVERYTHING AWAY ALREADY?
LOOK WHAT I FOUND IN THE OLD CHINA CABINET!
WHAT IS IT?
OLD PHOTOS, FROM WHEN I WAS LITTLE.
IT WAS SO LONG AGO, I'D TOTALLY FORGOTTEN ABOUT ALL THAT.
WHO'S THAT?
THIS IS ME WITH YOUR GRANDPARENTS. I MUST HAVE BEEN ABOUT THREE.
HA! YOU'RE SO CUTE WITH YOUR PIGTAILS!
THAT'S MY MOM. SHE WAS PROBABLY ABOUT MY AGE IN THE PHOTO.
IT'S CRAZY HOW MUCH SHE LOOKS LIKE YOU!
THAT'S WHAT SUZANNE SAID THE OTHER DAY.
THAT'S YOUR GRANDPA ON THE LEFT.
HEY, I SAW A LOT OF THOSE WEIRD ROCKS ON THE CLIFF!
THIS LITTLE GUY HERE'S BLACKIE. MY DAD CALLED HIM THAT BECAUSE THE DAY HE FOUND HIM, HE WAS SO DIRTY HE WAS ALMOST ALL BLACK!
CAN WE GET A DOG, MOM?
WE'LL SEE... MAYBE IF YOU'RE GOOD.
YOUR GRANDPA AGAIN... PROBABLY ABOUT TO SET OFF ON ANOTHER FISHING EXPEDITION.
WAS HE A CAPTAIN?

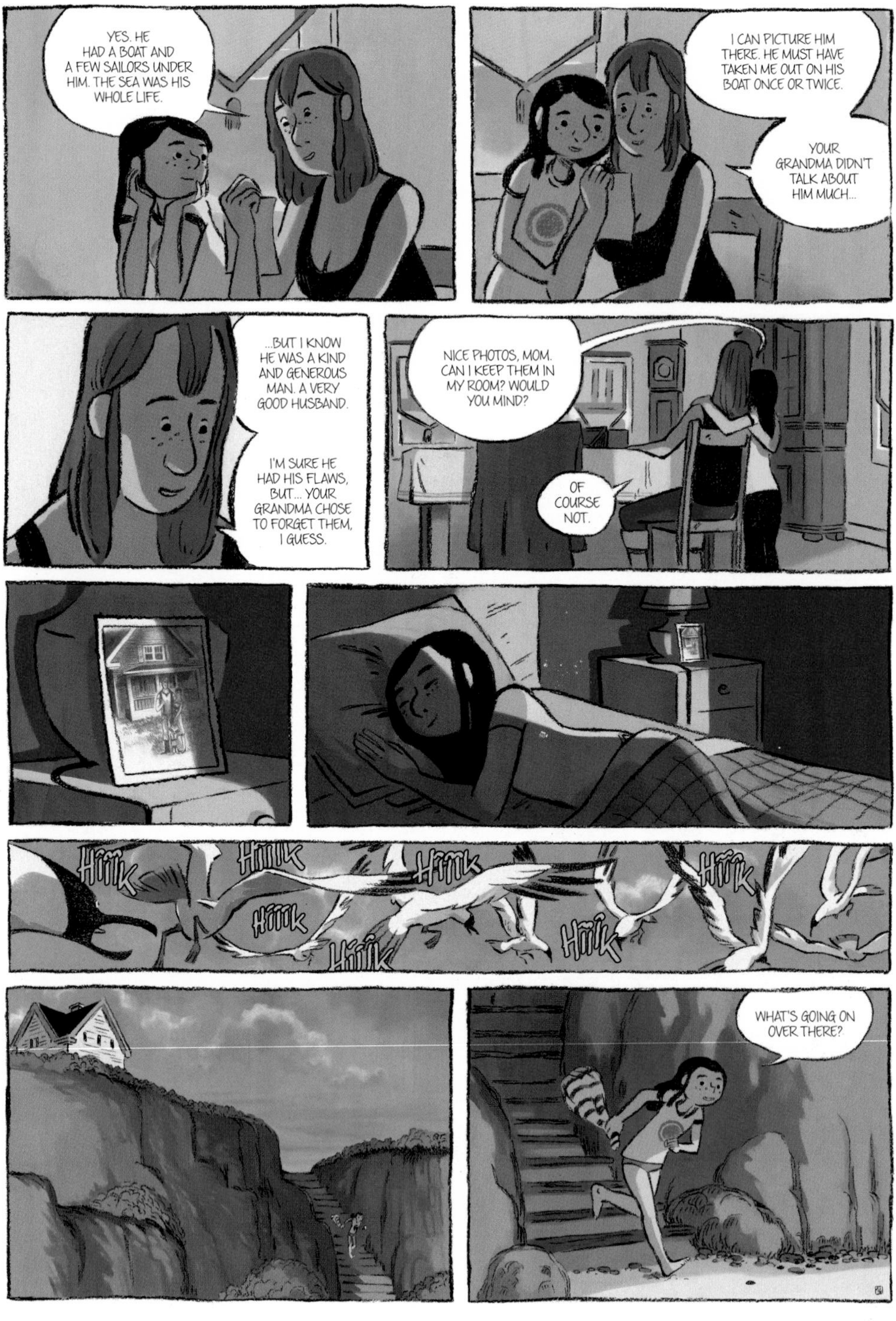
YES. HE HAD A BOAT AND A FEW SAILORS UNDER HIM. THE SEA WAS HIS WHOLE LIFE.
I CAN PICTURE HIM THERE. HE MUST HAVE TAKEN ME OUT ON HIS BOAT ONCE OR TWICE.
YOUR GRANDMA DIDN'T TALK ABOUT HIM MUCH...
...BUT I KNOW HE WAS A KIND AND GENEROUS MAN. A VERY GOOD HUSBAND.
I'M SURE HE HAD HIS FLAWS, BUT... YOUR GRANDMA CHOSE TO FORGET THEM, I GUESS.
NICE PHOTOS, MOM. CAN I KEEP THEM IN MY ROOM? WOULD YOU MIND?
OF COURSE NOT.
HIIIK
HIIIK
HIIIK
HIIIK
HIIIK
HIIIK
HIIIK
WHAT'S GOING ON OVER THERE?

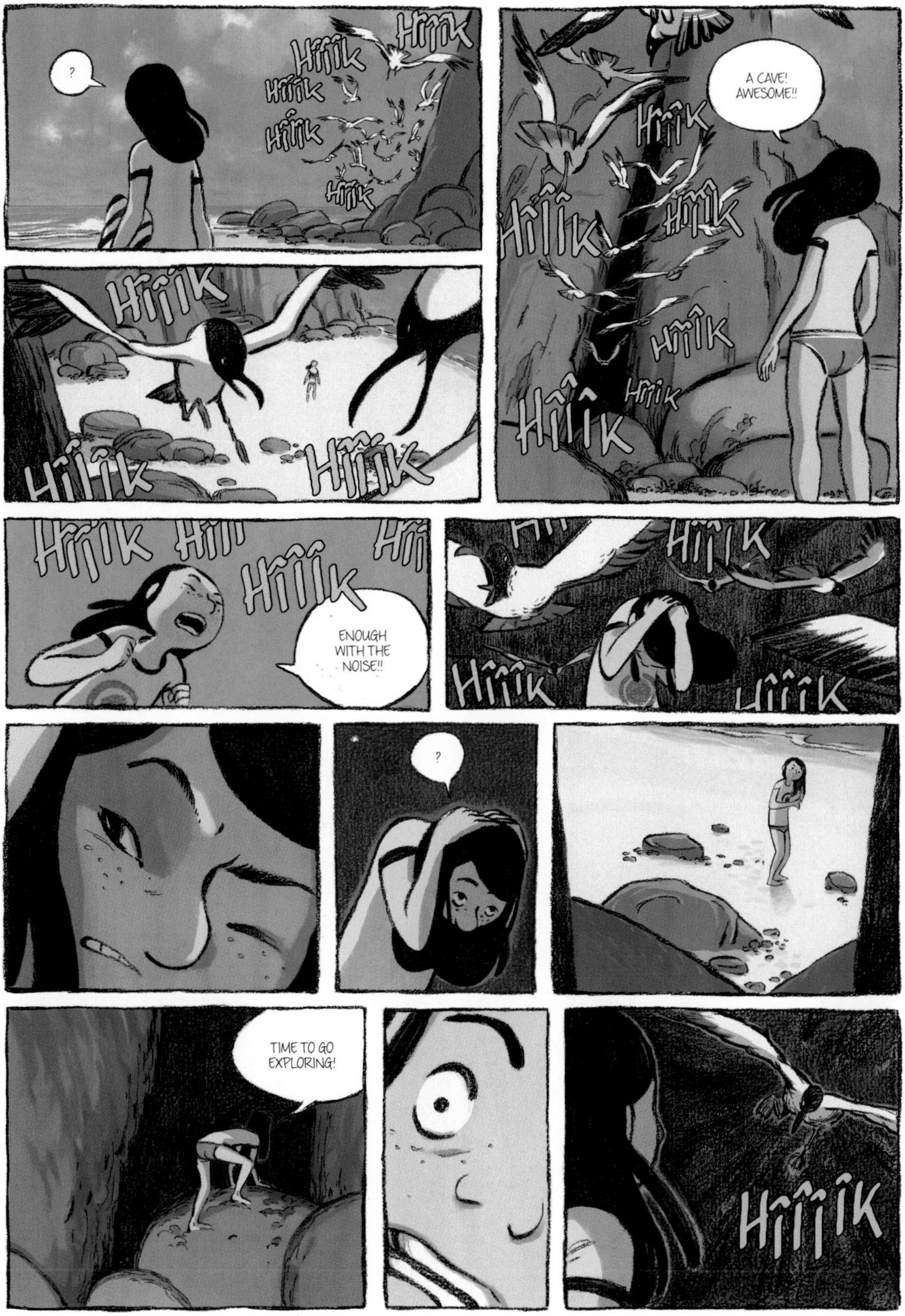
?
Hiîîk
A CAVE! AWESOME!!
Hiîîk
ENOUGH WITH THE NOISE!!
Hiîîk
?
TIME TO GO EXPLORING!
Hiîîk

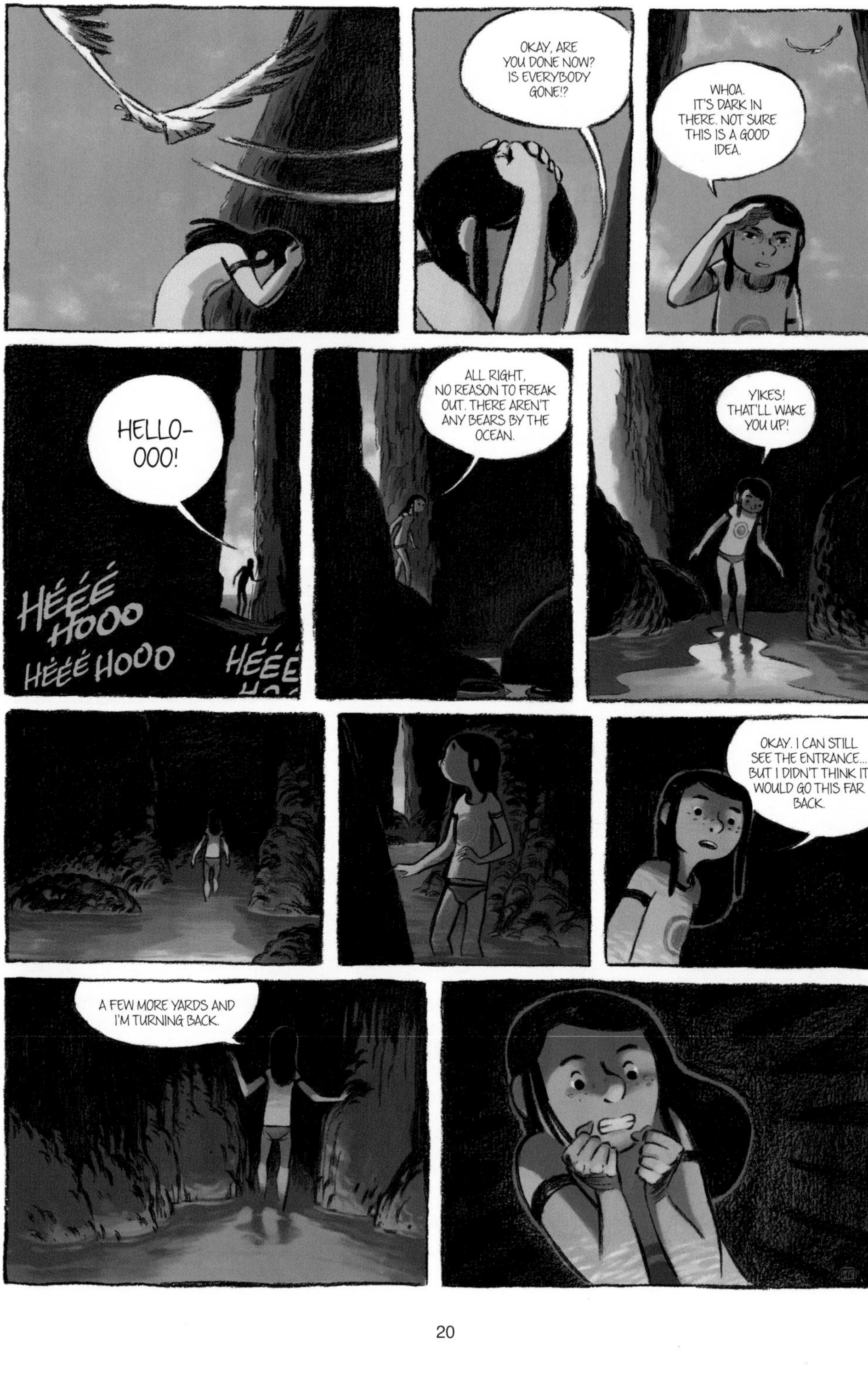
OKAY, ARE YOU DONE NOW? IS EVERYBODY GONE!?
WHOA. IT'S DARK IN THERE. NOT SURE THIS IS A GOOD IDEA.
HELLO-OOO!
HÉÉÉ HOOO
HÉÉÉ HOOO
ALL RIGHT, NO REASON TO FREAK OUT. THERE AREN'T ANY BEARS BY THE OCEAN.
YIKES! THAT'LL WAKE YOU UP!
OKAY. I CAN STILL SEE THE ENTRANCE... BUT I DIDN'T THINK IT WOULD GO THIS FAR BACK.
A FEW MORE YARDS AND I'M TURNING BACK.

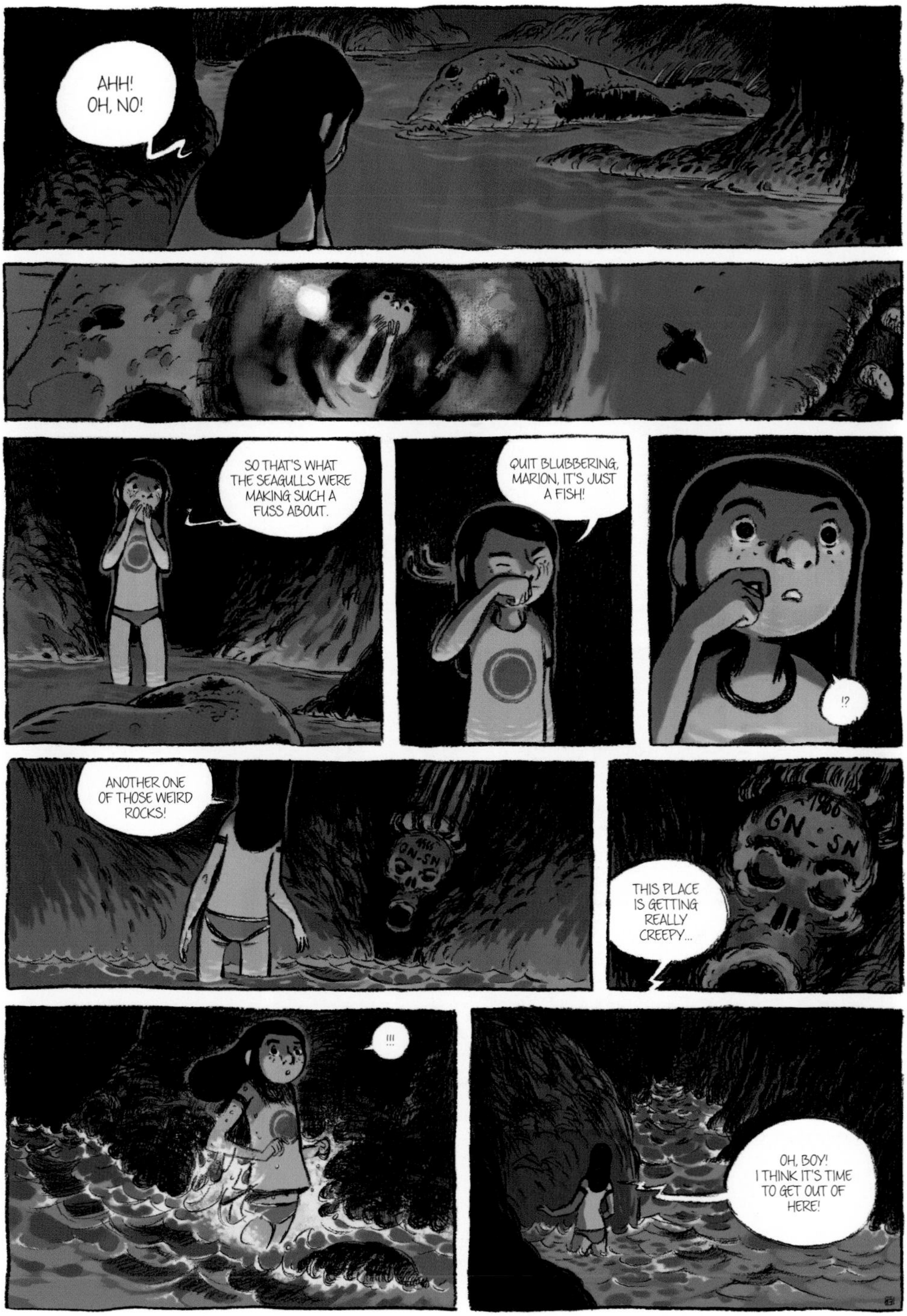
AHH! OH, NO!
SO THAT'S WHAT THE SEAGULLS WERE MAKING SUCH A FUSS ABOUT.
QUIT BLUBBERING, MARION, IT'S JUST A FISH!
!?
ANOTHER ONE OF THOSE WEIRD ROCKS!
GN - SN
THIS PLACE IS GETTING REALLY CREEPY...
!!!
OH, BOY! I THINK IT'S TIME TO GET OUT OF HERE!

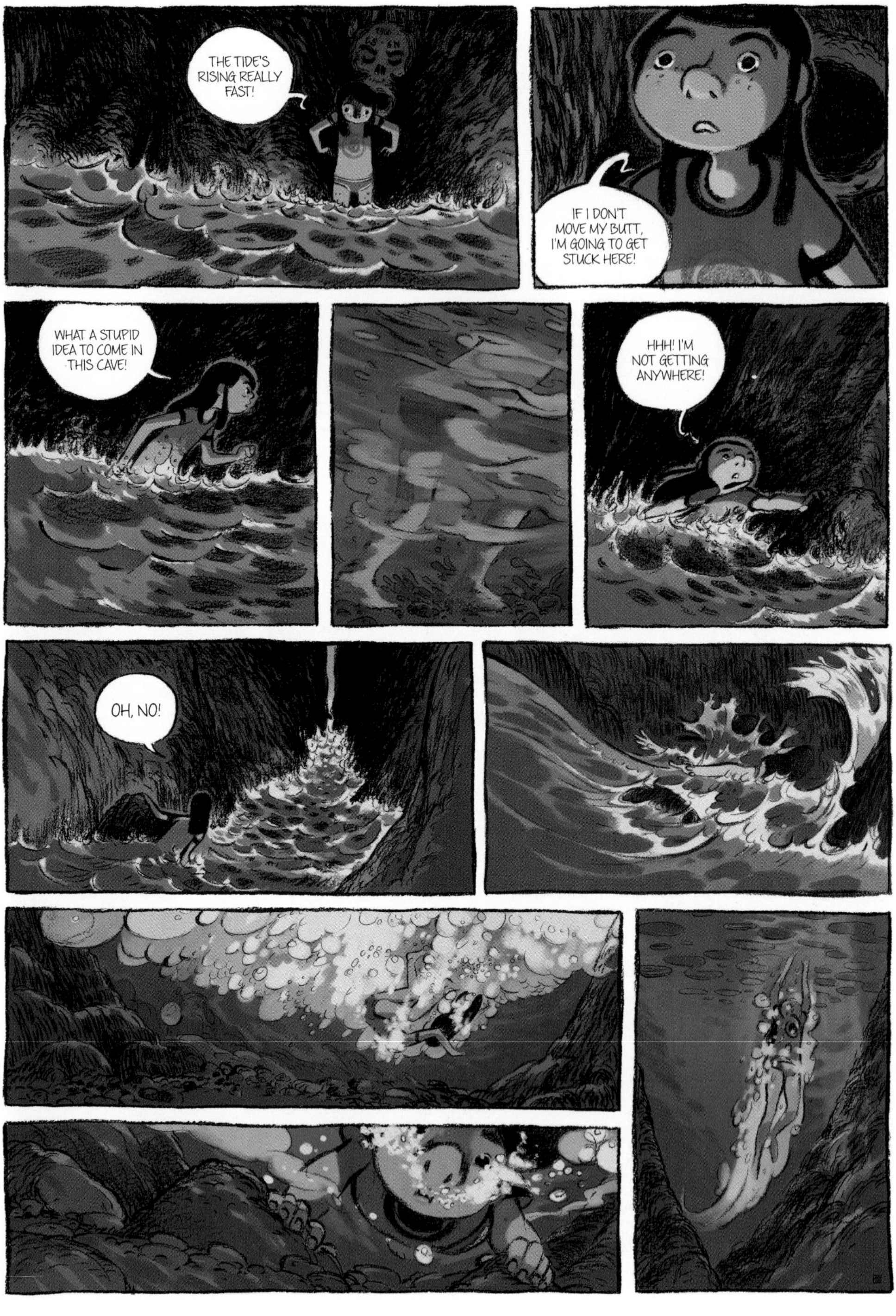
THE TIDE'S RISING REALLY FAST!
IF I DON'T MOVE MY BUTT, I'M GOING TO GET STUCK HERE!
WHAT A STUPID IDEA TO COME IN THIS CAVE!
HHH! I'M NOT GETTING ANYWHERE!
OH, NO!

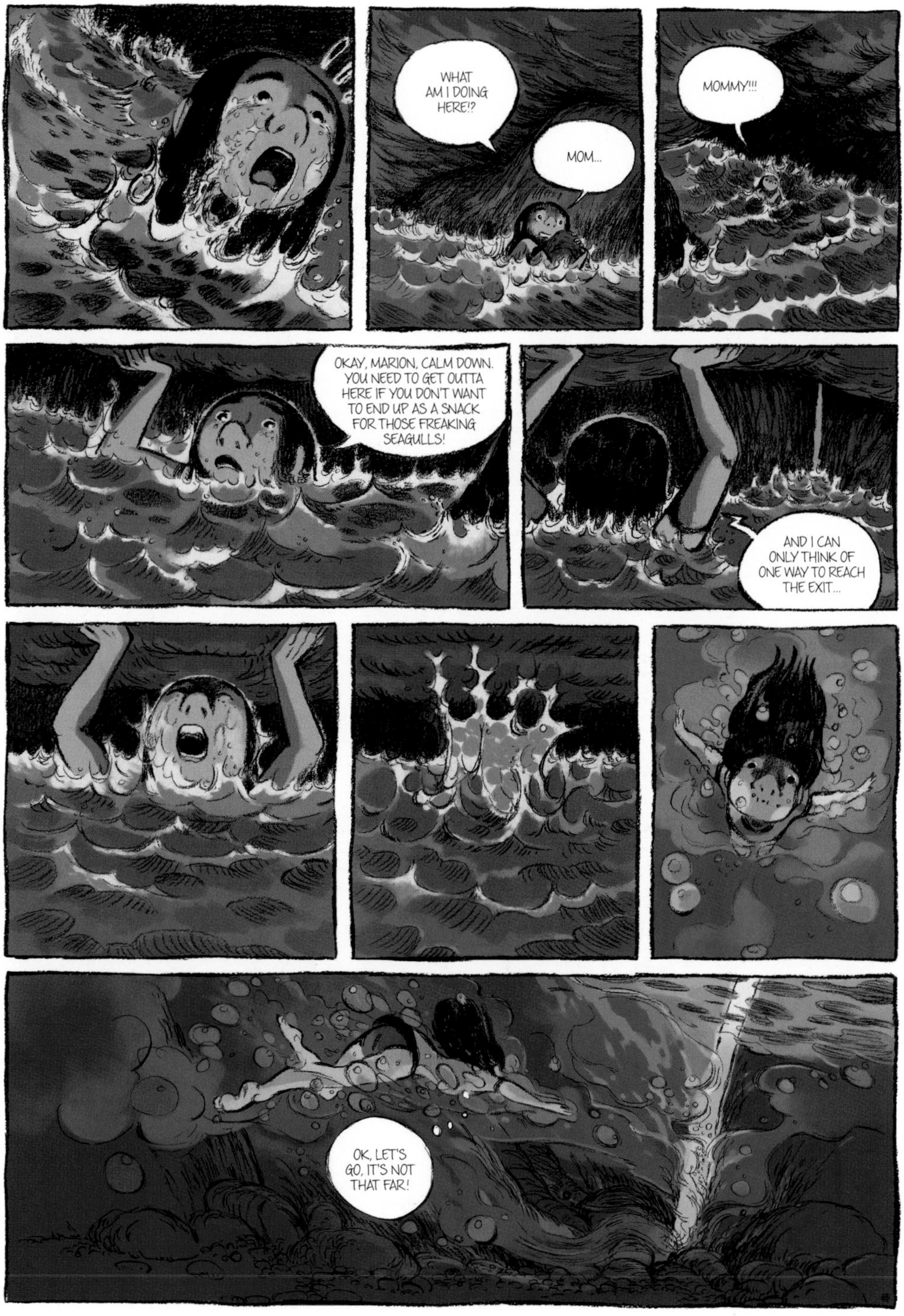
WHAT AM I DOING HERE!?
MOM...
MOMMY!!!
OKAY, MARION, CALM DOWN. YOU NEED TO GET OUTTA HERE IF YOU DON'T WANT TO END UP AS A SNACK FOR THOSE FREAKING SEAGULLS!
AND I CAN ONLY THINK OF ONE WAY TO REACH THE EXIT...
OK, LET'S GO, IT'S NOT THAT FAR!

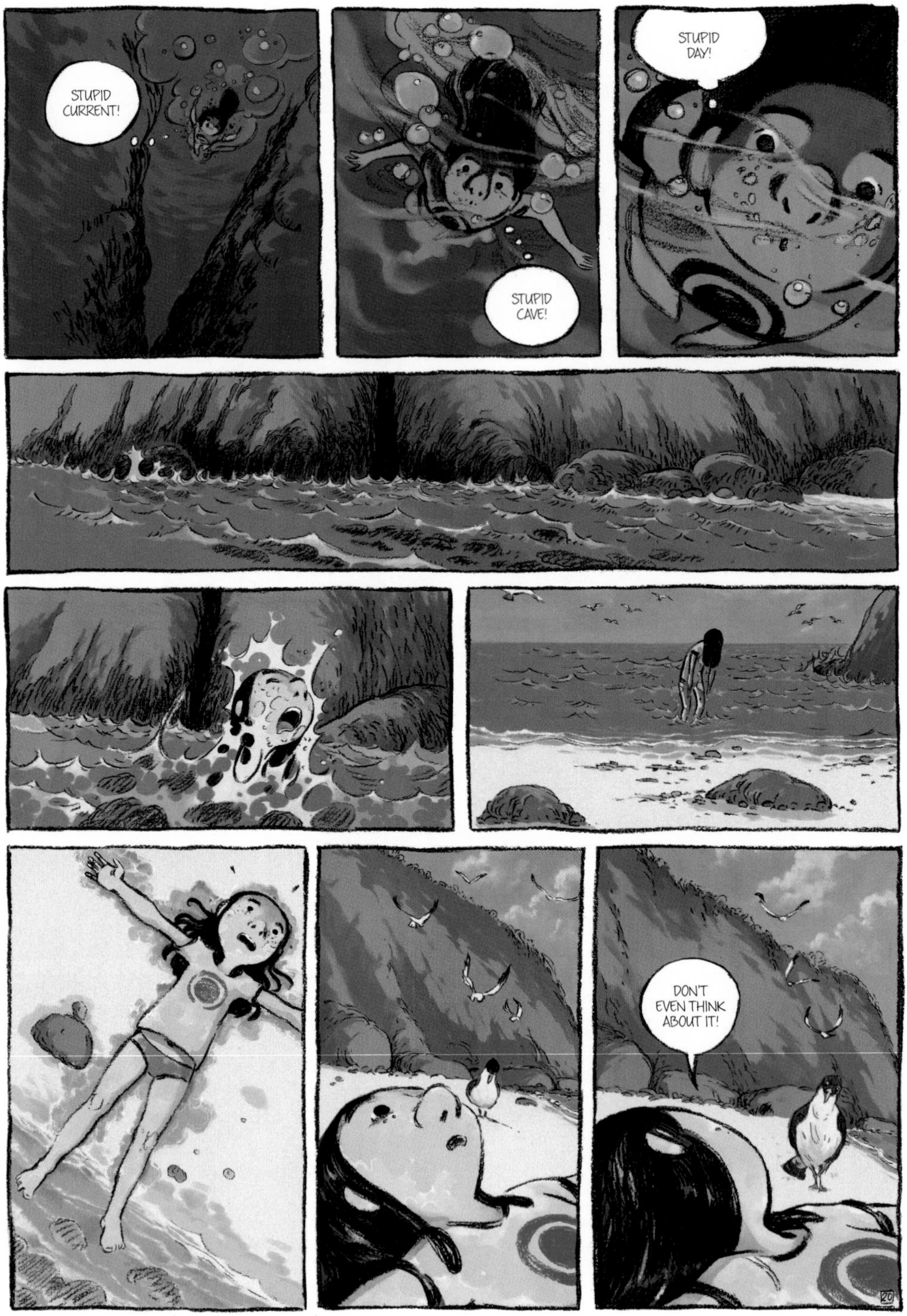
STUPID CURRENT!
STUPID CAVE!
STUPID DAY!
DON'T EVEN THINK ABOUT IT!
20

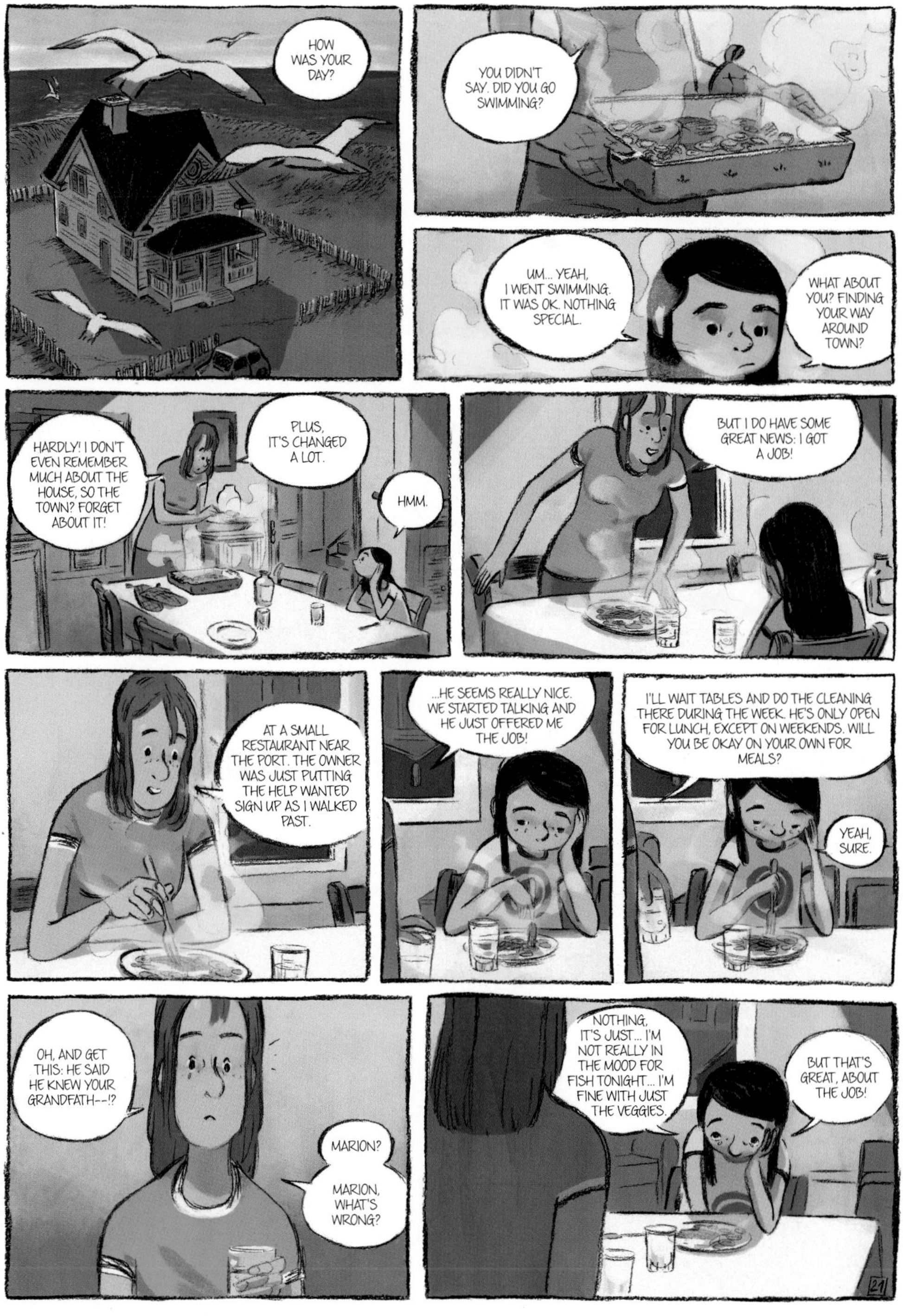
HOW WAS YOUR DAY?
YOU DIDN'T SAY. DID YOU GO SWIMMING?
UM... YEAH, I WENT SWIMMING. IT WAS OK. NOTHING SPECIAL.
WHAT ABOUT YOU? FINDING YOUR WAY AROUND TOWN?
HARDLY! I DON'T EVEN REMEMBER MUCH ABOUT THE HOUSE, SO THE TOWN? FORGET ABOUT IT!
PLUS, IT'S CHANGED A LOT.
HMM.
BUT I DO HAVE SOME GREAT NEWS: I GOT A JOB!
AT A SMALL RESTAURANT NEAR THE PORT. THE OWNER WAS JUST PUTTING THE HELP WANTED SIGN UP AS I WALKED PAST.
...HE SEEMS REALLY NICE. WE STARTED TALKING AND HE JUST OFFERED ME THE JOB!
I'LL WAIT TABLES AND DO THE CLEANING THERE DURING THE WEEK. HE'S ONLY OPEN FOR LUNCH, EXCEPT ON WEEKENDS. WILL YOU BE OKAY ON YOUR OWN FOR MEALS?
YEAH, SURE.
OH, AND GET THIS: HE SAID HE KNEW YOUR GRANDFATH--!?
MARION?
MARION, WHAT'S WRONG?
NOTHING, IT'S JUST... I'M NOT REALLY IN THE MOOD FOR FISH TONIGHT... I'M FINE WITH JUST THE VEGGIES.
BUT THAT'S GREAT, ABOUT THE JOB!
21

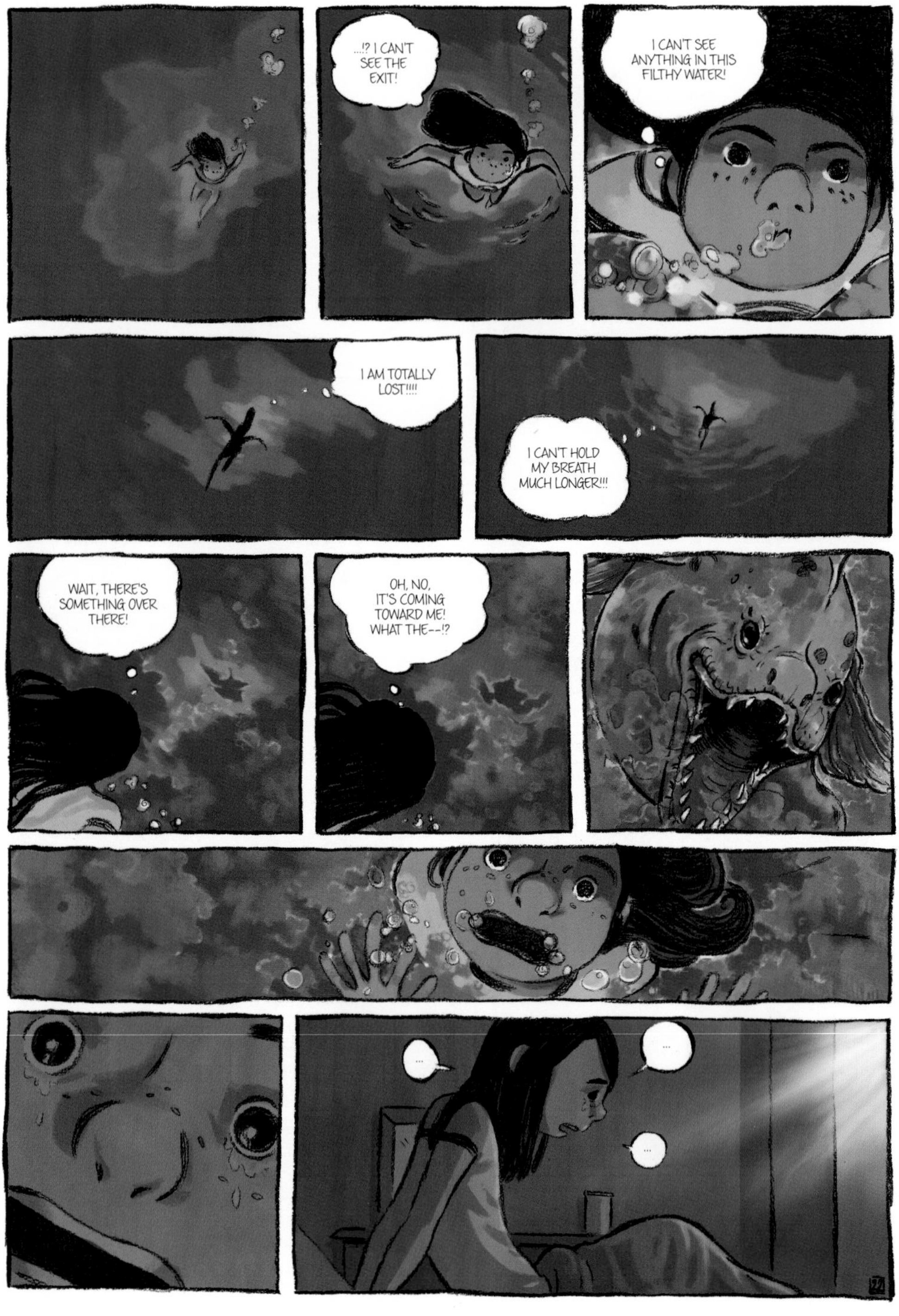

...!? I CAN'T SEE THE EXIT!
I CAN'T SEE ANYTHING IN THIS FILTHY WATER!
I AM TOTALLY LOST!!!!
I CAN'T HOLD MY BREATH MUCH LONGER!!!
WAIT, THERE'S SOMETHING OVER THERE!
OH, NO, IT'S COMING TOWARD ME! WHAT THE--!?
...
...
...

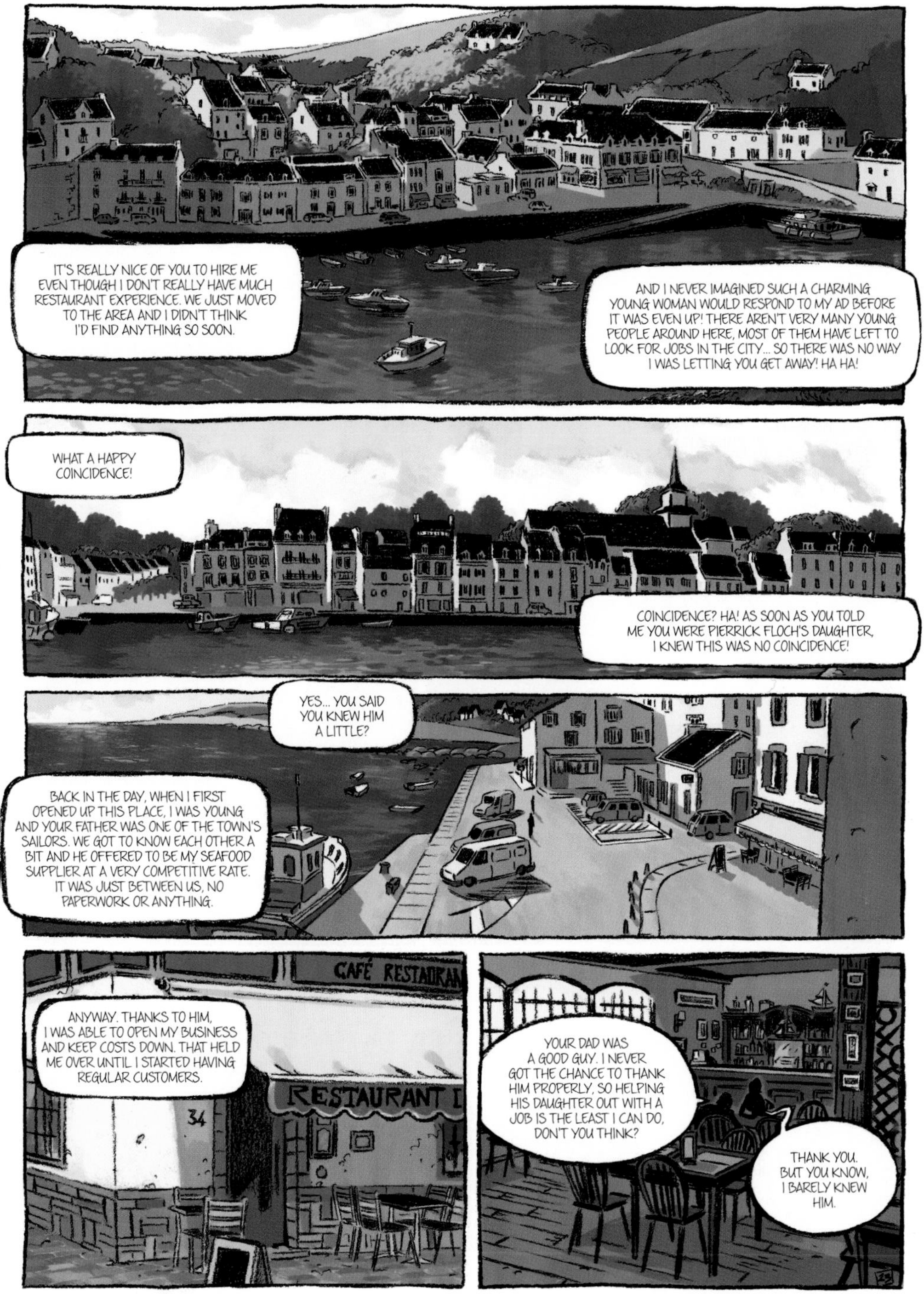
IT'S REALLY NICE OF YOU TO HIRE ME EVEN THOUGH I DON'T REALLY HAVE MUCH RESTAURANT EXPERIENCE. WE JUST MOVED TO THE AREA AND I DIDN'T THINK I'D FIND ANYTHING SO SOON.
AND I NEVER IMAGINED SUCH A CHARMING YOUNG WOMAN WOULD RESPOND TO MY AD BEFORE IT WAS EVEN UP! THERE AREN'T VERY MANY YOUNG PEOPLE AROUND HERE, MOST OF THEM HAVE LEFT TO LOOK FOR JOBS IN THE CITY... SO THERE WAS NO WAY I WAS LETTING YOU GET AWAY! HA HA!
WHAT A HAPPY COINCIDENCE!
COINCIDENCE? HA! AS SOON AS YOU TOLD ME YOU WERE PIERRICK FLOCH'S DAUGHTER, I KNEW THIS WAS NO COINCIDENCE!
YES... YOU SAID YOU KNEW HIM A LITTLE?
BACK IN THE DAY, WHEN I FIRST OPENED UP THIS PLACE, I WAS YOUNG AND YOUR FATHER WAS ONE OF THE TOWN'S SAILORS. WE GOT TO KNOW EACH OTHER A BIT AND HE OFFERED TO BE MY SEAFOOD SUPPLIER AT A VERY COMPETITIVE RATE. IT WAS JUST BETWEEN US, NO PAPERWORK OR ANYTHING.
CAFÉ RESTAURAN
ANYWAY. THANKS TO HIM, I WAS ABLE TO OPEN MY BUSINESS AND KEEP COSTS DOWN. THAT HELD ME OVER UNTIL I STARTED HAVING REGULAR CUSTOMERS.
RESTAURANT
34
YOUR DAD WAS A GOOD GUY. I NEVER GOT THE CHANCE TO THANK HIM PROPERLY, SO HELPING HIS DAUGHTER OUT WITH A JOB IS THE LEAST I CAN DO, DON'T YOU THINK?
THANK YOU. BUT YOU KNOW, I BARELY KNEW HIM.

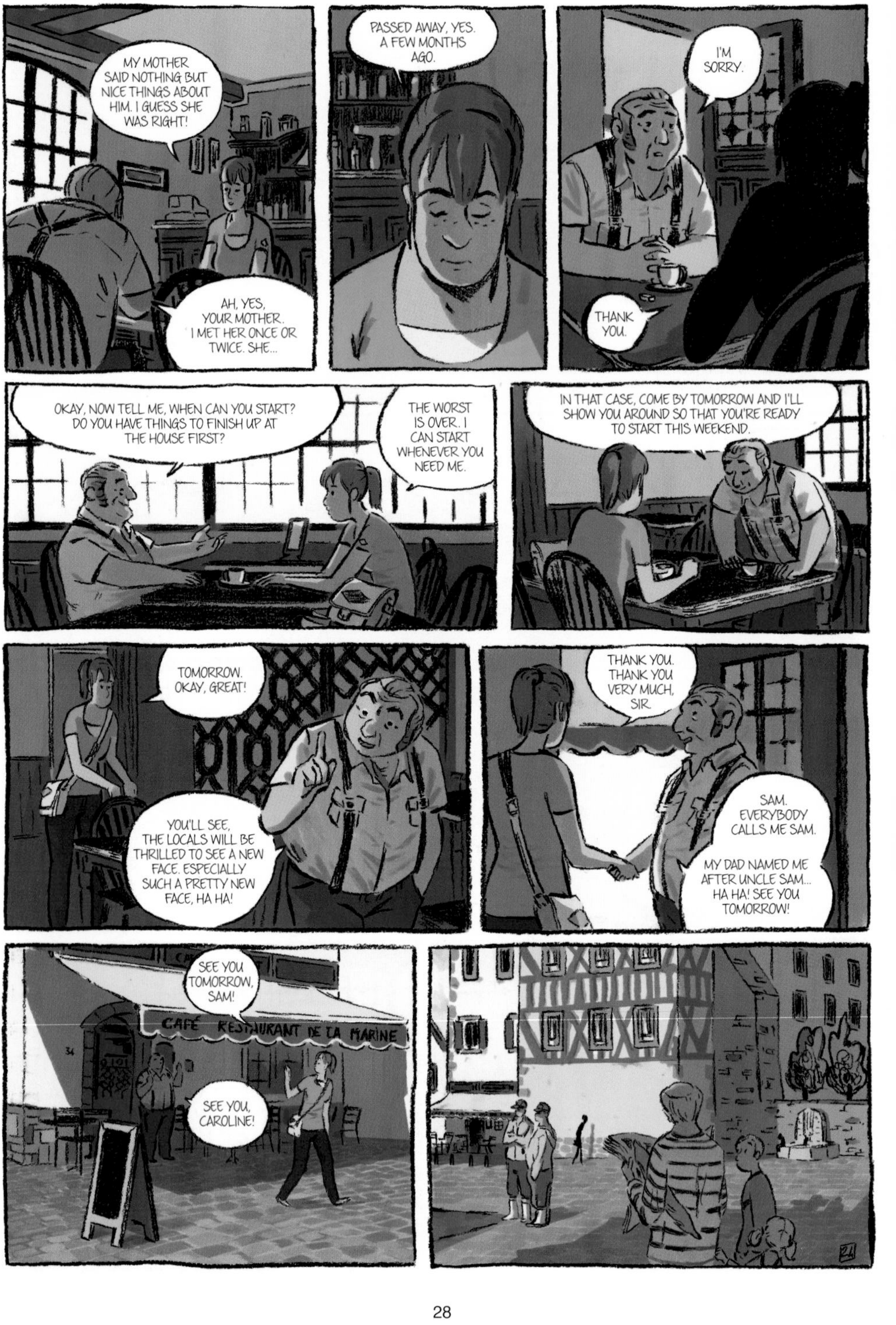
MY MOTHER SAID NOTHING BUT NICE THINGS ABOUT HIM. I GUESS SHE WAS RIGHT!
AH, YES, YOUR MOTHER. I MET HER ONCE OR TWICE. SHE...
PASSED AWAY, YES. A FEW MONTHS AGO.
I'M SORRY.
THANK YOU.
OKAY, NOW TELL ME, WHEN CAN YOU START? DO YOU HAVE THINGS TO FINISH UP AT THE HOUSE FIRST?
THE WORST IS OVER. I CAN START WHENEVER YOU NEED ME.
IN THAT CASE, COME BY TOMORROW AND I'LL SHOW YOU AROUND SO THAT YOU'RE READY TO START THIS WEEKEND.
TOMORROW. OKAY, GREAT!
YOU'LL SEE, THE LOCALS WILL BE THRILLED TO SEE A NEW FACE. ESPECIALLY SUCH A PRETTY NEW FACE, HA HA!
THANK YOU. THANK YOU VERY MUCH, SIR.
SAM. EVERYBODY CALLS ME SAM.
MY DAD NAMED ME AFTER UNCLE SAM... HA HA! SEE YOU TOMORROW!
SEE YOU TOMORROW, SAM!
CAFÉ RESTAURANT DE LA MARINE
34
SEE YOU, CAROLINE!

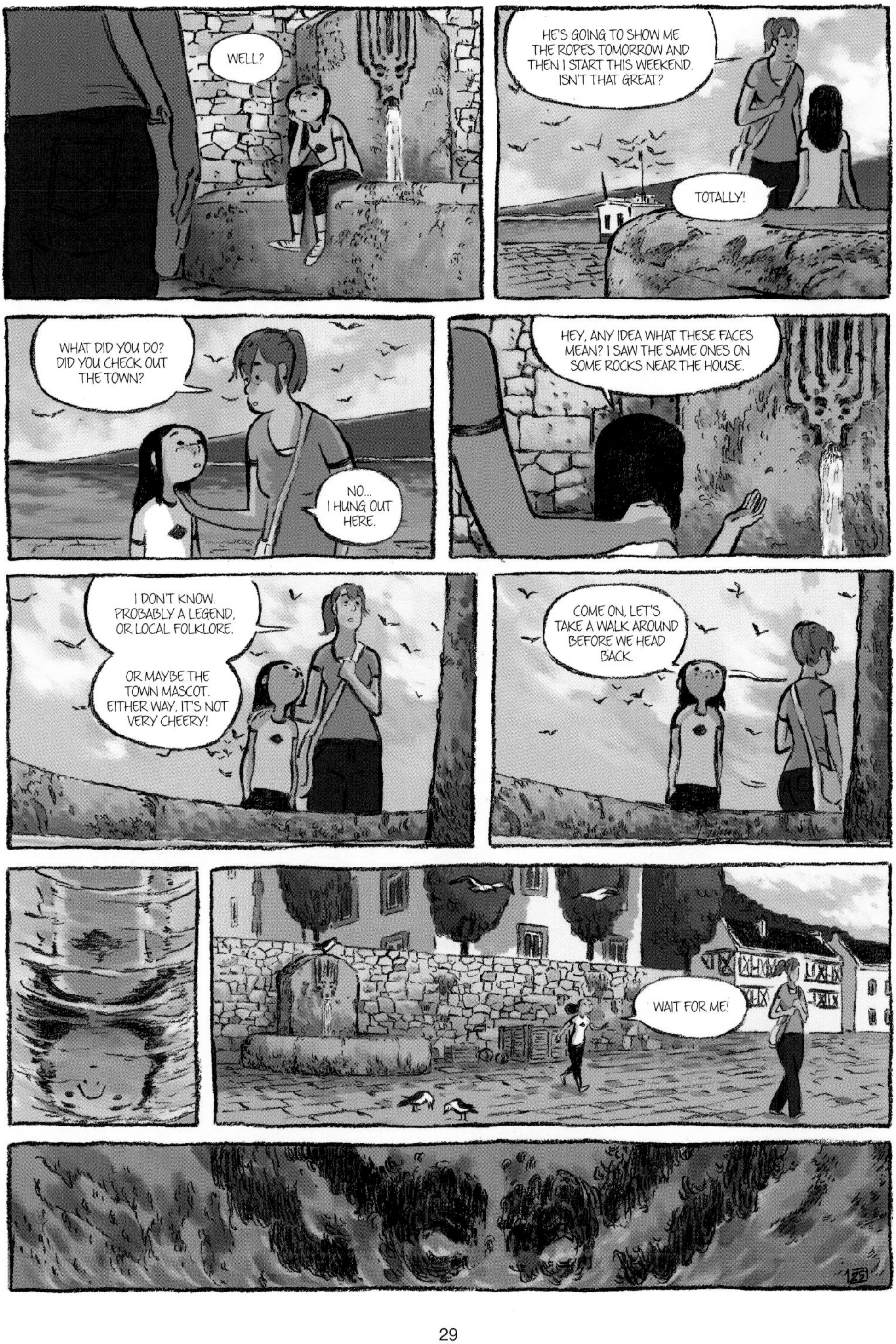
WELL?
HE'S GOING TO SHOW ME THE ROPES TOMORROW AND THEN I START THIS WEEKEND. ISN'T THAT GREAT?
TOTALLY!
WHAT DID YOU DO? DID YOU CHECK OUT THE TOWN?
NO... I HUNG OUT HERE.
HEY, ANY IDEA WHAT THESE FACES MEAN? I SAW THE SAME ONES ON SOME ROCKS NEAR THE HOUSE.
I DON'T KNOW. PROBABLY A LEGEND, OR LOCAL FOLKLORE.
OR MAYBE THE TOWN MASCOT. EITHER WAY, IT'S NOT VERY CHEERY!
COME ON, LET'S TAKE A WALK AROUND BEFORE WE HEAD BACK.
WAIT FOR ME!

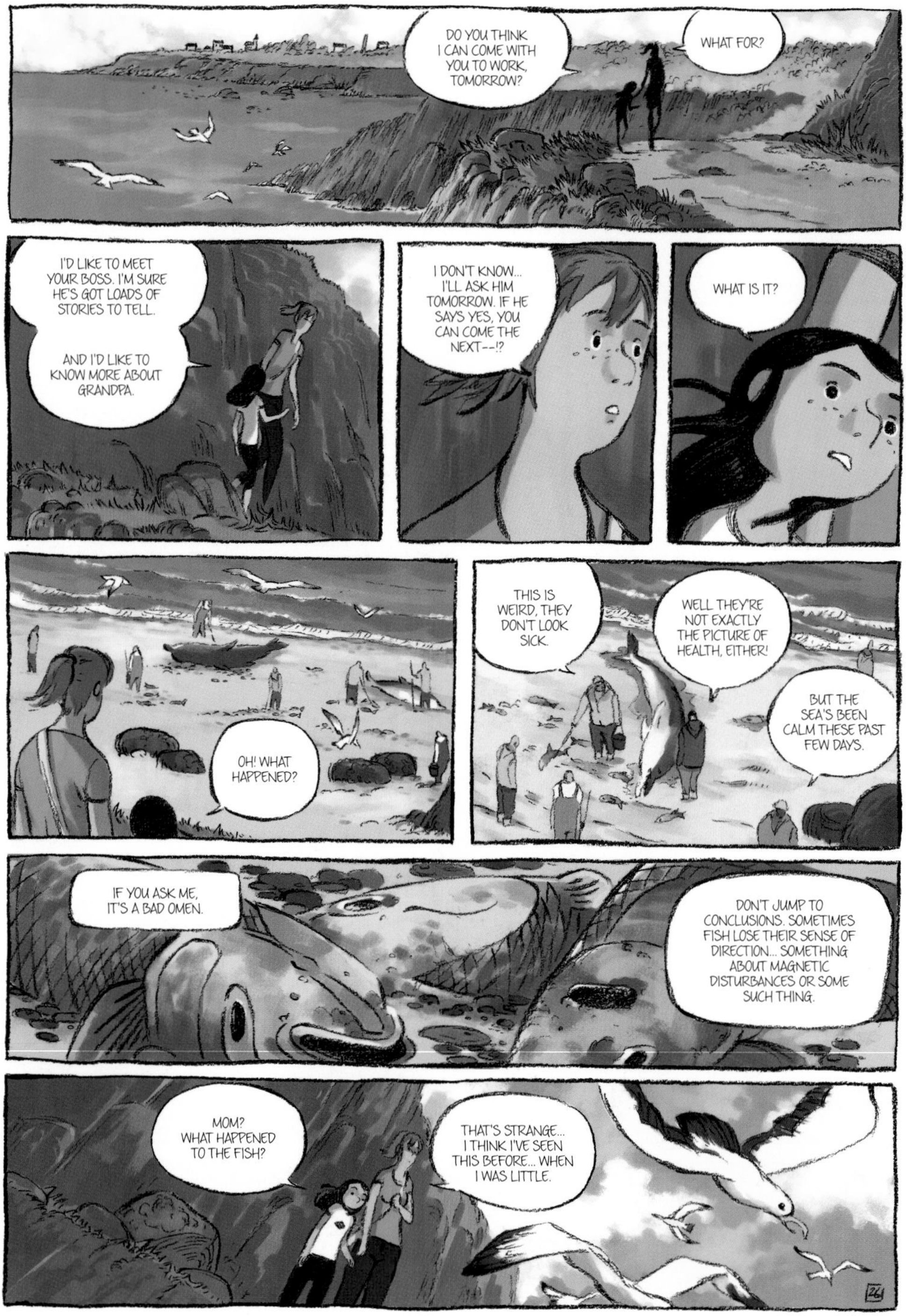
DO YOU THINK I CAN COME WITH YOU TO WORK, TOMORROW?
WHAT FOR?
I'D LIKE TO MEET YOUR BOSS. I'M SURE HE'S GOT LOADS OF STORIES TO TELL.
AND I'D LIKE TO KNOW MORE ABOUT GRANDPA.
I DON'T KNOW... I'LL ASK HIM TOMORROW. IF HE SAYS YES, YOU CAN COME THE NEXT--!?
WHAT IS IT?
OH! WHAT HAPPENED?
THIS IS WEIRD, THEY DON'T LOOK SICK.
WELL THEY'RE NOT EXACTLY THE PICTURE OF HEALTH, EITHER!
BUT THE SEA'S BEEN CALM THESE PAST FEW DAYS.
IF YOU ASK ME, IT'S A BAD OMEN.
DON'T JUMP TO CONCLUSIONS. SOMETIMES FISH LOSE THEIR SENSE OF DIRECTION... SOMETHING ABOUT MAGNETIC DISTURBANCES OR SOME SUCH THING.
MOM? WHAT HAPPENED TO THE FISH?
THAT'S STRANGE... I THINK I'VE SEEN THIS BEFORE... WHEN I WAS LITTLE.
26

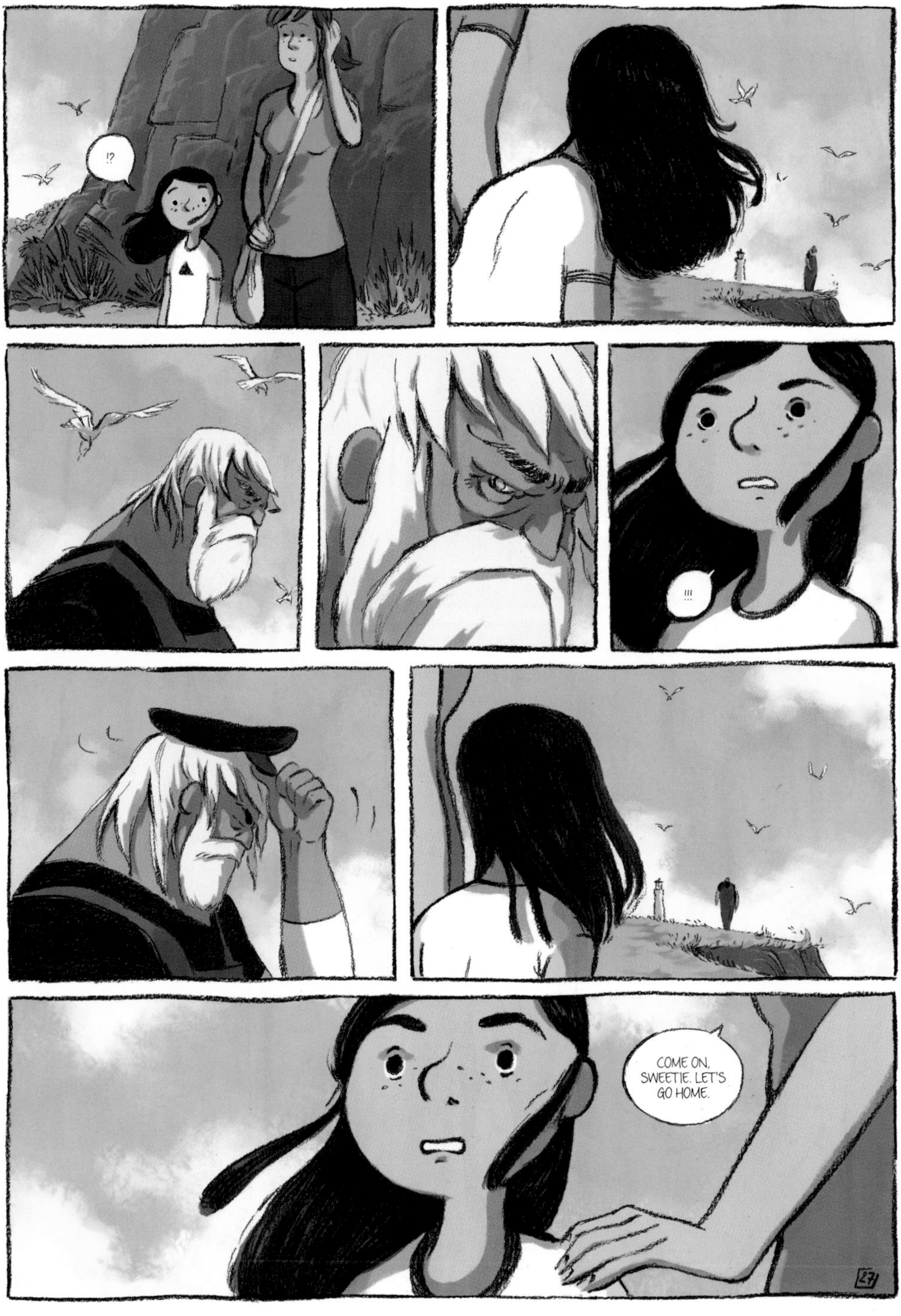
!?
!!!
COME ON, SWEETIE. LET'S GO HOME.
27

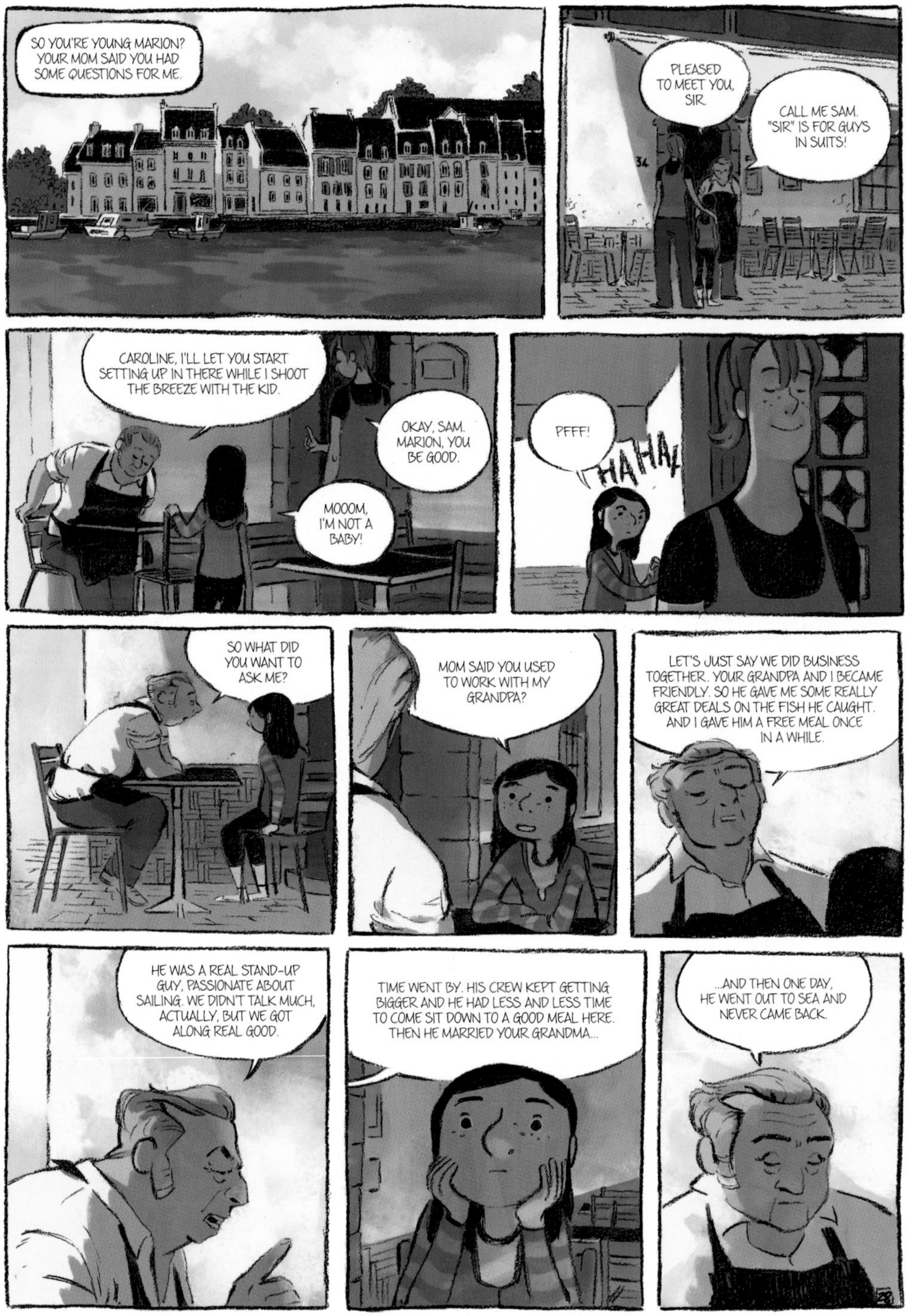
SO YOU'RE YOUNG MARION? YOUR MOM SAID YOU HAD SOME QUESTIONS FOR ME.
PLEASED TO MEET YOU, SIR.
CALL ME SAM. "SIR" IS FOR GUYS IN SUITS!
CAROLINE, I'LL LET YOU START SETTING UP IN THERE WHILE I SHOOT THE BREEZE WITH THE KID.
OKAY, SAM. MARION, YOU BE GOOD.
MOOOM, I'M NOT A BABY!
PFFF!
HAHA!
SO WHAT DID YOU WANT TO ASK ME?
MOM SAID YOU USED TO WORK WITH MY GRANDPA?
LET'S JUST SAY WE DID BUSINESS TOGETHER. YOUR GRANDPA AND I BECAME FRIENDLY. SO HE GAVE ME SOME REALLY GREAT DEALS ON THE FISH HE CAUGHT. AND I GAVE HIM A FREE MEAL ONCE IN A WHILE.
HE WAS A REAL STAND-UP GUY, PASSIONATE ABOUT SAILING. WE DIDN'T TALK MUCH, ACTUALLY, BUT WE GOT ALONG REAL GOOD.
TIME WENT BY. HIS CREW KEPT GETTING BIGGER AND HE HAD LESS AND LESS TIME TO COME SIT DOWN TO A GOOD MEAL HERE. THEN HE MARRIED YOUR GRANDMA...
...AND THEN ONE DAY, HE WENT OUT TO SEA AND NEVER CAME BACK.

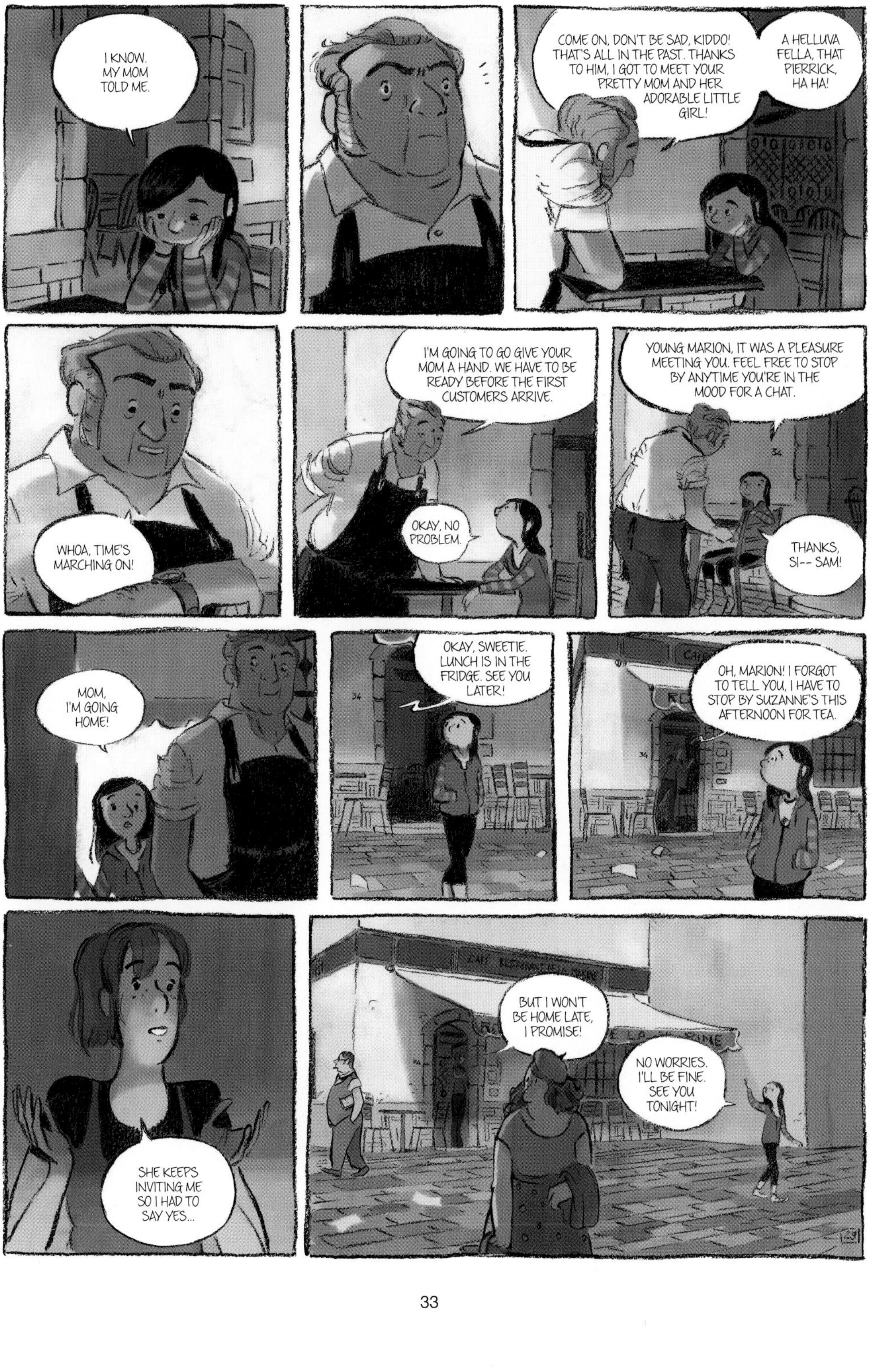
I KNOW. MY MOM TOLD ME.
COME ON, DON'T BE SAD, KIDDO! THAT'S ALL IN THE PAST. THANKS TO HIM, I GOT TO MEET YOUR PRETTY MOM AND HER ADORABLE LITTLE GIRL!
A HELLUVA FELLA, THAT PIERRICK, HA HA!
WHOA, TIME'S MARCHING ON!
I'M GOING TO GO GIVE YOUR MOM A HAND. WE HAVE TO BE READY BEFORE THE FIRST CUSTOMERS ARRIVE.
OKAY, NO PROBLEM.
YOUNG MARION, IT WAS A PLEASURE MEETING YOU. FEEL FREE TO STOP BY ANYTIME YOU'RE IN THE MOOD FOR A CHAT.
THANKS, SI-- SAM!
MOM, I'M GOING HOME!
OKAY, SWEETIE. LUNCH IS IN THE FRIDGE. SEE YOU LATER!
OH, MARION! I FORGOT TO TELL YOU, I HAVE TO STOP BY SUZANNE'S THIS AFTERNOON FOR TEA.
SHE KEEPS INVITING ME SO I HAD TO SAY YES...
BUT I WON'T BE HOME LATE, I PROMISE!
NO WORRIES. I'LL BE FINE. SEE YOU TONIGHT!

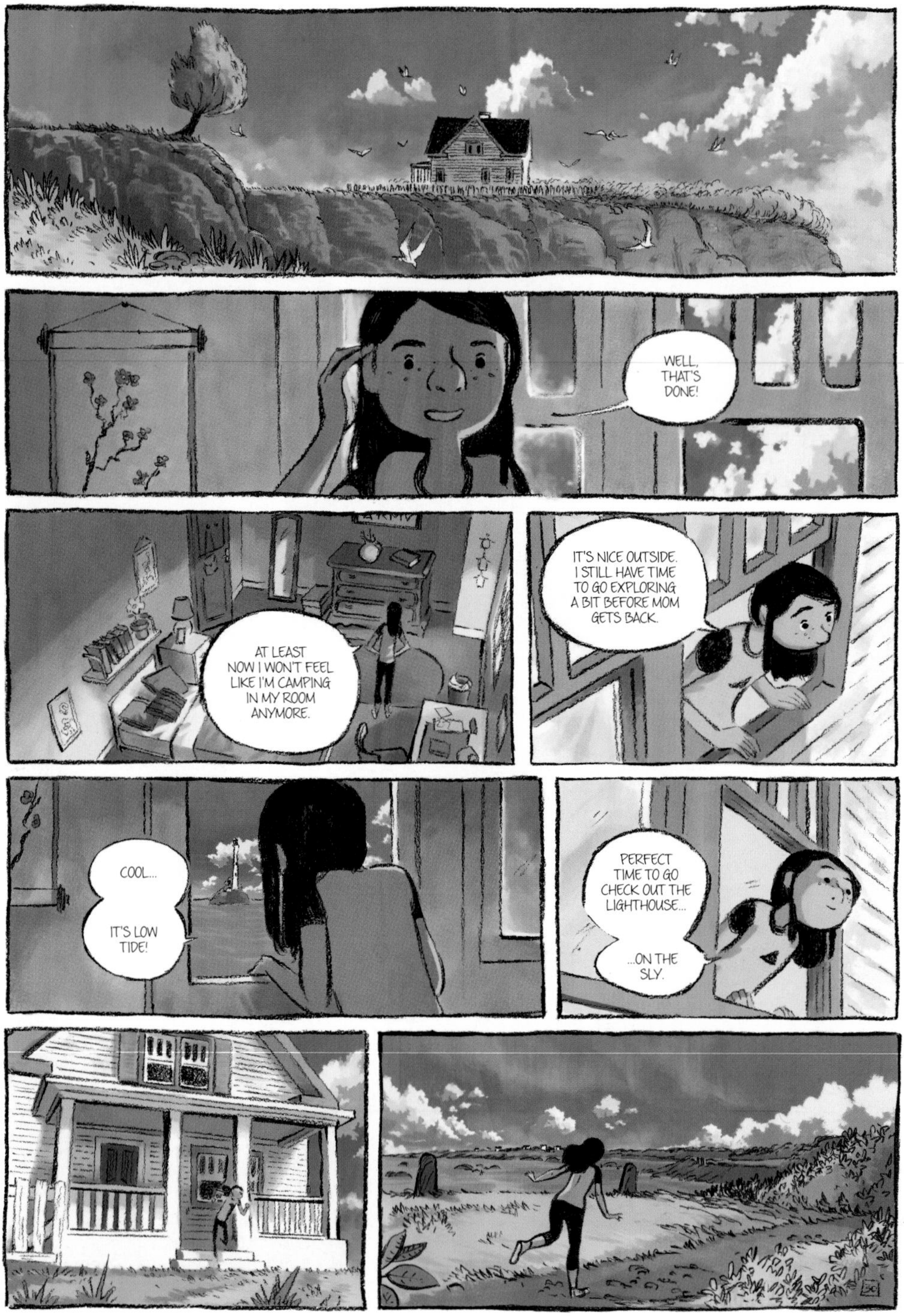
WELL, THAT'S DONE!
AT LEAST NOW I WON'T FEEL LIKE I'M CAMPING IN MY ROOM ANYMORE.
IT'S NICE OUTSIDE. I STILL HAVE TIME TO GO EXPLORING A BIT BEFORE MOM GETS BACK.
COOL...
IT'S LOW TIDE!
PERFECT TIME TO GO CHECK OUT THE LIGHTHOUSE...
...ON THE SLY.

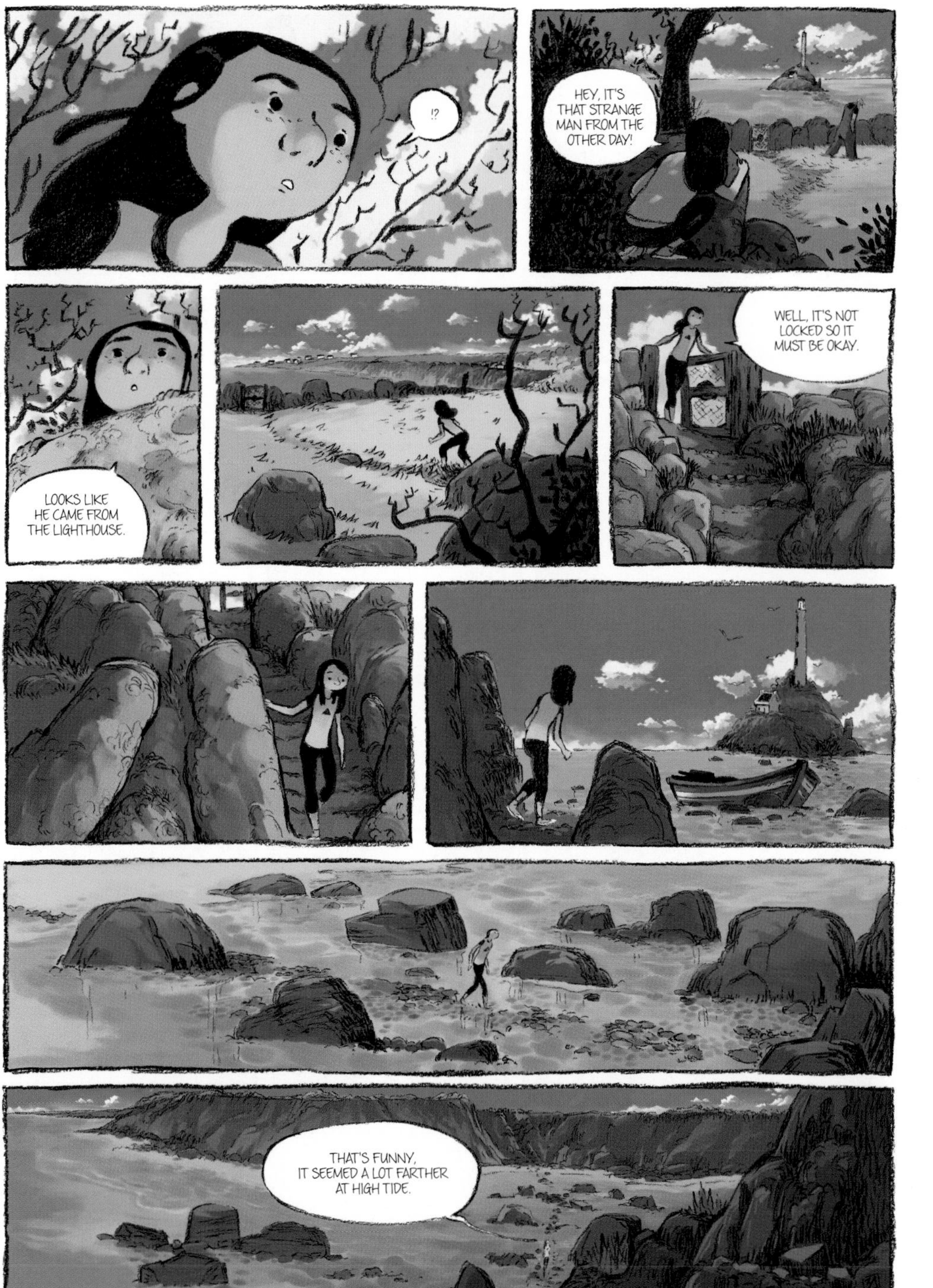
!?
HEY, IT'S THAT STRANGE MAN FROM THE OTHER DAY!
LOOKS LIKE HE CAME FROM THE LIGHTHOUSE.
WELL, IT'S NOT LOCKED SO IT MUST BE OKAY.
THAT'S FUNNY, IT SEEMED A LOT FARTHER AT HIGH TIDE.

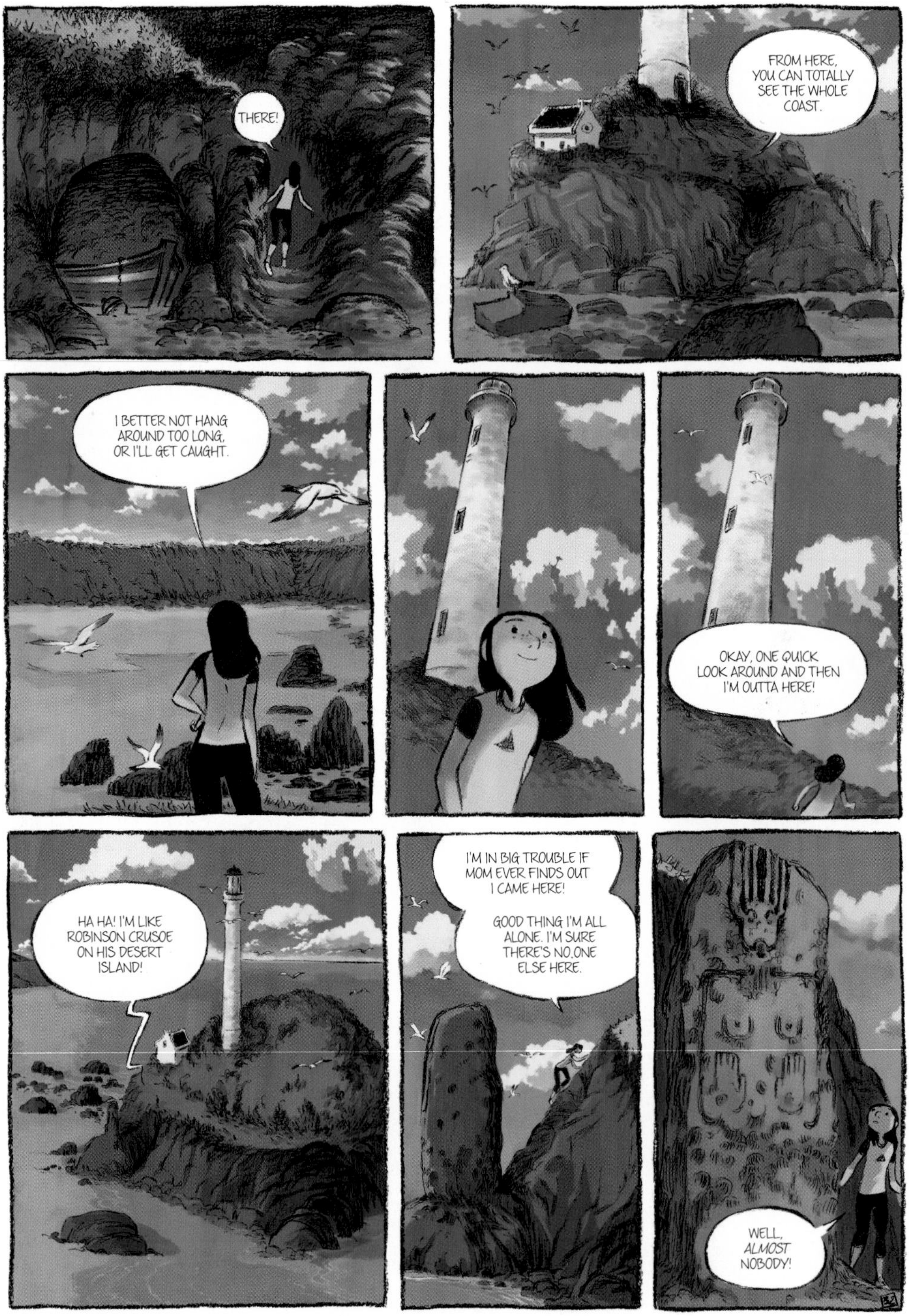
THERE!
FROM HERE, YOU CAN TOTALLY SEE THE WHOLE COAST.
I BETTER NOT HANG AROUND TOO LONG, OR I'LL GET CAUGHT.
OKAY, ONE QUICK LOOK AROUND AND THEN I'M OUTTA HERE!
HA HA! I'M LIKE ROBINSON CRUSOE ON HIS DESERT ISLAND!
I'M IN BIG TROUBLE IF MOM EVER FINDS OUT I CAME HERE!
GOOD THING I'M ALL ALONE. I'M SURE THERE'S NO ONE ELSE HERE.
WELL, *ALMOST* NOBODY!

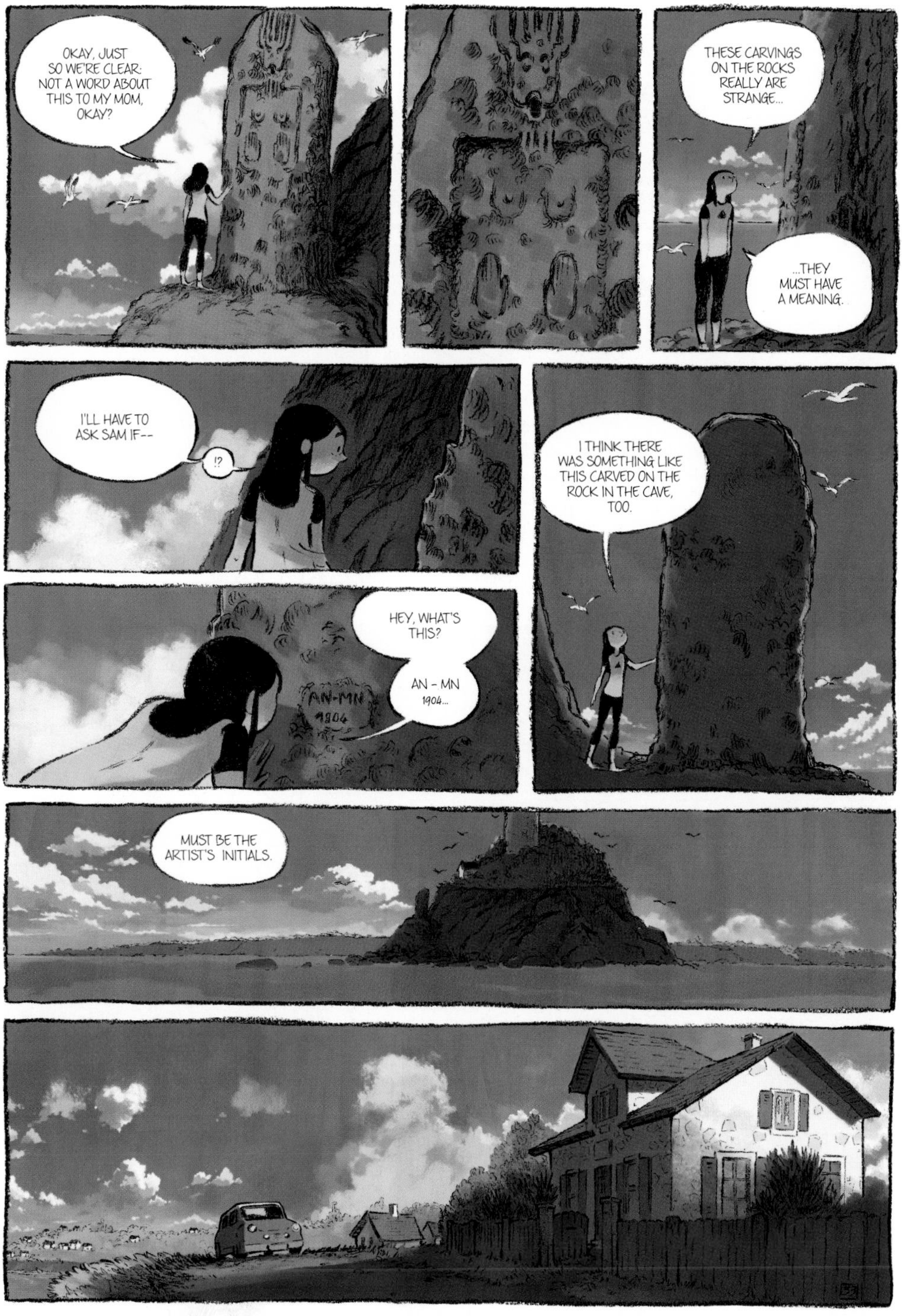
OKAY, JUST SO WE'RE CLEAR: NOT A WORD ABOUT THIS TO MY MOM, OKAY?
THESE CARVINGS ON THE ROCKS REALLY ARE STRANGE...
...THEY MUST HAVE A MEANING.
I'LL HAVE TO ASK SAM IF--
!?
I THINK THERE WAS SOMETHING LIKE THIS CARVED ON THE ROCK IN THE CAVE, TOO.
HEY, WHAT'S THIS?
AN-MN
1904
AN - MN 1904...
MUST BE THE ARTIST'S INITIALS.

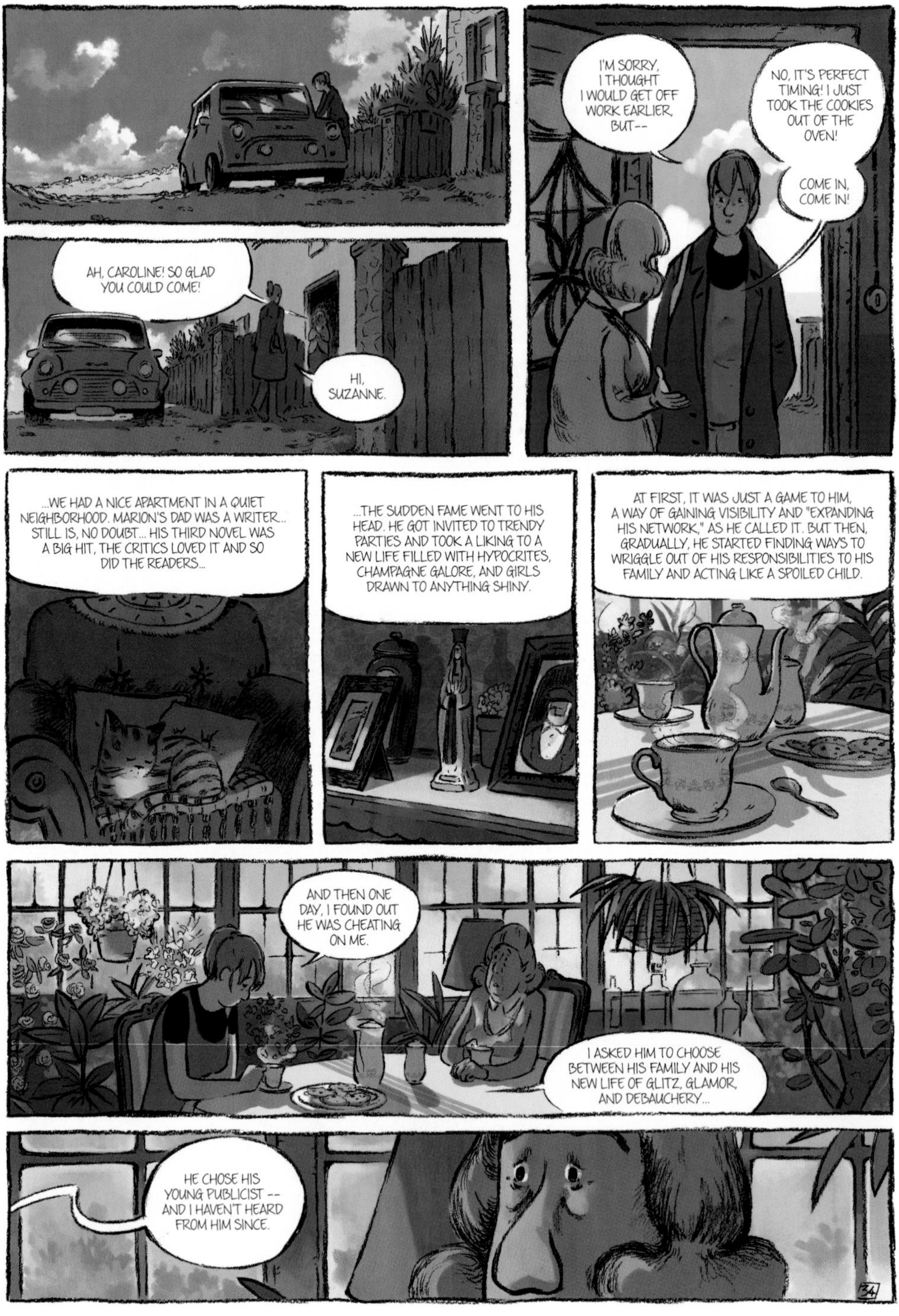
I'M SORRY, I THOUGHT I WOULD GET OFF WORK EARLIER, BUT--
NO, IT'S PERFECT TIMING! I JUST TOOK THE COOKIES OUT OF THE OVEN!
COME IN, COME IN!
AH, CAROLINE! SO GLAD YOU COULD COME!
HI, SUZANNE.
...WE HAD A NICE APARTMENT IN A QUIET NEIGHBORHOOD. MARION'S DAD WAS A WRITER... STILL IS, NO DOUBT... HIS THIRD NOVEL WAS A BIG HIT, THE CRITICS LOVED IT AND SO DID THE READERS...
...THE SUDDEN FAME WENT TO HIS HEAD. HE GOT INVITED TO TRENDY PARTIES AND TOOK A LIKING TO A NEW LIFE FILLED WITH HYPOCRITES, CHAMPAGNE GALORE, AND GIRLS DRAWN TO ANYTHING SHINY.
AT FIRST, IT WAS JUST A GAME TO HIM, A WAY OF GAINING VISIBILITY AND "EXPANDING HIS NETWORK," AS HE CALLED IT. BUT THEN, GRADUALLY, HE STARTED FINDING WAYS TO WRIGGLE OUT OF HIS RESPONSIBILITIES TO HIS FAMILY AND ACTING LIKE A SPOILED CHILD.
AND THEN ONE DAY, I FOUND OUT HE WAS CHEATING ON ME.
I ASKED HIM TO CHOOSE BETWEEN HIS FAMILY AND HIS NEW LIFE OF GLITZ, GLAMOR, AND DEBAUCHERY...
HE CHOSE HIS YOUNG PUBLICIST -- AND I HAVEN'T HEARD FROM HIM SINCE.
34

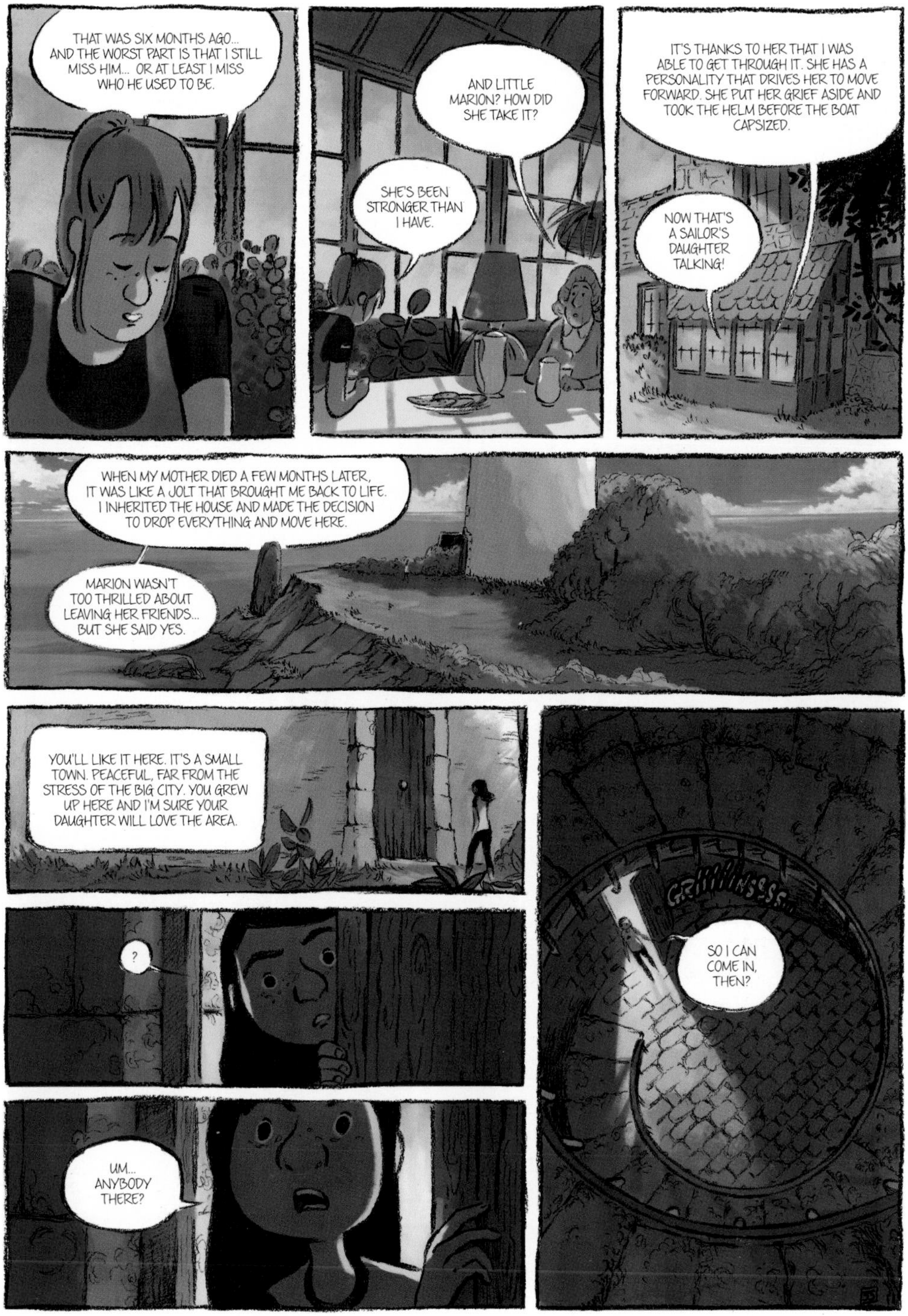
THAT WAS SIX MONTHS AGO... AND THE WORST PART IS THAT I STILL MISS HIM... OR AT LEAST I MISS WHO HE USED TO BE.
AND LITTLE MARION? HOW DID SHE TAKE IT?
SHE'S BEEN STRONGER THAN I HAVE.
IT'S THANKS TO HER THAT I WAS ABLE TO GET THROUGH IT. SHE HAS A PERSONALITY THAT DRIVES HER TO MOVE FORWARD. SHE PUT HER GRIEF ASIDE AND TOOK THE HELM BEFORE THE BOAT CAPSIZED.
NOW THAT'S A SAILOR'S DAUGHTER TALKING!
WHEN MY MOTHER DIED A FEW MONTHS LATER, IT WAS LIKE A JOLT THAT BROUGHT ME BACK TO LIFE. I INHERITED THE HOUSE AND MADE THE DECISION TO DROP EVERYTHING AND MOVE HERE.
MARION WASN'T TOO THRILLED ABOUT LEAVING HER FRIENDS... BUT SHE SAID YES.
YOU'LL LIKE IT HERE. IT'S A SMALL TOWN. PEACEFUL, FAR FROM THE STRESS OF THE BIG CITY. YOU GREW UP HERE AND I'M SURE YOUR DAUGHTER WILL LOVE THE AREA.
?
UM... ANYBODY THERE?
GRIIIINSSS...
SO I CAN COME IN, THEN?

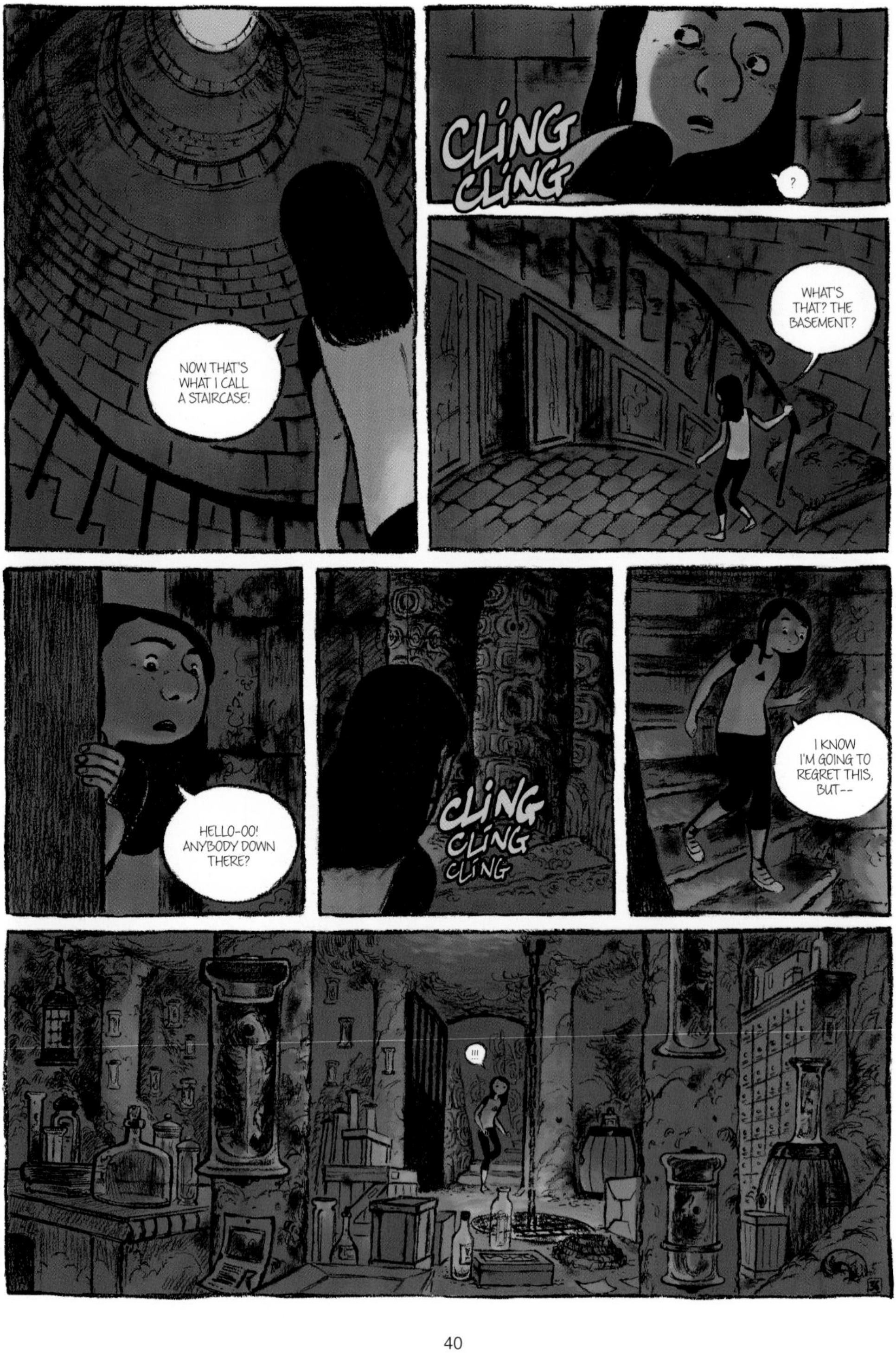
NOW THAT'S WHAT I CALL A STAIRCASE!
CLING
CLING
?
WHAT'S THAT? THE BASEMENT?
HELLO-OO! ANYBODY DOWN THERE?
CLING
CLING
CLING
I KNOW I'M GOING TO REGRET THIS, BUT--
!!!

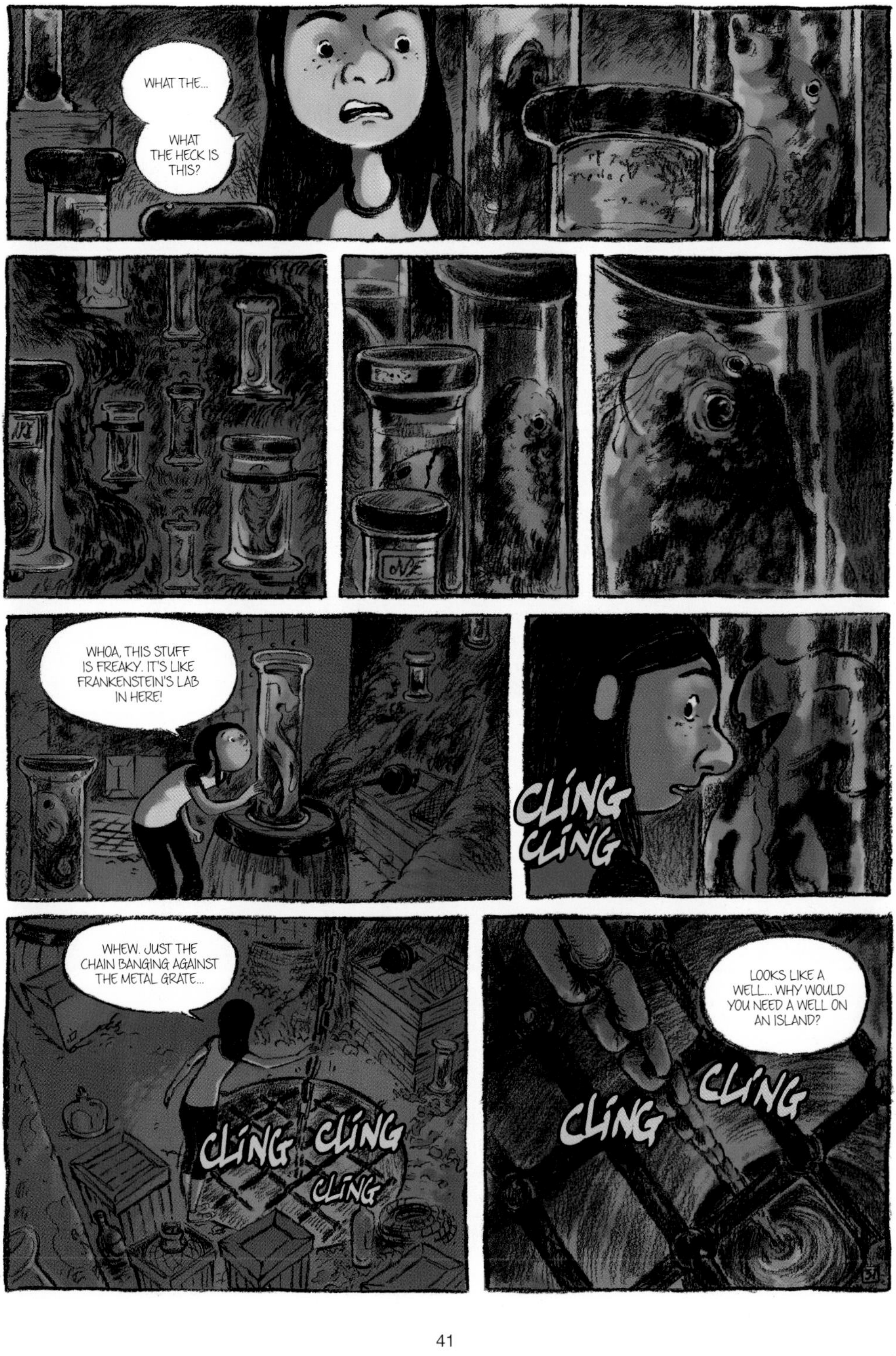
WHAT THE...
WHAT THE HECK IS THIS?
WHOA, THIS STUFF IS FREAKY. IT'S LIKE FRANKENSTEIN'S LAB IN HERE!
CLING CLING
WHEW. JUST THE CHAIN BANGING AGAINST THE METAL GRATE...
CLING CLING CLING
LOOKS LIKE A WELL... WHY WOULD YOU NEED A WELL ON AN ISLAND?
CLING CLING

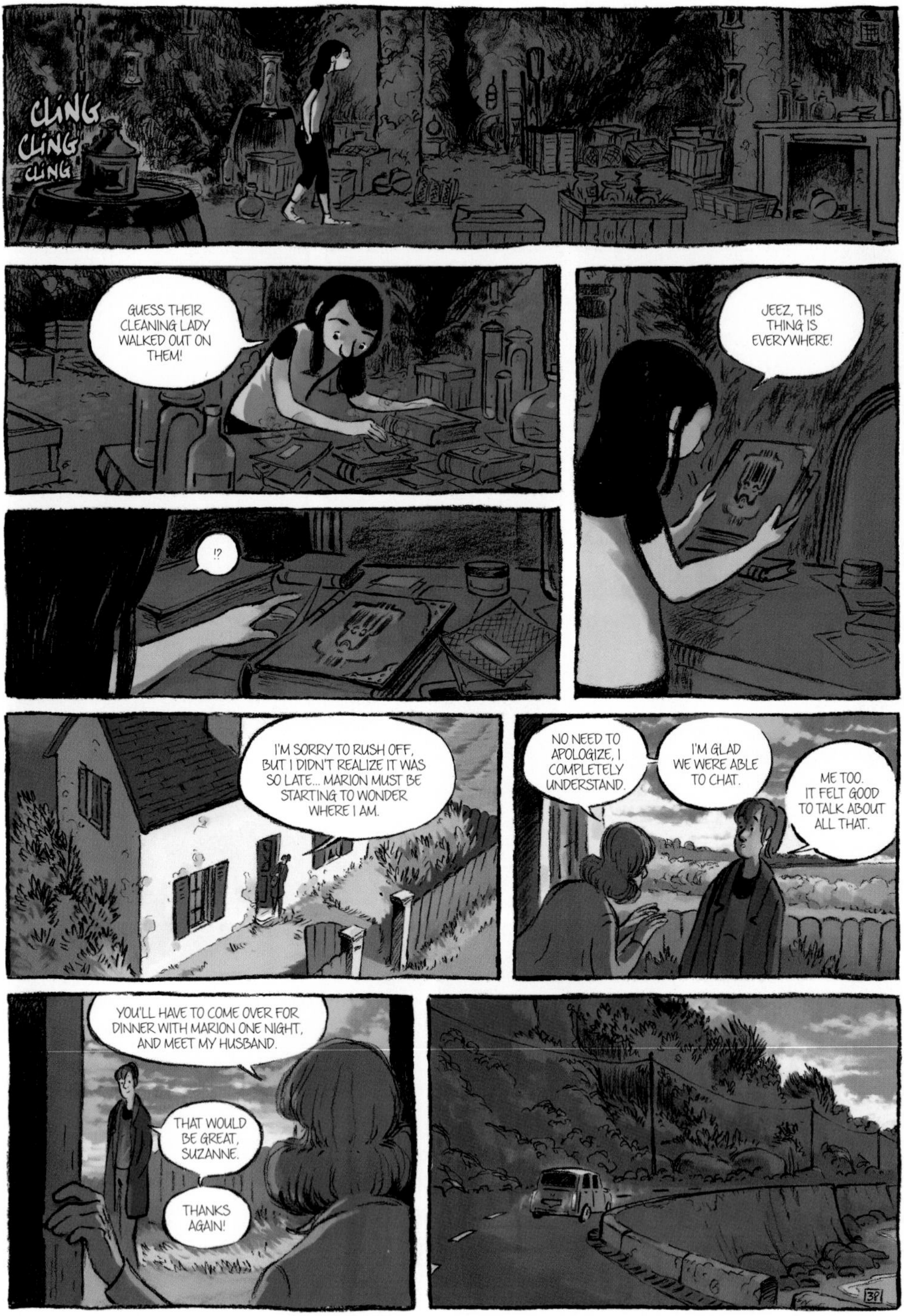
CLING
CLING
CLING
GUESS THEIR CLEANING LADY WALKED OUT ON THEM!
JEEZ, THIS THING IS EVERYWHERE!
!?
I'M SORRY TO RUSH OFF, BUT I DIDN'T REALIZE IT WAS SO LATE... MARION MUST BE STARTING TO WONDER WHERE I AM.
NO NEED TO APOLOGIZE, I COMPLETELY UNDERSTAND.
I'M GLAD WE WERE ABLE TO CHAT.
ME TOO. IT FELT GOOD TO TALK ABOUT ALL THAT.
YOU'LL HAVE TO COME OVER FOR DINNER WITH MARION ONE NIGHT, AND MEET MY HUSBAND.
THAT WOULD BE GREAT, SUZANNE.
THANKS AGAIN!
38

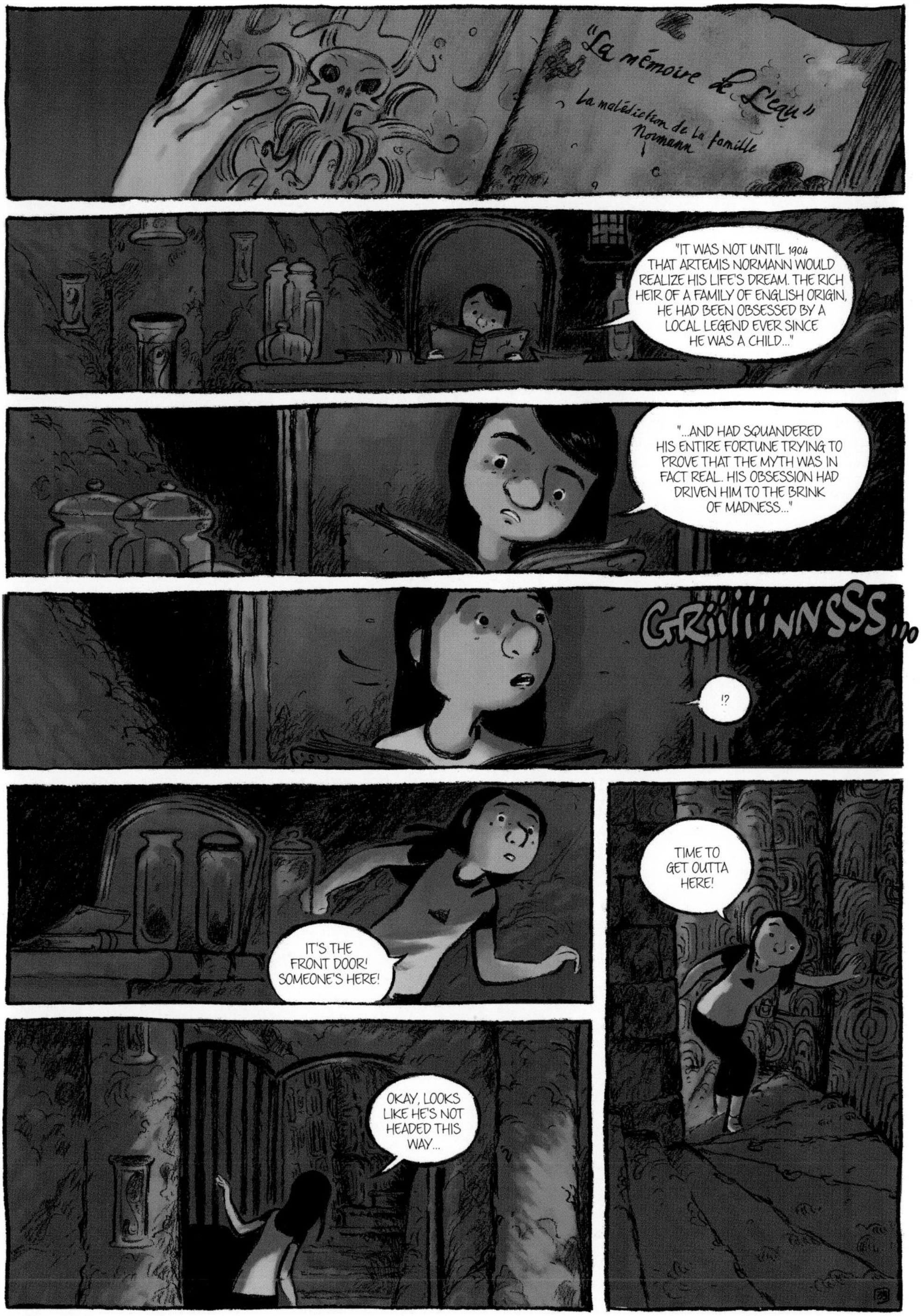
"La mémoire de L'eau"
La malédiction de la famille Normann
"IT WAS NOT UNTIL 1904 THAT ARTEMIS NORMANN WOULD REALIZE HIS LIFE'S DREAM. THE RICH HEIR OF A FAMILY OF ENGLISH ORIGIN, HE HAD BEEN OBSESSED BY A LOCAL LEGEND EVER SINCE HE WAS A CHILD..."
"...AND HAD SQUANDERED HIS ENTIRE FORTUNE TRYING TO PROVE THAT THE MYTH WAS IN FACT REAL. HIS OBSESSION HAD DRIVEN HIM TO THE BRINK OF MADNESS..."
GRIIIIINNSSS...
!?
IT'S THE FRONT DOOR! SOMEONE'S HERE!
OKAY, LOOKS LIKE HE'S NOT HEADED THIS WAY...
TIME TO GET OUTTA HERE!

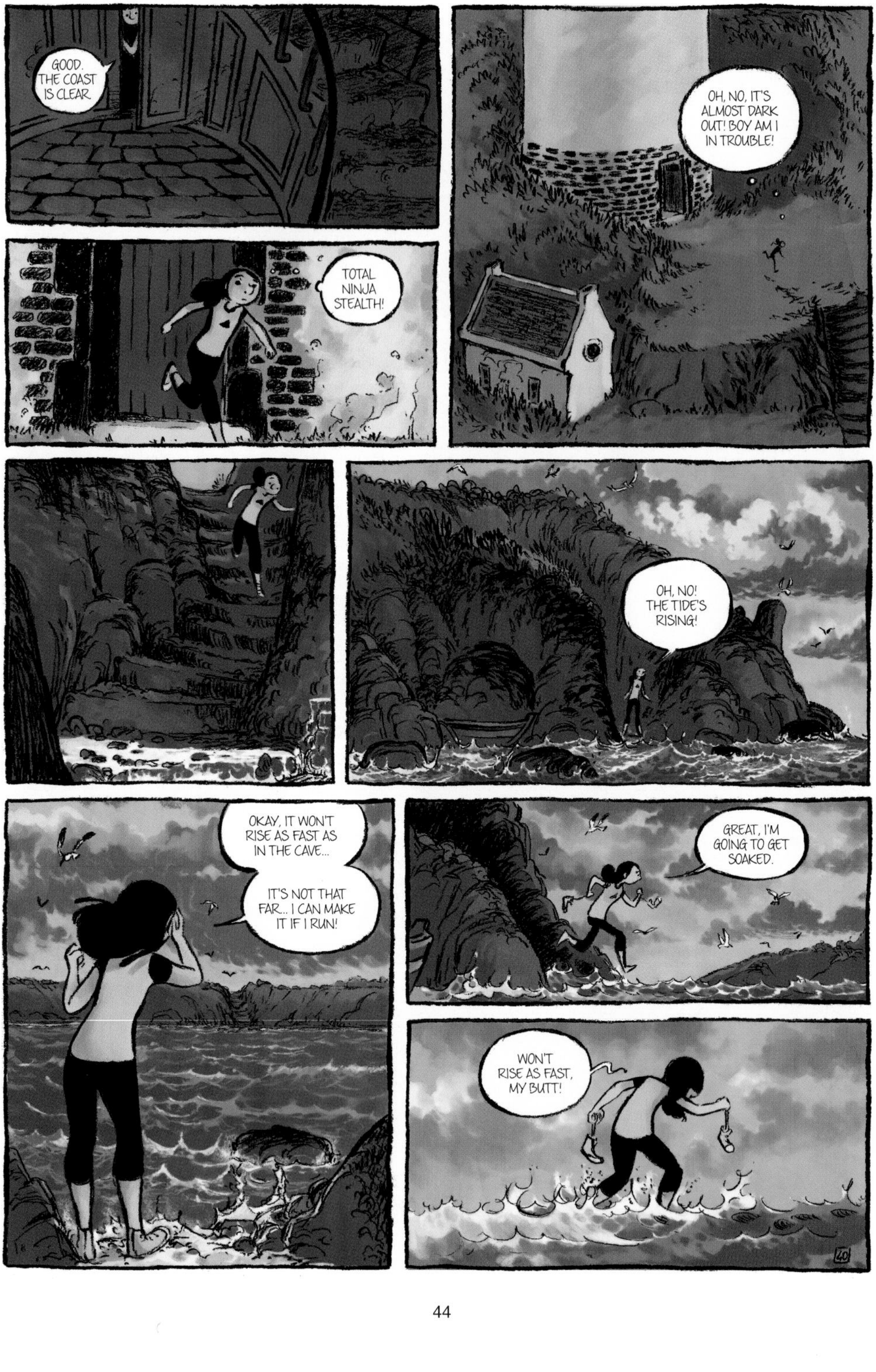
GOOD. THE COAST IS CLEAR.
OH, NO, IT'S ALMOST DARK OUT! BOY AM I IN TROUBLE!
TOTAL NINJA STEALTH!
OH, NO! THE TIDE'S RISING!
OKAY, IT WON'T RISE AS FAST AS IN THE CAVE...
IT'S NOT THAT FAR... I CAN MAKE IT IF I RUN!
GREAT, I'M GOING TO GET SOAKED.
WON'T RISE AS FAST, MY BUTT!
40

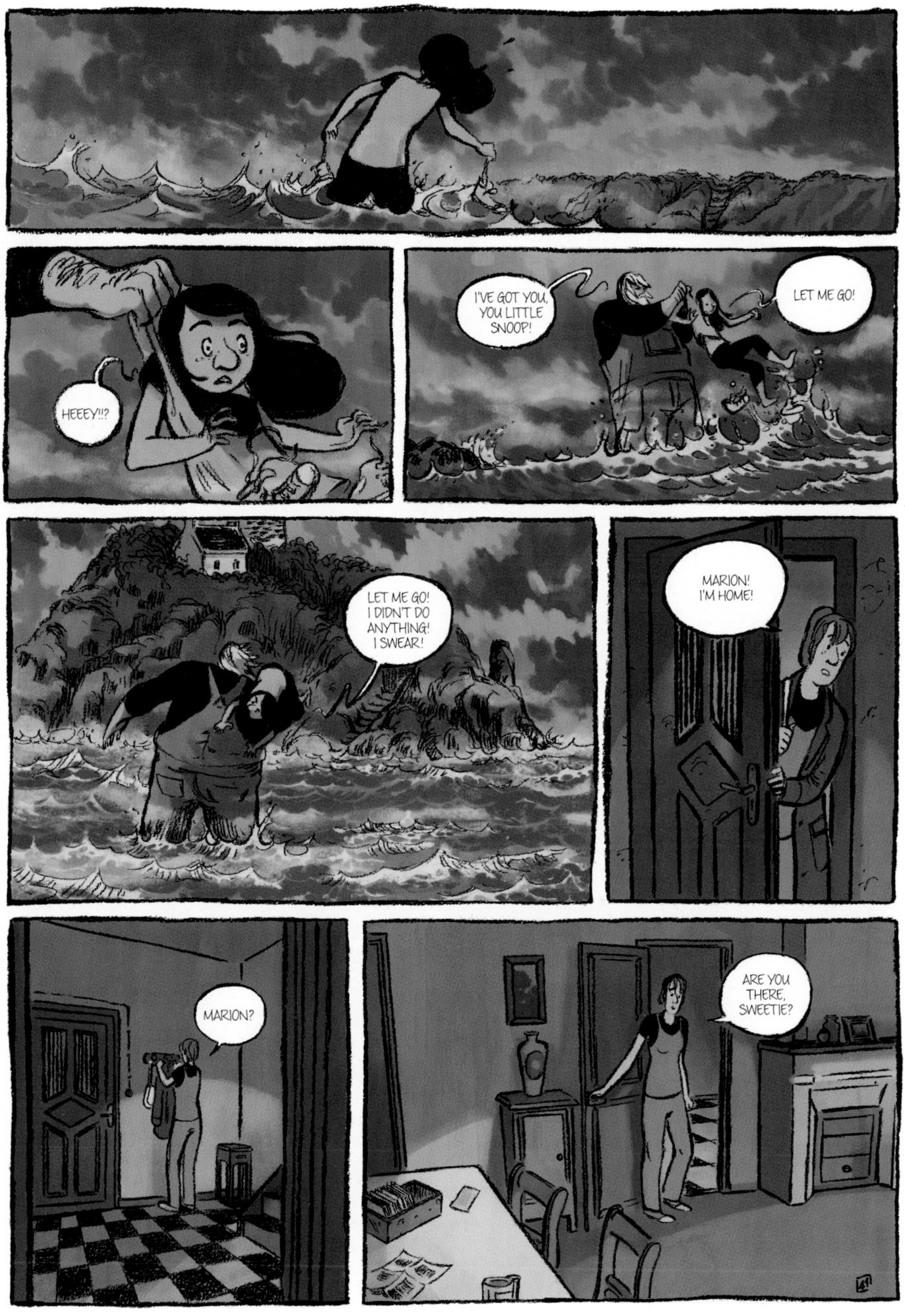
HEEEY!!?
I'VE GOT YOU, YOU LITTLE SNOOP!
LET ME GO!
LET ME GO! I DIDN'T DO ANYTHING! I SWEAR!
MARION! I'M HOME!
MARION?
ARE YOU THERE, SWEETIE?

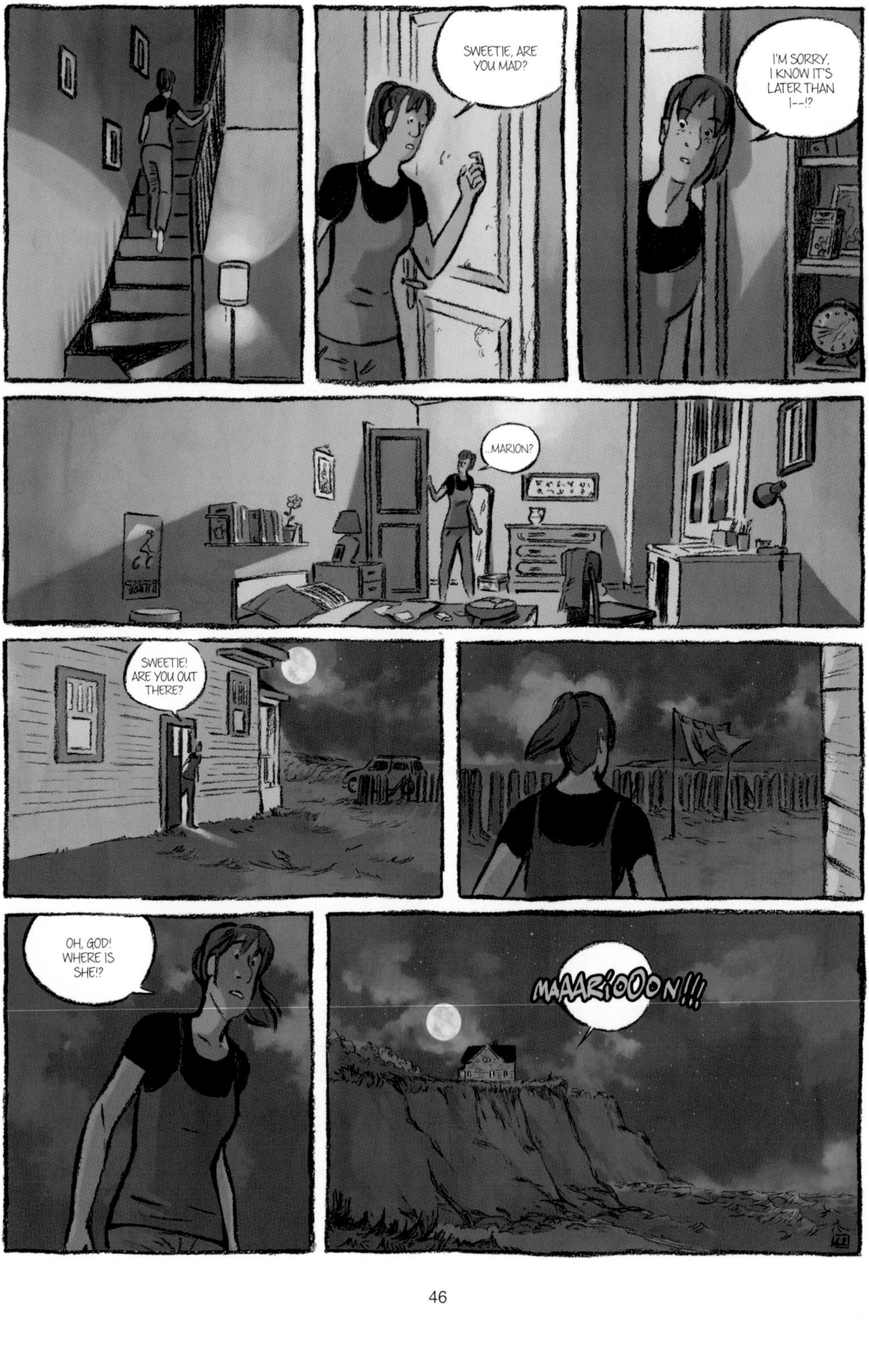
SWEETIE, ARE YOU MAD?
I'M SORRY, I KNOW IT'S LATER THAN I--!?
...MARION?
SWEETIE! ARE YOU OUT THERE?
OH, GOD! WHERE IS SHE!?
MAAARiOOON!!!

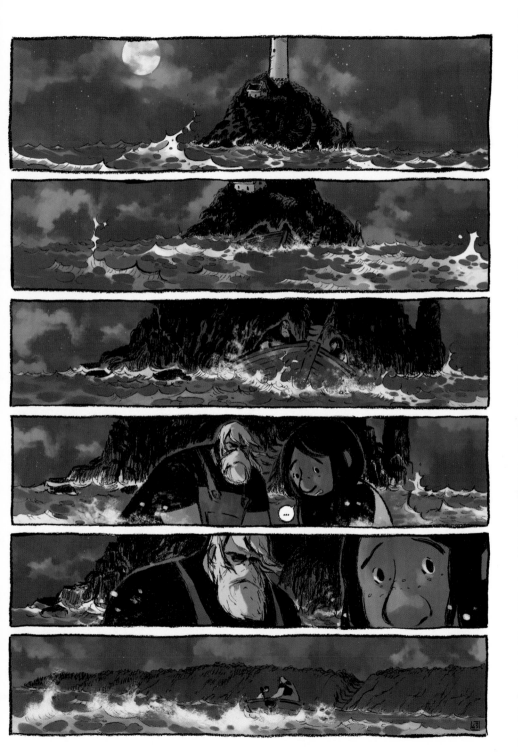

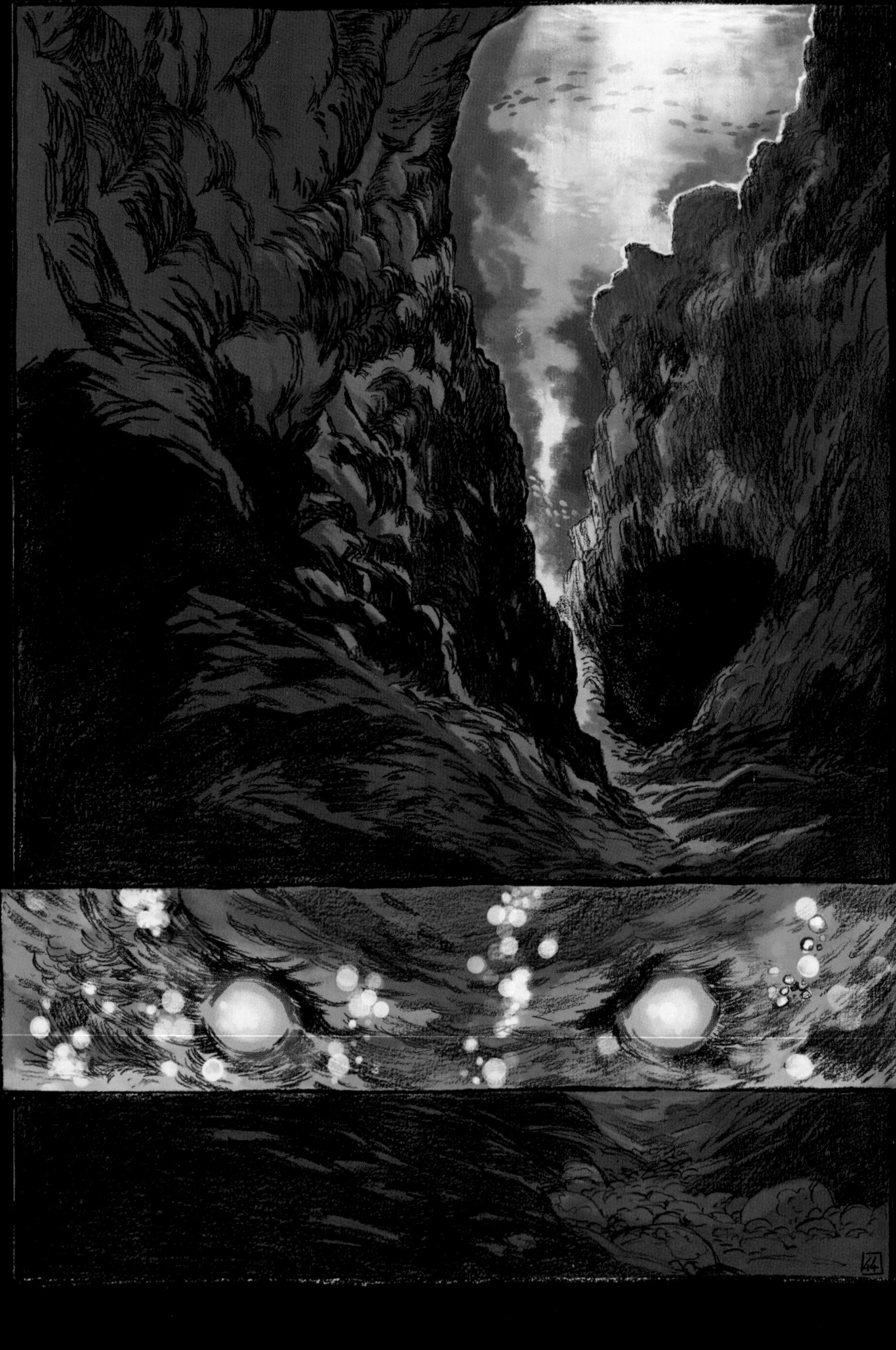

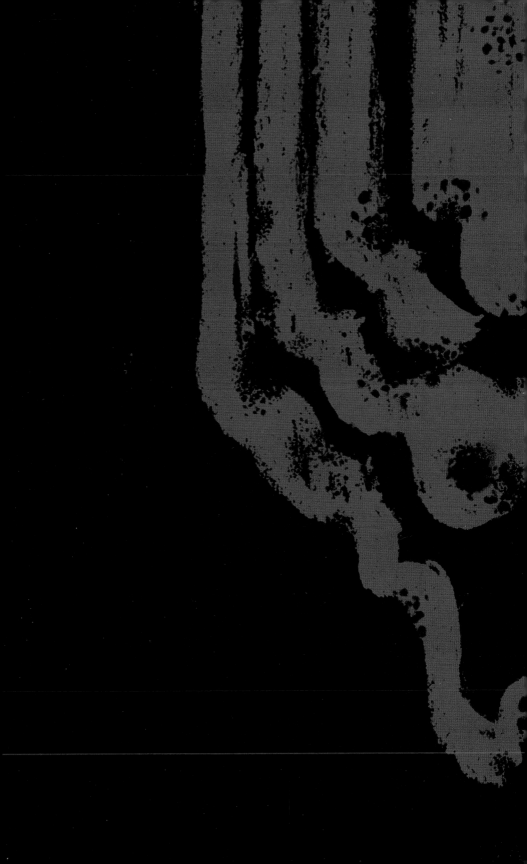

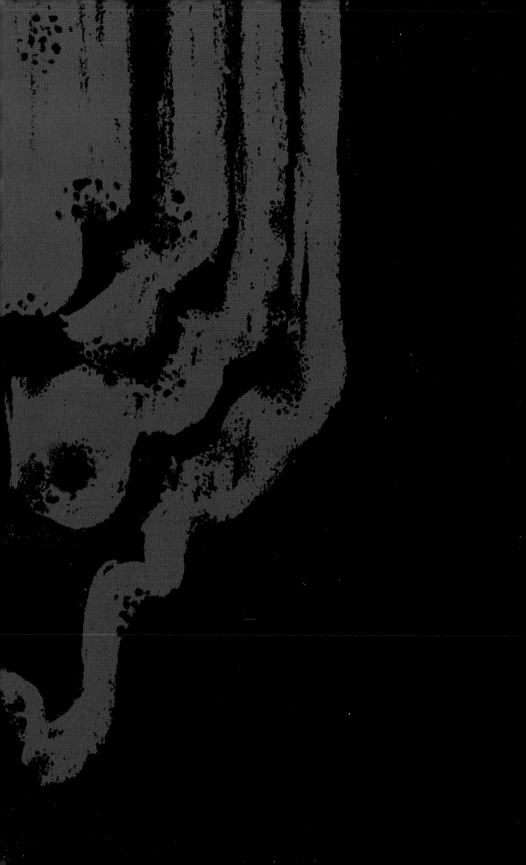

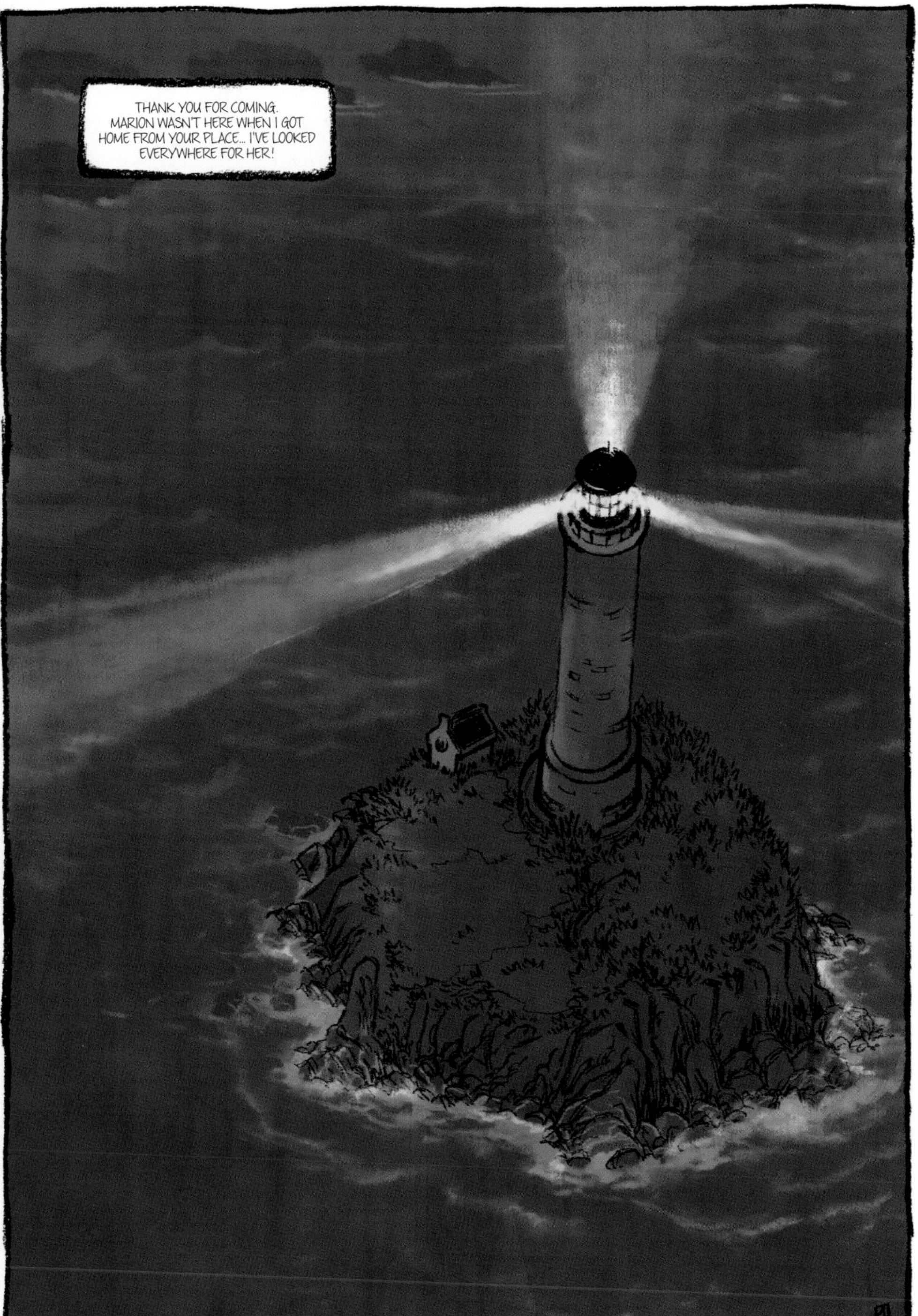
THANK YOU FOR COMING. MARION WASN'T HERE WHEN I GOT HOME FROM YOUR PLACE... I'VE LOOKED EVERYWHERE FOR HER!

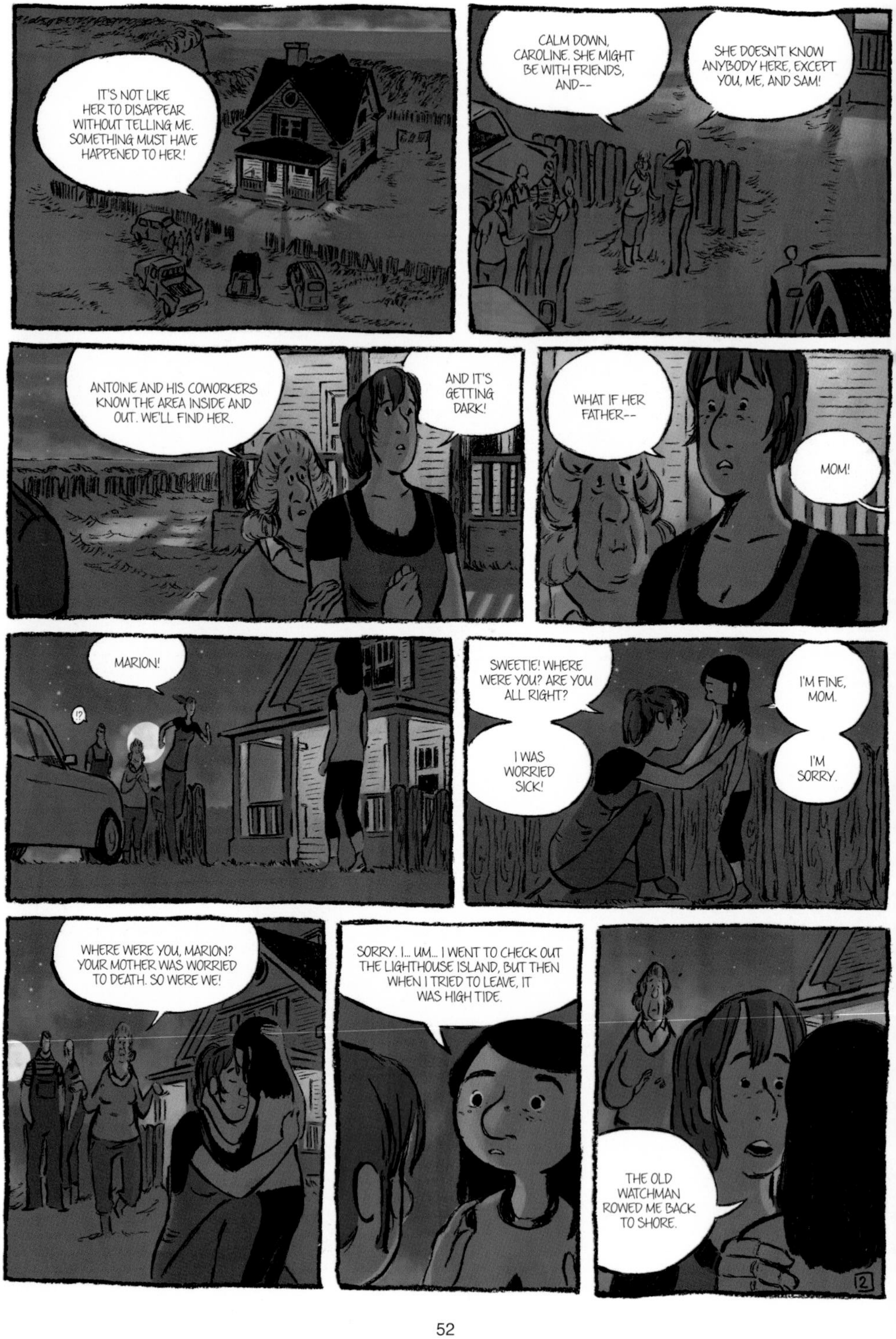
IT'S NOT LIKE HER TO DISAPPEAR WITHOUT TELLING ME. SOMETHING MUST HAVE HAPPENED TO HER!
CALM DOWN, CAROLINE. SHE MIGHT BE WITH FRIENDS, AND--
SHE DOESN'T KNOW ANYBODY HERE, EXCEPT YOU, ME, AND SAM!
ANTOINE AND HIS COWORKERS KNOW THE AREA INSIDE AND OUT. WE'LL FIND HER.
AND IT'S GETTING DARK!
WHAT IF HER FATHER--
MOM!
MARION!
!?
SWEETIE! WHERE WERE YOU? ARE YOU ALL RIGHT?
I WAS WORRIED SICK!
I'M FINE, MOM.
I'M SORRY.
WHERE WERE YOU, MARION? YOUR MOTHER WAS WORRIED TO DEATH. SO WERE WE!
SORRY. I... UM... I WENT TO CHECK OUT THE LIGHTHOUSE ISLAND, BUT THEN WHEN I TRIED TO LEAVE, IT WAS HIGH TIDE.
THE OLD WATCHMAN ROWED ME BACK TO SHORE.
2

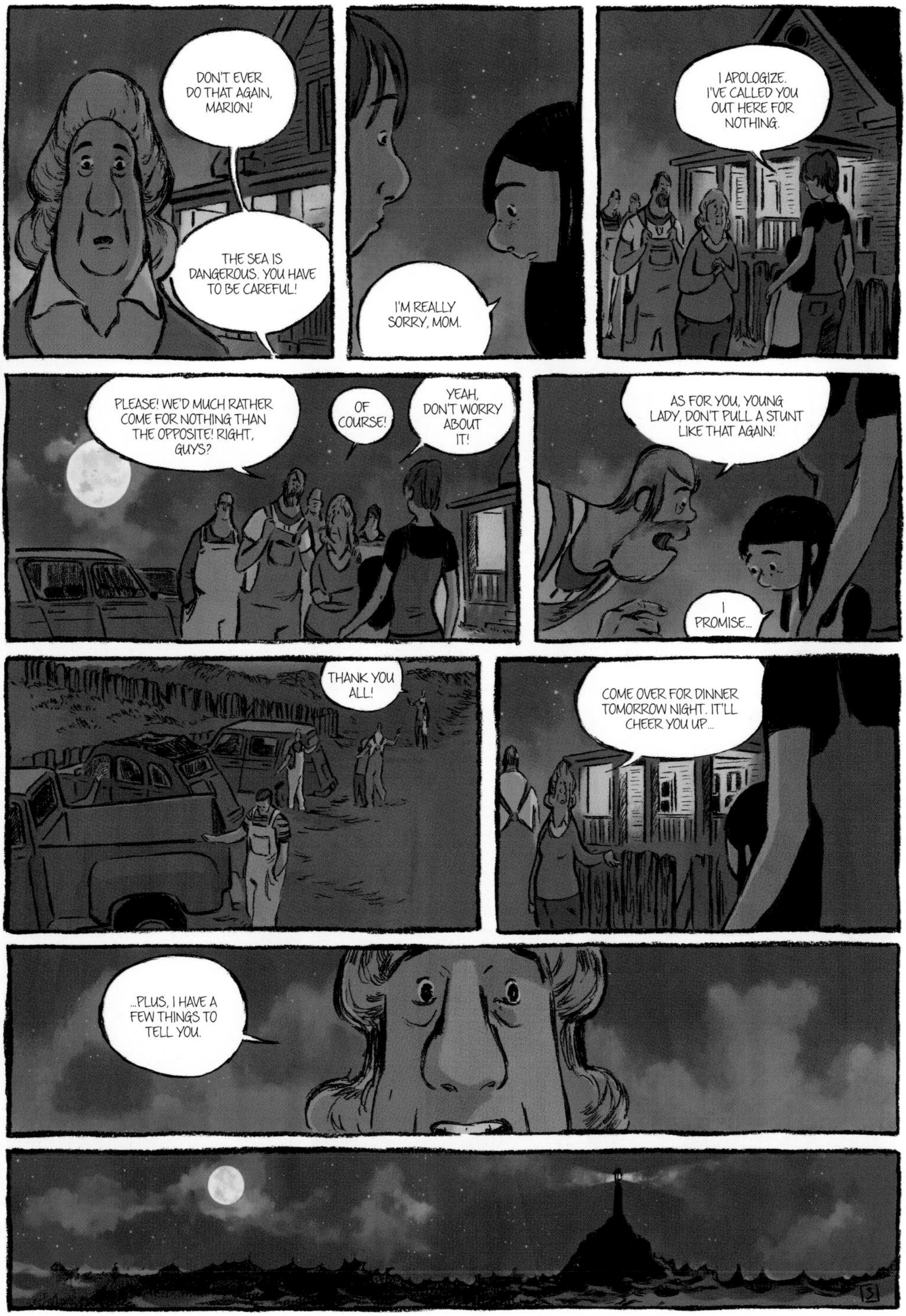
DON'T EVER DO THAT AGAIN, MARION!
THE SEA IS DANGEROUS. YOU HAVE TO BE CAREFUL!
I'M REALLY SORRY, MOM.
I APOLOGIZE. I'VE CALLED YOU OUT HERE FOR NOTHING.
PLEASE! WE'D MUCH RATHER COME FOR NOTHING THAN THE OPPOSITE! RIGHT, GUYS?
OF COURSE!
YEAH, DON'T WORRY ABOUT IT!
AS FOR YOU, YOUNG LADY, DON'T PULL A STUNT LIKE THAT AGAIN!
I PROMISE...
THANK YOU ALL!
COME OVER FOR DINNER TOMORROW NIGHT. IT'LL CHEER YOU UP...
...PLUS, I HAVE A FEW THINGS TO TELL YOU.

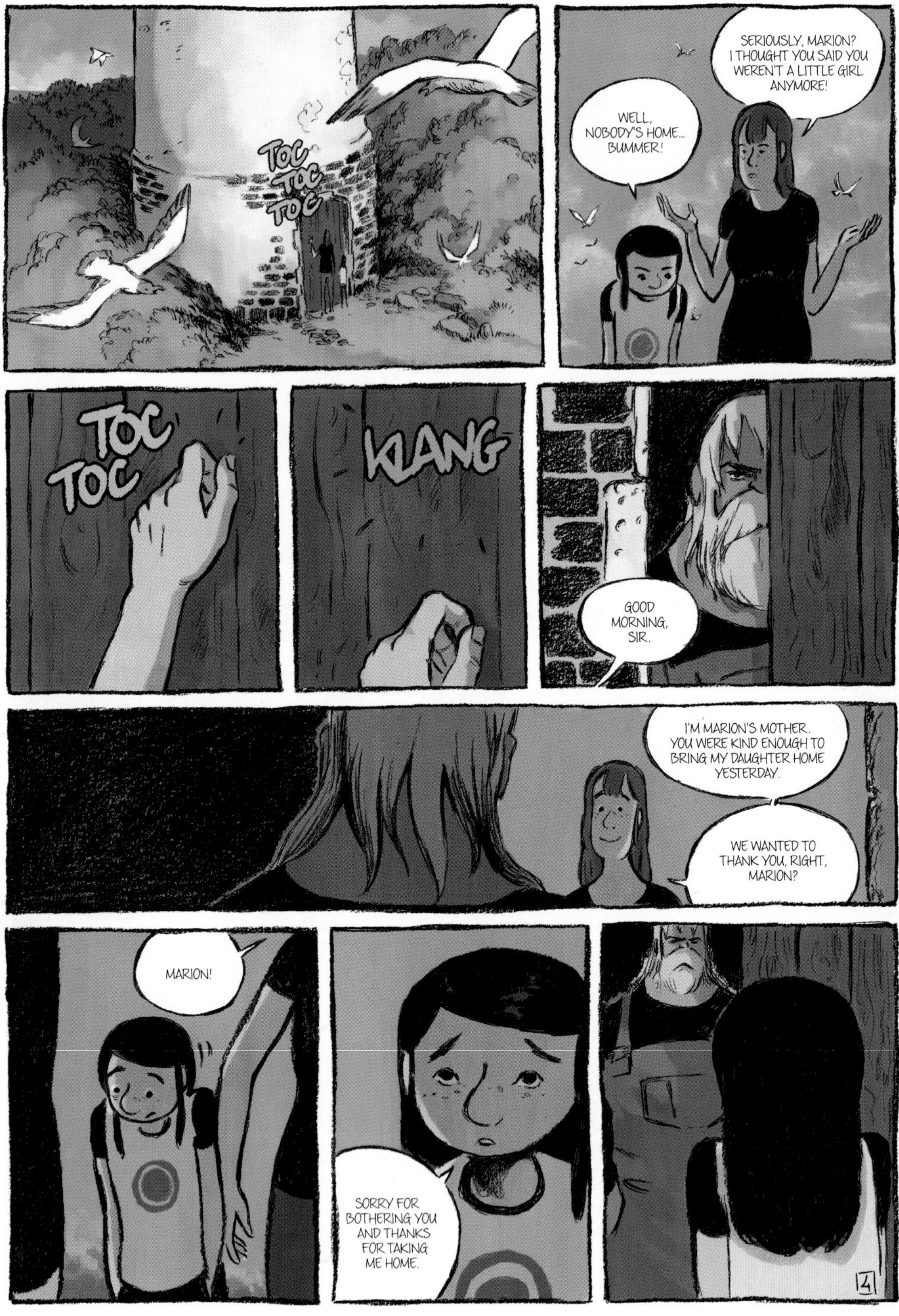
TOC TOC TOC
SERIOUSLY, MARION? I THOUGHT YOU SAID YOU WEREN'T A LITTLE GIRL ANYMORE!
WELL, NOBODY'S HOME... BUMMER!
TOC TOC
KLANG
GOOD MORNING, SIR.
I'M MARION'S MOTHER. YOU WERE KIND ENOUGH TO BRING MY DAUGHTER HOME YESTERDAY.
WE WANTED TO THANK YOU, RIGHT, MARION?
MARION!
SORRY FOR BOTHERING YOU AND THANKS FOR TAKING ME HOME.
4

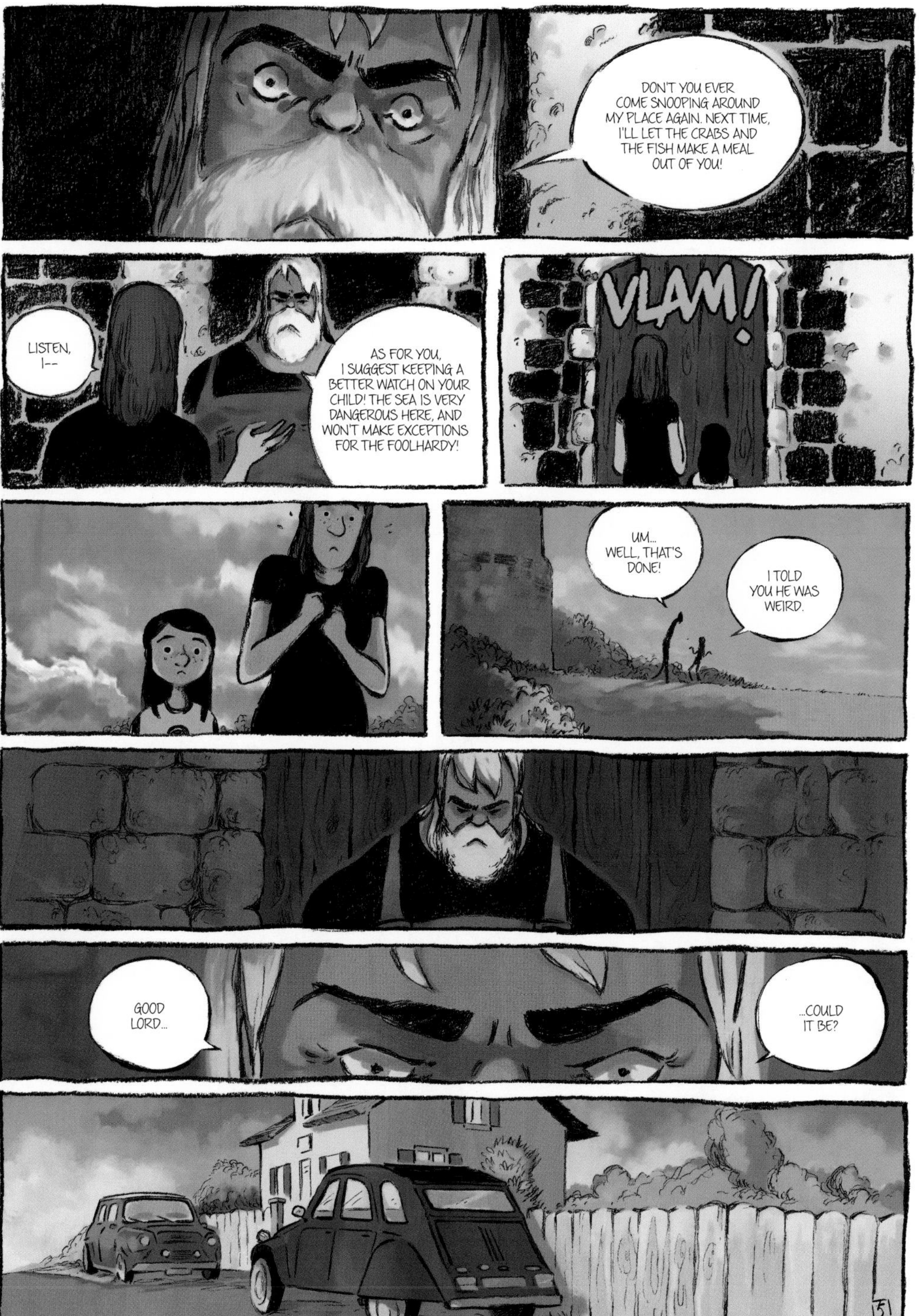
DON'T YOU EVER COME SNOOPING AROUND MY PLACE AGAIN. NEXT TIME, I'LL LET THE CRABS AND THE FISH MAKE A MEAL OUT OF YOU!
LISTEN, I--
AS FOR YOU, I SUGGEST KEEPING A BETTER WATCH ON YOUR CHILD! THE SEA IS VERY DANGEROUS HERE, AND WON'T MAKE EXCEPTIONS FOR THE FOOLHARDY!
VLAM!
UM... WELL, THAT'S DONE!
I TOLD YOU HE WAS WEIRD.
GOOD LORD...
...COULD IT BE?
5

...IT MUST HAVE BEEN ABOUT THIRTY YEARS AGO. IS THAT RIGHT, MATEY? ABOUT THIRTY YEARS?

MORE THAN THAT, CAPTAIN! WHEN ANNICK AND YOUNG CAROLINE HERE MOVED AWAY, WE'D ALREADY BEEN LIVING HERE A FEW YEARS.

RIGHT... IT'S EASY, IT'S THE YEAR I WON THE FISHING COMPETITION. REMEMBER THAT?

HOW COULD I FORGET? YOU REMIND ME EVERY CHANCE YOU GET!

PFFF! SHE EXAGGERATES.

STILL THOUGH, A 500-POUND TUNA! YOU SHOULD HAVE SEEN IT!

IT WAS TOUGH REELING IT IN, I'LL TELL YOU THAT MUCH!

BUT BACK IN THE DAY, I WAS A PRETTY STRONG FELLA. RIGHT, MATEY?

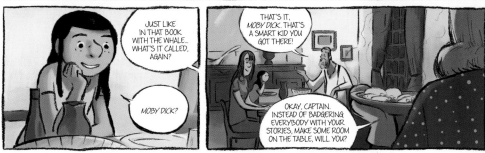

JUST LIKE IN THAT BOOK WITH THE WHALE... WHAT'S IT CALLED, AGAIN?

MOBY DICK?

THAT'S IT, MOBY DICK. THAT'S A SMART KID YOU GOT THERE!

OKAY, CAPTAIN. INSTEAD OF BADGERING EVERYBODY WITH YOUR STORIES, MAKE SOME ROOM ON THE TABLE, WILL YOU?

HA HA! YOU SHOULD HAVE SEEN THE LOOK ON THEIR FACES WHEN I CAME BACK WITH THAT THING!

I MADE BAKED FLOUNDER. I HOPE YOU LIKE IT!

IT SMELLS DELICIOUS, SUZANNE.

BASICALLY, I OBLITERATED THE PREVIOUS RECORD!

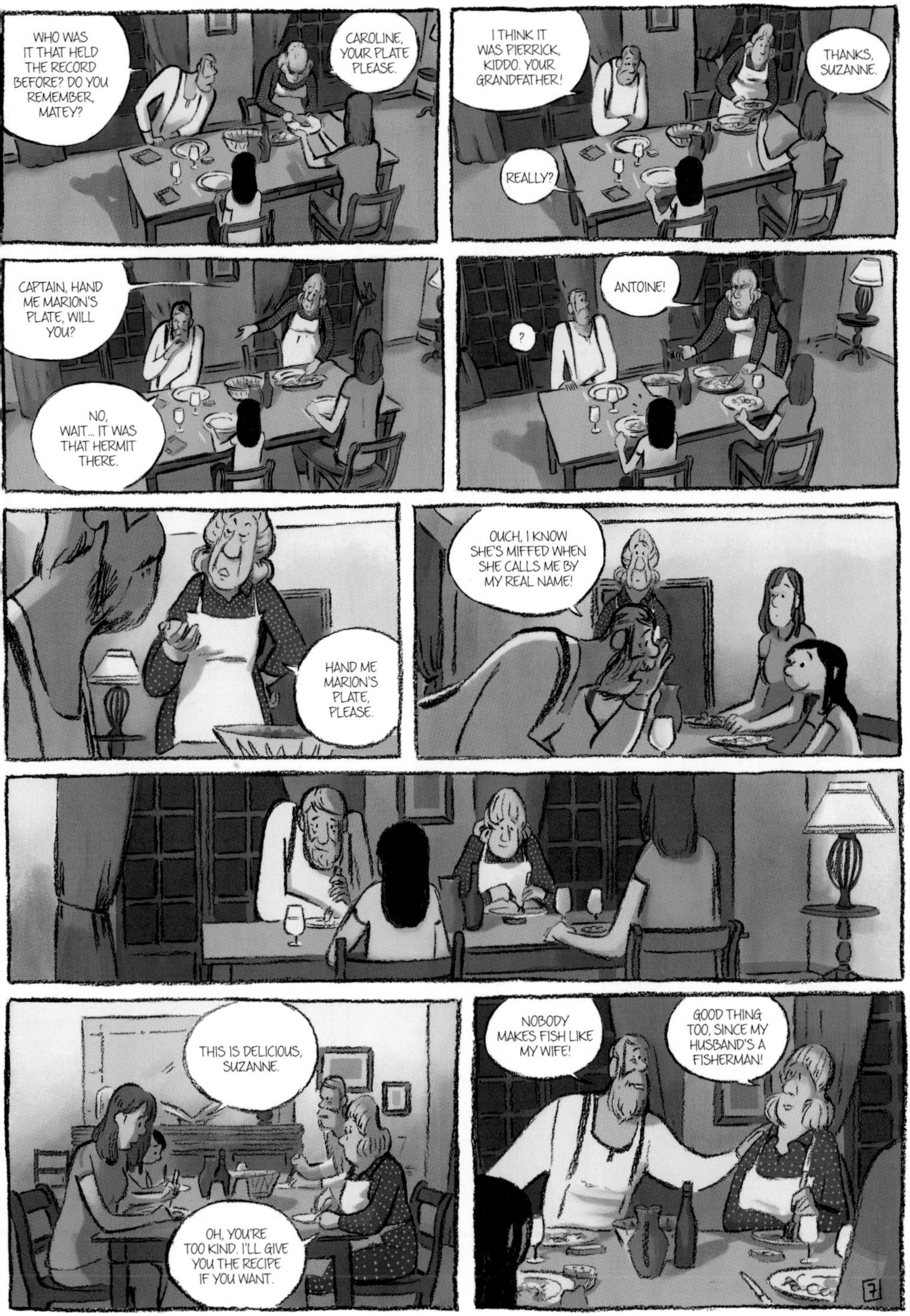
WHO WAS IT THAT HELD THE RECORD BEFORE? DO YOU REMEMBER, MATEY?
CAROLINE, YOUR PLATE PLEASE.
I THINK IT WAS PIERRICK, KIDDO. YOUR GRANDFATHER!
THANKS, SUZANNE.
REALLY?
CAPTAIN, HAND ME MARION'S PLATE, WILL YOU?
NO, WAIT... IT WAS THAT HERMIT THERE.
ANTOINE!
?
HAND ME MARION'S PLATE, PLEASE.
OUCH, I KNOW SHE'S MIFFED WHEN SHE CALLS ME BY MY REAL NAME!
THIS IS DELICIOUS, SUZANNE.
OH, YOU'RE TOO KIND. I'LL GIVE YOU THE RECIPE IF YOU WANT.
NOBODY MAKES FISH LIKE MY WIFE!
GOOD THING TOO, SINCE MY HUSBAND'S A FISHERMAN!

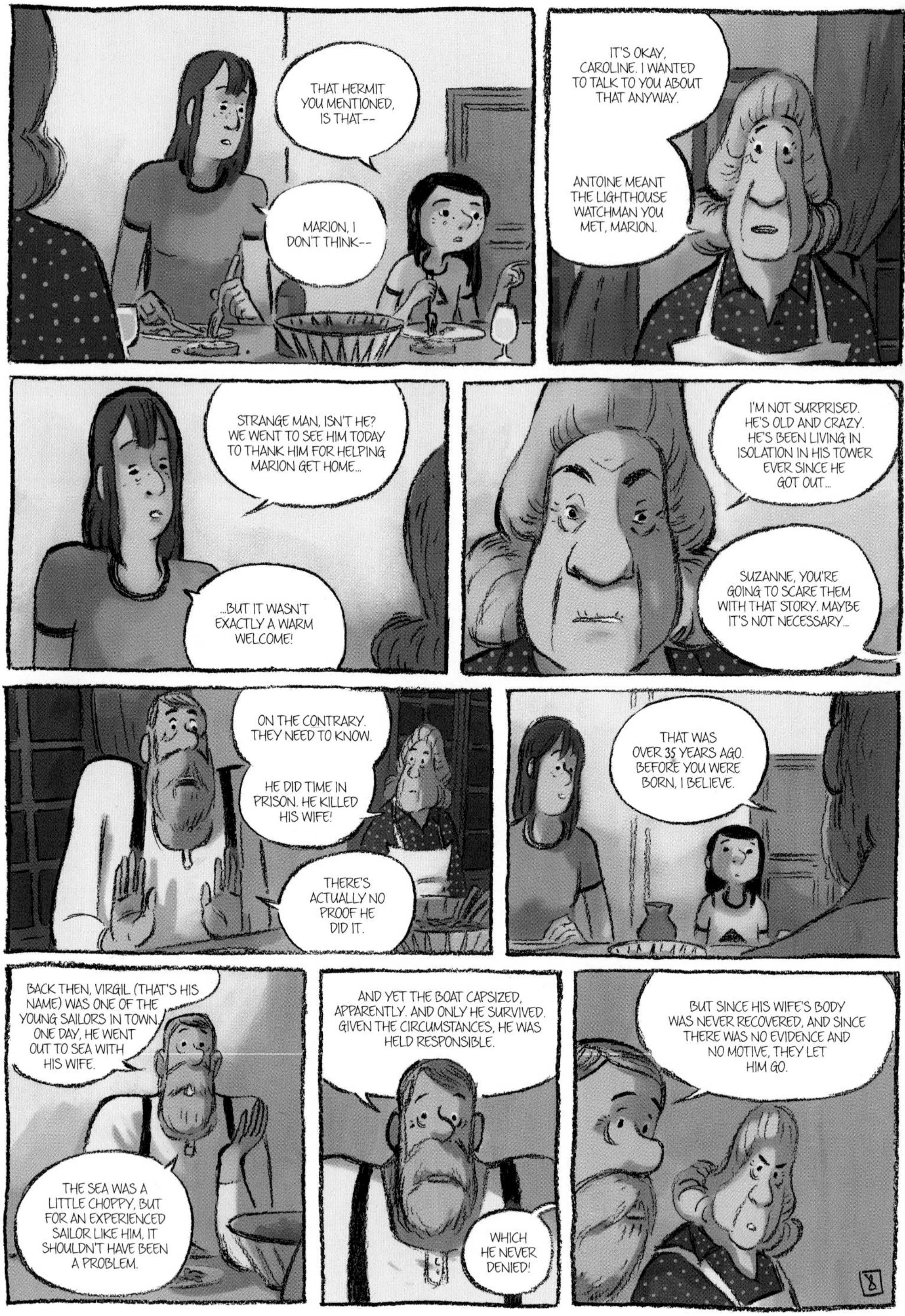
THAT HERMIT YOU MENTIONED, IS THAT--
MARION, I DON'T THINK--
IT'S OKAY, CAROLINE. I WANTED TO TALK TO YOU ABOUT THAT ANYWAY.
ANTOINE MEANT THE LIGHTHOUSE WATCHMAN YOU MET, MARION.
STRANGE MAN, ISN'T HE? WE WENT TO SEE HIM TODAY TO THANK HIM FOR HELPING MARION GET HOME...
...BUT IT WASN'T EXACTLY A WARM WELCOME!
I'M NOT SURPRISED. HE'S OLD AND CRAZY. HE'S BEEN LIVING IN ISOLATION IN HIS TOWER EVER SINCE HE GOT OUT...
SUZANNE, YOU'RE GOING TO SCARE THEM WITH THAT STORY. MAYBE IT'S NOT NECESSARY...
ON THE CONTRARY. THEY NEED TO KNOW.
HE DID TIME IN PRISON. HE KILLED HIS WIFE!
THERE'S ACTUALLY NO PROOF HE DID IT.
THAT WAS OVER 35 YEARS AGO. BEFORE YOU WERE BORN, I BELIEVE.
BACK THEN, VIRGIL (THAT'S HIS NAME) WAS ONE OF THE YOUNG SAILORS IN TOWN. ONE DAY, HE WENT OUT TO SEA WITH HIS WIFE.
THE SEA WAS A LITTLE CHOPPY, BUT FOR AN EXPERIENCED SAILOR LIKE HIM, IT SHOULDN'T HAVE BEEN A PROBLEM.
AND YET THE BOAT CAPSIZED, APPARENTLY. AND ONLY HE SURVIVED. GIVEN THE CIRCUMSTANCES, HE WAS HELD RESPONSIBLE.
WHICH HE NEVER DENIED!
BUT SINCE HIS WIFE'S BODY WAS NEVER RECOVERED, AND SINCE THERE WAS NO EVIDENCE AND NO MOTIVE, THEY LET HIM GO.

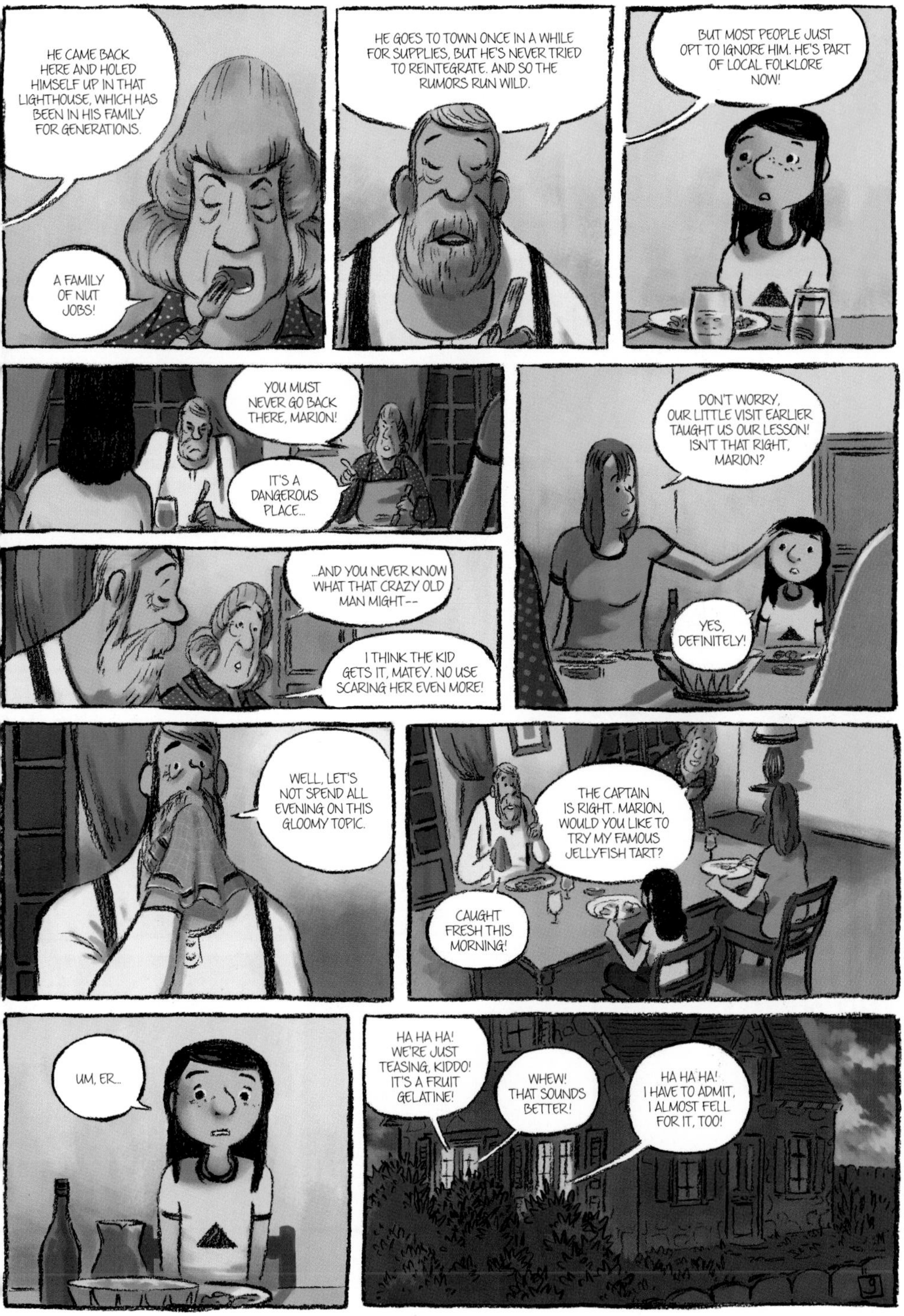
HE CAME BACK HERE AND HOLED HIMSELF UP IN THAT LIGHTHOUSE, WHICH HAS BEEN IN HIS FAMILY FOR GENERATIONS.
A FAMILY OF NUT JOBS!
HE GOES TO TOWN ONCE IN A WHILE FOR SUPPLIES, BUT HE'S NEVER TRIED TO REINTEGRATE. AND SO THE RUMORS RUN WILD.
BUT MOST PEOPLE JUST OPT TO IGNORE HIM. HE'S PART OF LOCAL FOLKLORE NOW!
YOU MUST NEVER GO BACK THERE, MARION!
IT'S A DANGEROUS PLACE...
...AND YOU NEVER KNOW WHAT THAT CRAZY OLD MAN MIGHT--
I THINK THE KID GETS IT, MATEY. NO USE SCARING HER EVEN MORE!
DON'T WORRY, OUR LITTLE VISIT EARLIER TAUGHT US OUR LESSON! ISN'T THAT RIGHT, MARION?
YES, DEFINITELY!
WELL, LET'S NOT SPEND ALL EVENING ON THIS GLOOMY TOPIC.
THE CAPTAIN IS RIGHT. MARION, WOULD YOU LIKE TO TRY MY FAMOUS JELLYFISH TART?
CAUGHT FRESH THIS MORNING!
UM, ER...
HA HA HA! WE'RE JUST TEASING, KIDDO! IT'S A FRUIT GELATINE!
WHEW! THAT SOUNDS BETTER!
HA HA HA! I HAVE TO ADMIT, I ALMOST FELL FOR IT, TOO!

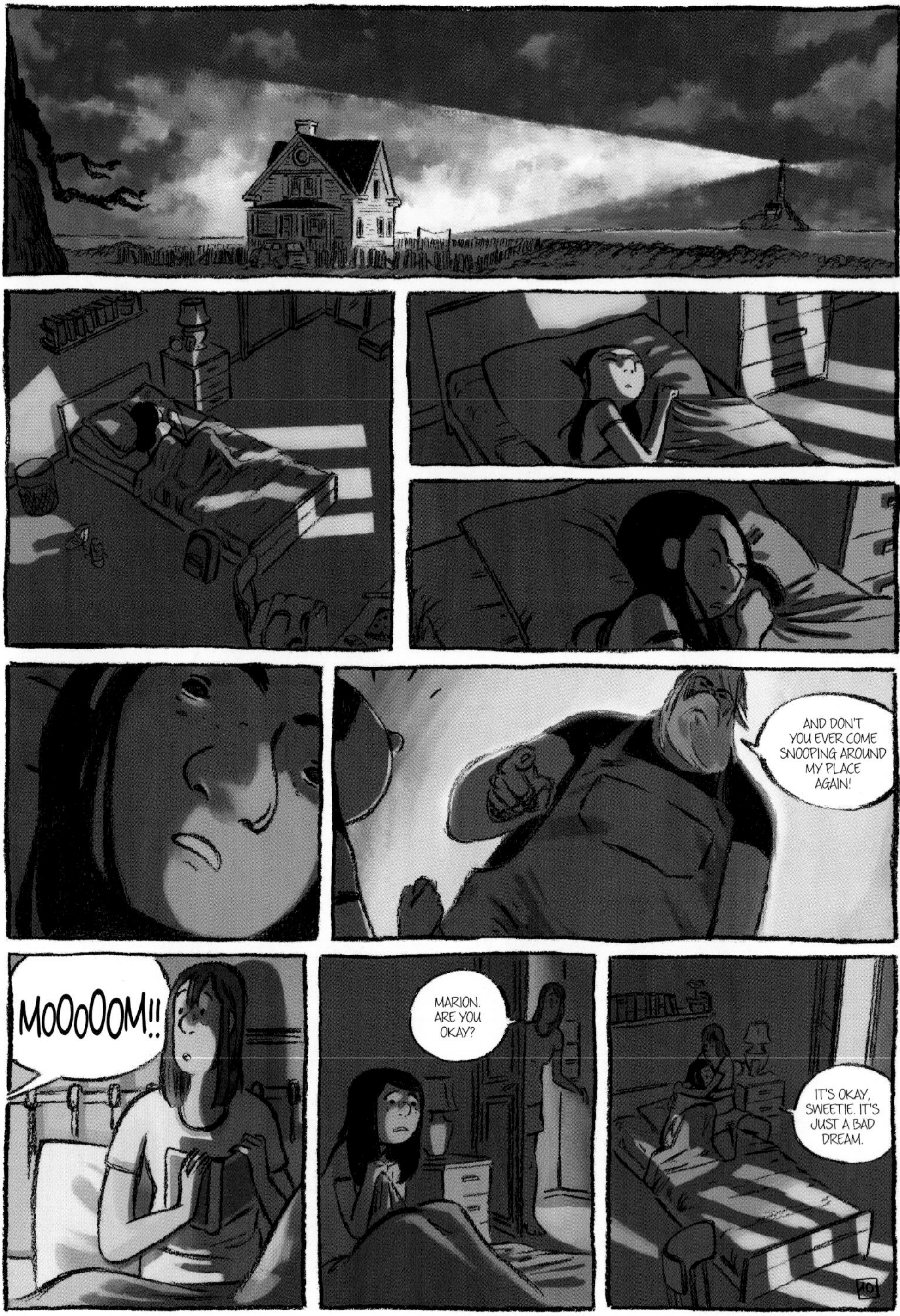
AND DON'T YOU EVER COME SNOOPING AROUND MY PLACE AGAIN!
MOOOOOM!!
MARION. ARE YOU OKAY?
IT'S OKAY, SWEETIE. IT'S JUST A BAD DREAM.
10

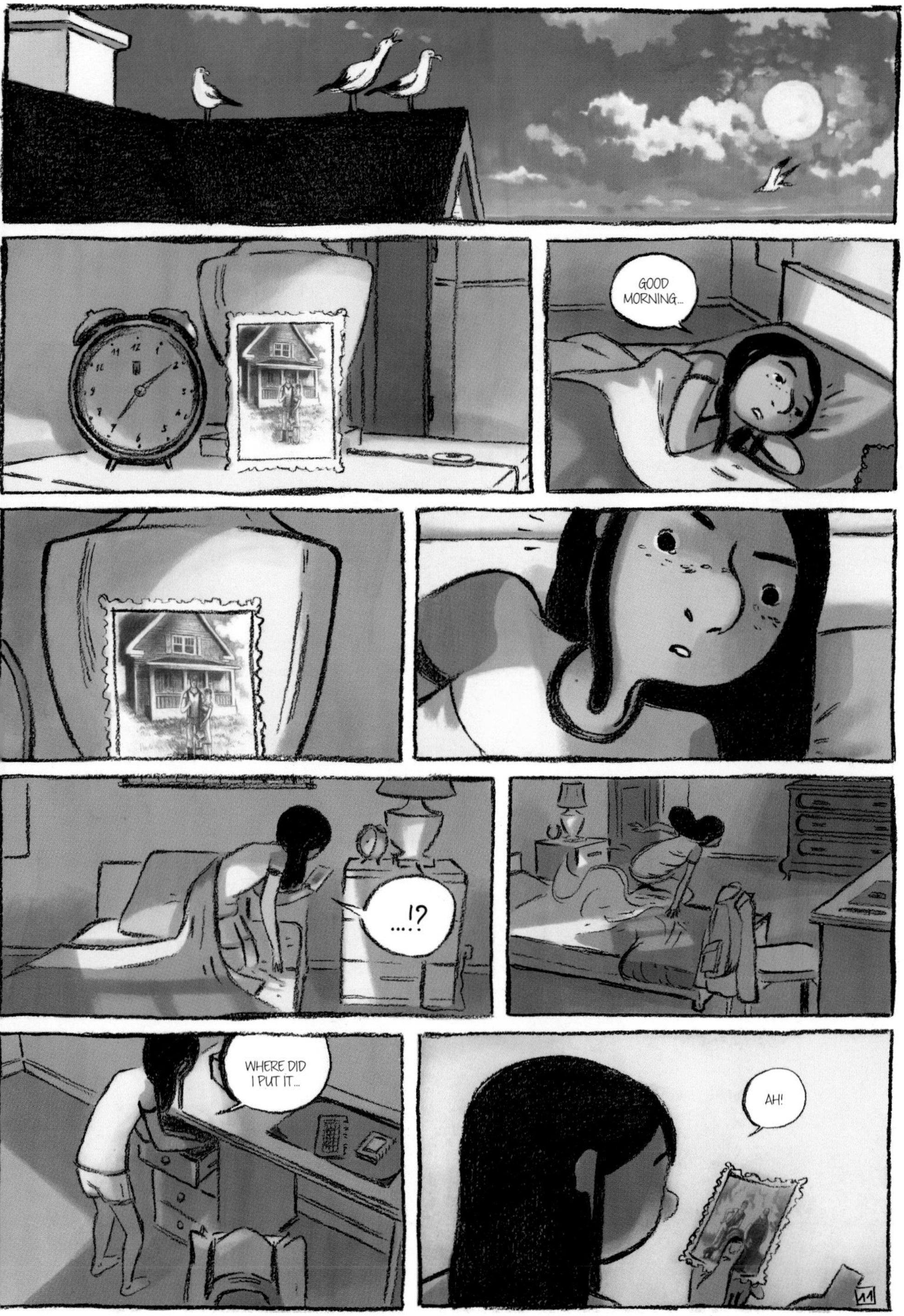
GOOD MORNING...
...!?
WHERE DID I PUT IT...
AH!

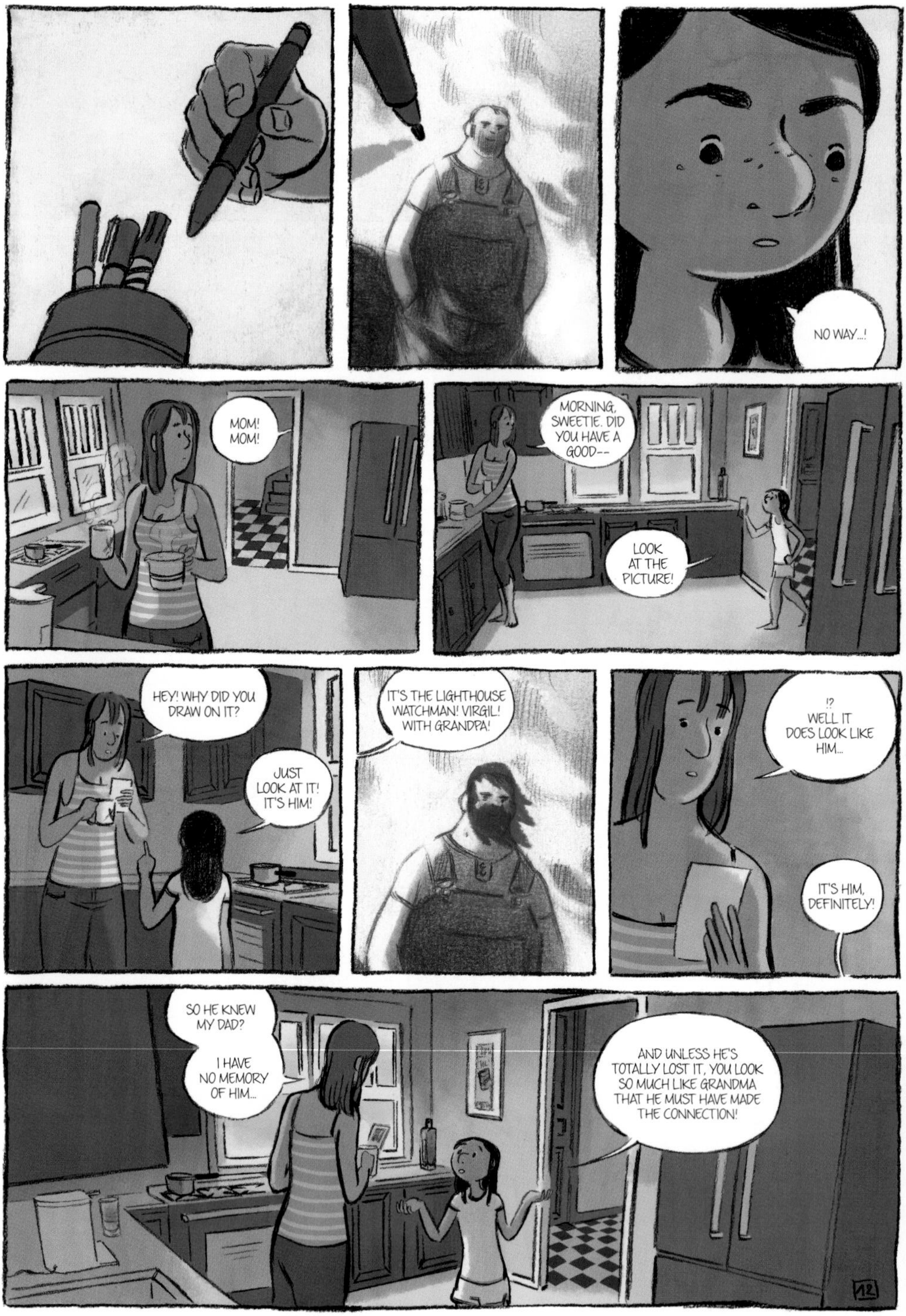
NO WAY...!
MOM! MOM!
MORNING, SWEETIE. DID YOU HAVE A GOOD--
LOOK AT THE PICTURE!
HEY! WHY DID YOU DRAW ON IT?
JUST LOOK AT IT! IT'S HIM!
IT'S THE LIGHTHOUSE WATCHMAN! VIRGIL! WITH GRANDPA!
!? WELL IT DOES LOOK LIKE HIM...
IT'S HIM, DEFINITELY!
SO HE KNEW MY DAD?
I HAVE NO MEMORY OF HIM...
AND UNLESS HE'S TOTALLY LOST IT, YOU LOOK SO MUCH LIKE GRANDMA THAT HE MUST HAVE MADE THE CONNECTION!
12

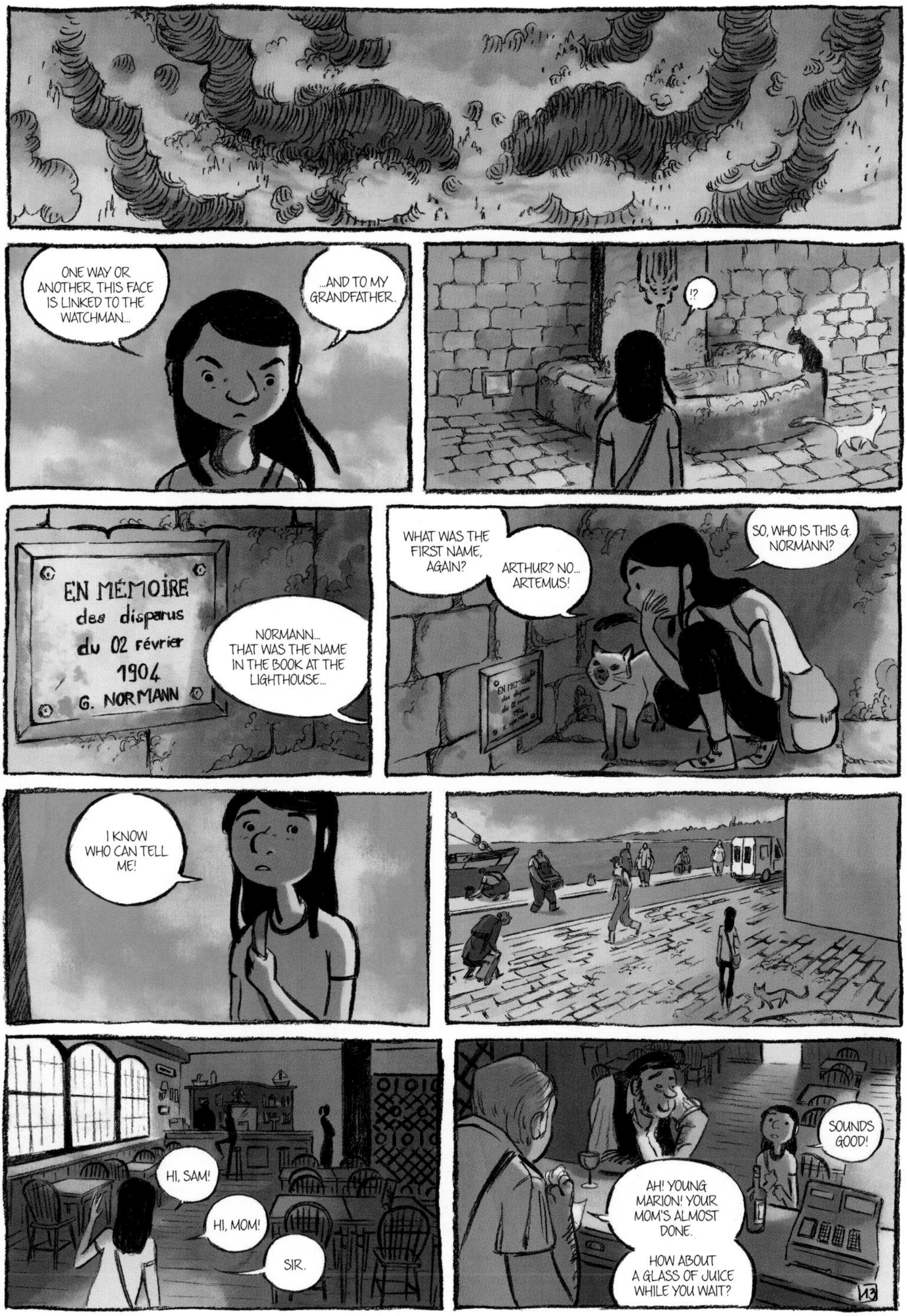
ONE WAY OR ANOTHER, THIS FACE IS LINKED TO THE WATCHMAN...
...AND TO MY GRANDFATHER.
!?
EN MÉMOIRE des disparus du 02 février 1904 G. NORMANN
NORMANN... THAT WAS THE NAME IN THE BOOK AT THE LIGHTHOUSE...
WHAT WAS THE FIRST NAME, AGAIN?
ARTHUR? NO... ARTEMUS!
SO, WHO IS THIS G. NORMANN?
I KNOW WHO CAN TELL ME!
HI, SAM!
HI, MOM!
SIR.
AH! YOUNG MARION! YOUR MOM'S ALMOST DONE.
HOW ABOUT A GLASS OF JUICE WHILE YOU WAIT?
SOUNDS GOOD!

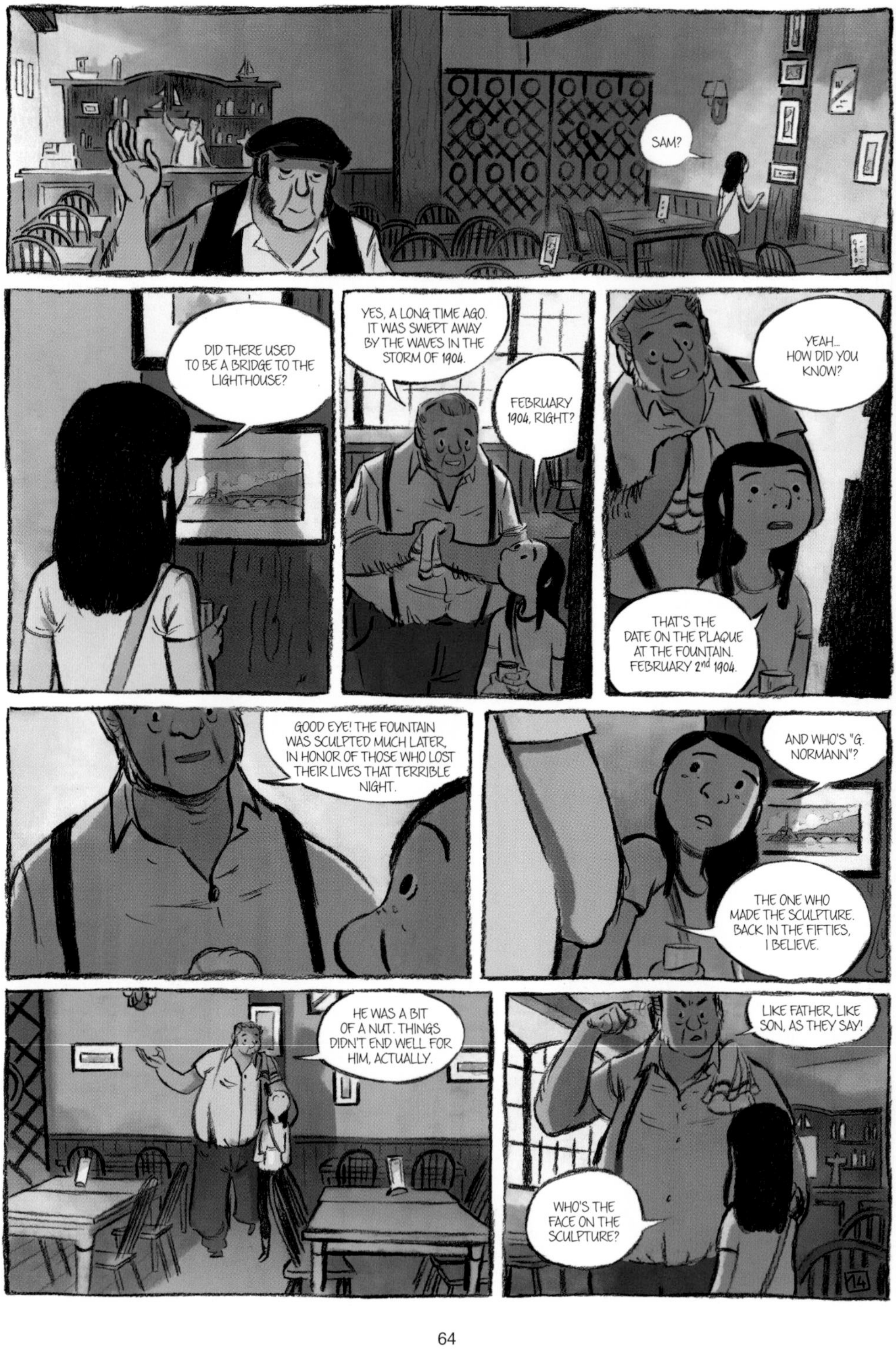
SAM?
DID THERE USED TO BE A BRIDGE TO THE LIGHTHOUSE?
YES, A LONG TIME AGO. IT WAS SWEPT AWAY BY THE WAVES IN THE STORM OF 1904.
FEBRUARY 1904, RIGHT?
YEAH... HOW DID YOU KNOW?
THAT'S THE DATE ON THE PLAQUE AT THE FOUNTAIN. FEBRUARY 2nd 1904.
GOOD EYE! THE FOUNTAIN WAS SCULPTED MUCH LATER, IN HONOR OF THOSE WHO LOST THEIR LIVES THAT TERRIBLE NIGHT.
AND WHO'S "G. NORMANN"?
THE ONE WHO MADE THE SCULPTURE. BACK IN THE FIFTIES, I BELIEVE.
HE WAS A BIT OF A NUT. THINGS DIDN'T END WELL FOR HIM, ACTUALLY.
LIKE FATHER, LIKE SON, AS THEY SAY!
WHO'S THE FACE ON THE SCULPTURE?
14

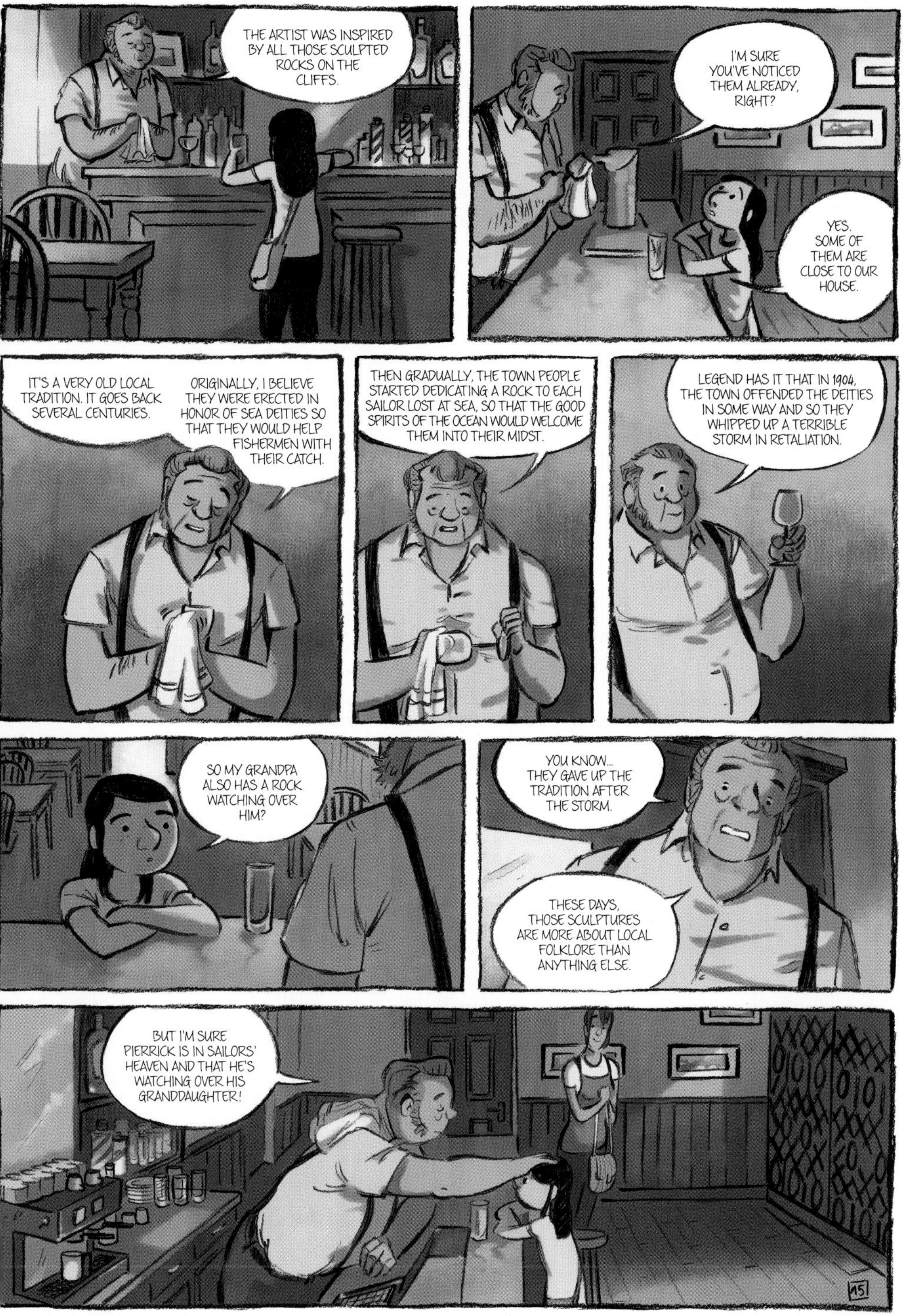
THE ARTIST WAS INSPIRED BY ALL THOSE SCULPTED ROCKS ON THE CLIFFS.
I'M SURE YOU'VE NOTICED THEM ALREADY, RIGHT?
YES. SOME OF THEM ARE CLOSE TO OUR HOUSE.
IT'S A VERY OLD LOCAL TRADITION. IT GOES BACK SEVERAL CENTURIES.
ORIGINALLY, I BELIEVE THEY WERE ERECTED IN HONOR OF SEA DEITIES SO THAT THEY WOULD HELP FISHERMEN WITH THEIR CATCH.
THEN GRADUALLY, THE TOWN PEOPLE STARTED DEDICATING A ROCK TO EACH SAILOR LOST AT SEA, SO THAT THE GOOD SPIRITS OF THE OCEAN WOULD WELCOME THEM INTO THEIR MIDST.
LEGEND HAS IT THAT IN 1904, THE TOWN OFFENDED THE DEITIES IN SOME WAY AND SO THEY WHIPPED UP A TERRIBLE STORM IN RETALIATION.
SO MY GRANDPA ALSO HAS A ROCK WATCHING OVER HIM?
YOU KNOW... THEY GAVE UP THE TRADITION AFTER THE STORM.
THESE DAYS, THOSE SCULPTURES ARE MORE ABOUT LOCAL FOLKLORE THAN ANYTHING ELSE.
BUT I'M SURE PIERRICK IS IN SAILORS' HEAVEN AND THAT HE'S WATCHING OVER HIS GRANDDAUGHTER!
15

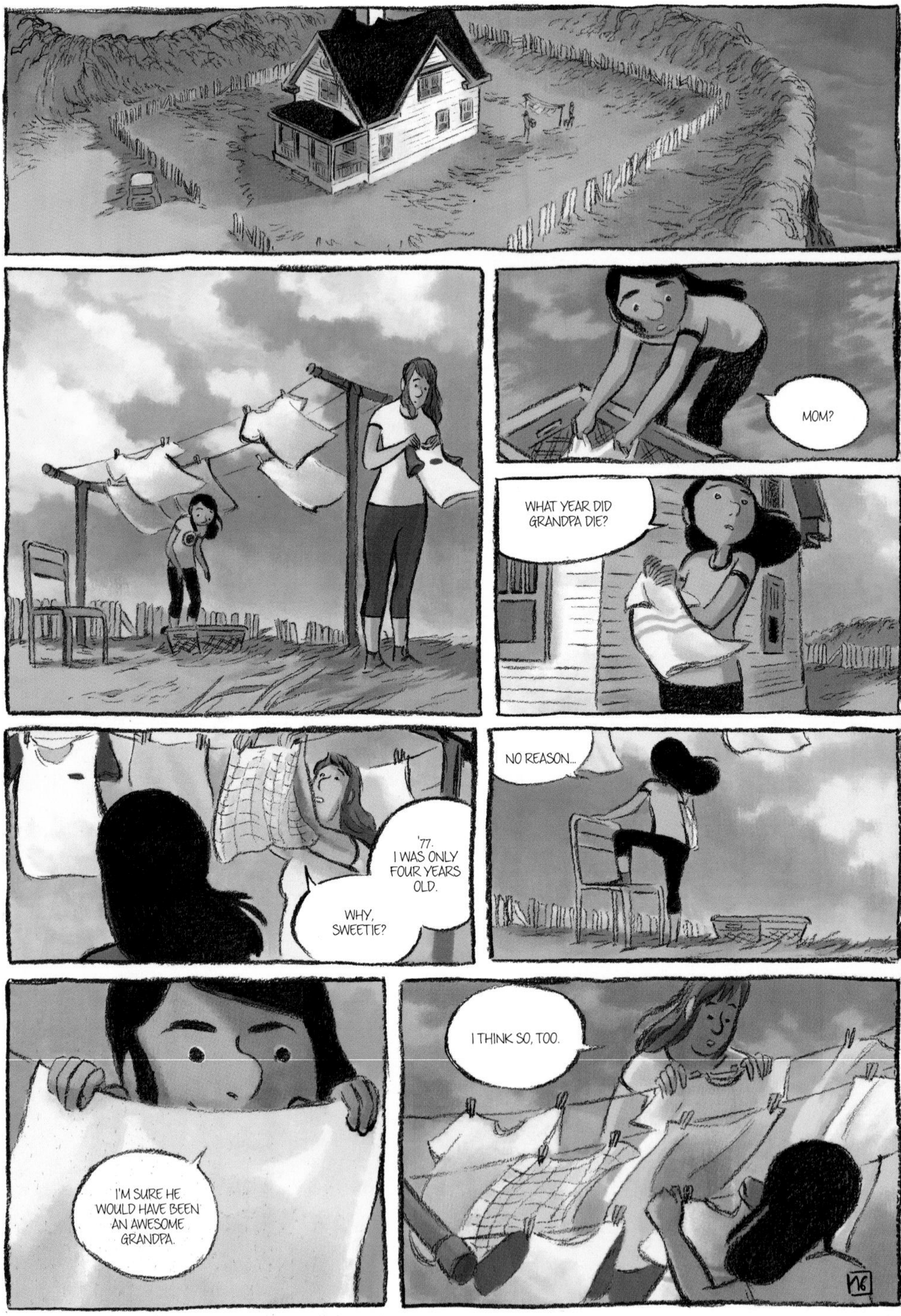
MOM?
WHAT YEAR DID GRANDPA DIE?
'77. I WAS ONLY FOUR YEARS OLD.
WHY, SWEETIE?
NO REASON...
I'M SURE HE WOULD HAVE BEEN AN AWESOME GRANDPA.
I THINK SO, TOO.

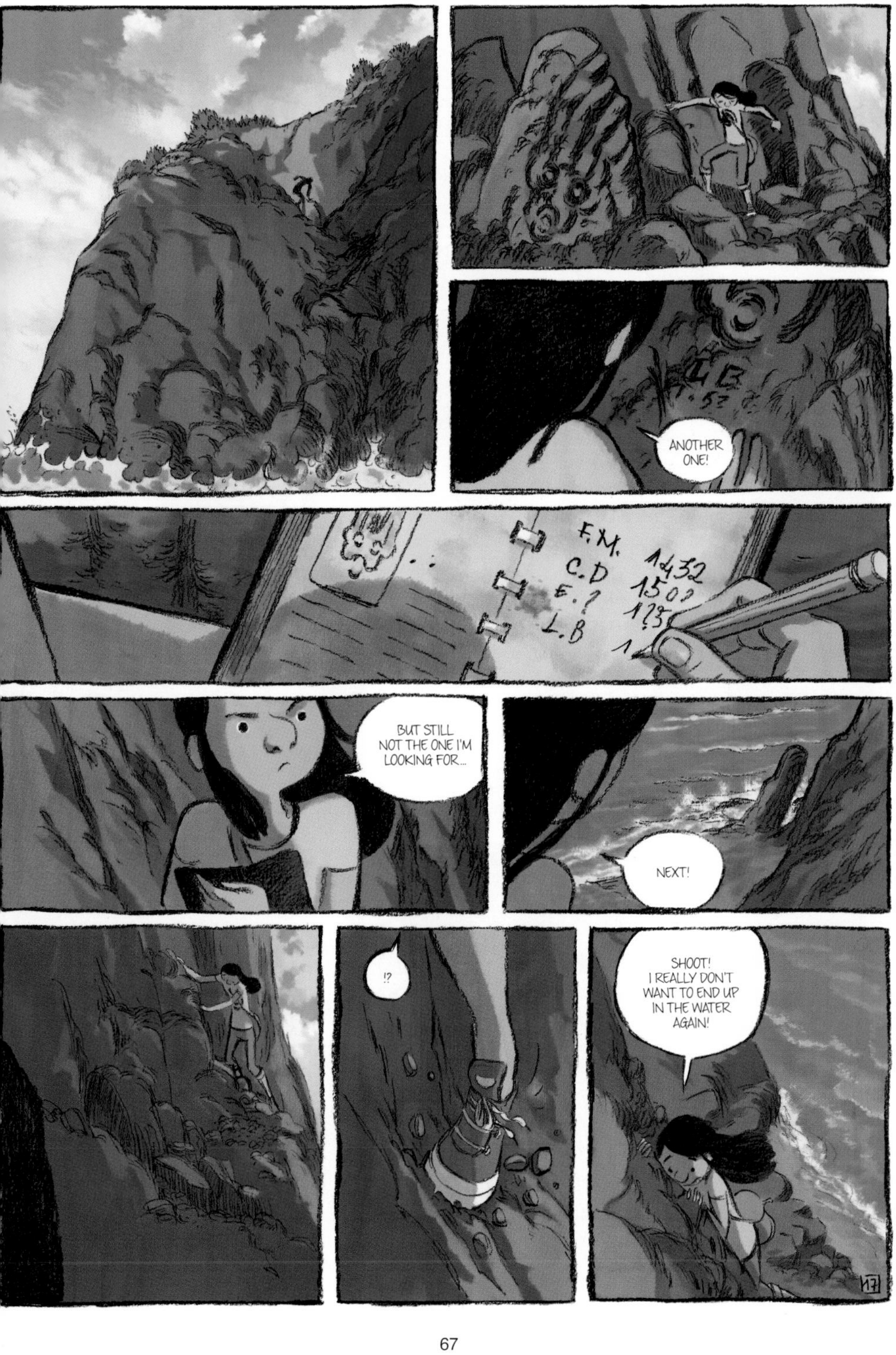
ANOTHER ONE!
BUT STILL NOT THE ONE I'M LOOKING FOR...
NEXT!
!?
SHOOT! I REALLY DON'T WANT TO END UP IN THE WATER AGAIN!

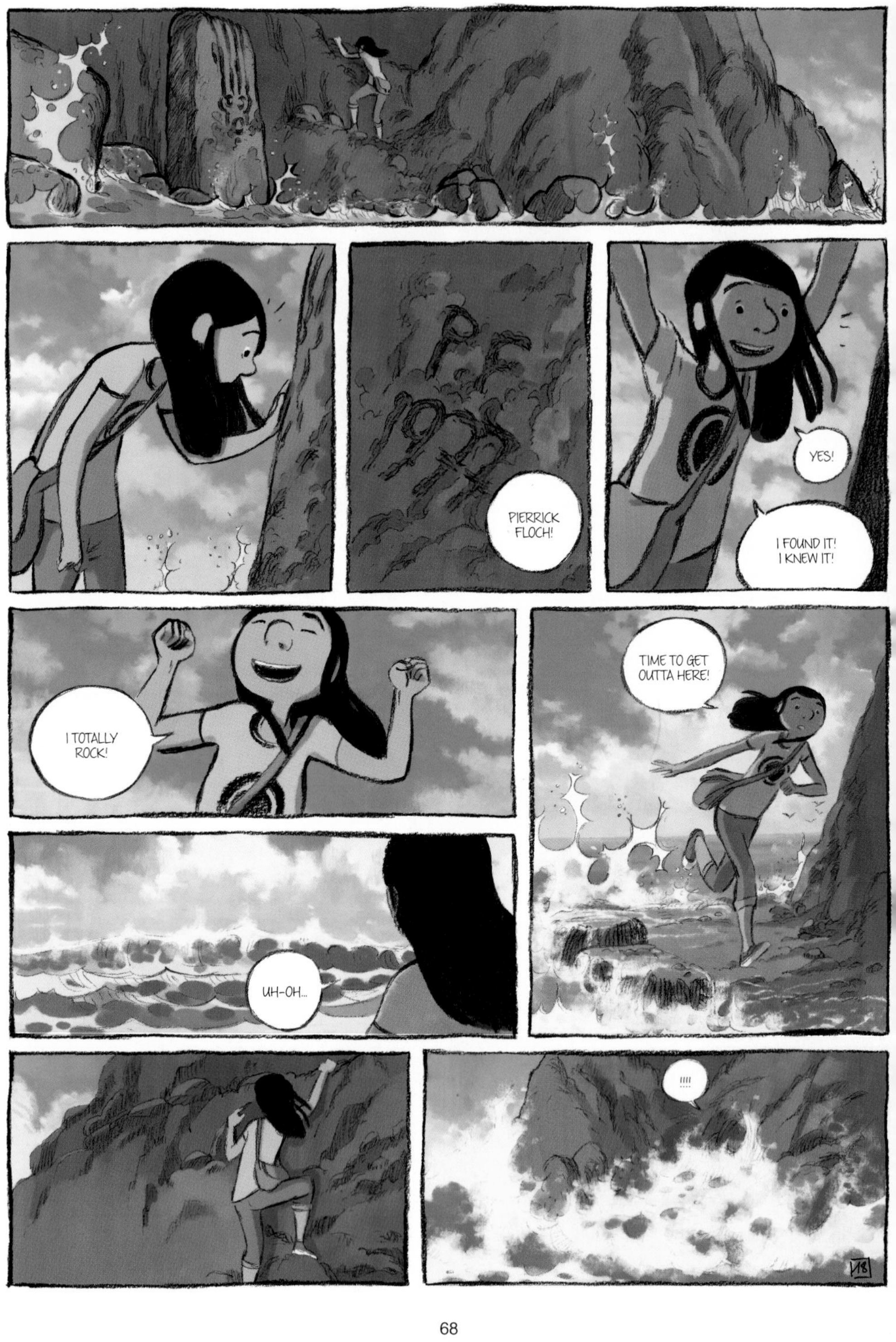
PIERRICK FLOCH!
YES!
I FOUND IT! I KNEW IT!
I TOTALLY ROCK!
TIME TO GET OUTTA HERE!
UH-OH...
!!!!

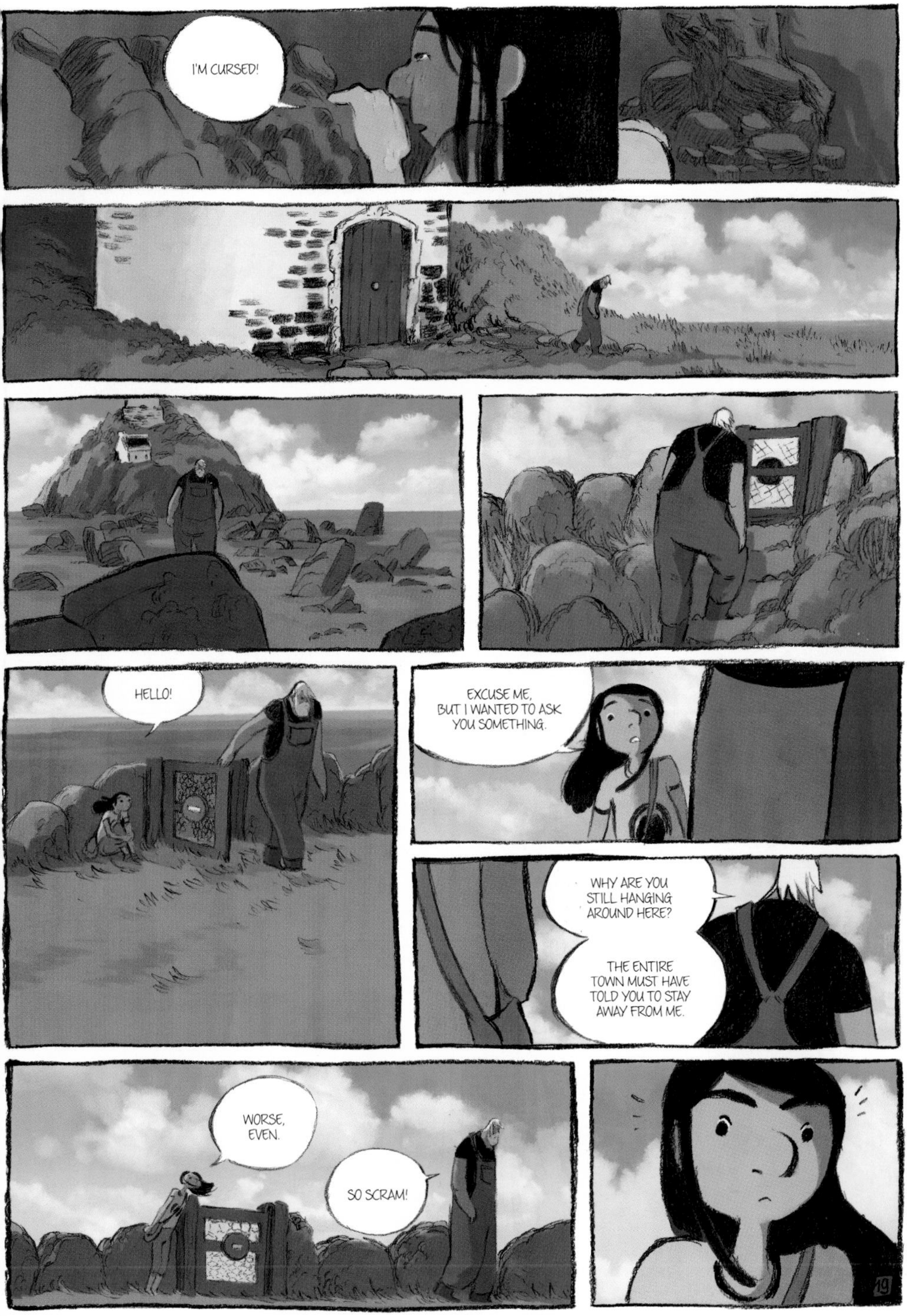
I'M CURSED!
HELLO!
EXCUSE ME, BUT I WANTED TO ASK YOU SOMETHING.
WHY ARE YOU STILL HANGING AROUND HERE?
THE ENTIRE TOWN MUST HAVE TOLD YOU TO STAY AWAY FROM ME.
WORSE, EVEN.
SO SCRAM!
19

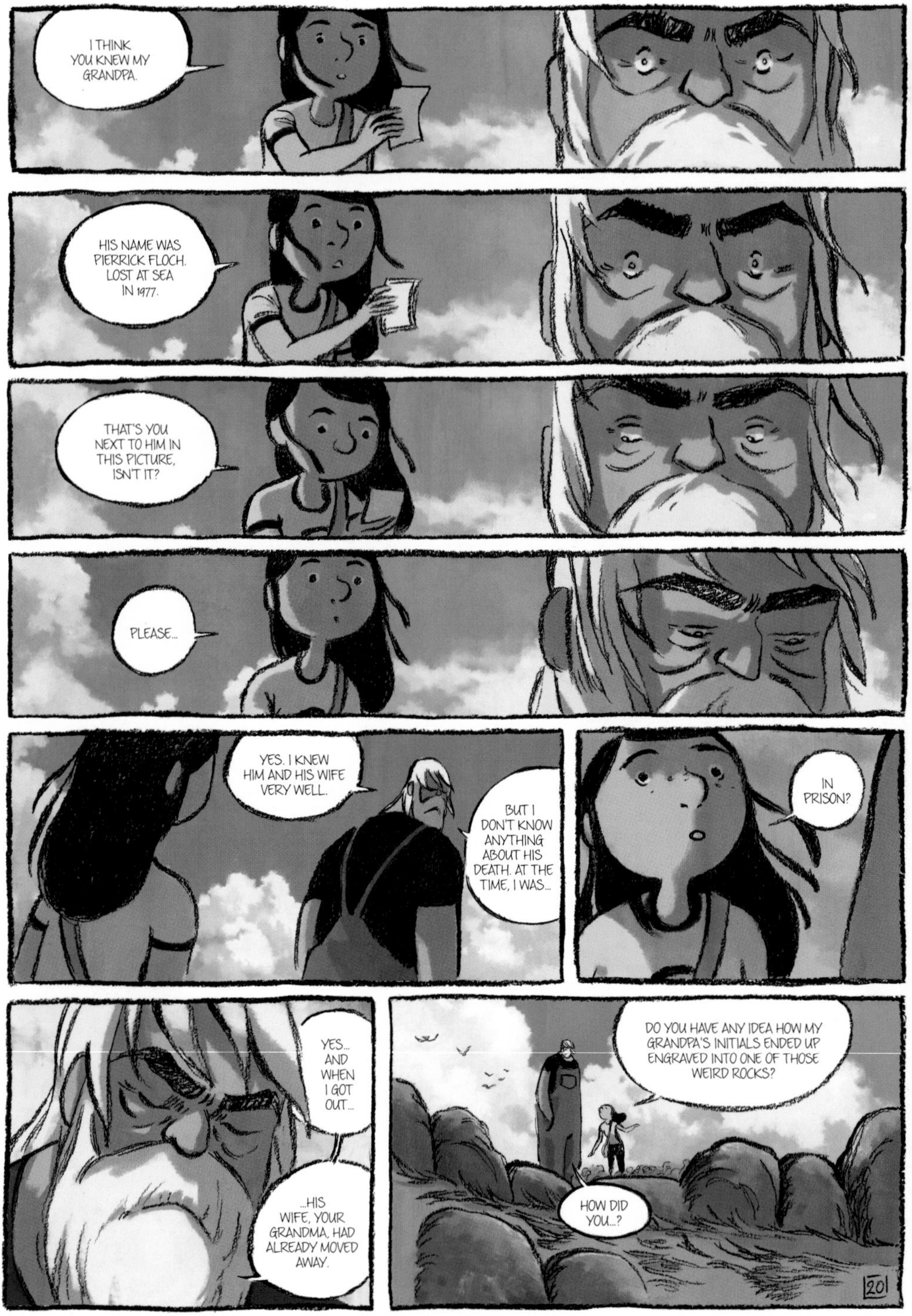
I THINK YOU KNEW MY GRANDPA.
HIS NAME WAS PIERRICK FLOCH. LOST AT SEA IN 1977.
THAT'S YOU NEXT TO HIM IN THIS PICTURE, ISN'T IT?
PLEASE...
YES. I KNEW HIM AND HIS WIFE VERY WELL.
BUT I DON'T KNOW ANYTHING ABOUT HIS DEATH. AT THE TIME, I WAS...
IN PRISON?
YES... AND WHEN I GOT OUT...
...HIS WIFE, YOUR GRANDMA, HAD ALREADY MOVED AWAY.
DO YOU HAVE ANY IDEA HOW MY GRANDPA'S INITIALS ENDED UP ENGRAVED INTO ONE OF THOSE WEIRD ROCKS?
HOW DID YOU...?
20

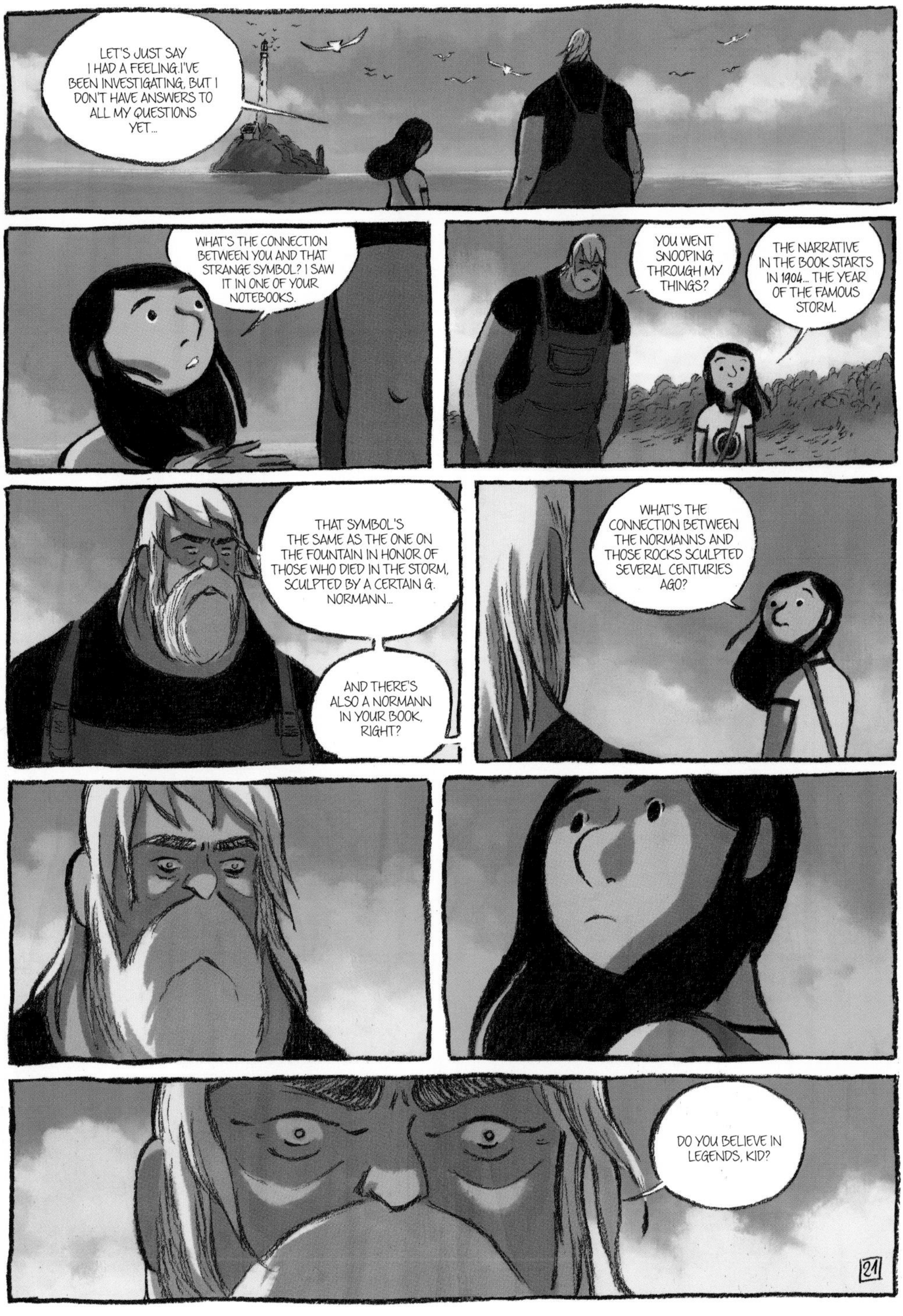
LET'S JUST SAY I HAD A FEELING. I'VE BEEN INVESTIGATING, BUT I DON'T HAVE ANSWERS TO ALL MY QUESTIONS YET...
WHAT'S THE CONNECTION BETWEEN YOU AND THAT STRANGE SYMBOL? I SAW IT IN ONE OF YOUR NOTEBOOKS.
YOU WENT SNOOPING THROUGH MY THINGS?
THE NARRATIVE IN THE BOOK STARTS IN 1904... THE YEAR OF THE FAMOUS STORM.
THAT SYMBOL'S THE SAME AS THE ONE ON THE FOUNTAIN IN HONOR OF THOSE WHO DIED IN THE STORM, SCULPTED BY A CERTAIN G. NORMANN...
AND THERE'S ALSO A NORMANN IN YOUR BOOK, RIGHT?
WHAT'S THE CONNECTION BETWEEN THE NORMANNS AND THOSE ROCKS SCULPTED SEVERAL CENTURIES AGO?
DO YOU BELIEVE IN LEGENDS, KID?
21

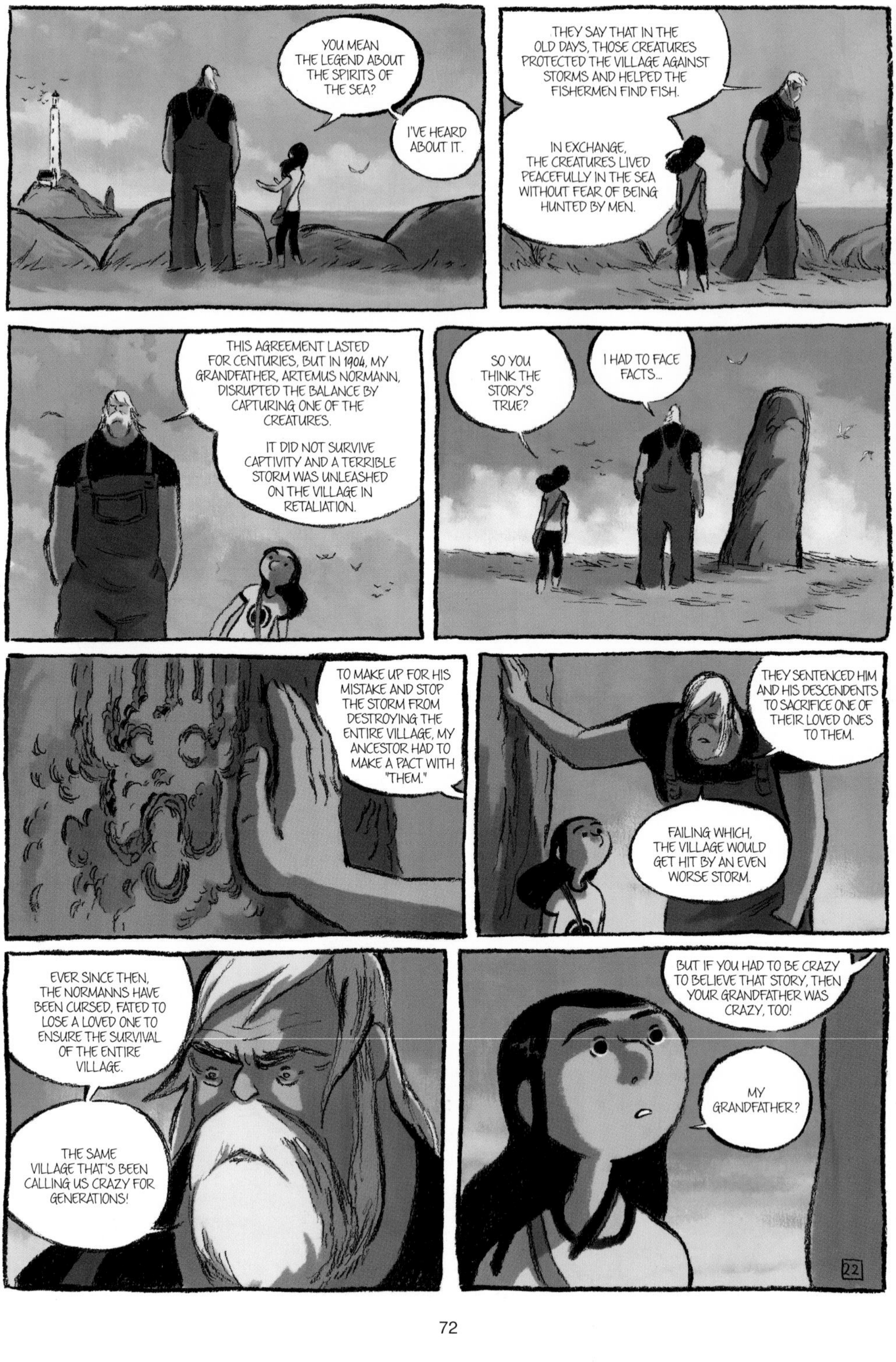
YOU MEAN THE LEGEND ABOUT THE SPIRITS OF THE SEA?
I'VE HEARD ABOUT IT.
THEY SAY THAT IN THE OLD DAYS, THOSE CREATURES PROTECTED THE VILLAGE AGAINST STORMS AND HELPED THE FISHERMEN FIND FISH.
IN EXCHANGE, THE CREATURES LIVED PEACEFULLY IN THE SEA WITHOUT FEAR OF BEING HUNTED BY MEN.
THIS AGREEMENT LASTED FOR CENTURIES, BUT IN 1904, MY GRANDFATHER, ARTEMUS NORMANN, DISRUPTED THE BALANCE BY CAPTURING ONE OF THE CREATURES.
IT DID NOT SURVIVE CAPTIVITY AND A TERRIBLE STORM WAS UNLEASHED ON THE VILLAGE IN RETALIATION.
SO YOU THINK THE STORY'S TRUE?
I HAD TO FACE FACTS...
TO MAKE UP FOR HIS MISTAKE AND STOP THE STORM FROM DESTROYING THE ENTIRE VILLAGE, MY ANCESTOR HAD TO MAKE A PACT WITH "THEM."
THEY SENTENCED HIM AND HIS DESCENDENTS TO SACRIFICE ONE OF THEIR LOVED ONES TO THEM.
FAILING WHICH, THE VILLAGE WOULD GET HIT BY AN EVEN WORSE STORM.
EVER SINCE THEN, THE NORMANNS HAVE BEEN CURSED, FATED TO LOSE A LOVED ONE TO ENSURE THE SURVIVAL OF THE ENTIRE VILLAGE.
THE SAME VILLAGE THAT'S BEEN CALLING US CRAZY FOR GENERATIONS!
BUT IF YOU HAD TO BE CRAZY TO BELIEVE THAT STORY, THEN YOUR GRANDFATHER WAS CRAZY, TOO!
MY GRANDFATHER?
22

YES. WE WERE REALLY GOOD FRIENDS BACK THEN. WE WORKED TOGETHER.

ONE DAY, HE TOLD ME HE WAS SURE HE HAD SEEN A STRANGE CREATURE ON THE HIGH SEAS.

I HAD ALREADY FOUND THE NOTEBOOKS OF MY GRANDFATHER AND FATHER WHEN I MOVED INTO THE FAMILY LIGHTHOUSE. THEY WROTE ABOUT SEA CREATURES AND THE CURSE ON OUR FAMILY.

I DIDN'T BELIEVE ANY OF IT, OF COURSE. I THOUGHT MY ANCESTORS WERE CRAZY MEN WHOSE OBSESSIONS HAD DRIVEN THEM TO THEIR DOWNFALL.

BUT YOUR GRANDPA WAS NOT THE TYPE TO TALK NONSENSE.

AND WHAT HE TOLD ME RATTLED MY BELIEFS.

ANY REMAINING DOUBTS I HAD WERE OBLITERATED A FEW WEEKS LATER.

I WAS OUT AT SEA WITH MY WIFE WHEN "THEY" CAME TO TAKE HER.

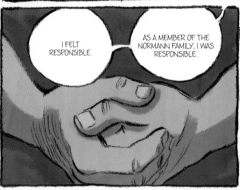

I FELT RESPONSIBLE.

AS A MEMBER OF THE NORMANN FAMILY, I WAS RESPONSIBLE.

DID YOU SEE THEM?

NO, BUT I COULD DEFINITELY FEEL THEIR PRESENCE.

THE BOAT WAS PICKED UP BY A WAVE THAT CAME OUT OF NOWHERE. MY WIFE FELL OVERBOARD AND NEVER RESURFACED.

I DOVE IN AND SWAM FOR HOURS LOOKING FOR HER, TO NO AVAIL.

WHAT ABOUT MY GRANDPA? WHAT HAPPENED TO HIM?

HE WAS LOST AT SEA, TOO, BUT I DON'T KNOW WHAT HAPPENED. AS YOU KNOW, I WAS... AWAY AT THE TIME.

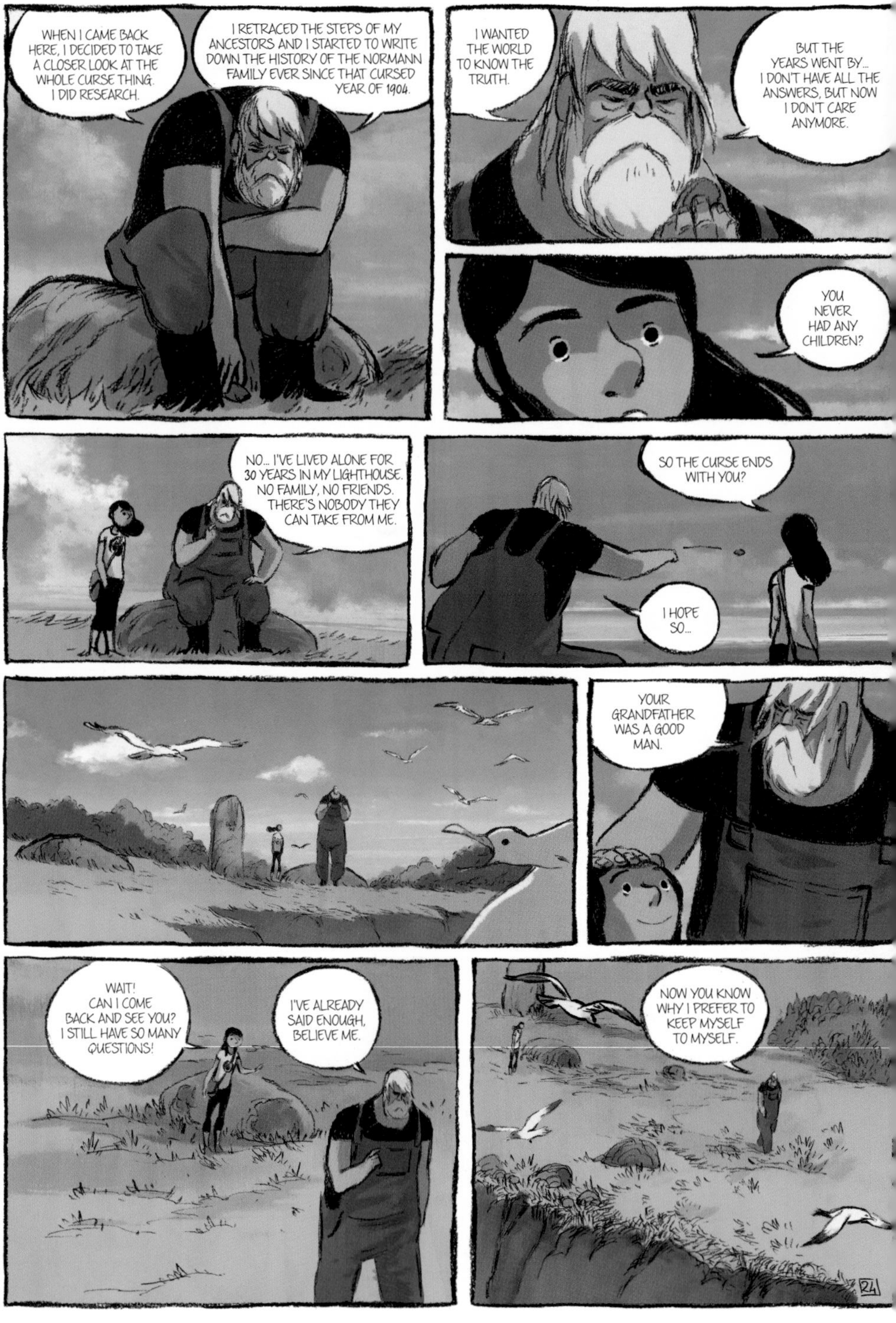

WHEN I CAME BACK HERE, I DECIDED TO TAKE A CLOSER LOOK AT THE WHOLE CURSE THING. I DID RESEARCH.
I RETRACED THE STEPS OF MY ANCESTORS AND I STARTED TO WRITE DOWN THE HISTORY OF THE NORMANN FAMILY EVER SINCE THAT CURSED YEAR OF 1904.
I WANTED THE WORLD TO KNOW THE TRUTH.
BUT THE YEARS WENT BY... I DON'T HAVE ALL THE ANSWERS, BUT NOW I DON'T CARE ANYMORE.
YOU NEVER HAD ANY CHILDREN?
NO... I'VE LIVED ALONE FOR 30 YEARS IN MY LIGHTHOUSE. NO FAMILY, NO FRIENDS. THERE'S NOBODY THEY CAN TAKE FROM ME.
SO THE CURSE ENDS WITH YOU?
I HOPE SO...
YOUR GRANDFATHER WAS A GOOD MAN.
WAIT! CAN I COME BACK AND SEE YOU? I STILL HAVE SO MANY QUESTIONS!
I'VE ALREADY SAID ENOUGH, BELIEVE ME.
NOW YOU KNOW WHY I PREFER TO KEEP MYSELF TO MYSELF.
24

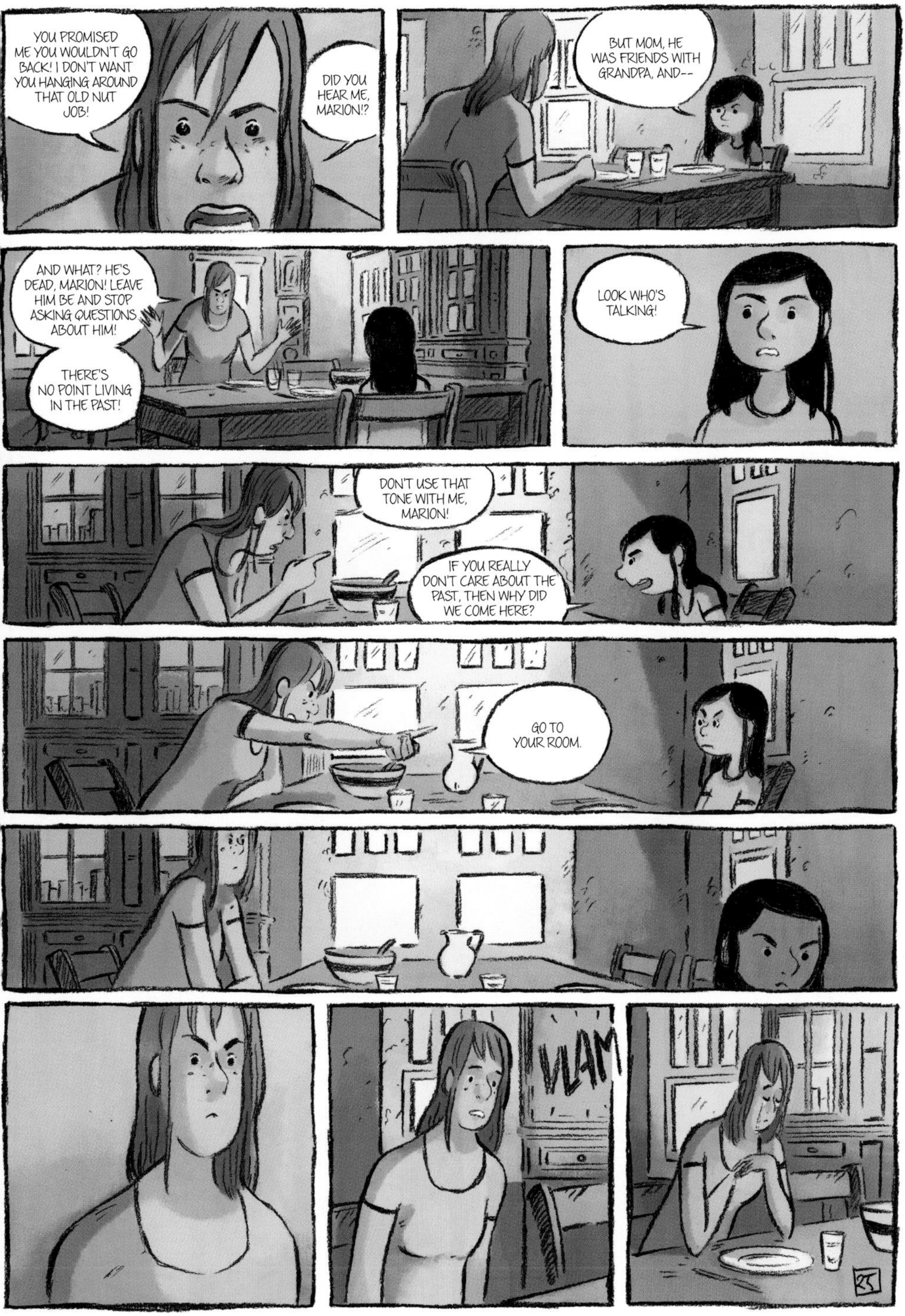
YOU PROMISED ME YOU WOULDN'T GO BACK! I DON'T WANT YOU HANGING AROUND THAT OLD NUT JOB!
DID YOU HEAR ME, MARION!?
BUT MOM, HE WAS FRIENDS WITH GRANDPA, AND--
AND WHAT? HE'S DEAD, MARION! LEAVE HIM BE AND STOP ASKING QUESTIONS ABOUT HIM!
THERE'S NO POINT LIVING IN THE PAST!
LOOK WHO'S TALKING!
DON'T USE THAT TONE WITH ME, MARION!
IF YOU REALLY DON'T CARE ABOUT THE PAST, THEN WHY DID WE COME HERE?
GO TO YOUR ROOM.
VLAM

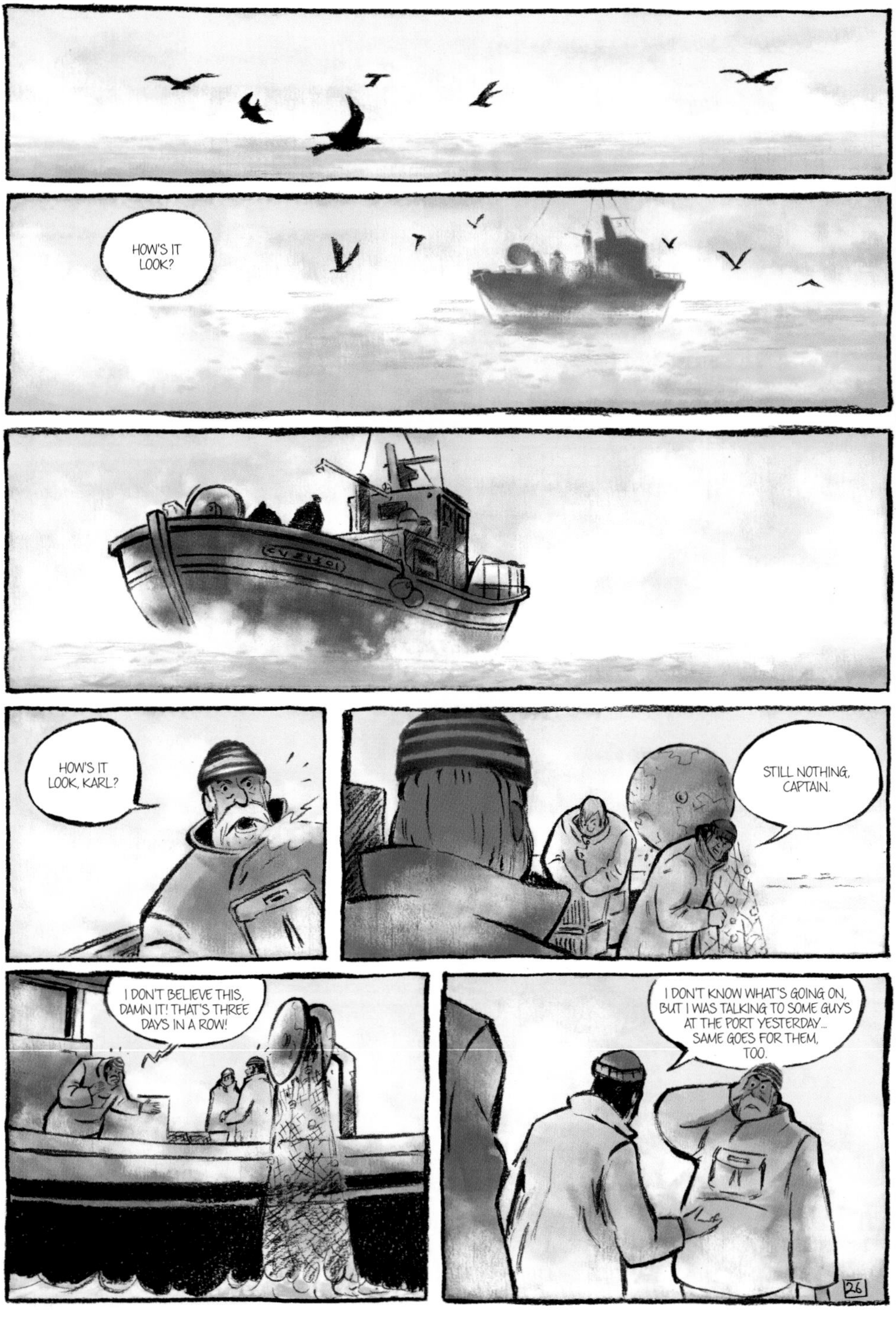
HOW'S IT LOOK?
HOW'S IT LOOK, KARL?
STILL NOTHING, CAPTAIN.
I DON'T BELIEVE THIS, DAMN IT! THAT'S THREE DAYS IN A ROW!
I DON'T KNOW WHAT'S GOING ON, BUT I WAS TALKING TO SOME GUYS AT THE PORT YESTERDAY... SAME GOES FOR THEM, TOO.
26

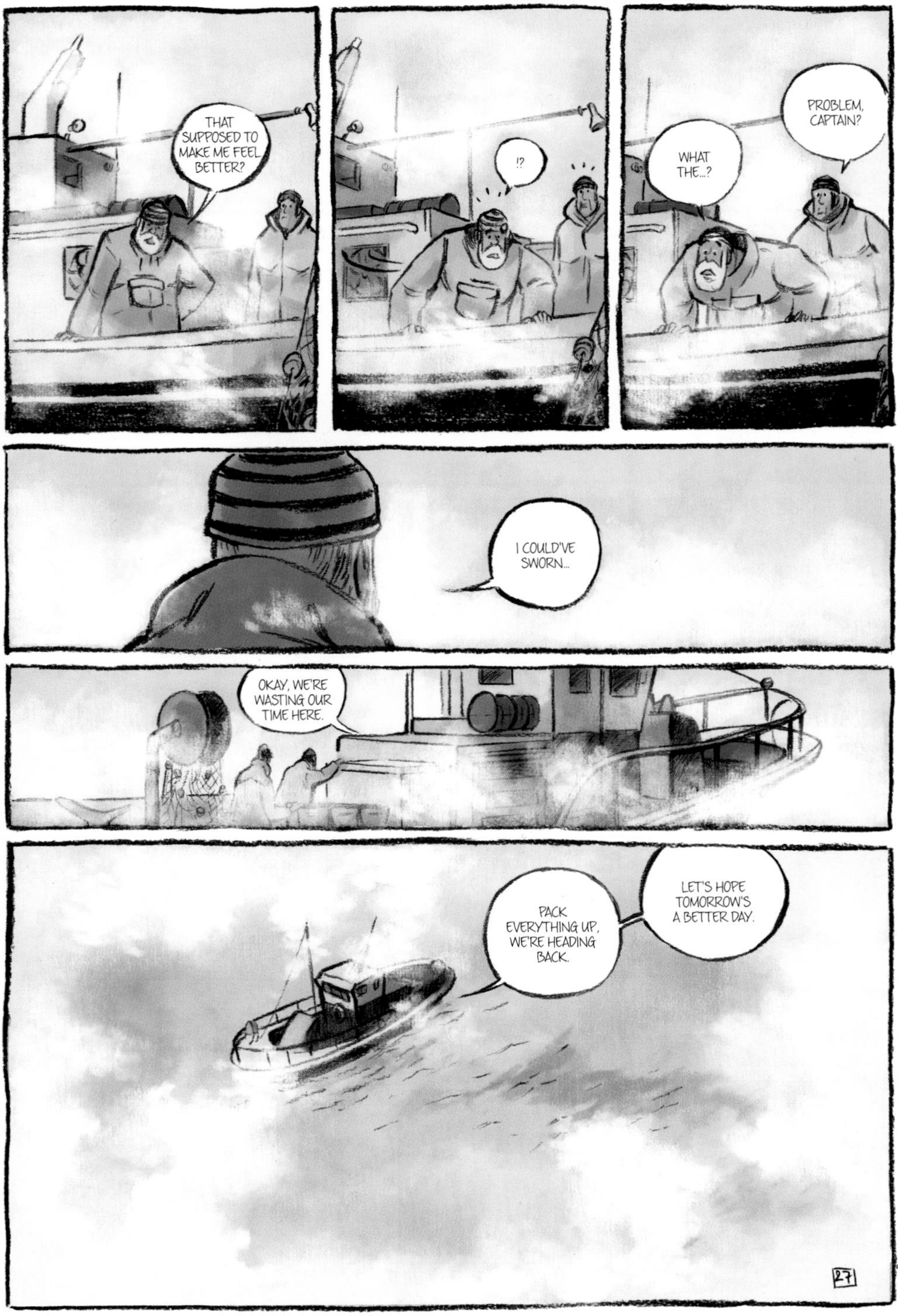
THAT SUPPOSED TO MAKE ME FEEL BETTER?
!?
WHAT THE...?
PROBLEM, CAPTAIN?
I COULD'VE SWORN...
OKAY, WE'RE WASTING OUR TIME HERE.
PACK EVERYTHING UP, WE'RE HEADING BACK.
LET'S HOPE TOMORROW'S A BETTER DAY.
27

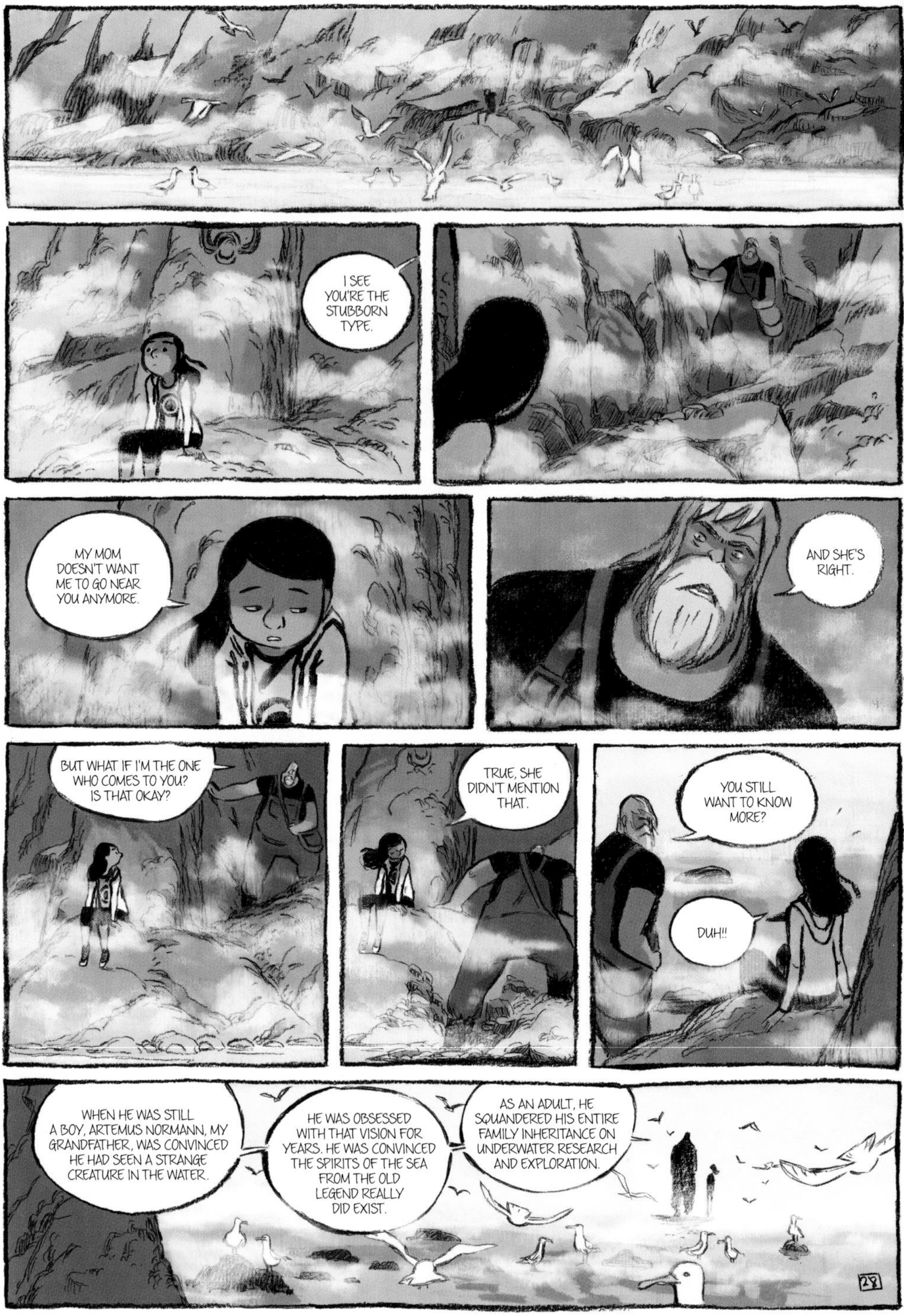
I SEE YOU'RE THE STUBBORN TYPE.
MY MOM DOESN'T WANT ME TO GO NEAR YOU ANYMORE.
AND SHE'S RIGHT.
BUT WHAT IF I'M THE ONE WHO COMES TO YOU? IS THAT OKAY?
TRUE, SHE DIDN'T MENTION THAT.
YOU STILL WANT TO KNOW MORE?
DUH!!
WHEN HE WAS STILL A BOY, ARTEMUS NORMANN, MY GRANDFATHER, WAS CONVINCED HE HAD SEEN A STRANGE CREATURE IN THE WATER.
HE WAS OBSESSED WITH THAT VISION FOR YEARS. HE WAS CONVINCED THE SPIRITS OF THE SEA FROM THE OLD LEGEND REALLY DID EXIST.
AS AN ADULT, HE SQUANDERED HIS ENTIRE FAMILY INHERITANCE ON UNDERWATER RESEARCH AND EXPLORATION.
28

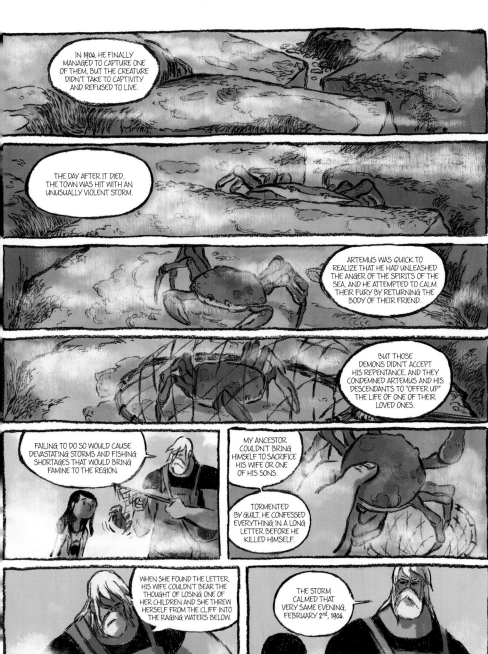

IN 1904, HE FINALLY MANAGED TO CAPTURE ONE OF THEM, BUT THE CREATURE DIDN'T TAKE TO CAPTIVITY AND REFUSED TO LIVE.

THE DAY AFTER IT DIED, THE TOWN WAS HIT WITH AN UNUSUALLY VIOLENT STORM.

ARTEMUS WAS QUICK TO REALIZE THAT HE HAD UNLEASHED THE ANGER OF THE SPIRITS OF THE SEA, AND HE ATTEMPTED TO CALM THEIR FURY BY RETURNING THE BODY OF THEIR FRIEND.

BUT THOSE DEMONS DIDN'T ACCEPT HIS REPENTANCE, AND THEY CONDEMNED ARTEMUS AND HIS DESCENDANTS TO "OFFER UP" THE LIFE OF ONE OF THEIR LOVED ONES.

FAILING TO DO SO WOULD CAUSE DEVASTATING STORMS AND FISHING SHORTAGES THAT WOULD BRING FAMINE TO THE REGION.

MY ANCESTOR COULDN'T BRING HIMSELF TO SACRIFICE HIS WIFE OR ONE OF HIS SONS.

TORMENTED BY GUILT, HE CONFESSED EVERYTHING IN A LONG LETTER BEFORE HE KILLED HIMSELF.

WHEN SHE FOUND THE LETTER, HIS WIFE COULDN'T BEAR THE THOUGHT OF LOSING ONE OF HER CHILDREN AND SHE THREW HERSELF FROM THE CLIFF INTO THE RAGING WATERS BELOW.

THE STORM CALMED THAT VERY SAME EVENING, FEBRUARY 2nd, 1904.

29

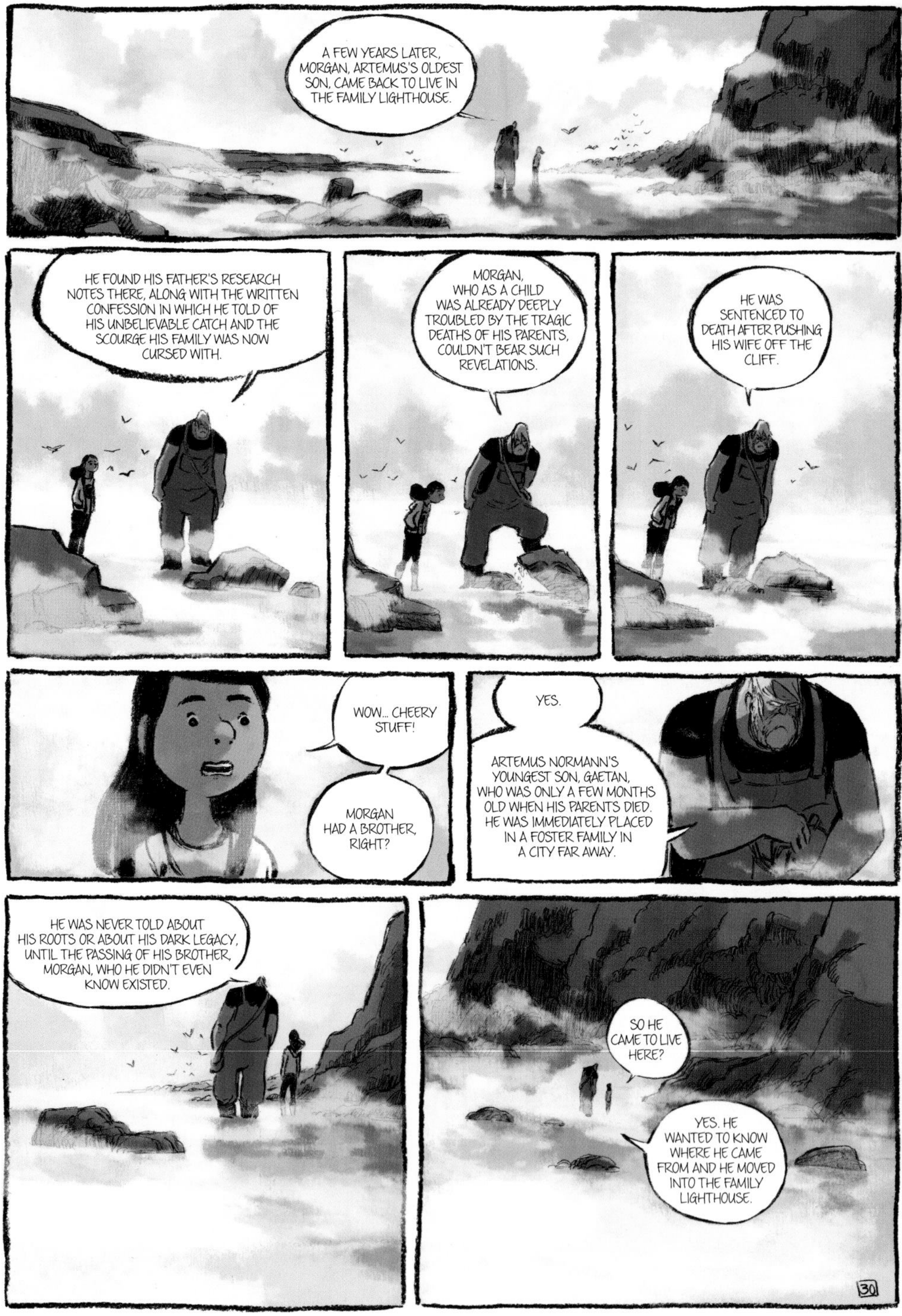
A FEW YEARS LATER, MORGAN, ARTEMUS'S OLDEST SON, CAME BACK TO LIVE IN THE FAMILY LIGHTHOUSE.
HE FOUND HIS FATHER'S RESEARCH NOTES THERE, ALONG WITH THE WRITTEN CONFESSION IN WHICH HE TOLD OF HIS UNBELIEVABLE CATCH AND THE SCOURGE HIS FAMILY WAS NOW CURSED WITH.
MORGAN, WHO AS A CHILD WAS ALREADY DEEPLY TROUBLED BY THE TRAGIC DEATHS OF HIS PARENTS, COULDN'T BEAR SUCH REVELATIONS.
HE WAS SENTENCED TO DEATH AFTER PUSHING HIS WIFE OFF THE CLIFF.
WOW... CHEERY STUFF!
MORGAN HAD A BROTHER, RIGHT?
YES.
ARTEMUS NORMANN'S YOUNGEST SON, GAETAN, WHO WAS ONLY A FEW MONTHS OLD WHEN HIS PARENTS DIED. HE WAS IMMEDIATELY PLACED IN A FOSTER FAMILY IN A CITY FAR AWAY.
HE WAS NEVER TOLD ABOUT HIS ROOTS OR ABOUT HIS DARK LEGACY, UNTIL THE PASSING OF HIS BROTHER, MORGAN, WHO HE DIDN'T EVEN KNOW EXISTED.
SO HE CAME TO LIVE HERE?
YES. HE WANTED TO KNOW WHERE HE CAME FROM AND HE MOVED INTO THE FAMILY LIGHTHOUSE.
30

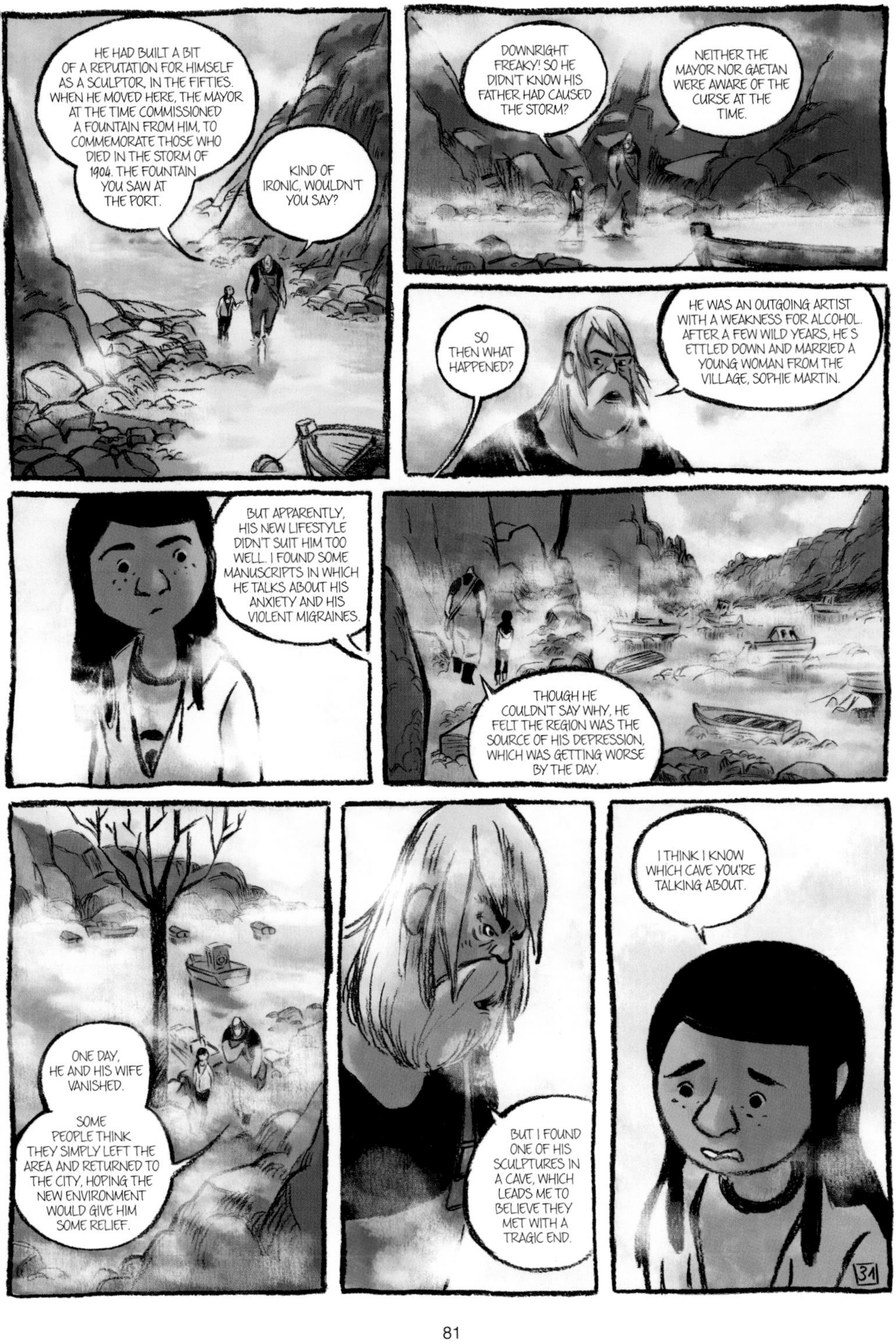
HE HAD BUILT A BIT OF A REPUTATION FOR HIMSELF AS A SCULPTOR, IN THE FIFTIES. WHEN HE MOVED HERE, THE MAYOR AT THE TIME COMMISSIONED A FOUNTAIN FROM HIM, TO COMMEMORATE THOSE WHO DIED IN THE STORM OF 1904. THE FOUNTAIN YOU SAW AT THE PORT.
KIND OF IRONIC, WOULDN'T YOU SAY?
DOWNRIGHT FREAKY! SO HE DIDN'T KNOW HIS FATHER HAD CAUSED THE STORM?
NEITHER THE MAYOR NOR GAETAN WERE AWARE OF THE CURSE AT THE TIME.
SO THEN WHAT HAPPENED?
HE WAS AN OUTGOING ARTIST WITH A WEAKNESS FOR ALCOHOL. AFTER A FEW WILD YEARS, HE S ETTLED DOWN AND MARRIED A YOUNG WOMAN FROM THE VILLAGE, SOPHIE MARTIN.
BUT APPARENTLY, HIS NEW LIFESTYLE DIDN'T SUIT HIM TOO WELL. I FOUND SOME MANUSCRIPTS IN WHICH HE TALKS ABOUT HIS ANXIETY AND HIS VIOLENT MIGRAINES.
THOUGH HE COULDN'T SAY WHY, HE FELT THE REGION WAS THE SOURCE OF HIS DEPRESSION, WHICH WAS GETTING WORSE BY THE DAY.
ONE DAY, HE AND HIS WIFE VANISHED.
SOME PEOPLE THINK THEY SIMPLY LEFT THE AREA AND RETURNED TO THE CITY, HOPING THE NEW ENVIRONMENT WOULD GIVE HIM SOME RELIEF.
BUT I FOUND ONE OF HIS SCULPTURES IN A CAVE, WHICH LEADS ME TO BELIEVE THEY MET WITH A TRAGIC END.
I THINK I KNOW WHICH CAVE YOU'RE TALKING ABOUT.
31

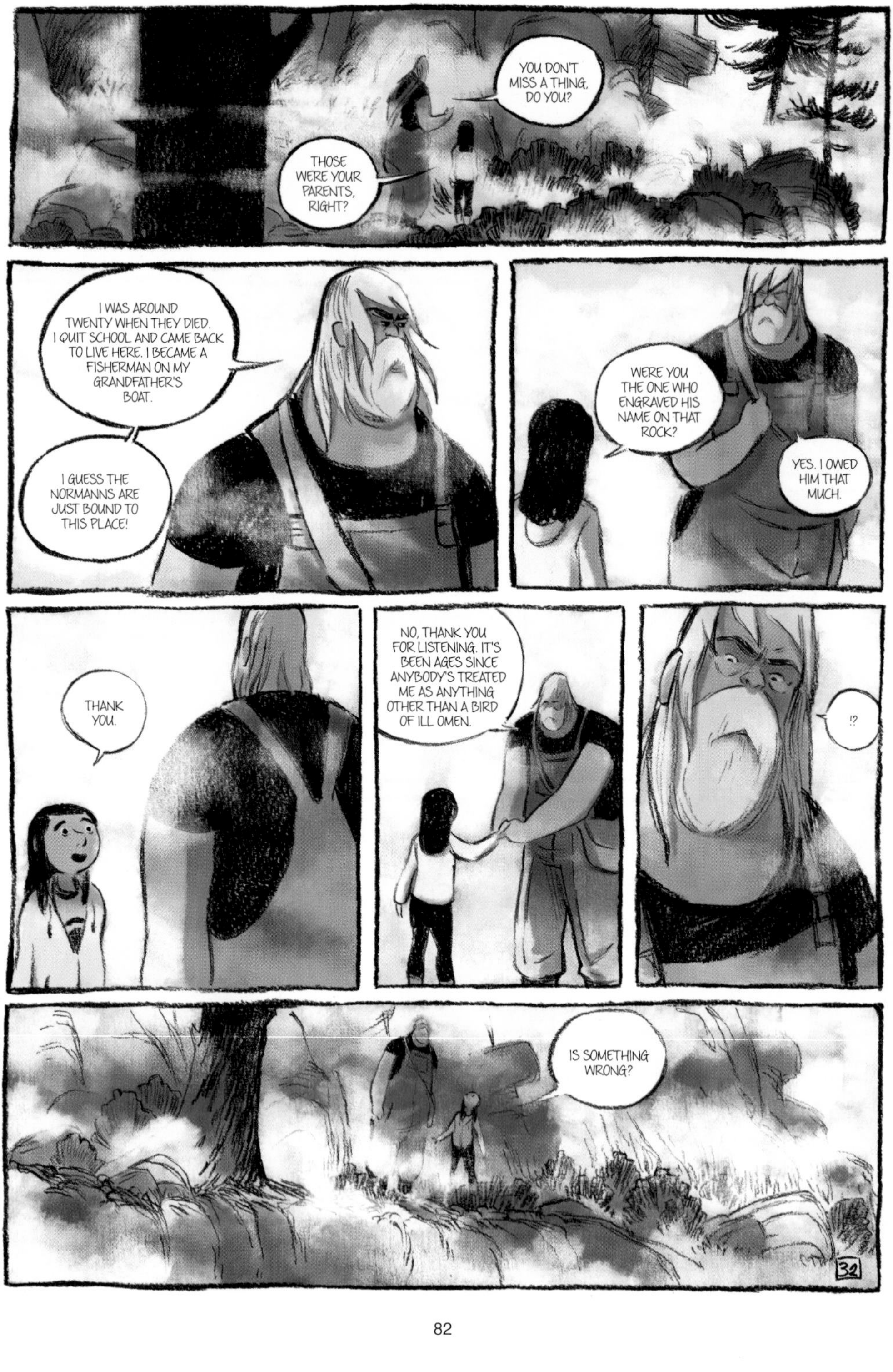
YOU DON'T MISS A THING, DO YOU?
THOSE WERE YOUR PARENTS, RIGHT?
I WAS AROUND TWENTY WHEN THEY DIED. I QUIT SCHOOL AND CAME BACK TO LIVE HERE. I BECAME A FISHERMAN ON MY GRANDFATHER'S BOAT.
I GUESS THE NORMANNS ARE JUST BOUND TO THIS PLACE!
WERE YOU THE ONE WHO ENGRAVED HIS NAME ON THAT ROCK?
YES. I OWED HIM THAT MUCH.
THANK YOU.
NO, THANK YOU FOR LISTENING. IT'S BEEN AGES SINCE ANYBODY'S TREATED ME AS ANYTHING OTHER THAN A BIRD OF ILL OMEN.
!?
IS SOMETHING WRONG?
32

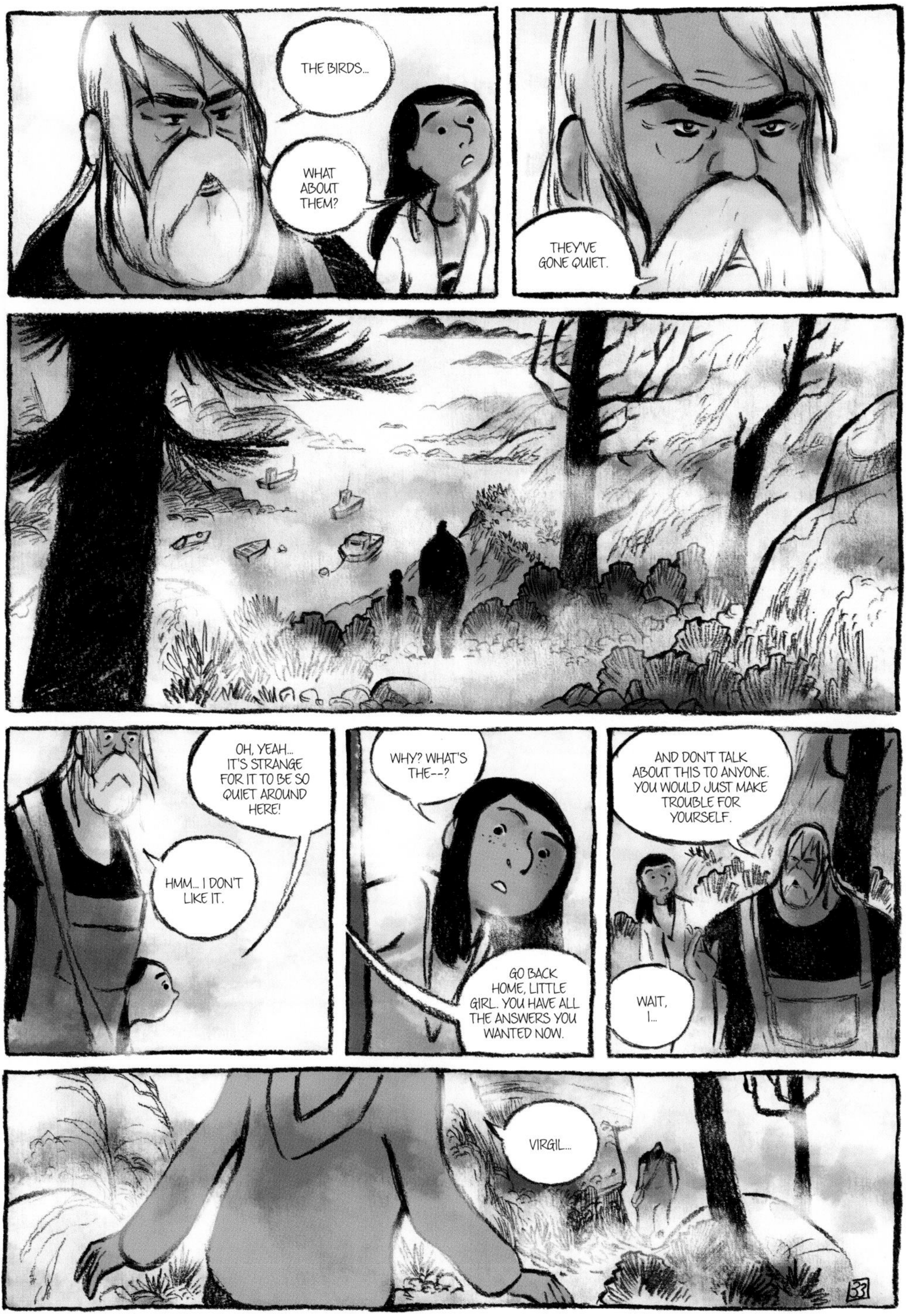
THE BIRDS...
WHAT ABOUT THEM?
THEY'VE GONE QUIET.
OH, YEAH... IT'S STRANGE FOR IT TO BE SO QUIET AROUND HERE!
HMM... I DON'T LIKE IT.
WHY? WHAT'S THE--?
GO BACK HOME, LITTLE GIRL. YOU HAVE ALL THE ANSWERS YOU WANTED NOW.
AND DON'T TALK ABOUT THIS TO ANYONE. YOU WOULD JUST MAKE TROUBLE FOR YOURSELF.
WAIT, I...
VIRGIL...
33

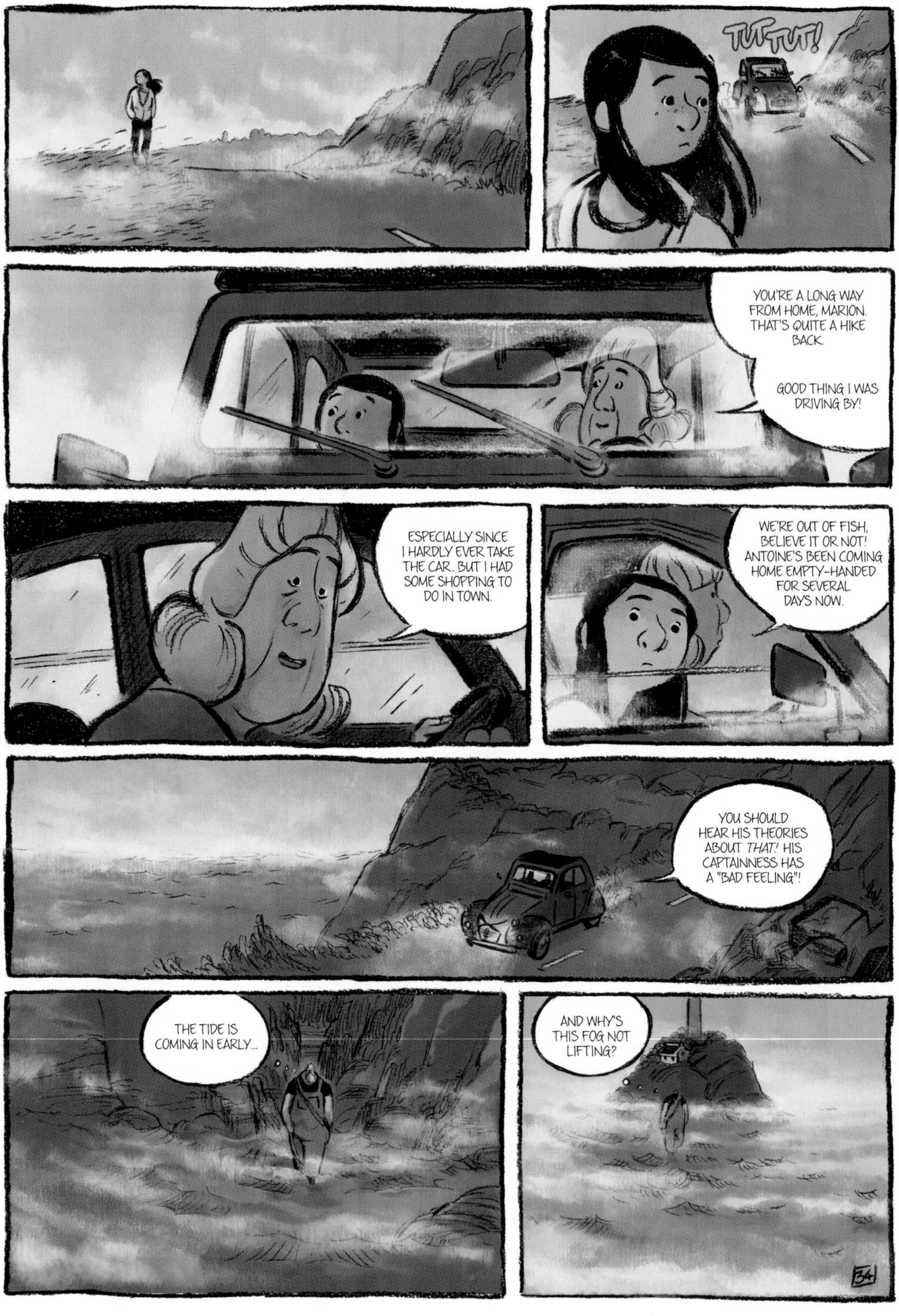
TUT TUT!
YOU'RE A LONG WAY FROM HOME, MARION. THAT'S QUITE A HIKE BACK.
GOOD THING I WAS DRIVING BY!
ESPECIALLY SINCE I HARDLY EVER TAKE THE CAR. BUT I HAD SOME SHOPPING TO DO IN TOWN.
WE'RE OUT OF FISH, BELIEVE IT OR NOT! ANTOINE'S BEEN COMING HOME EMPTY-HANDED FOR SEVERAL DAYS NOW.
YOU SHOULD HEAR HIS THEORIES ABOUT *THAT!* HIS CAPTAINNESS HAS A "BAD FEELING"!
THE TIDE IS COMING IN EARLY...
AND WHY'S THIS FOG NOT LIFTING?
34

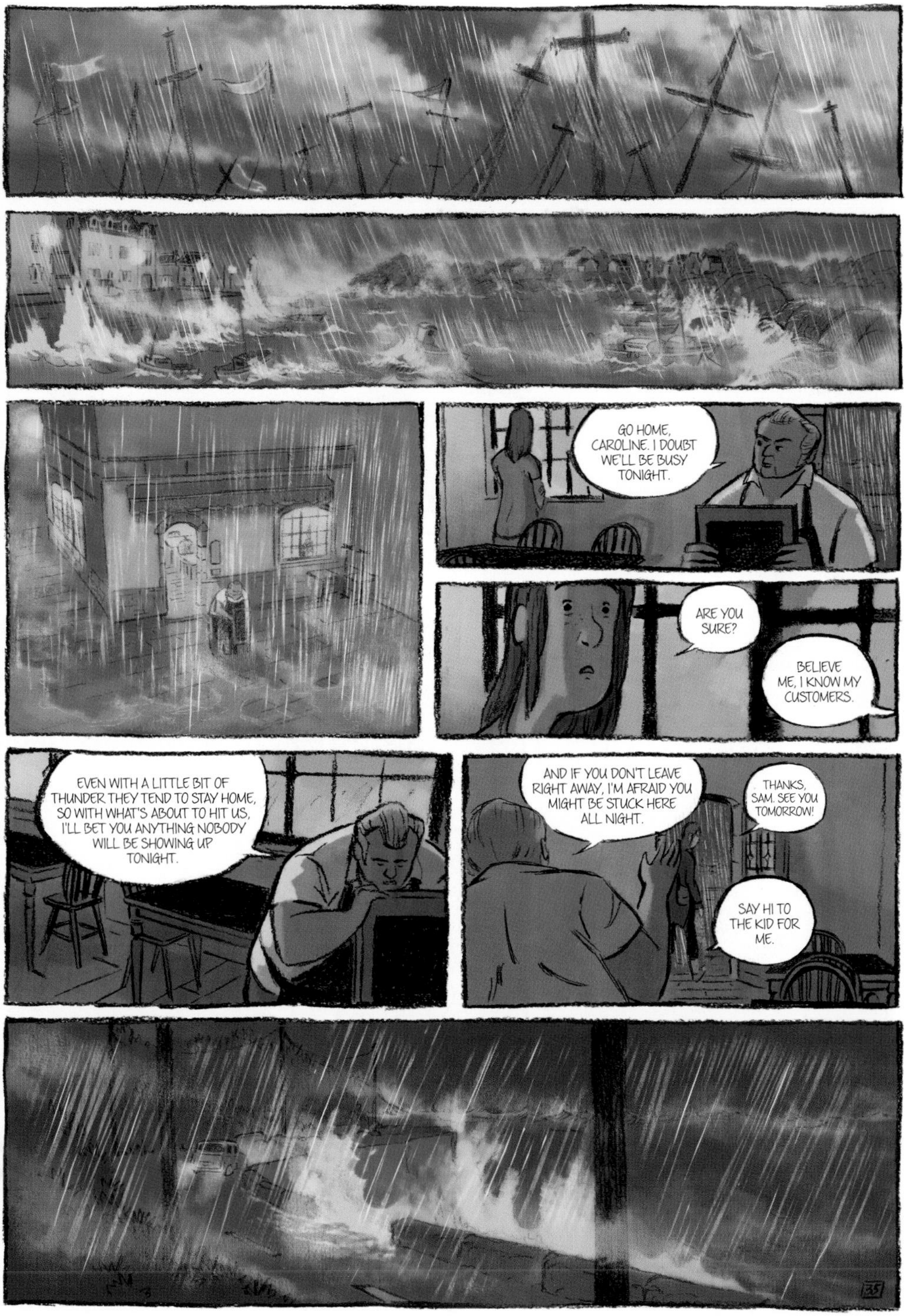
GO HOME, CAROLINE. I DOUBT WE'LL BE BUSY TONIGHT.
ARE YOU SURE?
BELIEVE ME, I KNOW MY CUSTOMERS.
EVEN WITH A LITTLE BIT OF THUNDER THEY TEND TO STAY HOME, SO WITH WHAT'S ABOUT TO HIT US, I'LL BET YOU ANYTHING NOBODY WILL BE SHOWING UP TONIGHT.
AND IF YOU DON'T LEAVE RIGHT AWAY, I'M AFRAID YOU MIGHT BE STUCK HERE ALL NIGHT.
THANKS, SAM. SEE YOU TOMORROW!
SAY HI TO THE KID FOR ME.
35

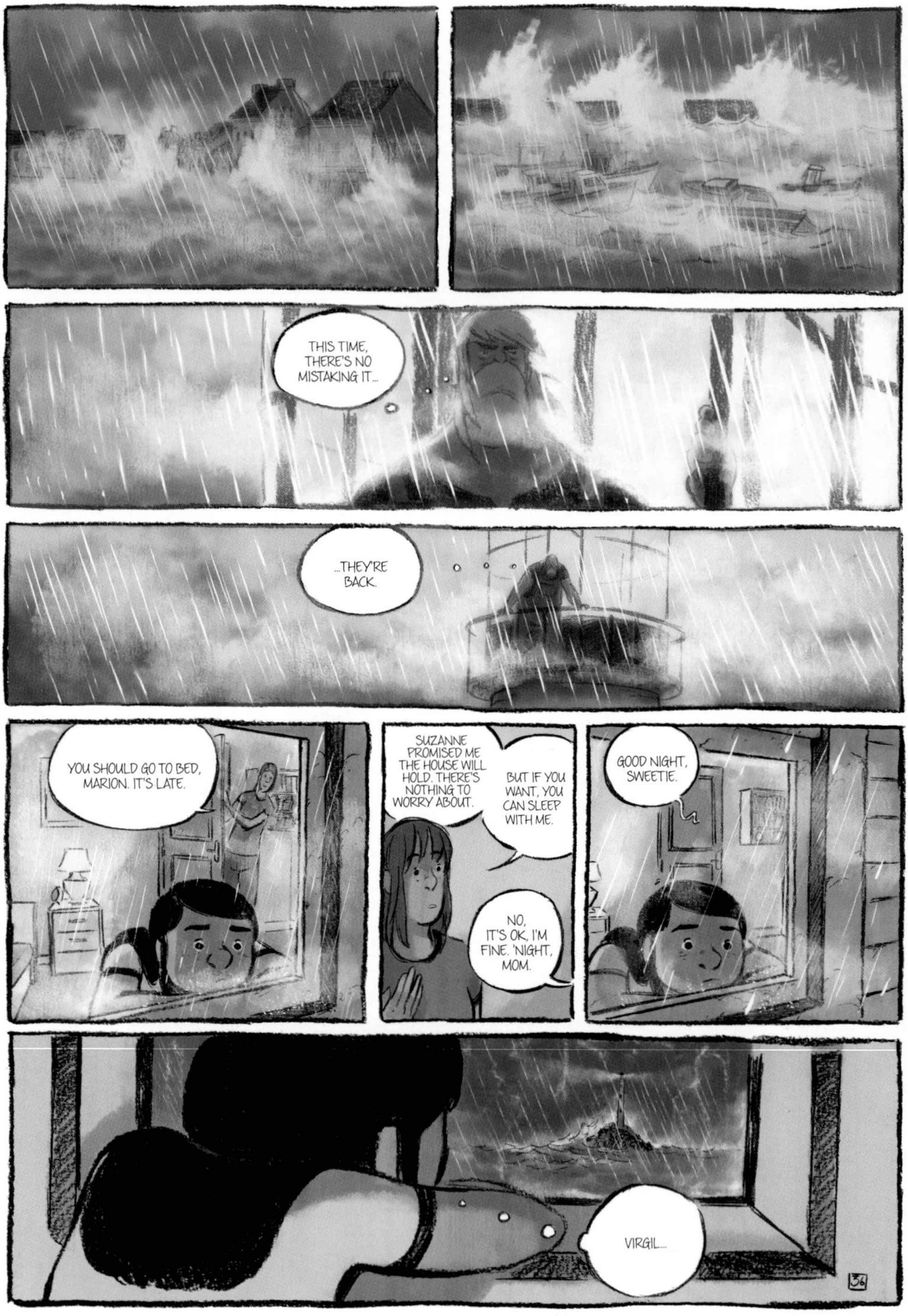
THIS TIME, THERE'S NO MISTAKING IT...
...THEY'RE BACK.
YOU SHOULD GO TO BED, MARION. IT'S LATE.
SUZANNE PROMISED ME THE HOUSE WILL HOLD. THERE'S NOTHING TO WORRY ABOUT.
BUT IF YOU WANT, YOU CAN SLEEP WITH ME.
NO, IT'S OK, I'M FINE. 'NIGHT, MOM.
GOOD NIGHT, SWEETIE.
VIRGIL...

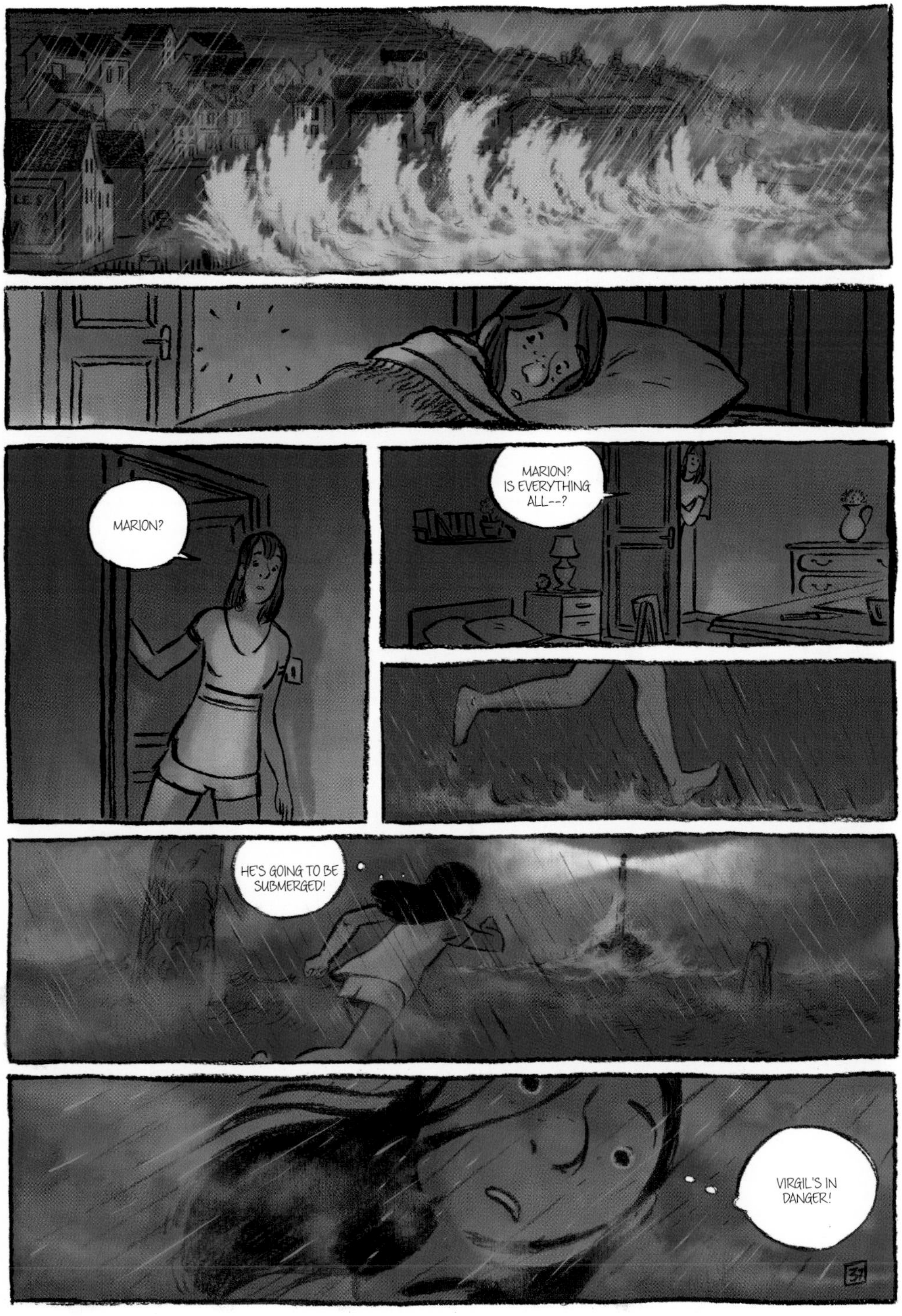
MARION?
MARION? IS EVERYTHING ALL--?
HE'S GOING TO BE SUBMERGED!
VIRGIL'S IN DANGER!

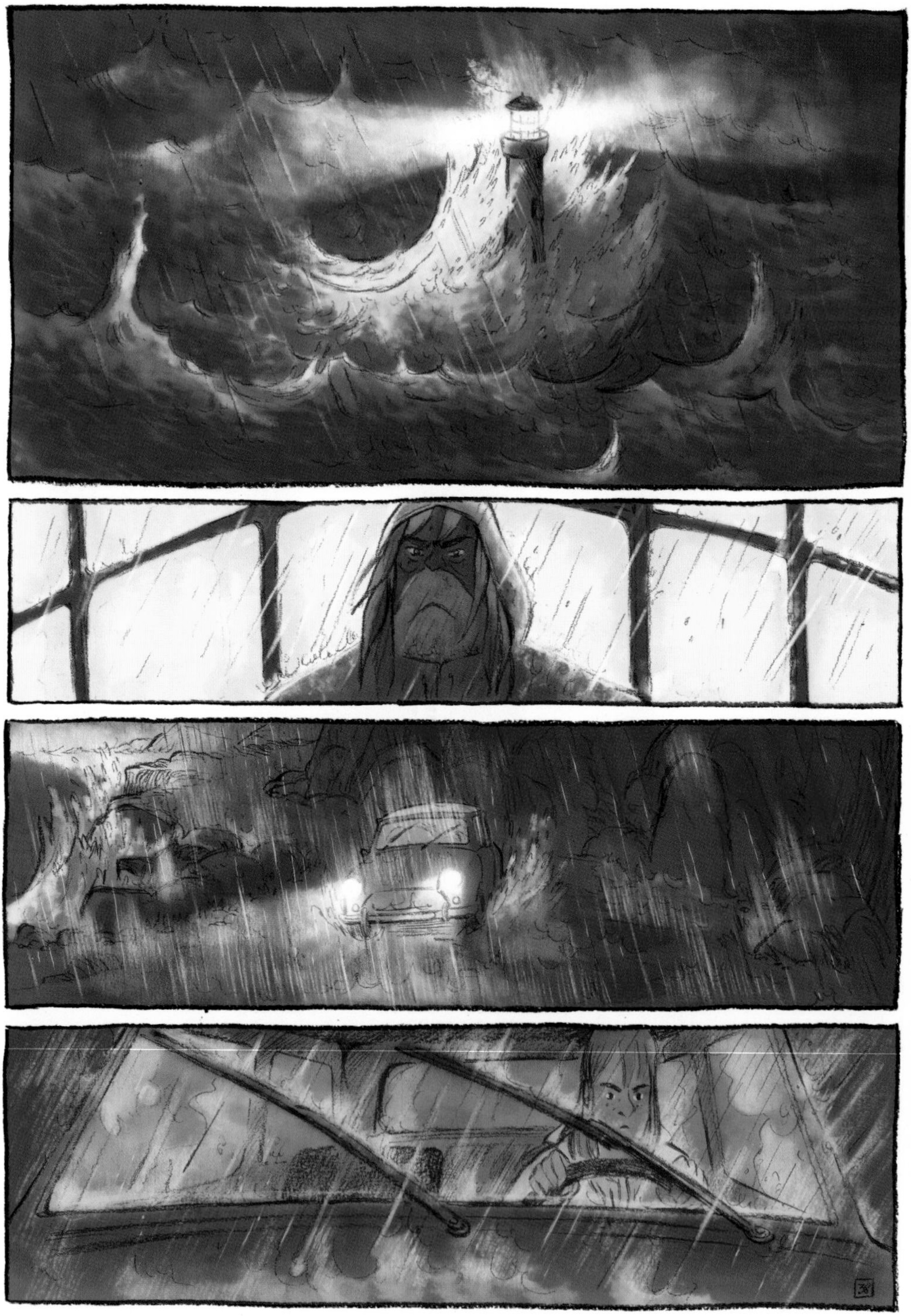

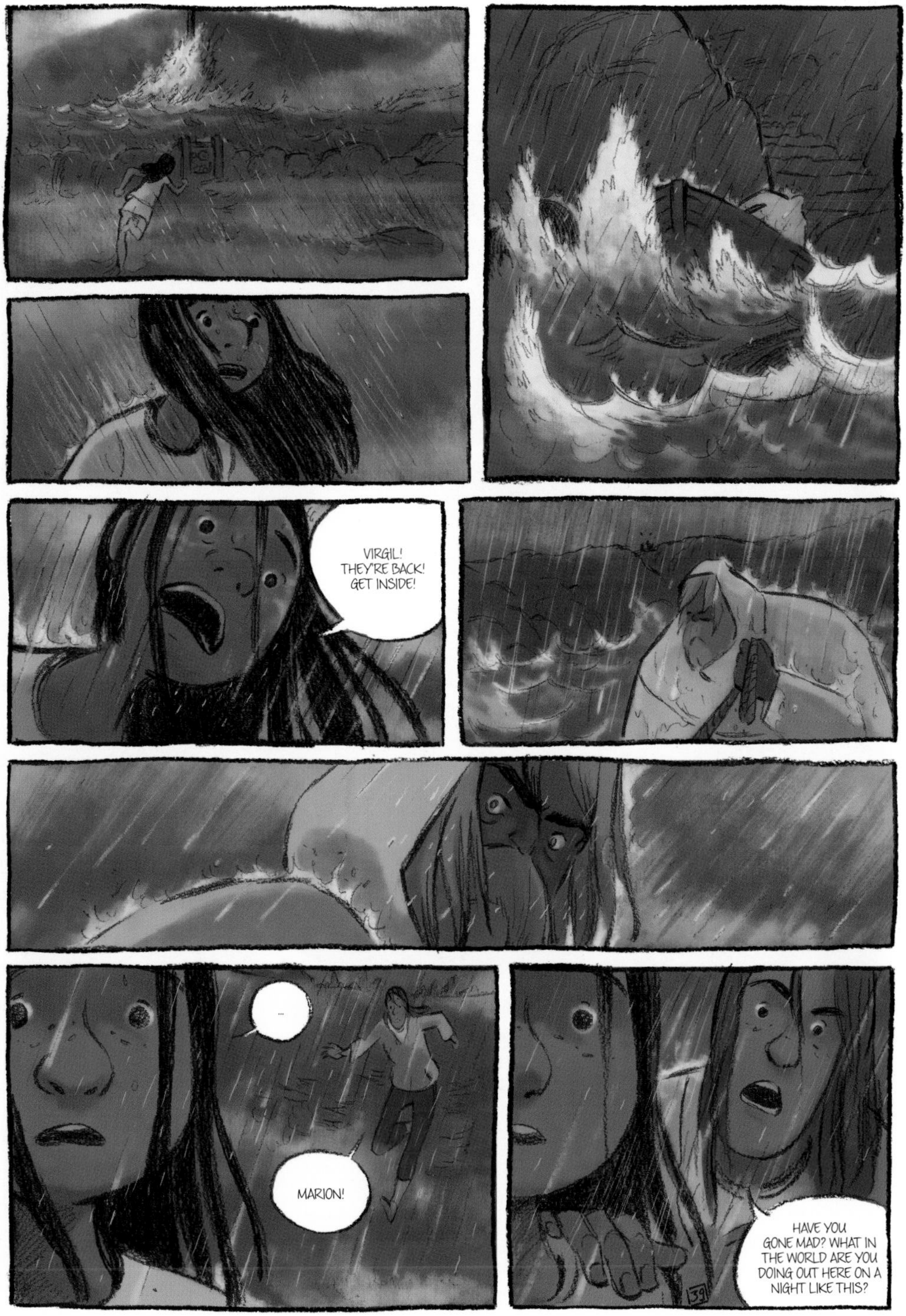
VIRGIL! THEY'RE BACK! GET INSIDE!
...
MARION!
HAVE YOU GONE MAD? WHAT IN THE WORLD ARE YOU DOING OUT HERE ON A NIGHT LIKE THIS?

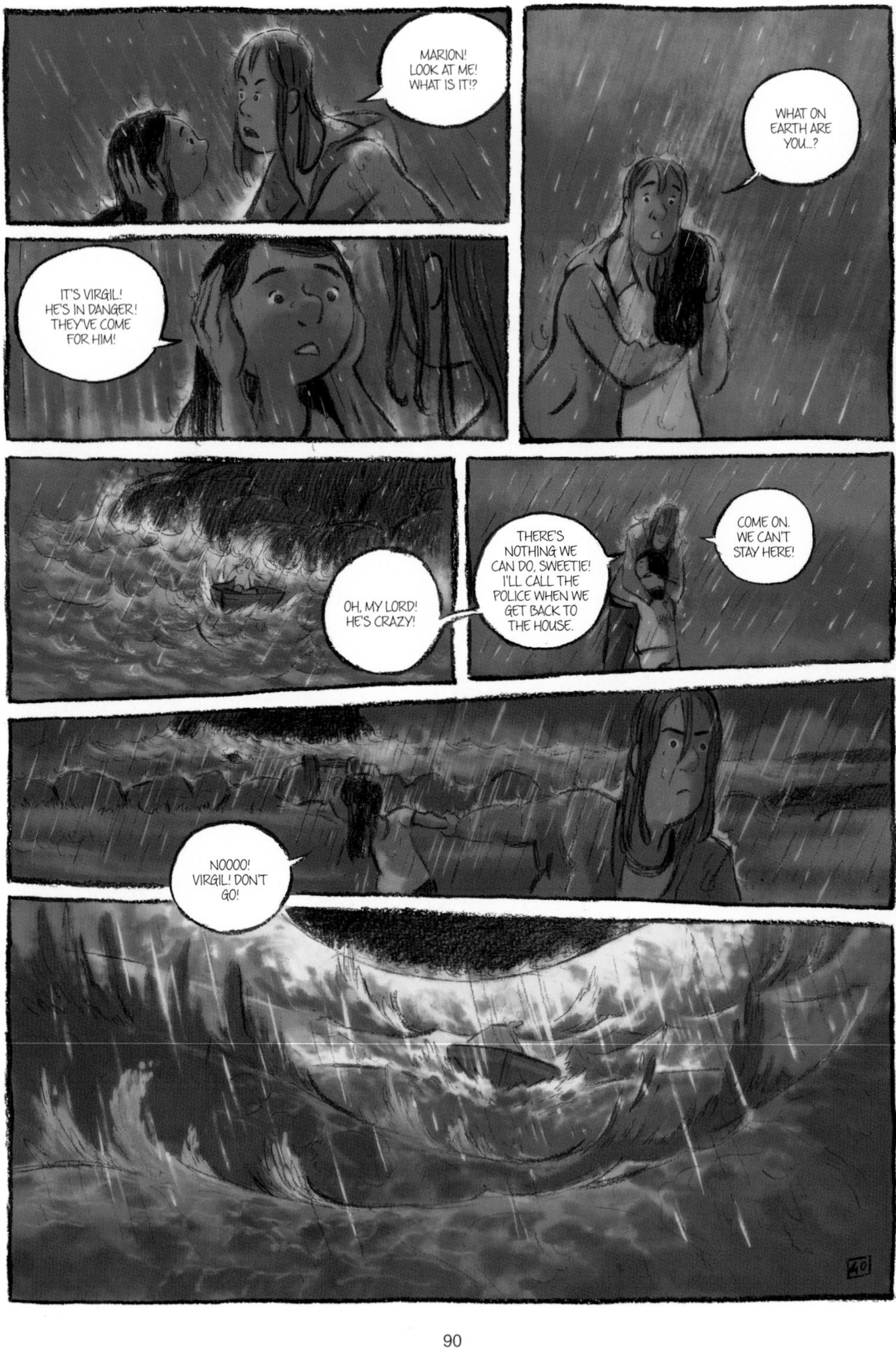
MARION! LOOK AT ME! WHAT IS IT!?
WHAT ON EARTH ARE YOU...?
IT'S VIRGIL! HE'S IN DANGER! THEY'VE COME FOR HIM!
OH, MY LORD! HE'S CRAZY!
THERE'S NOTHING WE CAN DO, SWEETIE! I'LL CALL THE POLICE WHEN WE GET BACK TO THE HOUSE.
COME ON. WE CAN'T STAY HERE!
NOOOO! VIRGIL! DON'T GO!
40

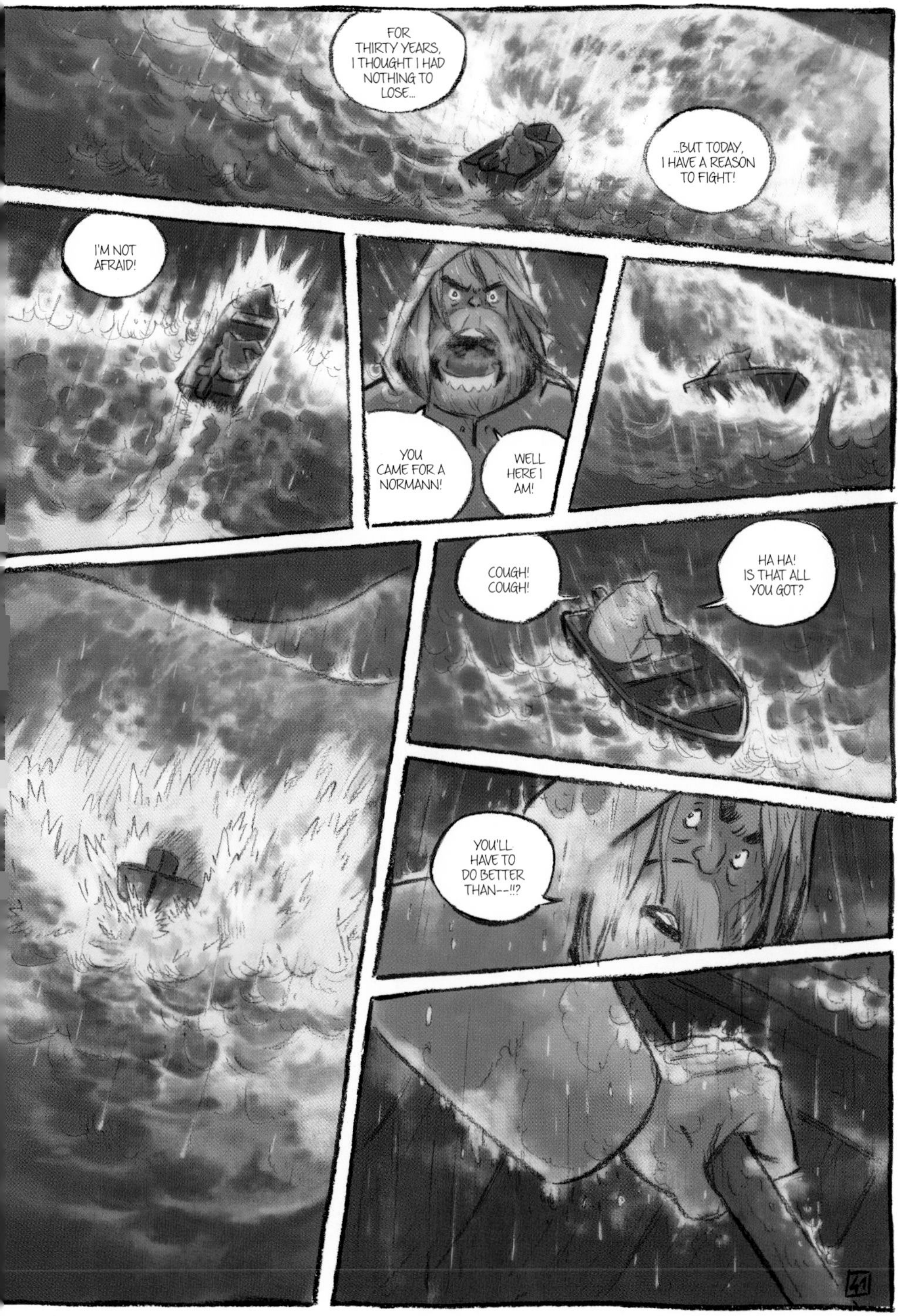
FOR THIRTY YEARS, I THOUGHT I HAD NOTHING TO LOSE...
...BUT TODAY, I HAVE A REASON TO FIGHT!
I'M NOT AFRAID!
YOU CAME FOR A NORMANN!
WELL HERE I AM!
COUGH! COUGH!
HA HA! IS THAT ALL YOU GOT?
YOU'LL HAVE TO DO BETTER THAN--!!?
41

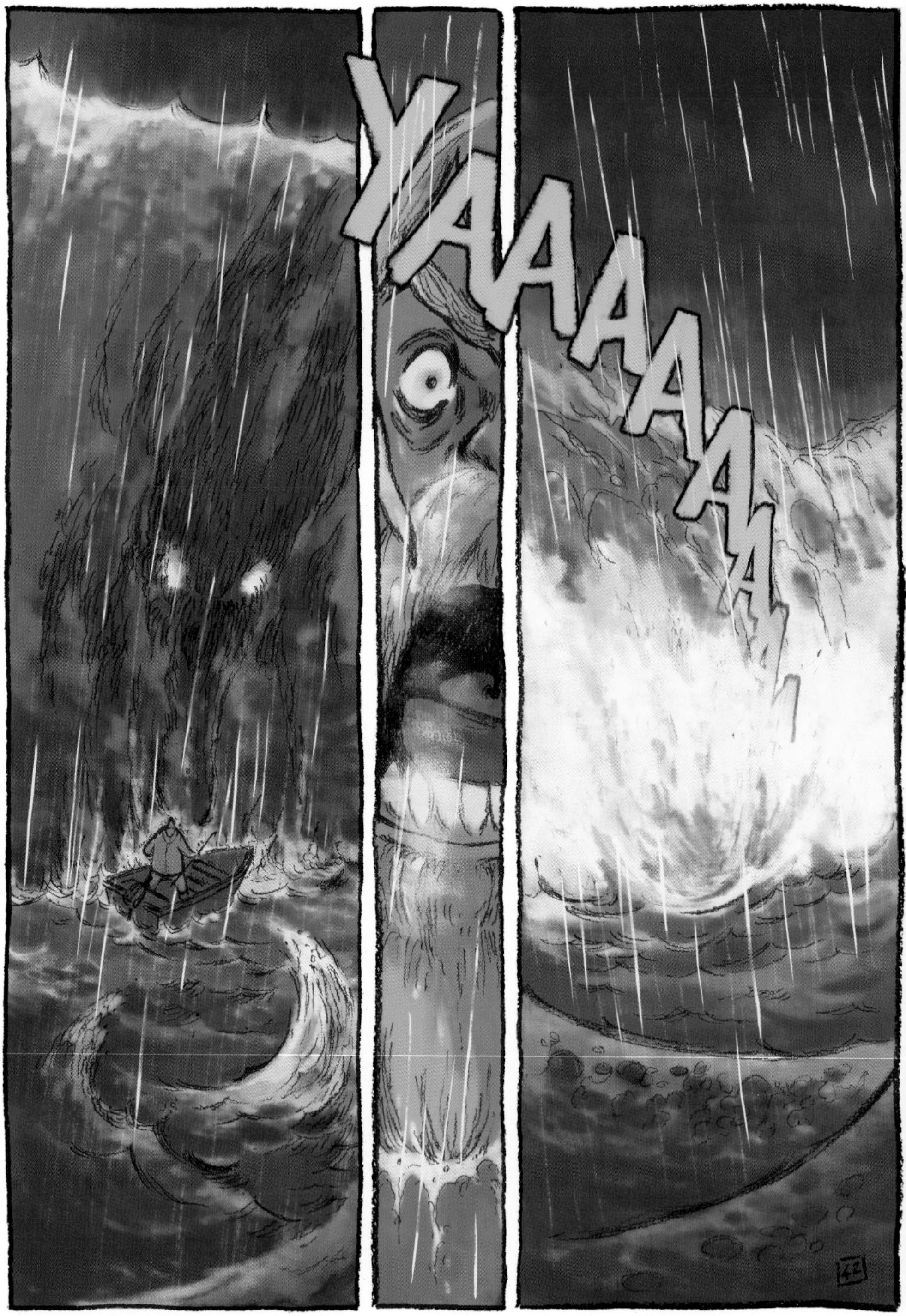
YAAAAAA

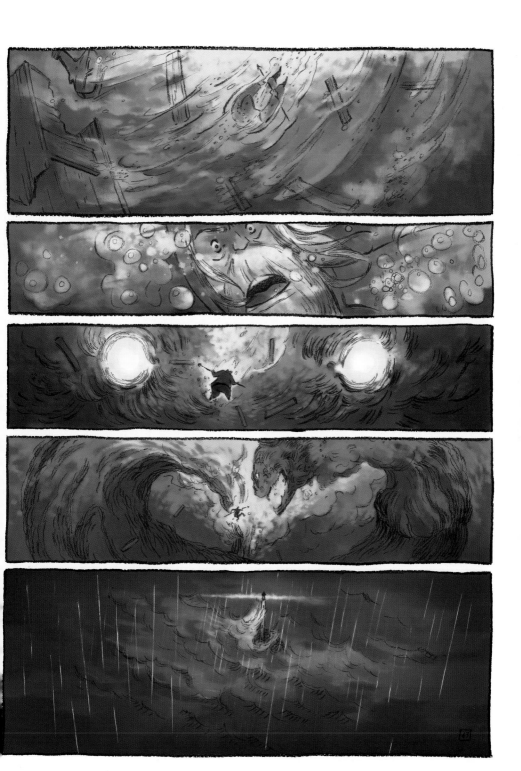

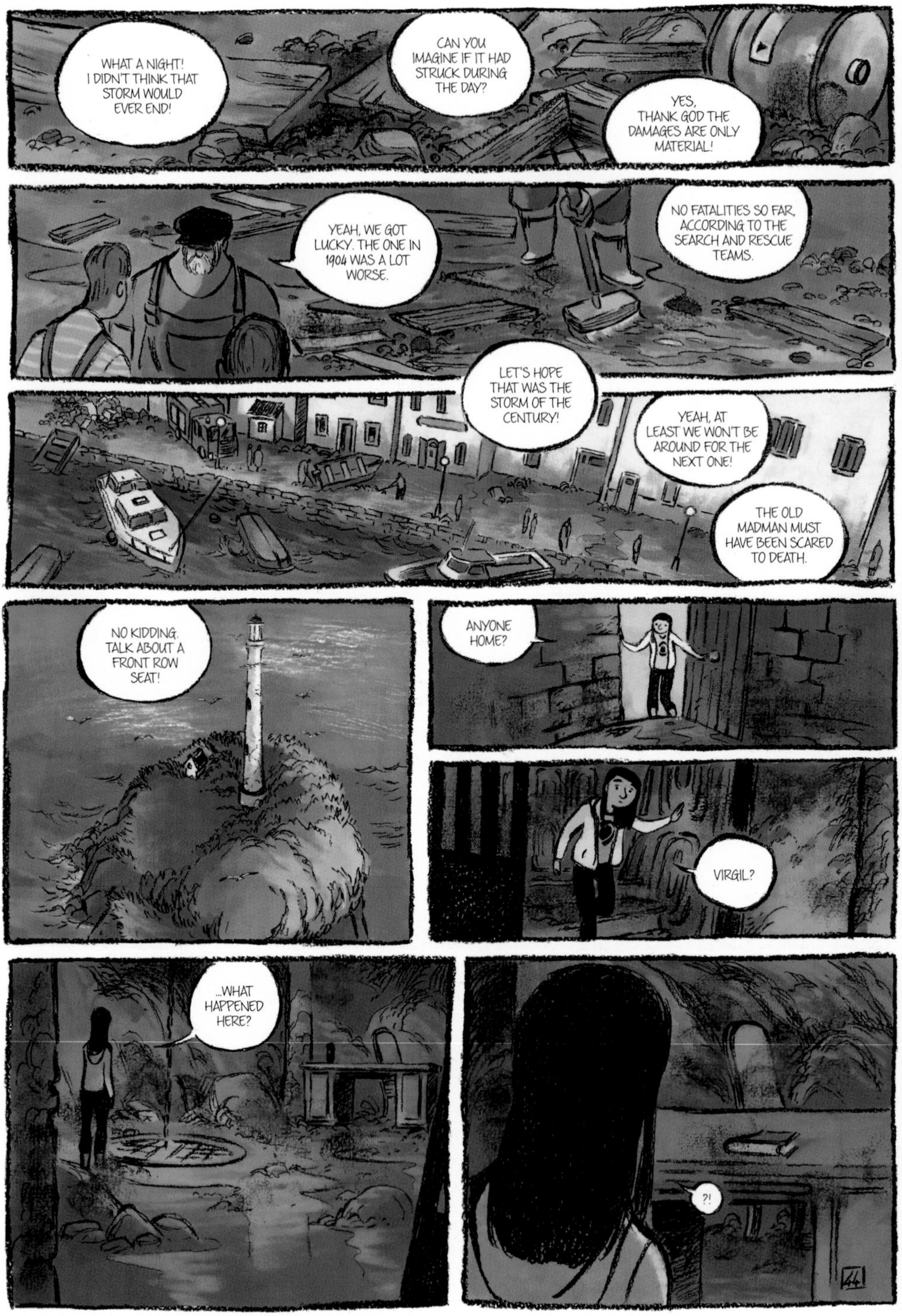
WHAT A NIGHT! I DIDN'T THINK THAT STORM WOULD EVER END!
CAN YOU IMAGINE IF IT HAD STRUCK DURING THE DAY?
YES, THANK GOD THE DAMAGES ARE ONLY MATERIAL!
YEAH, WE GOT LUCKY. THE ONE IN 1904 WAS A LOT WORSE.
NO FATALITIES SO FAR, ACCORDING TO THE SEARCH AND RESCUE TEAMS.
LET'S HOPE THAT WAS THE STORM OF THE CENTURY!
YEAH, AT LEAST WE WON'T BE AROUND FOR THE NEXT ONE!
THE OLD MADMAN MUST HAVE BEEN SCARED TO DEATH.
NO KIDDING. TALK ABOUT A FRONT ROW SEAT!
ANYONE HOME?
VIRGIL?
...WHAT HAPPENED HERE?
?!

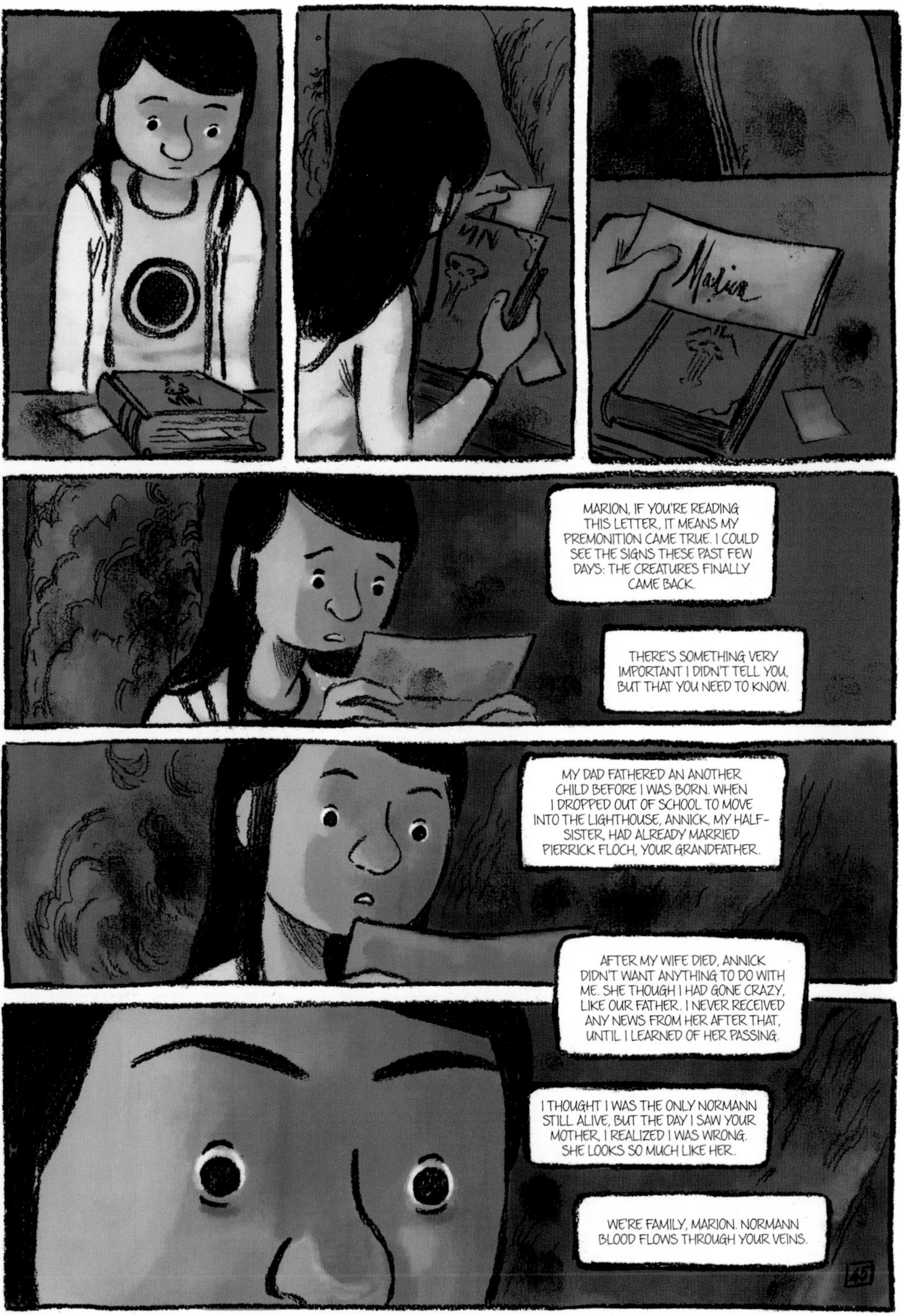
Marion
MARION, IF YOU'RE READING THIS LETTER, IT MEANS MY PREMONITION CAME TRUE. I COULD SEE THE SIGNS THESE PAST FEW DAYS: THE CREATURES FINALLY CAME BACK.
THERE'S SOMETHING VERY IMPORTANT I DIDN'T TELL YOU, BUT THAT YOU NEED TO KNOW.
MY DAD FATHERED AN ANOTHER CHILD BEFORE I WAS BORN. WHEN I DROPPED OUT OF SCHOOL TO MOVE INTO THE LIGHTHOUSE, ANNICK, MY HALF-SISTER, HAD ALREADY MARRIED PIERRICK FLOCH, YOUR GRANDFATHER.
AFTER MY WIFE DIED, ANNICK DIDN'T WANT ANYTHING TO DO WITH ME. SHE THOUGH I HAD GONE CRAZY, LIKE OUR FATHER. I NEVER RECEIVED ANY NEWS FROM HER AFTER THAT, UNTIL I LEARNED OF HER PASSING.
I THOUGHT I WAS THE ONLY NORMANN STILL ALIVE, BUT THE DAY I SAW YOUR MOTHER, I REALIZED I WAS WRONG. SHE LOOKS SO MUCH LIKE HER.
WE'RE FAMILY, MARION. NORMANN BLOOD FLOWS THROUGH YOUR VEINS.

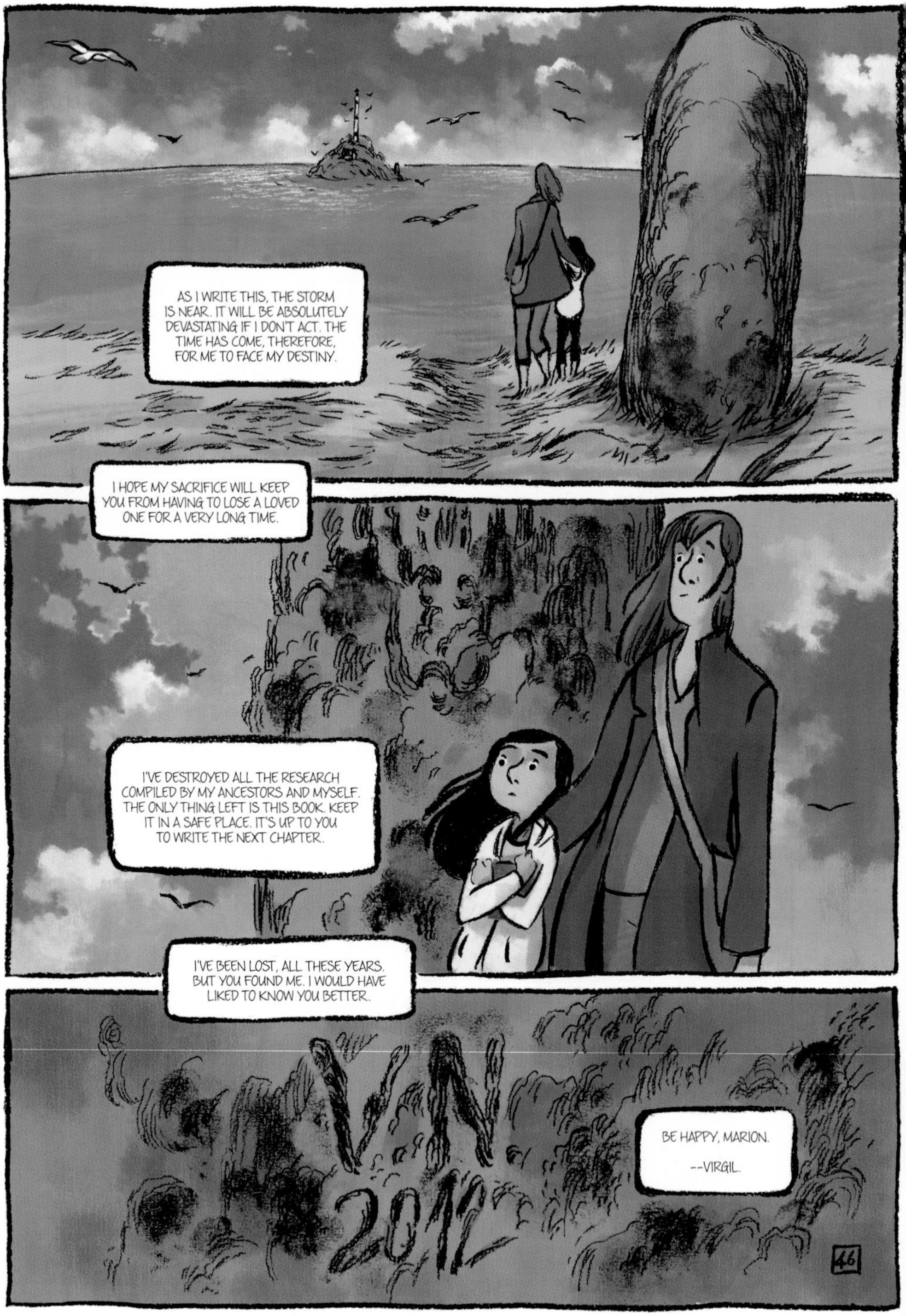
AS I WRITE THIS, THE STORM IS NEAR. IT WILL BE ABSOLUTELY DEVASTATING IF I DON'T ACT. THE TIME HAS COME, THEREFORE, FOR ME TO FACE MY DESTINY.
I HOPE MY SACRIFICE WILL KEEP YOU FROM HAVING TO LOSE A LOVED ONE FOR A VERY LONG TIME.
I'VE DESTROYED ALL THE RESEARCH COMPILED BY MY ANCESTORS AND MYSELF. THE ONLY THING LEFT IS THIS BOOK. KEEP IT IN A SAFE PLACE. IT'S UP TO YOU TO WRITE THE NEXT CHAPTER.
I'VE BEEN LOST, ALL THESE YEARS. BUT YOU FOUND ME. I WOULD HAVE LIKED TO KNOW YOU BETTER.
V.N.
2012
BE HAPPY, MARION.
--VIRGIL.
46
VERNAY 2012

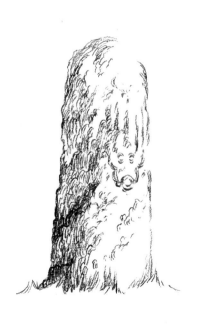

Water Memory

Graphic Journal

The idea for this story was born out of a desire Valérie and I had to work together. We both hold a deep appreciation for fantastical worlds, so it was only natural that we tended toward this kind of story.

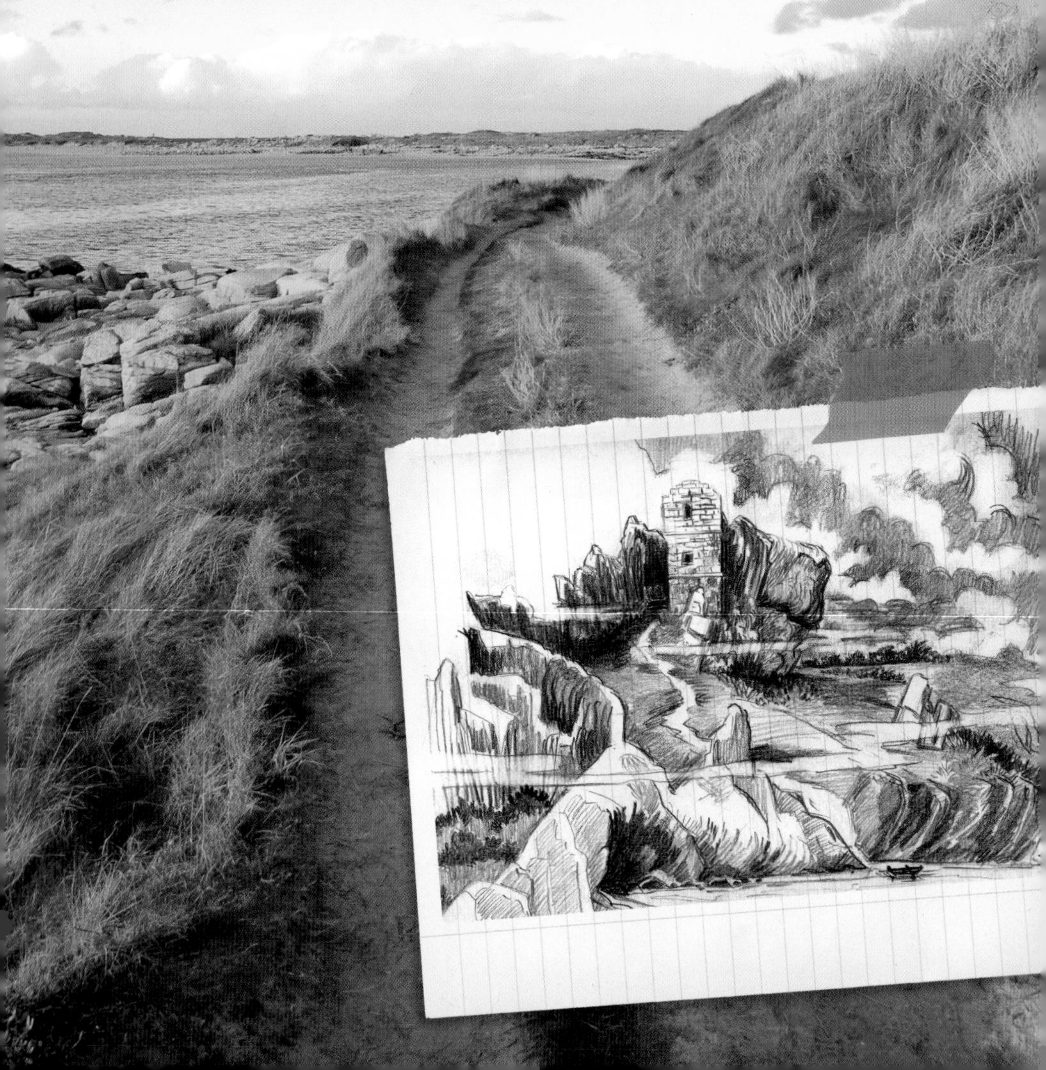

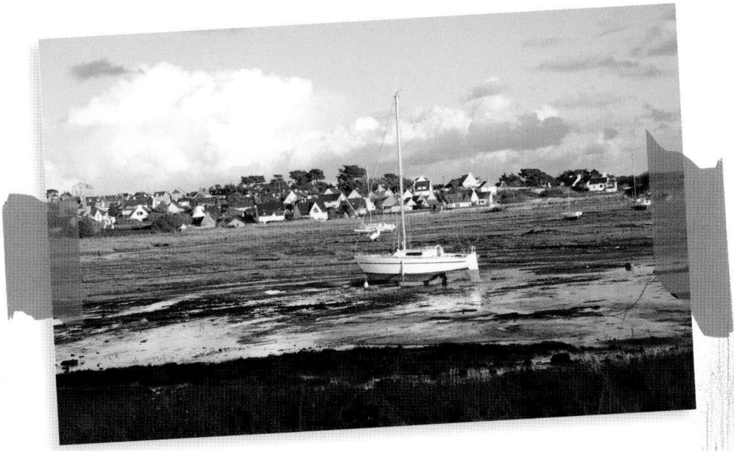

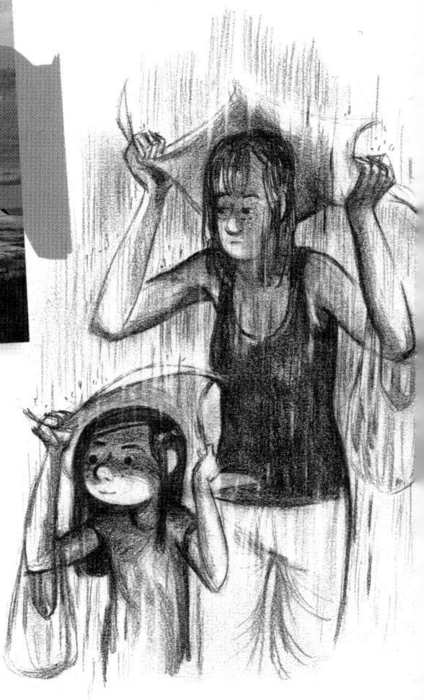

I'm more of an artist than a writer, but I wanted to write and Valérie wanted to get out of her comfort zone. It was our chance to experiment, to try something new, and break new ground.

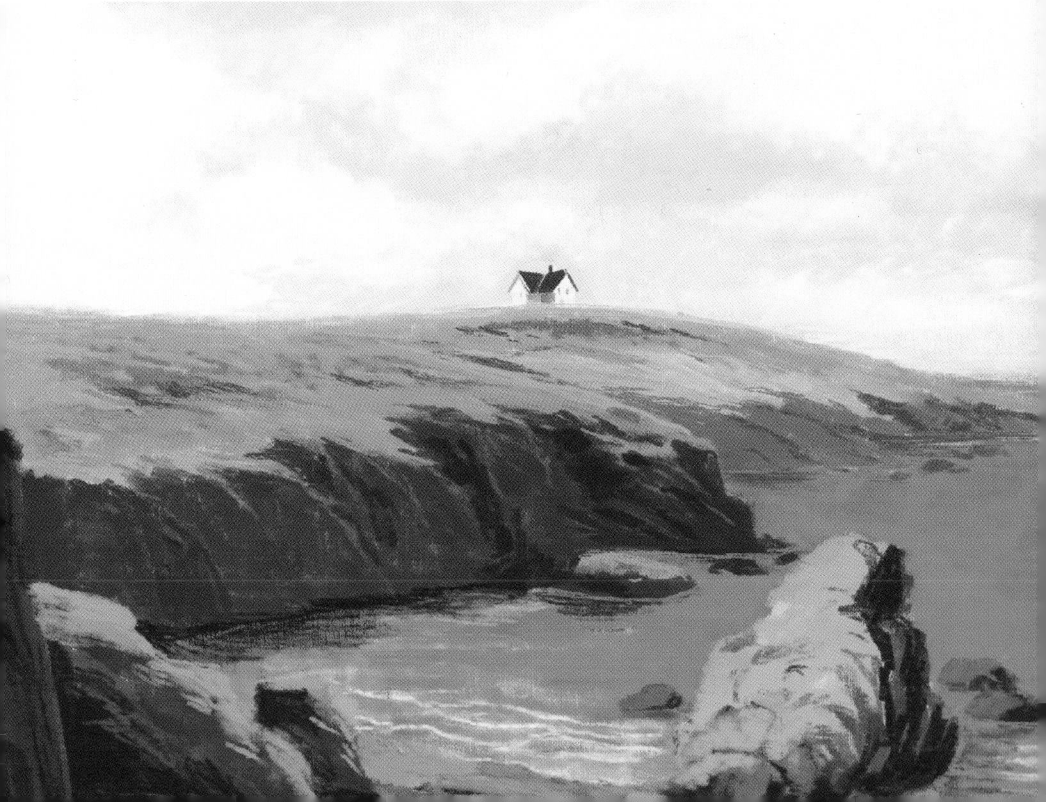

We live in the middle of a forest, a few miles away from the coast of the Atlantic. Nature holds an important place in our lives, and we believe it's an essential part of history.

The worlds created by Hayao Miyazaki, where nature and the fantastic coexisted served as our reference. We wanted mystery, adventure, strong characters and a certain poetry to the story.

When it came time to choose a setting for this story, Brittany came to mind. It's a land of legends and it gave an air of credibility to our story.

We visited several times to soak in the area. We took pictures and did our best to discover for ourselves the richness of the countryside, the light and energy they give off.

Research on Caroline and Marion's house.

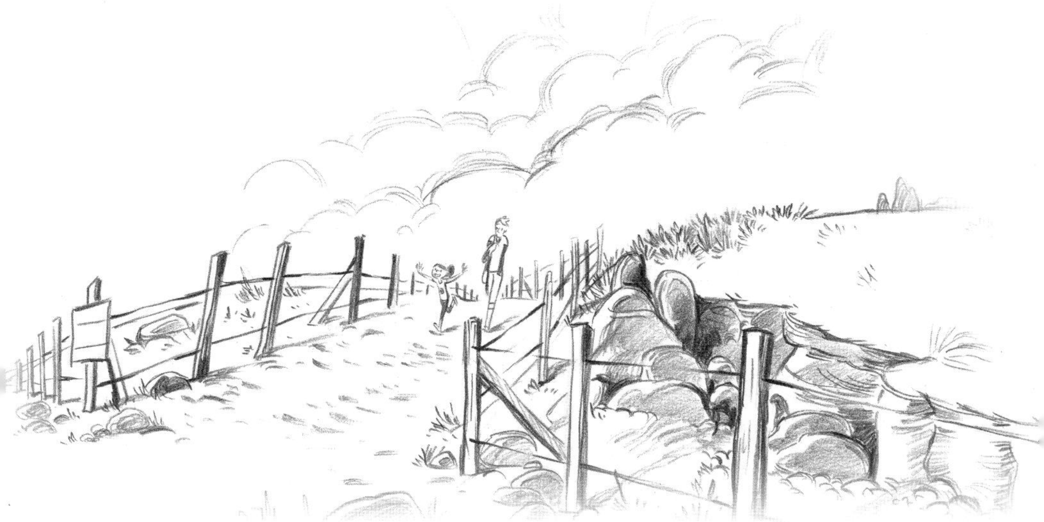

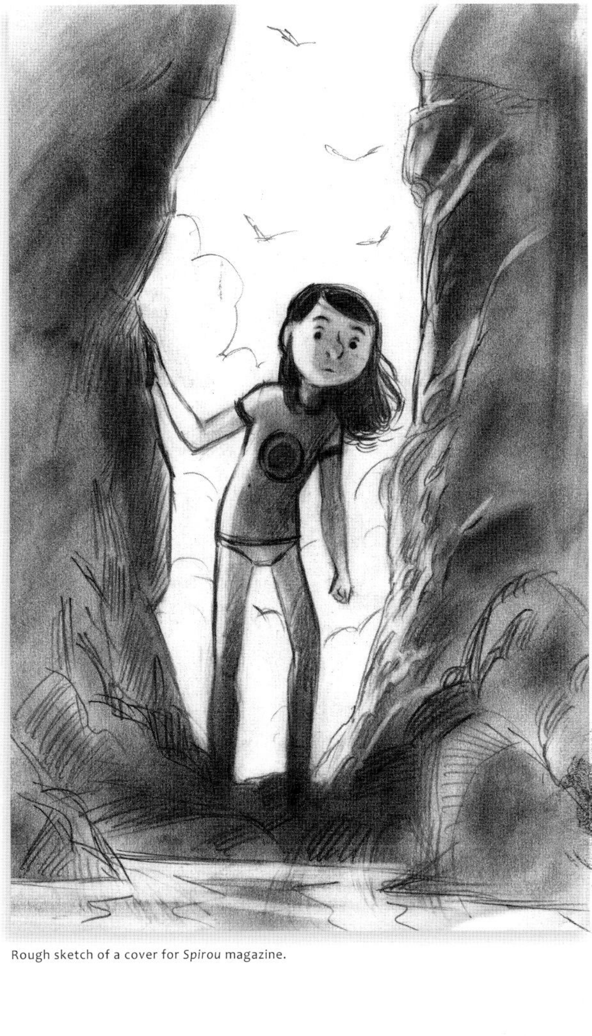

Rough sketch of a cover for *Spirou* magazine.

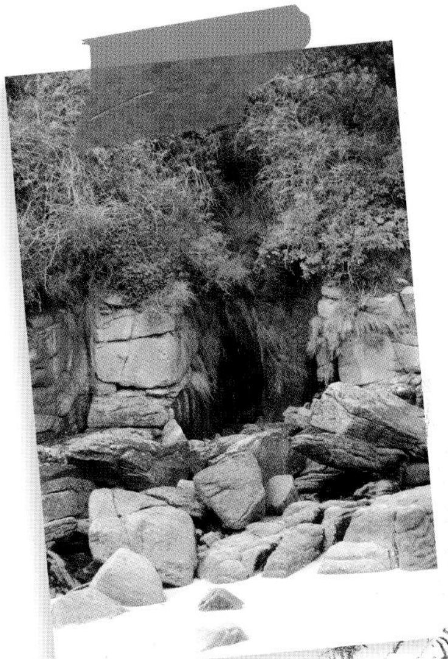

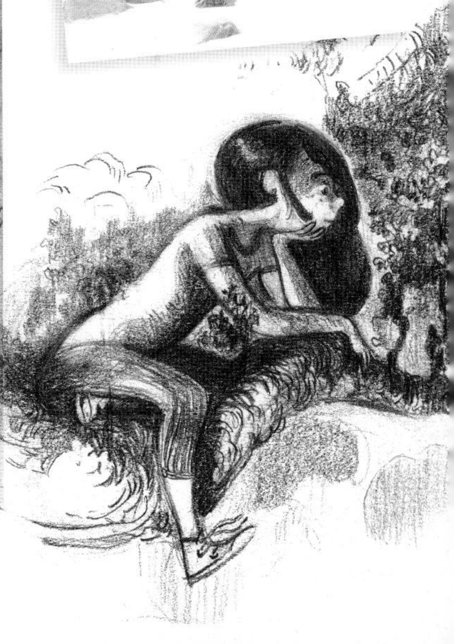

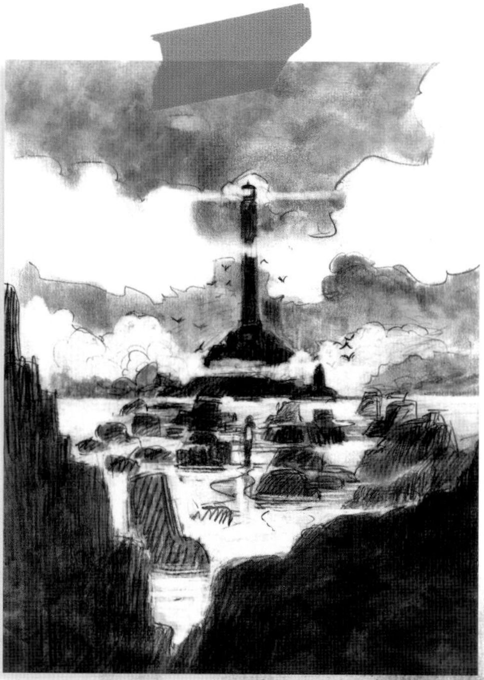

We made a clear choice not to represent a specific place, instead preferring to be inspired by different areas that we discovered along the course of our time there, like the island of Louët which inspired the lighthouse island we imagined.

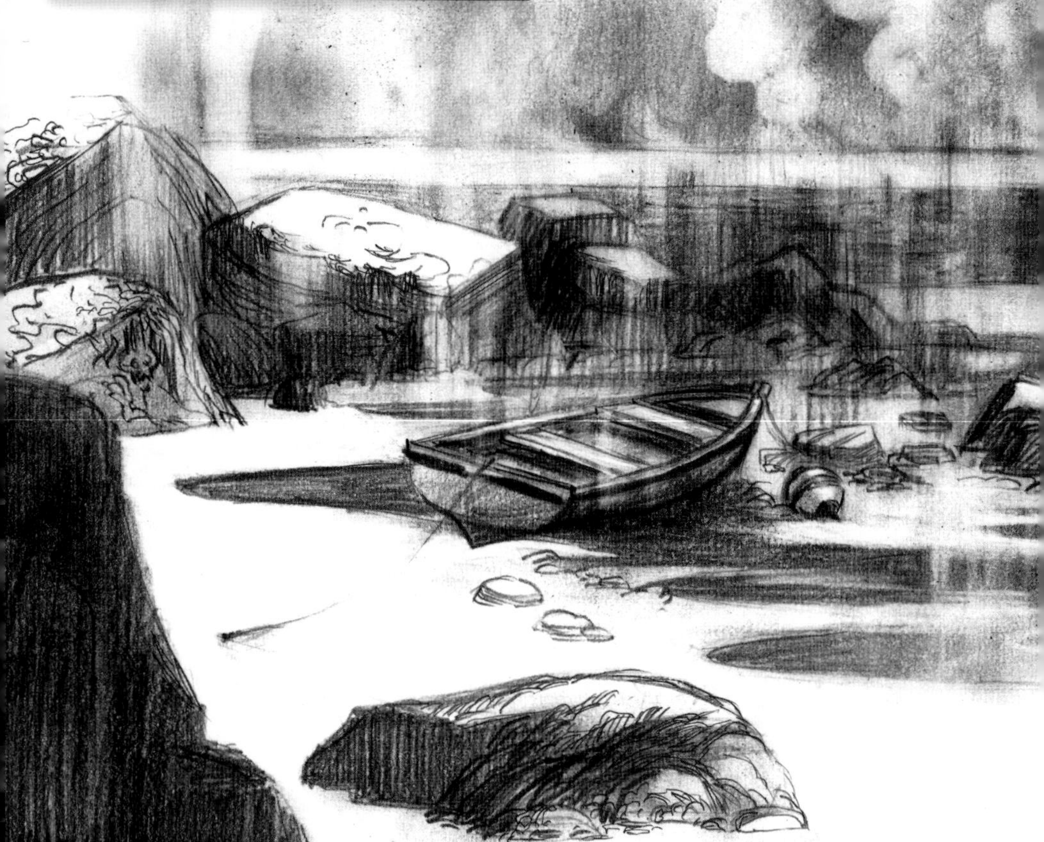

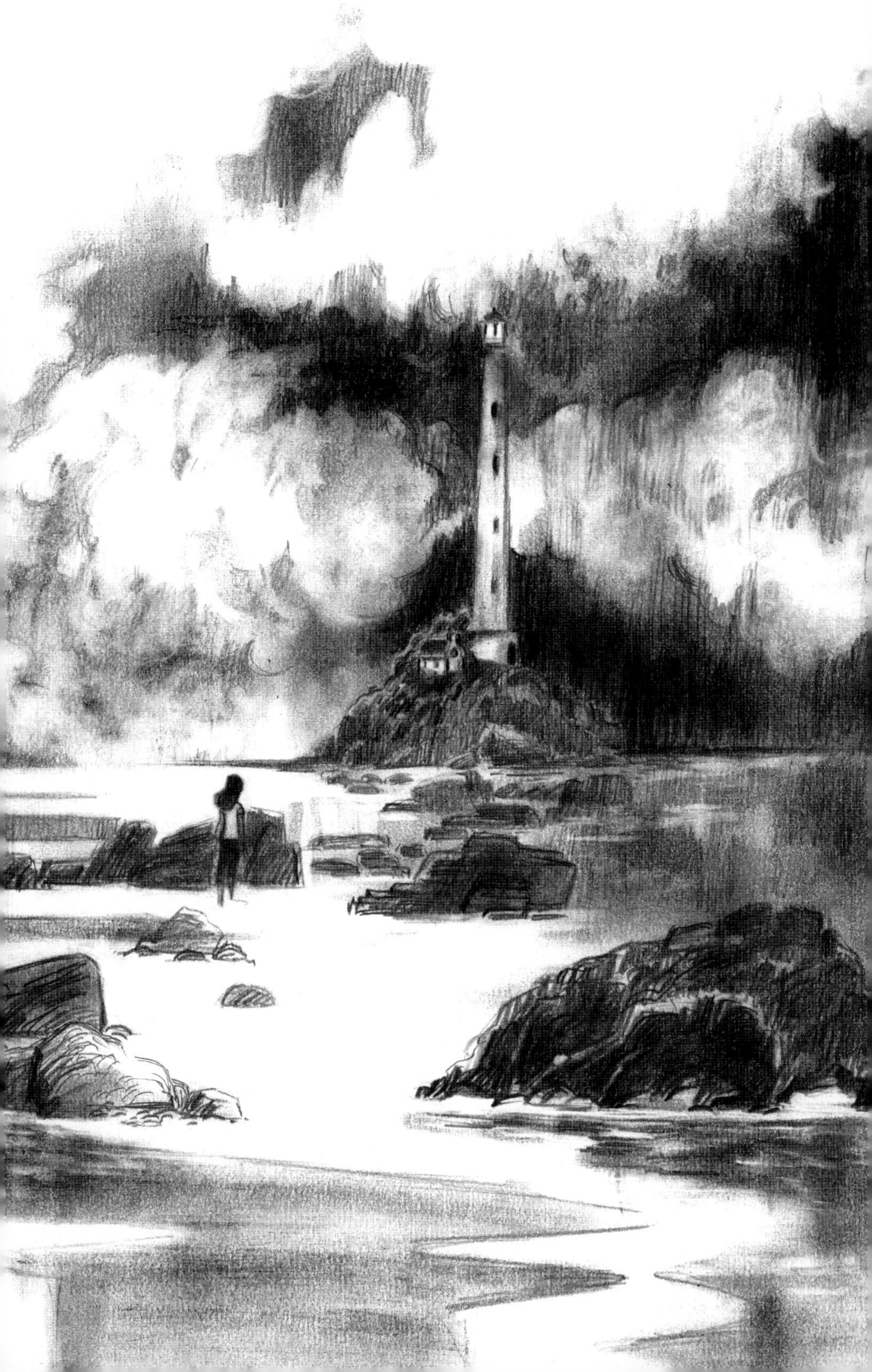

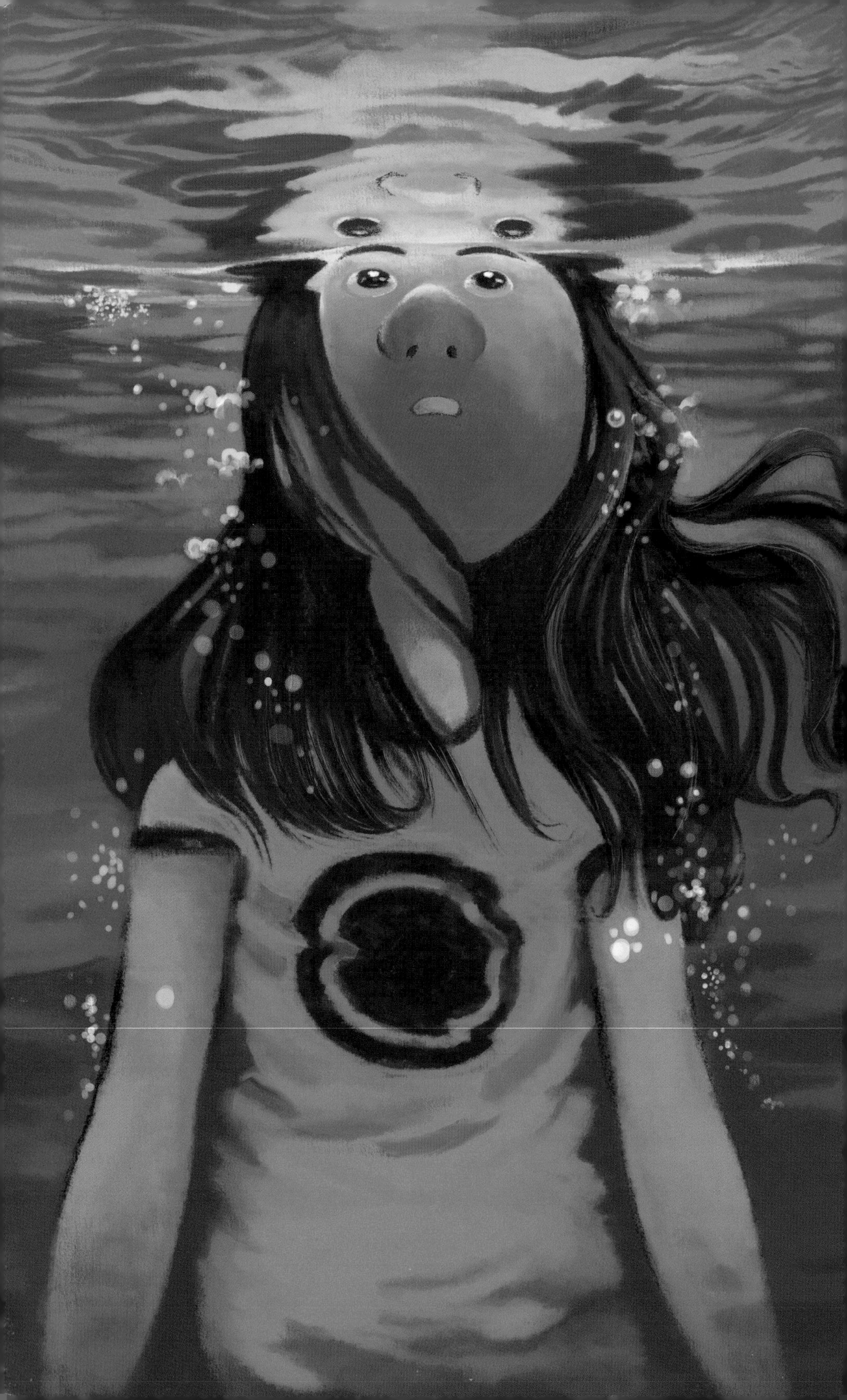

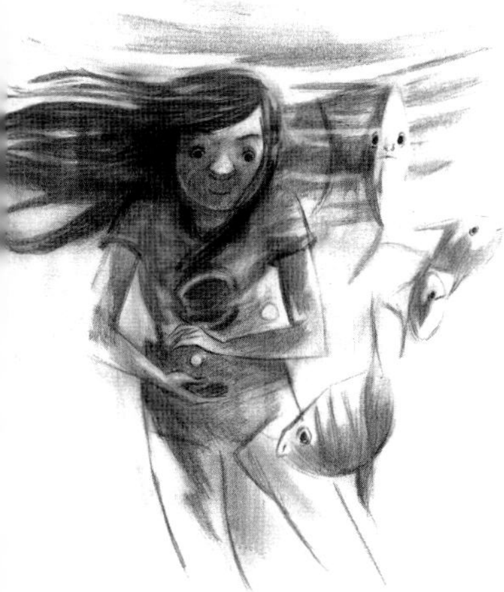

The most important thing was bringing the characters to life and creating strong relationships between them. I had a strong conviction that in order to keep the reader holding their breath in awe until the end, I needed to hint at the fantastical elements of the world, rather than show them outright.

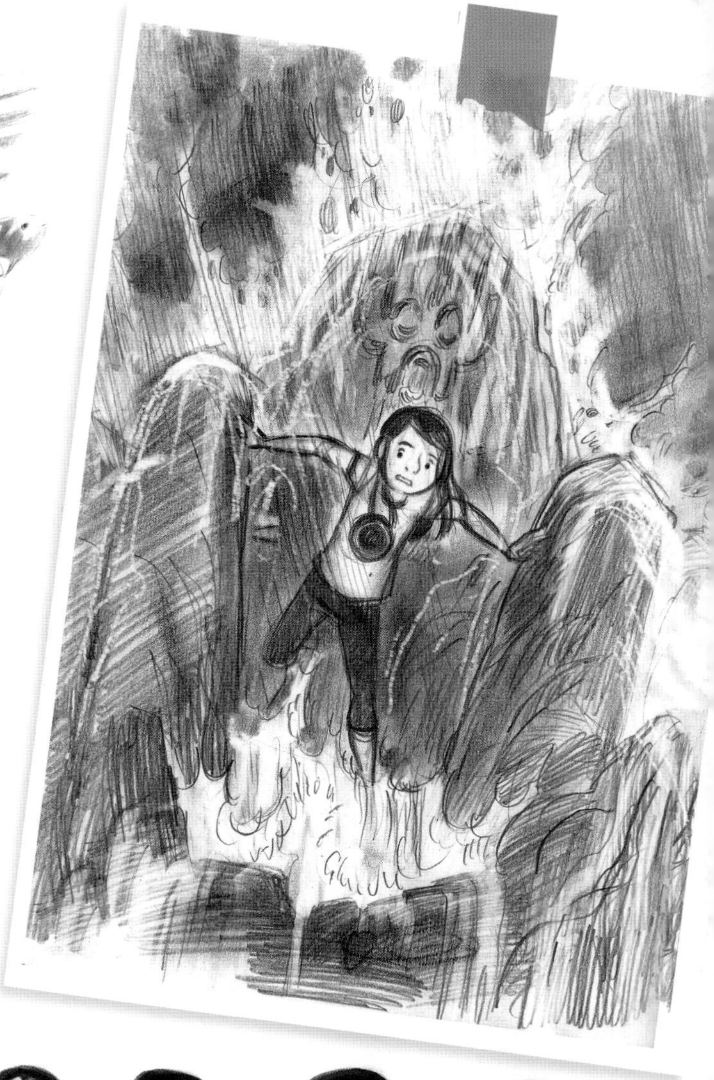

A cover concept for *Spirou* magazine.

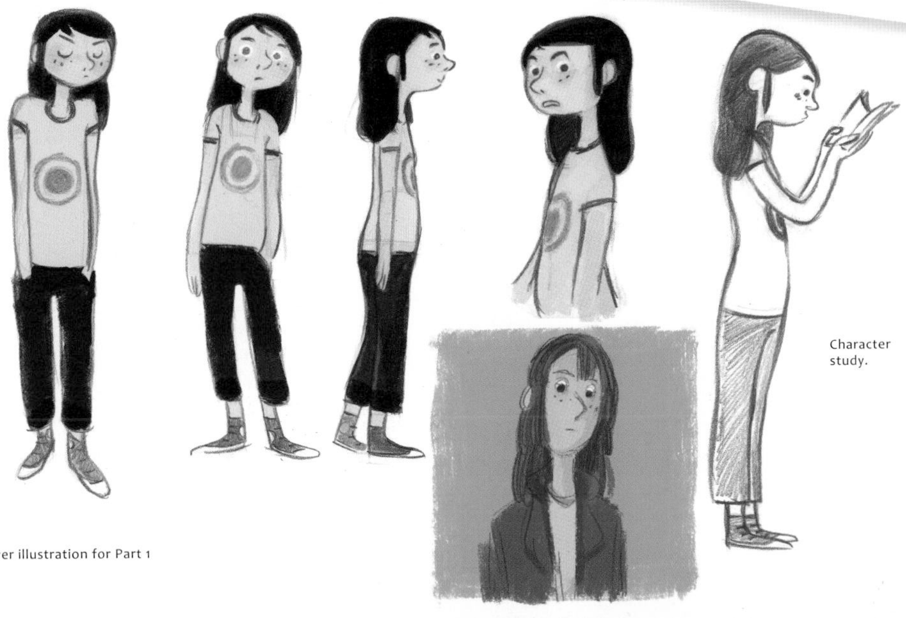

Character study.

Left page:
Original cover illustration for Part 1

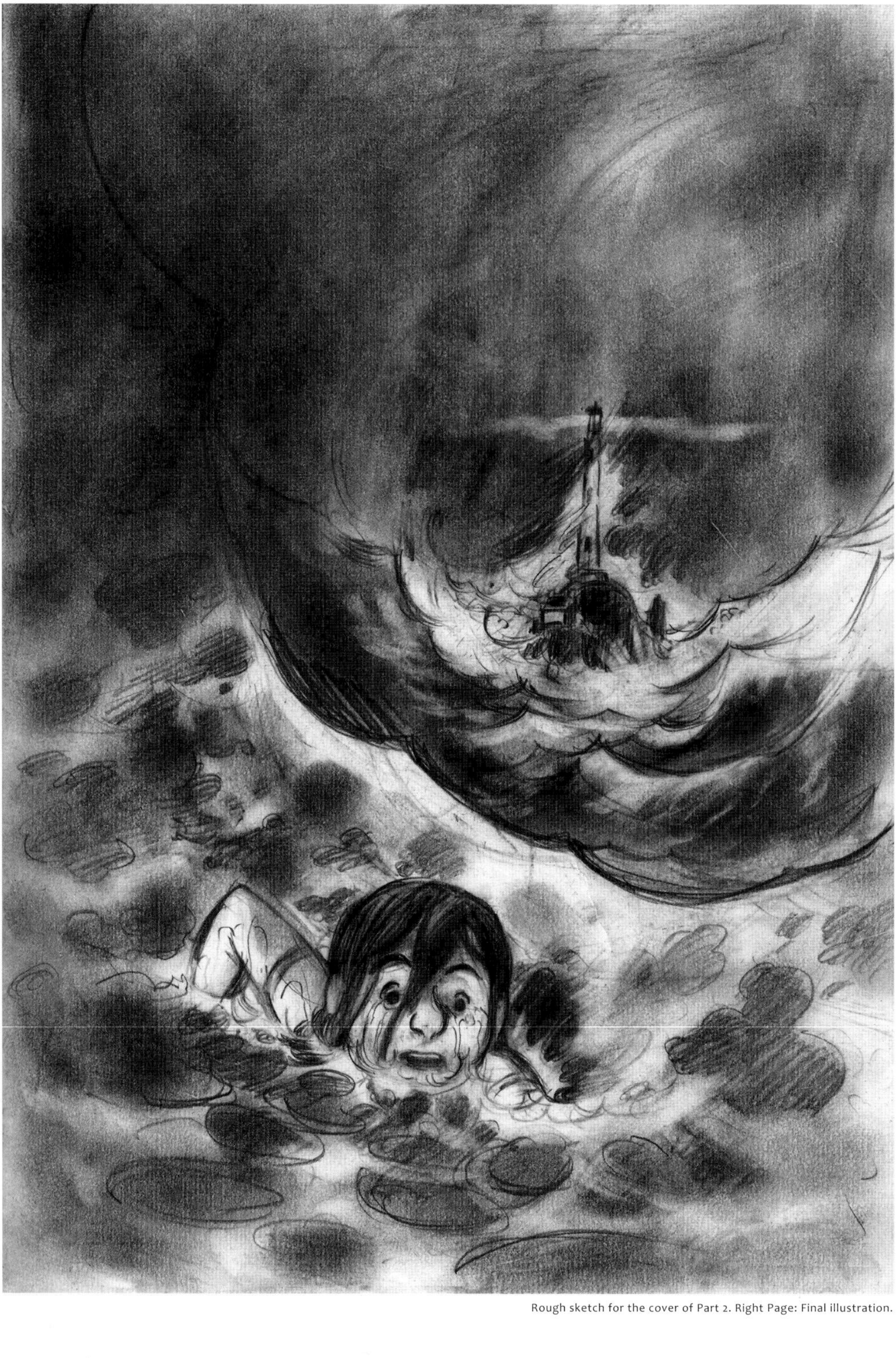

Rough sketch for the cover of Part 2. Right Page: Final illustration.

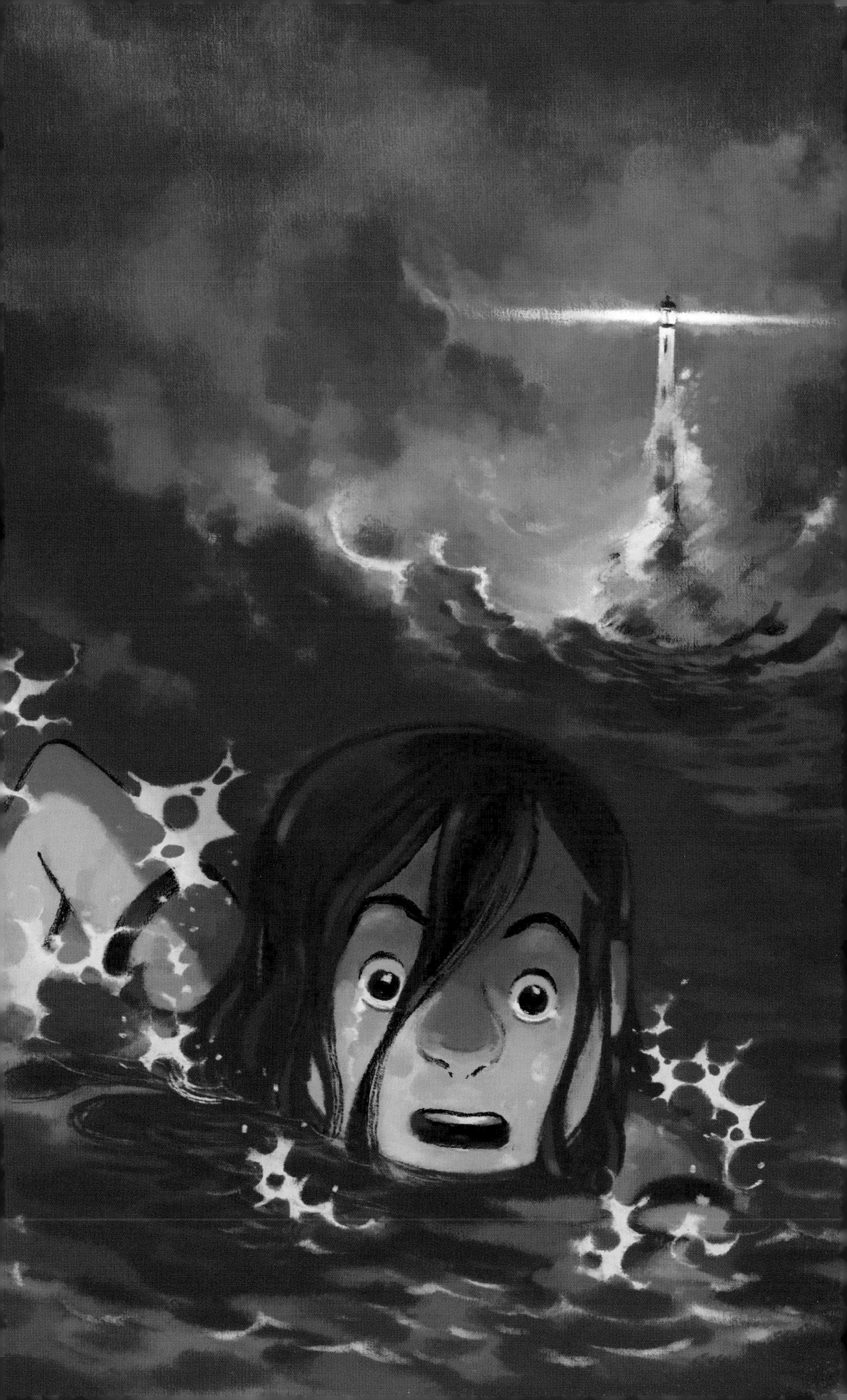

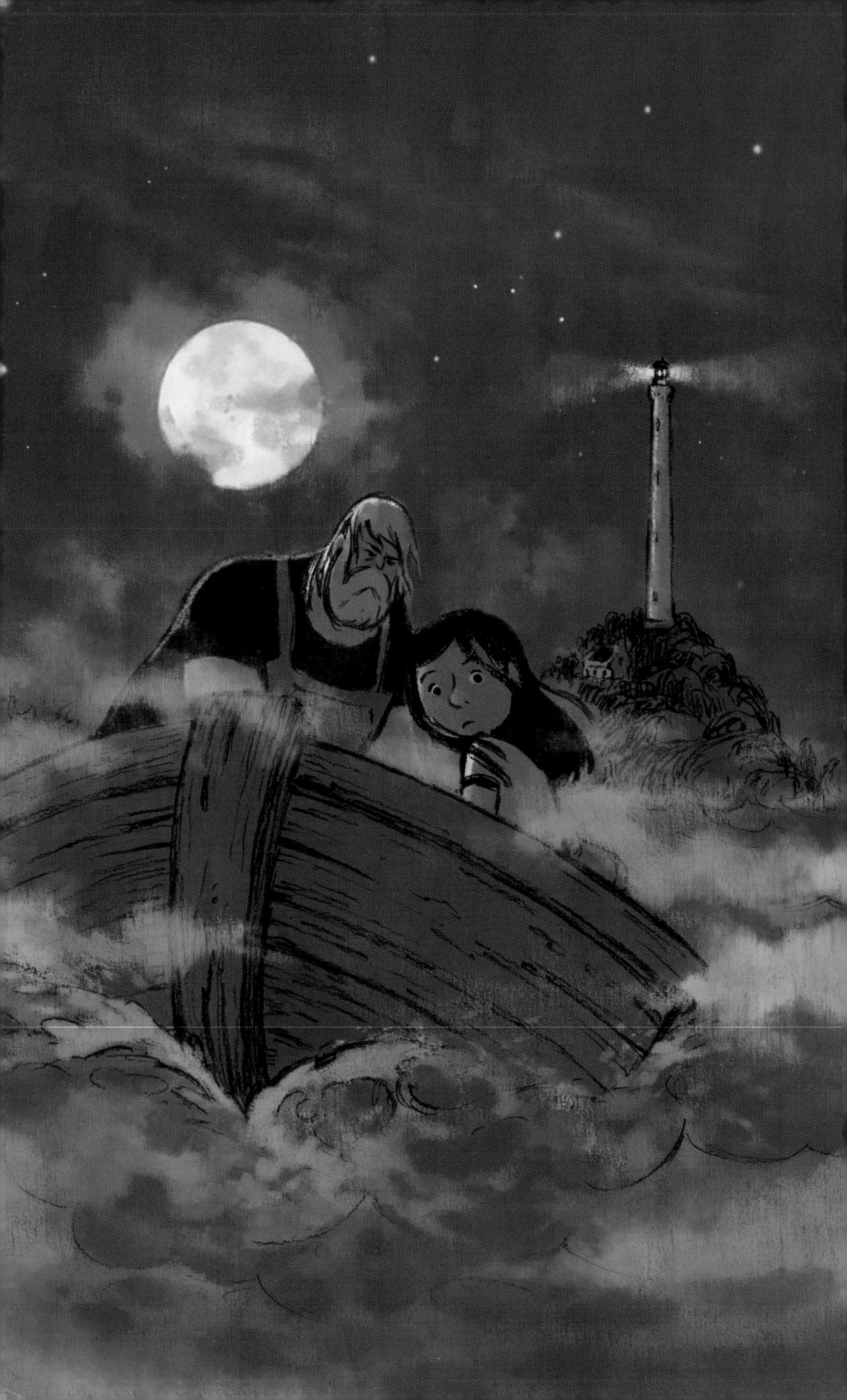

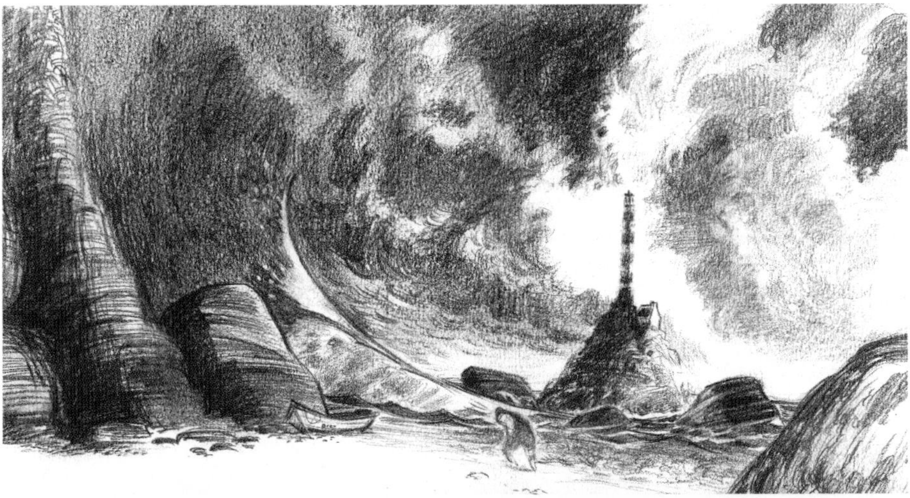

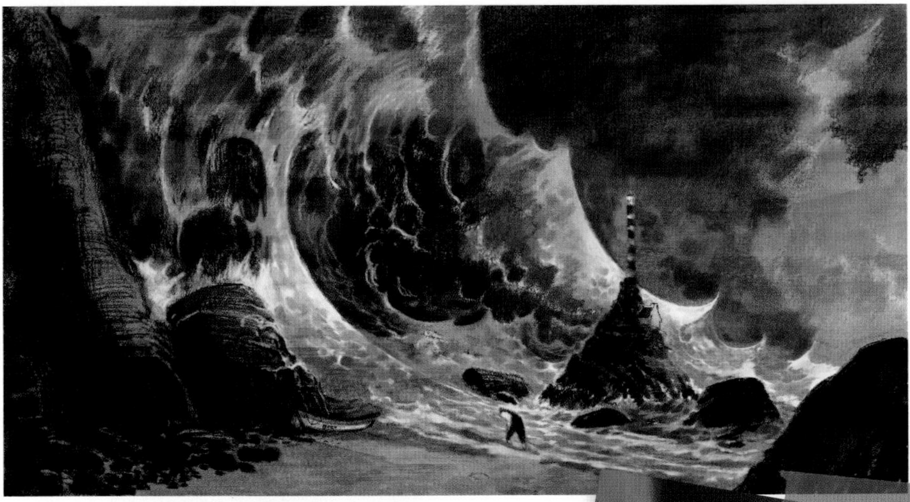

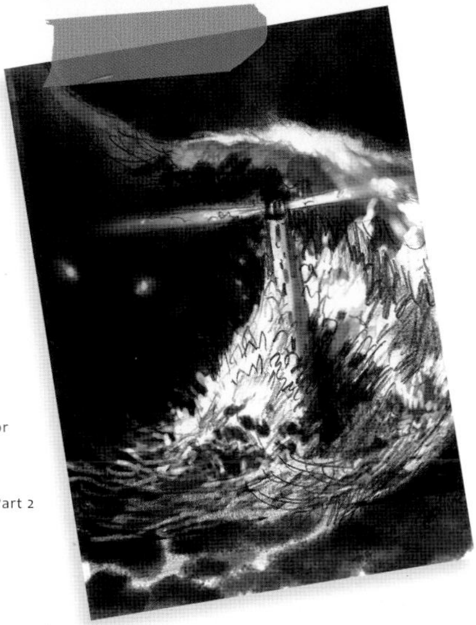

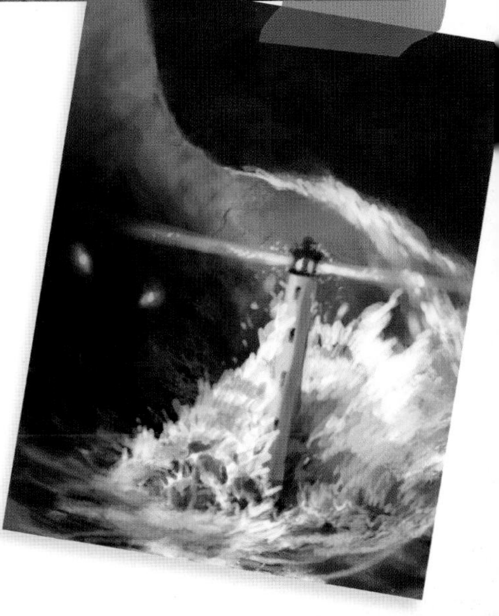

Left page:
Cover illustration for
Spirou magazine.

Opposite:
Cover concept for Part 2

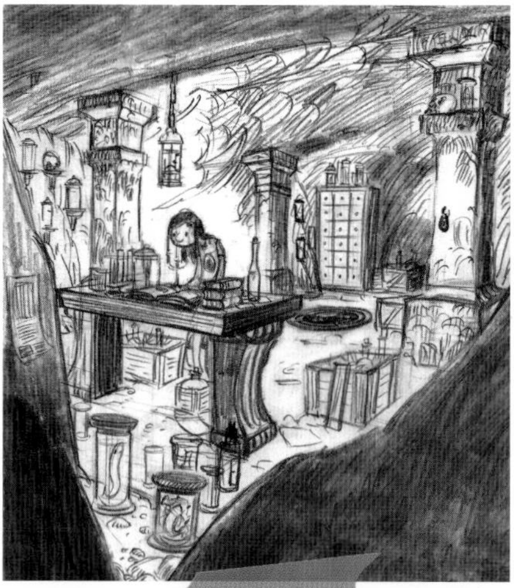

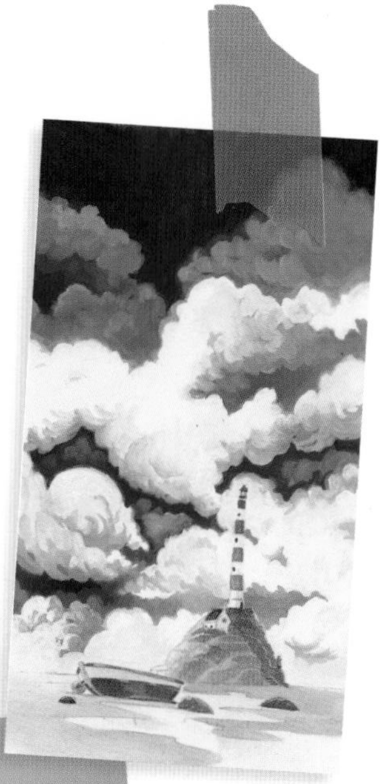

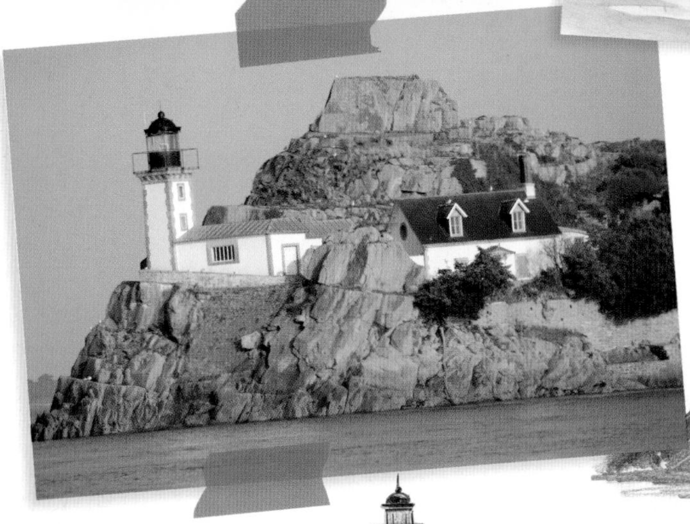

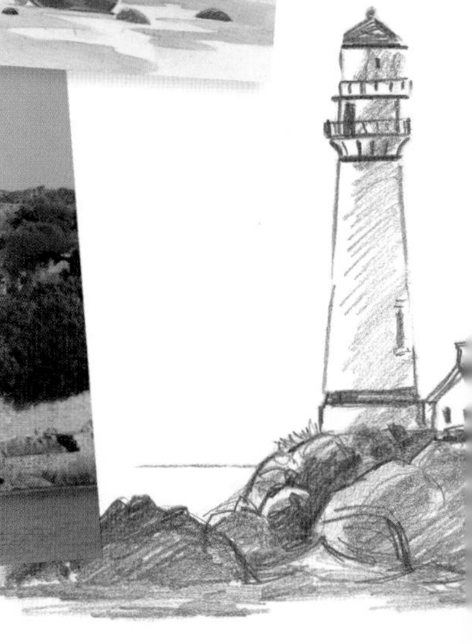

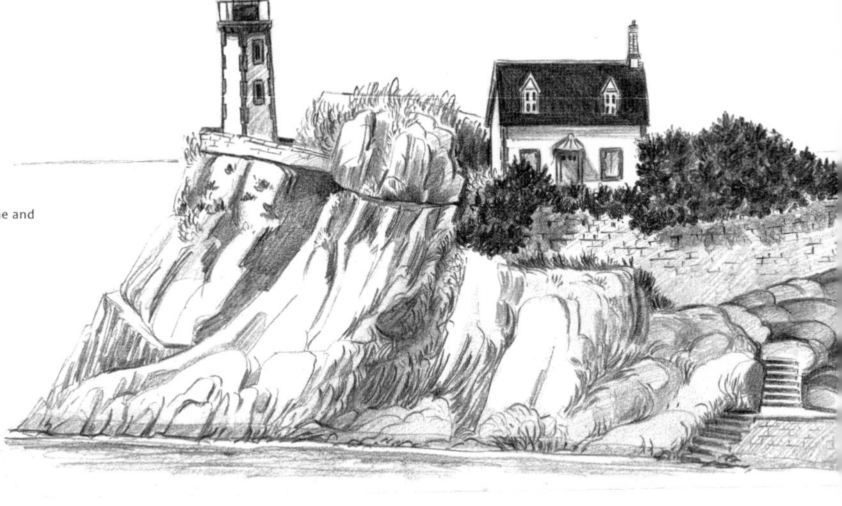

Research on Caroline and Marion's house.

For more than two years, we spent every day living with Marion and Caroline.

At the end of the adventure, we had a hard time separating ourselves from them, and we hope to be able to spend time with them again in the future!

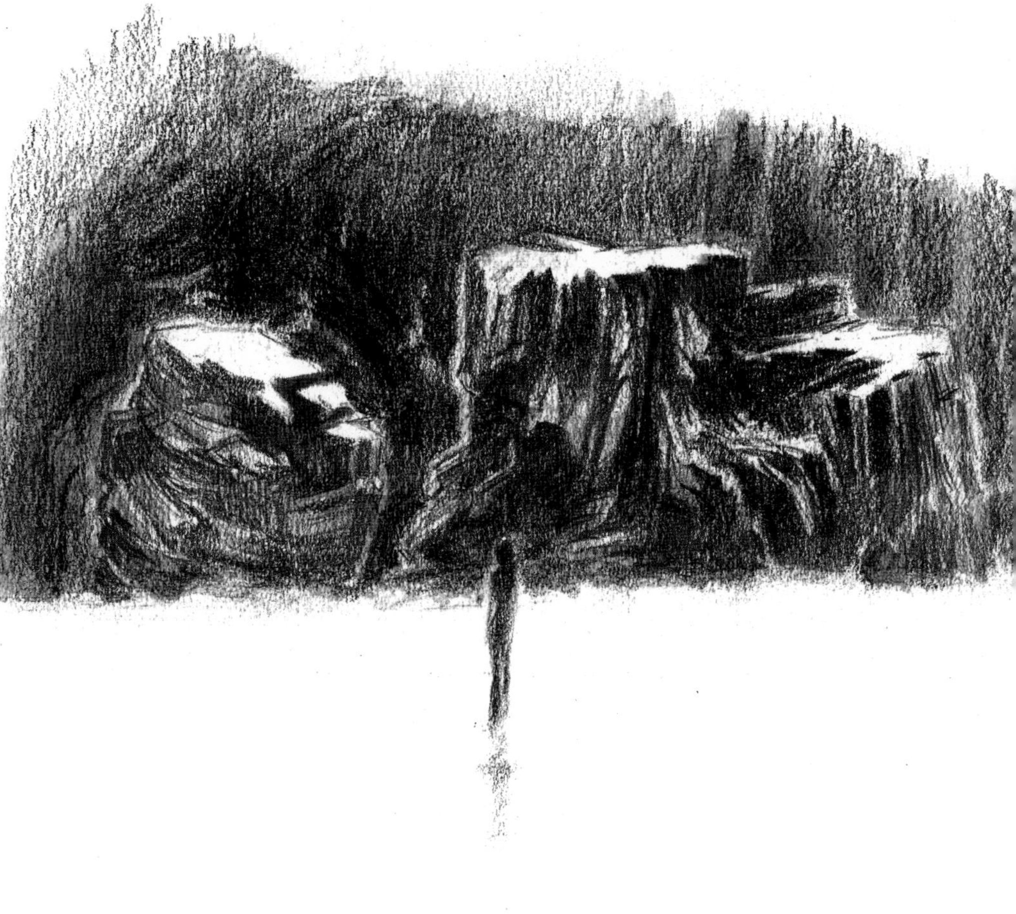

Thanks to Laurence for all the support she showed from the very start of this project,
thanks to Denis for his sharp eye and great advice, and thanks to the Kuglers, our beta testers!
Salem is in our thoughts.

Valérie and Mathieu

Publisher's Cataloging-In-Publication Data

(Prepared by The Donohue Group, Inc.)

Names: Reynès, Mathieu, 1977- | Vernay, Valérie, illustrator.
Title: Water memory / Valérie Vernay and Mathieu Reynès.
Other Titles: Mémoire de l'eau. English
Description: [St. Louis, Missouri] : The Lion Forge, LLC, 2017. | Translation of: La mémoire de l'eau. Marcinelle
    (Belgique) : Dupuis, ©2014.
Identifiers: ISBN 978-1-941302-43-9
Subjects: LCSH: Mothers and daughters--Comic books, strips, etc. | Fishing villages--Comic books, strips, etc. |
    Blessing and cursing--Comic books, strips, etc. | LCGFT: Graphic novels.
Classification: LCC PN6747.R49 M4613 2017 | DDC 741.5944--dc23